THIRD FORCE

"There is no road from Torcadino," said Tarl to the mercenary commander. "You have trapped yourself here. The walls are surrounded. Your army is small. Cos will maintain a considerable force in the area, at least compared to what is at your disposal. I do not think you will be able to fight your way out. I am sure you do not have enough tarns to evacuate your men.

"Obviously you have made strict arrangements with Ar," Tarl went on.

"No," the mercenary said. "I have no understanding with Ar."

"You must have!" Tarl said. "Are you not in the pay of Ar?"

"No," the commander said. "The powers of Ar and Cos must be balanced. The victory of either means the end of the free companies. . . ."

MERCENARIES OF GOR

John Norman

DAW BOOKS, INC.

DONALD A. WOLLHEIM, PUBLISHER

1633 Broadway, New York, NY 10019

First Printing, March 1985

1 2 3 4 5 6 7 8 9

PRINTED IN U.S.A.

Contents

1: What Occurred Outside Samnium 7

2: There Are Hardships in these Times 15

3: Tula 24

4: Feiqa Serves in the Alar Camp 43

5: We Are on the Genesian Road 65

6: Hurtha's Feast 80

7: We Get a Late Start;
   Boabissia Is Encouraged to Silence 89

8: Evidence of a Disquieting Event Is Found 93

9: Torcodino 99

10: We Proceed to the Wagon Yards 108

11: We Decide Boabissia Will Help Out
    with our Finances 111

12: It Is a Standard, That of a Silver Tarn 123

13: We Proceed to the Semnium 129

14: The Semnium; The Outer Office 140

15: The Semnium; What Transpired in the Inner Offices 146

16: A Night in the Semnium 171

17: Slavery Agrees with Feiqa 227

18: The Treasure Road 229

19: The Checkpoint 238

20: We See the City of Ar 255

21: Within the Walls of Ar 260

22: The Insula of Achiates 273

23: The Day of Generosity and Petitions 284

24: The Origins of Boabissia 291

25: The Tunnels 311

26: I Take my Leave of the Tunnels 378

27: I Sell a Blonde 432

28: Tenalion Accords Me a Favor 438

29: Soldiers 441

1: What Occurred Outside Samnium

"I do not know about other women," she said, "but I am one who wishes to belong to a man, *wholly*."

"Beware your words," I cautioned her.

"I am a free woman," she said. "I can speak as I please."

I could not gainsay her in this. She was free. She could, accordingly, say what she wished, and without requiring permission. She stood before me. She had dared to brush back her hood. She had unpinned her shimmering veils, permitting them to fall about her throat and shoulders. A soft movement of her hands and a shake of her head had thrown her long, dark hair behind her back. She had dark eyes. Her face was softly rounded. It was delicate and beautiful.

"You have unpinned your veil," I observed.

"Yes," she said.

"You are brazen," I said.

"Yes," she said, insolently.

I mused, considering this. It is not difficult, of course, to take insolence from a woman.

"Why have you unpinned your veil before me?" I asked.

"Perhaps you will like what you see," she said.

"Bold female," I observed.

She tossed her head, impatiently.

"Do you have the least inkling as to what it might be, to belong to a man, *wholly*?" I asked.

"Do you find me pleasing?" she asked.

"Answer my question," I said.

"Yes," she said.

I wondered if this were true. It might be. She was Gorean.

"Now," she said. "Answer mine!"

"Do not court an alteration in your condition, unless you are prepared to accept it, in its full consequences," I said.

She shuddered. She lowered her eyes. "It is said that there is in every woman that which I sense so fearfully, yet so longingly, in myself."

"I wonder if that is true," I said.

"I do not know," she said, "but I know that it is in me, passionately, strongly, irresistibly."

"You are bold," I said.

"A free woman may be bold," she said.

"True," I granted her.

"I need this for my fulfillment, to be one with myself," she said.

"Speak clearly," I said. She was free. I saw no point in making it easy for her.

"I want to be a total woman, in the order of nature," she said.

I shrugged.

"My heart cries out," she wept, "with the need to be accepted, to be acquired, to be owned, to be mastered, to be forced to submit, to be forced to will-lessly and selflessly serve and love!"

I did not respond to her.

"I beg this of you, for you are a man," she said.

"Speak with greater precision," I said.

"What sort of man are you?" she wept.

"Speak with greater precision," I said.

She shook her head. "Please, no," she said.

I shrugged.

"Mine is the slave sex!" she said, angrily, defiantly.

"The slave sex?" I asked.

"Yes!" she said.

"And you are a member of that sex?" I asked.

"Yes!" she said, angrily.

"I see," I said.

"I am tired of trying to be like a man!" she said. "It is a lie which robs me of myself!"

I said nothing.

"I want to be true to myself," she said. "I want to be fulfilled!"

"Such a thing is not reversible by your will," I said.

"I am well aware of that," she said.

"There are many sorts of masters," I said, "and you would be at the disposal of any of them, and totally."

"I know," she whispered.

I said nothing.

"You have still not answered my question," she said. "Do you find me pleasing?"

"It is difficult to say," I said, "bundled and covered as you are."

She looked at me, frightened.

"Strip," I said. She would be assessed.

She reached to the veils about her throat and shoulders and, taking them, dropped them softly to the grass. She stood not more than a hundred yards from the gate of Tesius, in the city of Samnium, some two hundred pasangs east and a bit south of Brundisium, both cities continental allies of the island ubarate of Cos. She slipped softly from her slippers. She must then have felt the touch of the grass blades on her ankles. She looked at me. Her hands went to the stiff, high brocaded collar of her robes, the robes of concealment, to the numerous eyes and hooks there, holding it tightly, protectively, about her throat, up high under her chin.

"Do not dally," I told her.

In a few moments she had parted her robes, and slipped them, first the street robe, that stiff, ornate fabric, and then the house robe, scarcely less inflexible and forbidding, from her small, soft shoulders. Clad now only in a silken sliplike undergarment, she then looked at me.

"Completely," I said, "absolutely."

She then stood before me, even more naked than many a girl up for vending, waiting to be thrust to the surface of the block, for she wore no collar, no chains, no brand. A merchant on his way to the gate of Tesius paused, to gaze upon her. So, too, did two soldiers, guardsmen of Samnium. She stood very straight, inspected. None of these wrinkled their noses nor spat upon the ground.

"What is your name?" I asked.

"Charlotte, Lady of Samnium," she said.

"Turn slowly before me, Lady Charlotte," I said. "Now, place your hands, clasped, behind the back of your head, and arch your back. Good. You may now kneel. Do you know the position of the pleasure slave? Good."

"How does it feel to be kneeling before a man?" I asked.

"I have never been like this before a man," she said.

"How does it feel?" I asked.

"I do not know," she said. "I am so confused. It is so overwhelming. I am uncertain. I do not know what I feel like. I am almost giddy."

"Lift your chin," I said.

She complied immediately, unhesitantly.

"Spread your knees more widely," I said. Again, unhesitantly, immediately, she complied.

I regarded Lady Charlotte. I saw that she might be suitable. She was beautiful, and extremely feminine. I saw one of the soldiers licking his lips.

"These are difficult and dark times," I told her. "I tell you nothing you do not know when I tell you that. Too, I now inform you that where I go, it will be dangerous."

She looked up at me.

"Remain in the city," I said. "There you will be safe, there you will be secure."

"No," she said.

"No?" I asked.

"No," she said, firmly. "I am not yours. I do not need to obey you."

"Assume a position on your hands and knees," I told her. "Yes," I said. I removed a slave whip from my pack.

"I am free!" she said.

"I think it will do you good to feel this," I said, shaking out the five, soft, broad blades. I then went behind her.

"Ai!" she cried, struck. "It hurts, so!" she wept, now, a moment later, beginning to feel the pain in its fullness, now on her stomach, disbelief in her eyes. "I did not know it was like that."

"I struck you but once, and not hard," I told her.

"That was not hard?" she gasped, striped, stung, sobbing, terrified.

"No," I told her. "Go back now to the city, and be safe."

"No," she sobbed. "No!"

I crouched near her, looking at her, closely.

"No," she said. "No, no!"

I regarded her.

"Please," she said.

"Very well," I said.

She looked at me, wildly, elated. I thrust her face down to the grass. She sobbed with relief, with pleasure. I drew forth a slave collar from my pack. Roughly, unceremoniously, I placed it on her neck, snapping it shut, locking it.

"Good," said the merchant, turning away. "Good," said the two soldiers, too, turning away.

I regarded her.

She was now collared. She was now a slave. She was now mine.

She looked up at me, frightened. "I am yours," she whispered.

"Yes," I said.

"Please strike me once more," she said, "that I may this time feel the blow as a slave."

I said nothing.

"I want to feel your whip, as your slave," she said.

"Very well," I said. I then, by the hair and an arm, drew her again to her hands and knees. I again then stood behind her but this time I did not strike her immediately, but let her wait, as a slave, that she might anticipate the blow, and grow apprehensive of it, and not know precisely when it would fall. Then the blades hissed suddenly down upon her and again she cried out, sobbing, flung to the grass, which she clutched with her fingers. "You punish me," she said. "You can do with me as you please. I am your slave! I am yours!"

I looked down upon her. She was not unattractive. I had not planned to take a slave with me from Samnium, but I did not truly object to doing so. She could cook for me, and serve me, and keep me warm in the furs. It was late in Se'Kara. I would find her a useful convenience, a lovely one. Every man needs such a convenience. Then, when I wished, I could give her away, or dispose of her in some market.

"Do you think you were struck hard?" I asked.

"I do not know, Master," she said.

"You were not," I informed her.

"Yes, Master," she whispered, frightened, sensing what might have been done to her but had not been. To be sure, I had struck her harder than the first time, for she was now a slave, and slaves, of course, are whipped differently from free women, but I had not, truly, struck her with great force.

"Can men strike harder than that?" she asked.

"Do not be absurd," I said. "I struck you with only a tiny fraction of the force that an average fellow, if he wished, might bring to such a task. Too, I struck you only once, and in only one area, one less sensitive to pain than many others."

"I see, Master," she said, shuddering. She had then sensed what it might be to be a whipped slave girl. And whipping, of course, is only one of the punishments to which such a girl might be subjected. "I will try to be a good slave, Master," she whispered, frightened, understanding now perhaps somewhat better than before something of the categorical and absolute nature of her new condition.

"Who were you?" I asked.

"Lady Charlotte, of Samnium," she said.

"Who are you?" I asked.

"A slave, only a slave, yours," she said.

"What is your name?" I asked.

"I have no name," she said. "I have not yet been given one. My master has not yet given me a name."

"Your responses are correct," I said.

She sobbed with relief.

"Do you wish a name?" I asked.

"It is all within the will of Master," she said. "I want only only what Master wants. I desire only to please."

"It will be a convenience for me to have a name for you," I said.

"Yes, Master," she said.

"You are 'Feiqa,' " I said, naming her.

"Thank you, Master," she breathed, elated. 'Feiqa' is a lovely name. It is not unknown among dancers in the Tahari. Other such names are 'Aytul', 'Benek', 'Emine', 'Faize', 'Mine', 'Yasemine' and 'Yasine'. The 'qa' in the name 'Feiqa', incidentally, is pronounced rather like 'kah' in English. I have not spelled it 'Feikah' in English because the letter in question, in the Gorean spelling, is a 'kwah' and not a 'kef'. The 'kwah' in Gorean, which I think is possibly related, directly or indirectly, to the English 'q', does not always have a 'kwah' sound. Sometimes it does; sometimes it does not; in the name 'Feiqa' it does not. Although this may seem strange to native English speakers, it is certainly not linguistically unprecedented. For example, in Spanish, certainly one of the major languages spoken on Earth, the letter 'q' seldom, if ever, has the 'kwah' sound. Even in English, of course, the letter 'q' itself is not pronounced with a 'kwah' sound, but rather with a 'k' or 'c' sound, as in 'kue' or 'cue'.

I gathered my shield and weapons from the grass near us, where they lay with my pack. I slung my helmet over my left shoulder. I set my eyes to the southeast, away from the high gray walls of Samnium.

"Fetch my pack, Feiqa," I said.

"Yes, Master," she aid. She would serve as my beast of burden.

I watched her as she, unaided, struggled with the pack. Then she had it on her back. Her back was bent. "It is heavy, Master," she said. I did not respond to her. She lowered her head, bearing the pack. The wind moved through the trampled grass. She shivered. It was now late in Se'Kara. Already on Thassa the winds would be chill and the cold waves would be dashing and plunging to the bulwarks and washing the decks with their cold floods. I regarded the girl. In warmer seasons, or warmer areas, one may take one's time in making the decision as to whether or not a female is to be permitted clothing. Some masters keep their slaves naked for a year or more. The girl is then grateful when, and if, she is permitted clothing, be it only a bit of cloth or some rag or other. In this latitude, however, and in this season, I would have to see to the slave's garmenture. I looked back at the discarded clothing on the grass. She could take none of that, of course. It was no longer proper for her. It was the clothing of a free woman. That sort of thing was now behind her. I could have her fashion something from a rough blanket perhaps, and find her something to wrap her feet in. Too, I might be able to find her something which might function as a cloak. That she could clutch about her head and shoulders.

"Do you know how to heel, Feiqa?" I asked.

"Yes, Master," she said. She was a Gorean woman, familiar at least superficially with the duties and obligations of slaves. To be sure, as a recently free woman, she might perhaps find herself astounded and horrified at some of the things that would now, even routinely, be required of her. I did not know. Certain things which are not only common knowledge to slaves but even a normal, familiar part of their lives seem to be scarcely suspected by free women. These are the sorts of things about which free women, horrified and scandalized, scarcely believing them, sometimes whisper, fearfully, delightedly, among themselves. Some Earth-girl slaves, brought to Gor, incidentally, do not even know how to heel. Incredibly, they must be taught. They learn quickly, of course, in the collar, and subject to the whip.

I looked back, again, to the walls of Samnium. It had been spared the savageries of the war, doubtless because of its relationship with Cos. I then set out, to the southeast. I did not look back. I was followed by Feiqa.

2: There Are Hardships in these Times

I looked up from Feiqa, moaning in my arms, clutching a me. I had heard a tiny noise. I thrust her back, and away, she whimpering. I reached to my knife, and stood up, in the darkness. I stood on the lowered circular floor, dug out of the earth, packed down and tiled with stone, behind a part of a wall. It was the remains of a calked, woven-stick wall. It was now broken and charred. I could see the dark sky, with the moons, over its jagged, serrated edge. Leaves, curled and dark, blew by, and, standing there, I could hear the whisper of other leaves outside. They were blown to and fro, like dry, brittle fugitives, on the small, central commons between the huts.

We had made our camp here, in the burnt, roofless, half-fallen ruins of one of the huts. It had given us shelter from the wind. The village had been deserted, perhaps, judging from the absence of crockery, household effects and furnish-gings, even before it had been burned. It stood like most Gorean villages at the hub of its wheel of fields, the fields, striplike, spanning out from it like spokes. Most Gorean peasants live in such villages, many of them palisaded, which they leave in the morning to tend their fields, to which they return at night after their day's labors. The fields about this village, however, and near other villages, too, in this part of the country, were now untended. They were untilled and desolate. Armies had passed here.

"Is there someone there?" asked a voice, a woman's voice.

I did not respond. I listened.

15

"Who is there?" she asked. The voice sounded hollow and weak. I heard the whimpering of a child.

I did not respond.

"Who is there?" she begged.

I moved a little in the shadows, slowly, and back and toward the center of the hut. In moving slowly one tends to convey, on a very basic level, that one is not intending harm; to be sure, even predators like the larl occasionally abuse this form of signaling, for example, in hunting tabuk, using it for purposes of deception; more rapid movement, of course, tends to precipitate defensive reactions. In moving back I had also tended to reassure the figure in the doorway that I meant no harm; this movement, too, of course, had the advantage of ensuring me reaction space; in moving toward the center of the hut I made it possible for her to see me better, this tending, too, one supposes, to allay suspicions; in this way, too, of course, I secured myself weapon space. These things seem to be instinctual, or, at least, to be done with very little conscious thought. They seem very natural. We tend to take them for granted. It is interesting, however, upon occasion, to speculate upon the possible origins of just such familiar and taken-for-granted accommodations and adjustments. It seems possible they have been selected for. At any rate, they, or their analogues, are found throughout the animal kingdom.

The small figure stood just outside what had once been the threshold of the hut. It had come there naturally, it seemed, as if perhaps by force of habit, or conviction, although the door was no longer there. It seemed forlorn, and weary. It clutched something in its arms.

"Are you a brigand?" she asked.

"No," I said.

"It is a free woman," whispered Feiqa, kneeling on the blankets.

"Cover your nakedness," I said. Feiqa pulled her tiny, coarse tunic about herself.

"This is my house," said the woman.

"Do you wish us to leave?" I asked.

"Do you have anything to eat?" she asked.

"A little," I said. "Are you hungry?"

"No," she said.

"Perhaps the child is hungry?" I asked.

"No," she said. "We have plenty."

I said nothing.

"I am a free woman!" she said, suddenly, piteously.

"We have food," I said. "We have used your house. Permit us to share it with you."

"Oh, I have begged at the wagons," she said suddenly, sobbing. "It is not a new thing for me! I have begged! I have been on my knees for a crust of bread. I have fought with other women for garbage beside the road."

"You shall not beg in your own house," I said.

She began to sob, and the small child, bundled in her arms, began to whimper.

I approached her very slowly, and drew back the edge of the coverlet about the child. Its eyes seemed very large. Its face was dirty.

"There are hundreds of us," she said, "following the wagons. In these times only soldiers can live."

"The forces of Ar," I said, "are even now being mustered, to repel the invaders. The soldiers of Cos, and their mercenary contingents, no matter how numerous, will be no match for the marshaled squares of Ar."

"My child is hungry," she said. "What do I care for the banners of Ar or Cos?"

"Are you companioned?" I asked.

"I do not know any longer," she said.

"Where are the men?" I asked.

"Gone," she said. "Fled, driven away, killed. Many were impressed into service. They are gone, all of them are gone."

"What happened here?" I asked.

"Foragers," she said. "They came for supplies, and men. They took what we had. Then they burned the village."

I nodded. I supposed things might not have been much different if the foragers had been soldiers of Ar.

"Would you like to stay in my house tonight?" she asked.

"Yes," I said.

"Build up the fire," I said to Feiqa, who was kneeling

back in the shadows. She had put her tunic about her. Too, she had pulled up the blanket about her body. As soon as I had spoken she crawled over the flat stones to the ashes of the fire, and began to prod among them, stirring them with a narrow stick, searching for covert vital embers.

"Surely you are a brigand," said the woman to me.

"No," I said.

"Then you are a deserter," she said. "It would be death for you to be found."

"No," I said. "I am not a deserter."

"What are you then?" she asked.

"A traveler," I said.

"What is your caste?" she asked.

"Scarlet is the color of my caste," I said.

"I thought it might be," she said. "Who but such as you can live in these times?"

I gave her some bread from my pack, from a rep-cloth draw-sack, and a bit of dried meat, paper thin, from its tied leather envelope.

"There, there," she crooned to the child, putting bits of bread into its mouth.

"I have water," I said, "but no broth, or soup."

"The ditches are filled with water," she said. "Here, here, little one."

"Why did you come back?" I asked.

"I have heard there are more wagons coming, she said. "Perhaps there will be fewer to follow these."

"You came back because you wanted to see the village again?" I speculated. "Perhaps you wanted to see if some of the men had returned."

"They are gone," she said.

"Why did you come back?" I asked.

"I came to look for roots," she said, chewing.

"Did you find any?" I asked.

She looked at me quickly, narrowly. "No," she said.

"Have more bread," I said, offering it.

She hesitated.

"It is a gift, like your hospitality." I said, "between free persons. Did you not accept it I should be shamed."

"You are kind," she said, "Not to make me beg in my own house."

"Eat," I said.

Feiqa had now succeeded in reviving the fire. It was now a small, sturdy, cheerful blaze. She knelt near it, on her bare knees, in the tiny, coarse tunic, on the flat, sooted, stained stones, tending it.

"She is collared!" cried the woman, suddenly, looking at Feiqa.

Feiqa shrank back, her hand inadvertently going to her collar. Too, her thigh now bore a brand, the common Kajira mark, high on her left thigh, just under the hip. I had had it put on her two days after leaving the vicinity of Samnium, at the town of Market of Semris, well known for its sales of tarsks. It had been put on in the house of the slaver, Teibar. He brands superbly, and his prices are competitive. No longer could the former Lady Charlotte, once of Samnium, be mistaken for a free woman.

The free woman looked at Feiqa, aghast.

"Belly," I said to Feiqa.

Immediately Feiqa, trembling, went to her belly on the stained, sooted stones near the fire.

"I will not have a slave in my house!" said the free woman.

Feiqa trembled.

"I know your sort!" cried the free woman. "I see them sometimes with the wagons, sleek, chained and well-fed, while free women starve!"

"It is natural that such women be cared for," I said. "They are salable animals, properties. They represent a form of wealth. It is as natural to look after them as it is to look after tharlarion or tarsks."

"You will not stay in my house!" cried the free woman to Feiqa. "I will not keep livestock in my house!"

Feiqa clenched her small fists beside her head. I could see she did not care to hear this sort of thing. In Samnium she had been a rich woman, of a family well known on its Street of Coins. Doubtless many times she would have held herself a thousand times superior to the poor peasant women, coming in from the villages, in their bleached woolen robes, bringing their sacks and baskets of grain and produce to the city's markets. Her clenched fists indicated that perhaps she did not yet fully understand that all that was now behind her.

"Animal!" screamed the free woman.

Feiqa looked up angrily, tears in her eyes, and lifted herself an inch or two from the floor on the palms of her hands. "I was once as free as you!" she said.

"Oh!" cried Feiqa, suddenly, sobbing, recoiling from my kick, and then "Aii!," she cried, in sharp pain, as, my hand in her hair, she was jerked up to a kneeling position.

"But no more!" I said. I was furious. I could not believe her insolence.

"No, Master," she wept, "no more!"

I then, with the back of my hand, and then its palm, first one, and then the other, back and forth, to and fro, again and again, lashed her head from side to side. Then I flung her on her belly before the free woman. The was blood on my hand, and about her mouth and lips.

"Forgive me!" she begged the free woman. "Forgive me!"

"Address her as 'Mistress,' " I said. It is customary for Gorean slaves to address free women as "Mistress" and free men as "Master."

"I beg your forgiveness, Mistress!" wept the girl. "Forgive me, please, I beg it of you!"

"She is new to the collar," I apologized to the free woman. "I think that perhaps even now she does not yet fully understand its import. Yet I think that perhaps she understands something more of its meanng now than she did a few moments ago. Shall I kill her?"

Hearing this question Feiqa cried out in fear and shuddered uncontrollably on her belly before the free woman. She then clutched at her ankles and, putting down her head, began to cover her feet with desperate, placatory kisses. "Please forgive the animal!" wept Feiqa. "The animal begs your forgiveness! Please, Mistress! Please, gracious, beautiful, noble Mistress! Forgive Feiqa, please forgive Feiqa, who is only a slave!" I looked down at Feiqa. I think she now

understood her collar better than before. I had, for her insolence and unconscionable behavior, literally placed her life in
the hands of the free woman. She now understood this sort of
thing could be done. Too, she would now understand even
more keenly how her life was completely and totally, absolutely,
at the mercy of a Master. It thus came home to her, I think,
fully, perhaps for the first time, what it could be to be a
Gorean slave.

"Are you sorry for what you have done?" asked the free
woman.

"Yes, yes, yes, yes, yes, Mistress!" wept Feiqa, her head
down, doing obeisance to one who was a thousand times,
nay, infinitely, her superior, the free woman of the peasants.

"You may live," said the free woman.

"Thank you, Mistress!" wept Feiqa, head down, shuddering and sobbing uncontrollably at the free woman's feet.

"Have you learned anything from this, Feiqa?" I asked.

"Yes, Master," she wept.

"What?" I asked.

"That I am a slave," she said.

"Do not forget it, Feiqa," I told her.

"No, Master," she sobbed, fervently.

"Will you stay the night?" asked the free woman.

"With your permission," I said.

"You are welcome here," she said. "But you will have to
sleep your animal outside."

I glanced down at Feiqa. She was still shuddering. It would
be difficult for her, I supposed, at least for a time, to cope
with her new comprehensions concerning the nature of her
condition.

"I do not allow livestock in my house," said the free
woman.

I smiled, looking down at Feiqa. To be sure, the former
rich young lady of Samnium was now livestock, that and
nothing more. Too I smiled because of the free woman's
concern, and outrage, at the very thought of having a slave in
the house. This seemed amusing to me for two reasons. First,
it is quite common for Goreans to keep slaves, a lovely form
of domestic animal, in the house. Indeed, the richer and more

well-to-do the Gorean the more likely it is that he will have slaves in the house. In the houses of administrators, in the domiciles of high merchants, in the palaces of Ubars, for example, slaves, and usually beautiful ones, for they can afford them, are often abundant. Secondly, it is not unusual either for many peasants to keep animals in the house, usually verr or bosk, sometimes tarsk, at least in the winter. The family lives in one section of the dwelling, and the animals are quartered in the other.

"Go outside," I told Feiqa.

"Yes, Master," she said.

"Would you like a little more food?" I asked the free woman. "I have some more."

She looked at me.

"Please," I said.

She took two more wedges of yellow Sa-Tarna bread. I put some more sticks on the fire.

"Here," she said, embarrassed. She drew some roots, and two suls, from her robe. They had been freshly dug. Dirt still clung to them. She put them down on the stones, between us. I sat down cross-legged, and she knelt down, opposite me, knees together, in the common fashion of the Gorean free woman. The roots, the two suls, were between us. She rocked the child in her arms.

"I thought you could find no roots." I smiled.

"Some were left in the garden," she said. "I remembered them. I came back for them. There was very little left though. Others obviously had come before me. These things were missed. They are poor stuff. We used to use the produce of that garden for tarsk feed."

"They are fine roots," I said, "and splendid suls."

"We even hunt for tarsk troughs," she said, wearily, "and dig in the cold dirt of the pens. The tarsk are gone, but sometimes a bit of feed remains, fallen between the cracks, or missed by the animals, having been trampled into the mud. There are many tricks we learn in these days."

"I do not want to take your food," I said.

"Would you shame me?" she asked.

"No," I said.

"Share my kettle," she said.

"Thank you," I said. I took one of the roots and broke off a bit of it in my hand. I rubbed the dirt from it. I bit into it. "Good," I said. I did not eat more, however. I would let her keep her food. I had done in this matter what would be sufficient. I had, in what I had done, acknowledged her as the mistress in her house; I had shown her honor; I had "shared her kettle."

"Little Andar is asleep," she said, looking at the bundled child.

I nodded.

"You may sleep your slave inside the threshold," she said.

3: Tula

"Throw back your hoods, pull down your veils, females!" laughed the wagoner.

The women crowding about the back of the wagon, many with their hands outstretched, the sleeves of their robes falling back, cried out in consternation.

"—if you would be fed!" he added.

These women must be new, I thought. Probably they had come only recently to the wagons, probably trekking overland from some contacted village, perhaps one from as far away as fifty pasangs, a common range for the excursions, the searches and collections of mounted foragers. Most of the women I had seen following the wagons, at any rate, knew enough by now to approach them only bareheaded, as female suppliants, too, to be more pleasing to the men who might possibly be persuaded to feed them, with their hair as visible and loose as that of slaves. Similarly, most had already discarded or hidden their veils, even when not begging. They did not even wear them in their own small, foul, often-fireless makeshift camps near the wagons, camps, to be sure, to which men might sometimes come. It had been discovered that a woman who is seen with a veil, even if she has lowered the veil, abjectly and piteously face-stripping herself, is less likely to be fed than one with no veil in evidence. Too, of course, it had been quickly noted that such women, too, tended to be less frequently selected for the pleasure of the drivers. The men with the wagons had not seen fit to permit the women the dignity of veiling. In this, of course, they treated them like slaves.

"Please!" cried a woman, thrusting back her hood and

tearing away her veil. "Feed me! Please, feed me!" The others, too, then, almost instantly, hastily, each seeming to hurry to be before the others, some moaning and crying out in misery, unhooded and unveiled themselves.

"That is better, females," laughed the driver.

Many of the women moaned and wept.

They were now, to be sure, I mused, in their predicament and helplessness, even though free women, as the driver had implied, little more than mere females. One could probably not be more a female unless one was a slave.

"Feed us!" they cried piteously to the driver, many of them with their arms outstretched, their hands lifted, their palms opened, crowding and pressing about the back of the wagon. "We beg food!" "We are hungry!" "Please!" "Feed us, please!" "Please!"

I looked at their faces. On the whole they seemed to be simple, plain women, peasant women, and peasant lasses. One or two of them, I thought, might be suitable for the collar.

"Here!" cried the driver, laughing, throwing pieces of bread from a sack to one and then another of the women. The first piece of bread he threw to the woman who had been the first to unhood and face-strip herself, perhaps thereby rewarding her for her intelligence and alacrity. He then threw pieces to certain others of the women, generally to those who were the prettiest and begged the hardest. Sometimes, not unoften, these pieces of bread were torn away from the prettier, more feminine women by their brawnier, huskier, more masculine fellows. Where there are no men, or no true men, to protect them, feminine women will, in a grotesque perversion of nature, be controlled, exploited and dominated by more masculine women, sometimes monsters and mere caricatures of men. Yet even such grosser women, sometimes little more than surrogates for males, can upon occasion, in the hands of a strong, uncompromising master, he forced to manifest and fulfil, realizing then for the first time, the depths of their long-denied, long-suppressed womanness. There are two sexes. They are not the same.

"More, more, please!" begged the females.

Then, amusing himself, the driver tossed some bits of

bread into the air and watched the desperate, anxious women crowd and bunch under it, pushing and shoving for position, and trying to leap upward, thrusting at one another, to snatch at it.

"More, please!" they screamed.

I saw again a large straight-hipped woman seize a piece of bread fiercely from a smaller woman, one with a delicious love cradle. Then with both of her hands she thrust it in her mouth and, bending over, shouldering and thrusting, fought her way back to where, crouching down, watching for others, she could eat it alone. None could take it from her, save a man, of course, who might have done it easily.

"That is all!" laughed the driver.

"No!" wept women.

"Bread!" wept others.

It was clear that something, in spite of what the driver had said, remained in the sack. He grinned and wiped his face with his arm. It had been a joke.

"Another crust, please!" begged a woman.

"Feed us!" cried another.

"You are the masters!" wept one of the women, suddenly. "Feed us! Please, feed us!"

The driver laughed and drew forth a handful of crusts from the sack, which crusts apparently constituted the remainder of its contents. Then he flung these over the heads of the women, well behind them. They turned about and, running, flinging themselves to their hands and knees in the dirt, scrambling about, snatching and screaming, fought for them.

The driver watched them for a time, amused. Then he turned away, and, stepping among the bundles in the wagon bed, went to the wagon box. This type of box serves both as the driver's seat, or bench, and as a literal box, in which various items may be stored, usually spare parts, tools and personal belongings. It ususally locks. He lifted the lid of the wagon box, which lid served also as the surface of his seat or bench, and dropped the empty sack within, and then shut the box. Also, from near the box, in front of it, near where his feet would rest in driving, he picked up a tharlarion whip. He had had experience with such women before, it seemed.

"No more!" he said, angrily. "No more!"

Women now again, pathetic and desperate, robes now wrinkled and dirty from where they had knelt, and crawled and fought for the crusts and crumbs in the dirt, began to approach the wagon. The whip lashed out, cracking over their heads. They fell back.

"More!" they begged. "Please!"

"It is all gone," said the driver. "It is all gone now! Get away, sluts!"

"You have bread!" wept one. This was true, of course. The wagon's lading was Sa-Tarna bread, and also, incidentally, Sa-Tarna meal and flour. It creaked under perhaps a hundred and fifty Gorean stone of such stores. These supplies, of course, were not intended for vagabonds or itinerants who might be encountered on the road but for the kitchens set up at the various nights' encampments.

"Back, sluts!" he cried. "I carry stores for soldiers!"

"Please!" wept more than one woman.

"I see that it was a mistake to have fed you anything!" he cried angrily.

"No, no!" cried a woman. "We are sorry! We beg your forgiveness, gencrous sir!"

"Please, more bread!" wept others.

He lifted the whip, menacingly. It was a tharlarion whip. I would not care to have been struck with it.

"Get back!" he cried.

Some crowded yet more closely about the wagon. "Bread!" they begged. "Please!" Then the whip fell amongst them and they, though free women, fell back, away from it, crying out in pain, and scattering.

"Tomorrow then," he cried, angrily, "if you wish, there will be nothing for any of you!"

"No, please!" wept the women.

"Kneel down," he said. Swiftly they fell on their knees, behind the wagon. "Heads down to the dirt," he commanded. They complied. I was not certain that it was proper to command free women in this fashion. It was rather as one might command slaves. Still, women, even free women, look well, obeying. The slave, of course, must obey. She has no choice.

"You may lift your heads," he said. "Are you contrite?" he inquired.

"Yes," moaned several of the women.

"Perhaps you are moved to beg my forgiveness?" he asked.

"We beg your forgiveness, generous and noble sir!" called a woman.

"Yes, yes!" said others.

"Well," he said, seemingly perhaps a bit mollified, "we shall see." He then put down the whip and took his place on the wagon box. He released the brake, pulling its wooden handle back on its pivot with his left hand, freeing its leather-lined shoe from the left front wheel. "Ho!" he cried to the tharlarion and, with a crack of the whip, a creak of wood, a rattle of chain traces, and a grunt from the beast, was on his way. I watched the wagon for a moment or two, trundling down the road on its wooden-spoked, iron-rimmed wheels. I tied a rope on Feiqa's neck. "Come along," I told her.

In a few moments I had caught up with the wagon. I looked back. The women in the road were only now getting to their feet. Doubtless they were still terribly hungry. Many, too, seemed weary and dazed. They had apparently come only this morning from some village to the road. They had now begun to learn what it was for a woman to follow the wagons.

I took my pack from Feiqa's back and threw it, and my spear and shield, into the wagon. I then climbed up to the wagon box beside the driver. "Tal," said he, looking over at me.

"Tal," said I to him. I tied Feiqa's neck rope to the side of the wagon. She stayed close to the side of the wagon, almost so close that I could reach out and touch her. She was frightened, I think, at the looks she received from some of the free women at the side of the road. "No!" said the driver, sternly, more than once, lifting his whip, as such women rose to their feet, as though to approach him. Not all of these women, of course, followed the wagons. Some, doubtless, merely came from their villages, or the remains of their villages, down to the side of the road to beg as the wagons passed. In such villages, I supposed, there might still be some food. When that was exhausted perhaps these women, too, would put their belongings in a bundle and trek after the wagons. One of the women did come up beside the wagon with a switch and struck Feiqa in fury three times. Feiqa, on her rope, moving, shrank small before her, trying to cover her face and body. There is little love lost between free women and slaves, particularly in these times.

"Oh!" cried Feiqa, suddenly stung by a stone, hurled by another woman. She then walked weeping, almost pressed against the side of the wagon. She could not even think of daring to object to such treatment, of course. In the hut of the free woman, last night, she had learned, unconditionally, that she was a slave. I wondered if the former rich young woman of Samnium had herself, in bygone days, accorded slaves similar treatment. I supposed so. It is not uncommon on the part of free women. Now, of course, as a slave herself, she would understand clearly what it was to be the one who is subjectable to such treatment. Perhaps free women would treat slaves somewhat differently if they understood that one day it might be they themselves whom they might find in the collar. In these attacks, of course, Feiqa was in no danger of being seriously injured, or disfigured or maimed. Accordingly, I did not take any official notice of them.

The wagons, for the most part, were well scattered apart on the road. Their intervals were irregular and sometimes one or another of them stopped. We had come to the vicinity of the road, the Genesian Road, early this morning. Surmounting a rise, we had seen it below us, and the wagons, in their long line, stretched out in the distance. We had then descended the gentle declivity slowly, through the wet grass, to its side. I had some idea of the forces of Cos which had made their landing at Brundisium earlier in Se'Kara. I had seen the invasion fleet entering upon its peaceful harborage at Brundisium. Never before on Gor, I suspected, had such forces been marshaled. It was an invasion, it seemed, not of an army, but of armies. To be sure, many of its contingents were composed of mercenaries sworn to the temporary service of diverse fee captains, and not Cosian regulars. It is difficult to manage such men. They do not fight for Home Stones. They are often little more than armed rabbles. Many are little better than thieves and cutthroats. They must be well paid and assured of ample booty. Accordingly the tactics and movements of such groups, functions of captains who know their men well, and must be wary of them, are often less indicative of sound military considerations, strategic or otherwise, than of organized brigandage. I did not think that such men would stand well, even in their numbers, against the well-trained soldiers of Ar.

"I trust you are not a brigand," said the driver, not looking at me.

"No," I said.

"You would not get much here," he said, "except Sa-Tarna meal and such."

"I am not a brigand," I said.

"Have you fled from some captain?" he asked.

"No," I said.

"You are a big fellow," he said. "Are you in service?"

"No," I said.

"Do you seek service?" he asked.

"No," I said.

"You own your own weapons?" he asked.

"Yes," I said.

"Raymond, he of Rive-de-Bois, is recruiting," he said. "So, too, is Conrad of Hochburg, and Pietro Vacchi." These men were mercenary captains. There were dozens of such companies. If one owns one's own weapons, of course, one need not be armed at the expense of the company. Too, if one owns one's own weapons, it may usually be fairly assumed that one knows how to use them. Such men, then, may receive a certain preference in being added to the rolls. They are likely to be experienced soldiers, not eager lads just in from the farms. In many mercenary companies, incidentally, there are no uniforms and no issuance of standard equipment. Too, many such companies are, for most practical purposes, disbanded during the winter, the captain retaining then only a cadre of officers and professionals. Then, in the spring, after obtaining a war contract, sometimes obtained by competitive bidding, they begin anew, almost from the beginning, with recruiting and training.

It is quite unusual, incidentally, for such men as Raymond and Conrad to be recruiting now, in Se'Kara. It was really a time in which most soldiers on Gor would be thinking about the pleasures of winter quarters or a return to their own villages and towns. There are usually diverse explanations, depending on the situation, for the type of forced recruiting to which men in some of the villages had been subjected. Sometimes a passing army desires merely to amplify its forces, or replace losses, particularly among the lighter arms, such as bowmen, slingers and javelin men. Sometimes the recruiting is done more for the purposes of obtaining a labor force, for siegeworks and entrenching camps, than for actual combat. Sometimes the mercenary captains, whose negotiated, signed contracts call for the furnishing of certain numbers of armed men for their various employers, have little choice but to impress some reluctant fellows, that their obligatory quotas may be met. More than one fellow has sworn an oath of allegiance with a sword at his throat. Most mercenaries, of course, join their captains voluntarily. Indeed, skilled and famous captains, ones noted for their military skill and profitable campaigns, must often close down their enlisting tables early in En'Kara.

"So, too, is Dietrich of Tarnburg," he said.

"Oh?" I said. "For what side?"

"Who knows?" chuckled the driver.

Dietrich of Tarnburg, of the high city of Tarnburg, some two hundred pasangs to the north and west of Hochburg, both substantially mountain fortresses, both in the more southern and civilized ranges of the Voltai, was well-known to the warriors of Gor. His name was almost a legend. It was he who had won the day on the fields of both Piedmont and Cardonicus, who had led the Forty Days' March, relieving the siege of Talmont, who had effected the crossing of the Issus in 10,122 C.A., in the night evacuation of Keibel Hill, when I had been in Torvaldsland, and who had been the victor in the battles of Rovere, Kargash, Edgington, Teveh Pass, Gordon Heights, and the Plains of Sanchez. His campaigns were studied in all the war schools of the high cities. I knew him from scrolls I had studied years ago in Ko-ro-ba, and from volumes in my library in Port Kar, such as the commentaries of Minicius and the anonymous analyses of "The Diaries," sometimes attributed to the military historian, Carl Commenius, of Argentum, rumored to have once been a mercenary himself.

It was Dietrich of Tarnburg who had first introduced the "harrow" to positional warfare on Gor, that formation named for the large, rakelike agricultural instrument, used for such tasks as the further leveling of ground after plowing and, sometimes, on the great farms, for the covering of seed. In this formation spikes of archers, protected by iron-shod stakes and sleen pits, project beyond the forward lines of the heavily armed warriors and their reserves. This formation, if approached head-on by tharlarion ground cavalry, is extremely effective. It constitutes, in effect, a set of corridors of death through which the cavalry must ride, in which it is commonly decimated before it can reach the main lines of the defenders. When the cavalry is disorganized, shattered and torn by missile fire, and turns about to retreat, the defenders, fresh and eager, initiate their own attack.

He was also the initiator of the oblique advance in Gorean field warfare, whereby large numbers of men may be concentrated at crucial points while the balance of the enemy remains unengaged. This formation makes it possible for a given army, choosing to attack only limited portions of the enemy, portions smaller than itself, to engage an army which, all told, may be three times its size, and, not unoften, to turn the flank of this much larger body, producing its confusion and rout. Too, if the attack fails, the advanced force may fall back, knowing that the balance of their army, indeed, its bulk, rested and fresh, not yet engaged, is fully prepared to cover their retreat.

Most impressive to me, perhaps, was Dietrich of Tarnburg's coordination of air and ground forces, and his transposition of certain techniques and weapons of siege warfare to the field. The common military response to aerial attack from tarnsmen is the "shield roof" or "shield shed," a formation the same as, or quite similar to, a formation once known on Earth as the *testudo*, or "tortoise." In this formation shields are held in such a way that they constitute a wall for the outer ranks and a roof for the inner ranks. This is primarily a defensive formation but it may also be used for advancing under fire. The common Gorean defense against tharlarion attack, if it must be met on open ground, is the stationary, defensive square, defended by braced spears. At Rovere and Kargash Dietrich coordinated his air and ground cavalry in such a way as to force his opponents into sturdy but relatively inflexible defensive squares. He then advanced his archers in long, enveloping lines; in this way they could muster a much broader front for low-level, point-blank firepower than could the narrower concentrated squares.

He then utilized, for the first time in Gorean field warfare, first at Rovere, and later at Kargash, mobile siege equipment, catapults mounted on wheeled platforms, which could fire over the heads of the draft animals. From these engines, hitherto employed only in siege warfare, now become a startling and devastating new weapon, in effect, a field artillery, tubs of burning pitch and flaming naphtha, and siege javelins, and giant boulders, fell in shattering torrents upon the immobilized squares. The shield shed was broken. The missiles of archers rained upon the confused, hapless defenders. Even mobile siege towers, pushed from within by straining tharlarion, pressing their weight against prepared harnesses, trundled toward them, their bulwarks swarming with archers and javelin men. The squares were broken. Then again the ponderous, earthshaking, bellowing, grunting, trampling thalarion ground cavalry charged, this time breaking through the walls like dried straw, followed by waves of screaming, heavily armed spearmen. The ranks of the enemy then irremediably broke. The air howled with panic. Rout was upon them. Spears and shields were cast away that men might flee the more rapidly. There was then little left to be done. It would be the cavalries which would attend to the fugitives.

"I had thought rather," I said, "of perhaps joining the wagons for a time."

"They need drivers," said the fellow. "Can you handle tharlarion?"

"I can handle high tharlarion," I said. Long ago I had ridden guard in a caravan of Mintar, a merchant of Ar.

"I mean the draft fellows," said the driver.

"I suppose so," I said. It seemed likely to me that I could handle these more docile, sluggish beasts, if I had been able to handle their more agile brothers, the saddle tharlarion.

"They take a great deal of beating about the head and neck," he said.

I nodded. That was not so much different from the high tharlarion, either. They are usually controlled by voice commands and the blows of a spear. The tharlarion, incidentally, at least compared to mammals, seems to have a very sluggish nervous system. It seems almost impervious to pain. Most of the larger varieties have two brains, or, perhaps better, a brain and a smaller brainlike organ. The brain, or one brain, is located in the head, and the other brain, or the brainlike organ, is located near the base of the spine.

I looked down to Feiqa, walking beside the wagon, the rope on her neck. "Tharlarion," I told her, expanding on the driver's remark, "show little susceptibility to pain."

"Yes, Master," she said.

"In this," I said, "they closely resemble female slaves."

"Oh, no, Master!" she cried. "No!"

"No?" I said.

"No," she said, looking up earnestly, frightened, "we are terribly susceptible to pain, truly!"

"Doubtless you were as a free woman," I said, "but now you are a slave."

"I am even more susceptible to pain now," she said, "for now I have felt pain, and know what it is like, and now I have a slave girl's total vulnerability and helplessness, and know that anything can be done to me! Too, my entire body has become a thousand times more responsive and sensitive, a thousand times more meaningful and alive, since I have been locked in the collar. I assure you, Master, I am a thousand times more susceptible to pain now than ever I was before!"

I smiled. Such transformations were common in the female slave. Just as their sensitivities to pleasure and feeling, sexual and otherwise, physical and psychological, conscious and subconscious, were greatly increased and intensified by being imbonded, so too, concomitantly, naturally, were their sensitivities to pain. The same changes that so considerably increased their capacities in certain directions increased them also in others, and put them ever more helplessly, and hopelessly, at the mercy of their masters.

"Ah," she said, chagrined, putting down her lovely head, "Master teases his girl."

"Perhaps," I said.

She kept her head down. She blushed. She looked lovely, the light, locked, steel collar on her throat.

I reached down and lifted her up, by the arms, swinging her up, and back, into the wagon. She would be weary from her walking. "Thank you, Master," she said, much pleased. She then knelt behind us, rather close to us, on some folded sacks in the wagon bed, the rope attaching her to the wagon still tied on her neck. I began to consider in what ways I should have her this evening.

"Bread! Bread!" cried a woman to one side. There another Sa-Tarna wagon had stopped. The driver, who had apparently been adjusting the harness of his beast, was now again on the wagon box, his reins and whip in hand.

"Away!" cried the driver.

She threw herself before the wagon. "Bread!" she screamed. He cracked the whip and the beast lurched forward, the woman screamed, barely scrambling from its path. I had little doubt that had she not moved as she had she would have been run over.

"They will try almost anything," said my driver, as our wagon rolled past the woman. She was shuddering. She had just escaped death or crippling. "Sometimes they will send their children out beside the road to do the begging. They themselves hide in the brush. Sometimes I throw them some bread. Sometimes I don't. It seems the women themselves should beg, if they want the bread."

"Perhaps they do not want to pay for it, in the way of women," I said.

"They will pay for it, and in the way of women, when they are hungry enough," said the driver.

I nodded. That was true, I supposed. This driver, incidentally, seemed to me a decent, good-hearted fellow. Certainly he had stopped and fed some of the women along the road. That I had seen. Too, he had doubtless done that in spite of the fact that he would now come in with a short load. Many of the drivers, I speculated, would not have behaved so. Also, he had not objected to my riding with him, nor to carrying Feiqa. Yes, he seemed a good fellow.

"How far ahead are the troops?" I asked.

"Their lines of march extend for pasangs, with intervals, too, of pasangs," he said.

I nodded. It would take days for them to pass through the country. They were apparently far from the vicinity of any enemy. Accordingly, they exhibited little concern with possible imperatives of assembly and concentration. Interestingly, not even raiding parties, as far as I knew, had delayed or harried their advance. They might as well have been marching through their own countries in a time of peace.

"The rearward contingents of the units before us will be some ten pasangs up the road," he said.

"How many troops are there, altogether?" I asked.

"A great many," he said. "Are you a spy?"

"No," I said.

"Look," he said, gesturing.

I glanced to the right, and upward. On the summit of a small hill I saw some seven or eight riders, riders of the high tharlarion, the tharlarion shifting and clawing about under them, with tharlarion lances. They were clad in dusty, soiled leather, riding leather, to protect their legs from the scaly hides of the beasts, and helmeted. Two had shields slung at their back. Shields of the others hung at the left sides of their saddles. They seemed an unkempt, dirty, grim lot. About the beasts' necks, and behind the saddles, hung panniers of grain and sacks of woven netting containing dried larmas and brown suls. Across the saddle of one were tied the hind feet, crossed, of two verr, their throats cut, the blood now brown on the sides of the tharlarion. Another fellow had a basket of vulos, tied shut. Another had strings of sausage hung about his neck and shoulders.

There were no herded tarsk or bosk with the group. Such animals were probably extremely rare now, at least within one or two day's ride of the march. Still the fellows seemed to have done very well. Doubtless they had fared far better than most engaged in their business. Too, I noted that their interests had not been confined merely to foodstuffs. From the saddle of more than one there dangled armlets, two-handled bowls and cups. Too, from the saddle of one a long tether looped back to the crossed bound wrists of a female. Doubtless she had been found pleasing. Thus she had been brought along. Doubtless she was destined for the collar. Near the pawing feet of the leader's tarlarion, in their tunics of white wool, there stood two stout peasant lads, bound, heavy sticks thrust before their elbows and behind their backs, their arms bound to these at the back, their wrists, a rope across their bellies, held back, tied at their sides. They would be recruits for some captain, requiring to fill gaps in his ranks. They would probably bring their captors in the neighborhood of a copper tarsk apiece.

The fellows on the tharlarion looked down at the wagons and then moved down the hill and forward. Two or three women, I now saw, coming over the hill, had apparently been following them, probably on foot from some village. One of the fellows, shouting angrily, turned his tharlarion about and, waving his lance, urging it up the slope toward them, charged them. They scattered before him, and he, not pursuing them, turned about and, in a moment, had rejoined his fellows. The women now hung back, daring to follow no further. I looked after the riders, now two or three wagons ahead of us, the two peasant lads, and the female, stumbling behind them on her tether.

"Foragers," said the driver.

I looked back at Feiqa, and she lowered her eyes, not meeting mine.

"The units ahead of us," I said, turning about, "are the rear guard of the army, I take it."

"No," he said.

"Oh?" I said.

"There are units," he said, "and wagons, and units. I do not know how far it goes on."

I was then silent, for a time. There must be an incredible amount of men, I surmised. I knew, of course, that considerable forces had been landed at Brundisium. What I was not sure of, however, was the current distribution, or deployment, of these forces.

"You are sure you are not a spy," he said.

"Yes," I smiled, "I am sure." I supposed, of course, that Ar must be attempting to keep itself apprised of the movements of the enemy. Presumably there would be spies, or informers of some sort, with the troops or the wagons. It is not difficult to infiltrate spies into mercenary troops, incidentally, where the men come from different backgrounds, castes and cities, and little is asked of them other than their ability to handle weapons and obey orders. Yet, if men of Ar, or men in the pay of Ar, were attending to these matters, and submitting current and accurate reports, Ar herself, for whatever reason, unpreparedness or whatever, had not acted.

I looked at the string of wagons ahead.

How different things seemed from the marches of the forces of Ar, and others of the high cities. When the men of Ar moved, for example, and whenever possible they would do so on the great military roads, such as the Viktel Aria, they used a measured pace, often kept by a drum, and, including rests, would each day cover a calculable distance, usually forty pasangs. At forty-pasang intervals there would generally, on the military roads, be a fortified camp, supplied in advance with ample provisions. Some of these camps became towns. Later some became cities. These roads and camps, and measures, made it possible to move troops not only efficiently and rapidly, but assisted in military planning. One could tell, for example, how long it would take to bring a certain number of men to bear on a certain point. The permanent garrisons of the fortified camps, too, of course, exercise a significant peace-keeping and holding role in the outer districts of a city's power. Too, training and recruiting often take place in such camps. To be sure, these forces of Cos could not be expected to have come over and taken a few months to attend to the leisurely construction of permanent camps along the route of their projected march. Still, judging from the nature of the supply column, or columns, their progress seemed very slow, almost leisurely. It was as though they feared nothing. Their numbers, I speculated, might have emboldened them. Why had Ar not acted, I wondered.

"Have you seen tarnsmen in the sky?" I asked.

"No," he said. Cos, of course, would have tarnsmen at her disposal. But even those, it seemed, were not patrolling the line of march.

"Why are there no guards with the supply train?" I asked. "Surely that is unusual."

"I do not know," he said. "I have wondered about it. Perhaps it is not thought that they are necessary."

"Have there been no attacks?" I asked. Surely it seemed that Ar might be expected to apply her tarnsmen to the effort to disrupt the enemy's lines of supply and communication. Perhaps her tarnsmen had not been able to reach the wagons. If command in Ar had been in the hands of Marlenus, her Ubar, I had little doubt that Ar would have acted by now. Marlenus, however, as the report went, was not in Ar. He was supposedly on an expedition into the Voltai, conducting a punitive expedition against raiders of Treve. Why he had not been recalled, if it were possible, I did not understand.

"What would you do if tarnsmen of Ar arrived?" I asked.

"I would leap under the wagon," he chuckled. "If they saw fit to land, I would take to my heels with all haste."

"You would not defend your lading, your freight?" I asked.

"That is not my job," he said. "That is the job of soldiers. I am paid to drive. That is what I do."

"What of the other drivers?" I asked.

"They would do the same, I would suppose," he said. "We are wagoners, not soldiers."

"The entire train then," I said, "or at least these wagons, is open to attack. Yet Ar has not attacked. That is interesting."

"Perhaps," he said.

"Why not?" I asked.

He shrugged. "I do not know. Perhaps they can't get here."

"Even with small strike forces, disguised as peasants?"

"Perhaps not," he said. "I do not know."

It was now growing dark along the road. Here and there, back from the road, on one side or the other, there were small camps of free women. In some of them there were tiny fires lit. Some small shelters had been pitched, too, in some of these camps, little more than tarpaulins or blankets stretched over sticks. Sometimes some of the women about these tiny fires stood up and watched us, as we rolled past. I recalled the free woman I had met last night in her hut. She had not come down to the wagons as far as I knew. We had left her before she had awakened. I had left some more food with her, and had tied a golden tarn disk of Port Kar, from my wallet, in the corner of the child's blanket. With that she might buy much. Too, with it, or its residue, she might be able to make her way to a distant village, far from the trekking of armies, where she could use it as a bride price, using it, in effect, to purchase herself a companion, a good fellow who could care for herself and her child. Peasants, unlike women of the cities, tend to be very practical about such matters. She had shown me hospitality.

"We will be coming to the camp soon," said the driver.

I heard Feiqa suddenly gasp in horror, shrinking back. Beside the road, on the right, a human figure, head and legs dangling downward, on each side, was fixed on an impaling stake. The stake was some ten feet in height, and some four inches in diameter. It had been wedged between rocks and braced with stones. Its point was roughly sharpened, probably with an adz. This point had been entered in the victim's back and thrust through with great force. It emerged from the belly, and protruded some two feet above the body.

"Perhaps that is a spy," I said.

"More likely it is a straggler or a deserter," said the driver.

"Perhaps," I said. This was the first sign I had had today, that there were truly soldiers ahead of us on the road.

A girl looked up from the small fire in one of the roadside camps, and then, suddenly, rose to her feet and, in the shadows, darted out to the road. "Sir!" she called. "Sir!" The driver did not stop the wagon. She began to run beside the wagon. "Sir!" she called. "Please! I am hungry!" Her face was lifted up to us. "Please, Sir!" she begged. "Look upon me! I am fair!" She hurried along beside us. "See!" she wept. She tore down her robes to her hips. "My breasts are well formed," she said. "My belly is wet and hot! I will serve you even as a slave. I will do whatever you want. I do not ask for food for nothing. I will pay! I will pay!"

"Away," said the driver, "before I use the whip on you!"

"Stop!" she wept. "Stop!" Then she ran to the head of the tharlarion and seized its halter. The beast grunting, slowed, dragging the girl's weight; she clung fiercely to the halter; it moved its head about, pulling her about, from side to side, shaking her; it tossed its head impatiently upward, lifting her literally from the ground. But she held firmly to the halter and was then, in a moment, still clinging to it, again on the ground. The beast stopped.

The driver angrily rose in his place and the long whip lashed out. "Ai!" she cried, in misery, struck for perhaps the first time with a whip. She released the halter and then stood there in misery, in the shadows, in the road, facing us, a foot or so from the jowls of the animal. "Let me please you!" she begged. Then the whip flashed forth again, like a striking snake, and she, struck once more, sobbing, stumbled back on the road. "Do you not know me?" she cried.

He lowered the whip, looking out into the shadows.

"I am Tula from your village," she wept, "she who was too good for you, she who refused your suit!"

"You shame the village!" he cried.

"Whip me!" she wept.

He leaped down from the wagon box. Another wagon, to one side of us, rolled by. He dragged her, two stripes on her body, gray in the shadows, by the arm, back, and to the rear of the wagon. He stood her by the back, right wheel of the wagon. "Face the wheel," he said. "Hold the wheel rim!" She seized it, putting her head down. He lifted the whip, in fury. "Whip me," she said. Three blows fell upon her. "But feed me!" she begged. Two more blows struck her. Then she clung to the wheel, gasping, sobbing. As a male of her village it was his duty to discipline her for what shame she had brought on the village.

"Do not strike me again!" she begged. She sank to her knees beside the wheel. Another wagon rolled by.

"So Tula, the proud, the beauty of our village, now bares her beauty before strangers," he said, "and begs to sell her body for a crust of bread!"

She leaned against the wheel, sobbing.

"Disgraceful!" he said.

She held the spokes of the wheel, her head down.

"Shameful!" he cried.

"The strong women take what food there is," she said. "I am hungry."

"Tula, the proud," he said, angrily, "has now become only another slut by the road."

"Yes," she said.

"What have you to say for yourself!" he demanded.

"Feed me," she said.

"Turn about," he said, angrily.

She turned about, facing him, on her knees.

"Pull down your robes," he said, "until they are about your knees, lying fallen, back upon your calves."

She did this and then lifted her head to him.

"On what conditions?" he asked.

"On yours, totally yours," she said.

"Pull up your robes, about your hips," he said. "You may follow the wagon."

Sobbing with gratitude, she clutched at her robes and drew them up about her hips. He angrily returned to his place on the wagon box and with an angry cry and a fierce snap of the whip put his ponderous draft beast once more into motion, taking his place between two other wagons. It was now rather dark but the road shone clearly in the moonlight. It glistened, too, from tiny chips and plates of mica ingredient in its surface. The girl followed the wagon.

"Is the camp far ahead?" I asked.

"No," he said.

4: Feiqa Serves in the Alar Camp

I heard the sudden, hesitant, choking cry of the newborn infant.

Genserix, broad-shouldered and powerful, in his furs and leather, with his heavy eyebrows, his long, braided blond hair and long, yellow, drooping mustache, looked up from the fire, about which we sat. The sound came from one of the wagons.

The bawling was now lusty.

"It will live," said one of the men, a sitting warrior near us.

Genserix shrugged. That would remain to be seen. Feiqa knelt behind me. We were now within the laager of Genserix, a chieftain of the Alars, a nomadic, wandering herding people, and one well-known, like the folks of Torvaldsland, for their skills with the ax. The laager of the Alars, like that of similar folks, is a fortress of wagons. They are ranged in a closed circle, or concentric, closed circles, draft animals, and women and children within. Also, not unoften, depending on the numbers involved, and particularly when traversing, or sojourning in, dangerous countries, verr, tarsk and bosk may also be found within the wagon enclosure. Sewage and sanitation, which might be expected to present serious problems, do not do so, because of the frequent moving of the camps.

"It is a son," said one of the women coming from the wagon, nearing the fire.

"Not yet," said Genserix.

The wagons often move. There must be new grazing for the bosk. There must be fresh rooting and browse for the tarsk and verr. The needs of these animals, on which the

43

Alars depend for their existence, are taken to justify movements, and sometimes even migrations, of the Alars and kindred peoples. Needless to say, these movements, particularly when they intrude into more settled areas, often bring the folk of the laagers into conflict with others peasants and, of course, shortly thereafter, townsfolk and city dwellers who depend on the peasants for their foodstuffs. Also, of course, their movements often, from a legal point of view, constitute actual invasions or indisputable territorial infringements, as when, uninvited, they enter areas technically within the jurisdiction or hegemony of given cities or towns.

Sometimes they pay for passage through a country, or pasturage within it, but this is the exception rather than the rule. They are a fierce folk and it would take a courageous town indeed to suggest the suitability or propriety of such an arrangement. From the point of view of the Alars, of course, they feel it is as absurd to pay for pasturage as it would be to pay for air, both of which are required for life. "Without grass the bosk will die," they say. "The bosk will live," they add. They often find themselves temporarily within the borders of a town's or city's lands, usually about their fringes, but sometimes, depending on the weather and grazing conditions, much deeper within them. Most often little official notice is taken of them, no war challenges being issued, and they are regarded merely as peripheral, unwelcome itinerants, uninvited guests, dangerous, temporary visitors with whom the local folks must for a time live uneasily. It is a rare council or citizenry that does not breathe more easily once the wagons have taken their way out of their lands.

The woman who had come to bear tidings to Genserix now turned about and returned to the wagon.

When there is weakness or chaos in an area, and when the ordinary structures of social order are disrupted, with the concurrent disorganization, failures of responsibility and discipline, it is natural for folks like the Alars to appear. They have a tendency to pour into such areas. Indeed, sometimes they can make them their own, settling within them, sometimes turning to the soil themselves, sometimes assuming the roles and prerogatives of a conquering aristocracy, and becoming, in their turn, the foundation of a new civilization. I had little doubt that it was the current weakness and disorder in this area, attendant on the Cosian invasion, which had drawn the Alars this far south. On the other hand, officially, as I had gathered from the driver with whom I had ridden on the Genesian Road, these Alars had been approached to serve as suppliers and wagoners to the troops. It was in this capacity that they were this close to the road. In accepting this arrangement, the Alars, of course, were in an excellent position to observe the course of events, and, if it seemed practical to them, take possible action. Here they could watch closely for opportunities, either monetary or territorial. Perhaps the men of Cos, no fools, had invited them inward that they might remain in this area, thus rendering more difficult its reoccupation by the forces of Ar. Perhaps, in virtue of gifts of lands, they hoped to make them grateful, pledged allies.

I could hear movement in the nearby wagon. A woman climbed into it carrying cloths and water. I heard the child crying again.

Besides the ax Alars are fond of the Alar sword, a long, heavy, double-edged weapon. Their shields tend to be oval, like those of Turians. Their most common mount is the medium-weight saddle tharlarion, a beast smaller and less powerful, but swifter and more agile, than the common high tharlarion. Their saddles, however, have stirrups, and thus make possible the use of the couched shock lance. Some cities use Alars in their tharlarion cavalries. Others, perhaps wisely, do not enlist them in their own forces, either as regulars or auxiliaries. When the Alars ride forth to do battle they normally have their laager behind them, to which, in the case of defeat, they swiftly retire. They are fierce and redoubtable warriors in the open field. They know little, however, of politics, or of siege work and the taking of cities. In the cities, normally one needs only to close the gates and wait for them to go away, compelled eventually to do so by the needs of their animals.

A woman now descended from the wagon, carrying a small object. She came near to the fire and Genserix motioned for her to put the object down, to lay it on the dirt before him, between himself and the fire. She did so. He then crouched down near it, and, gently, with his large hands, put back the edges of the blanket in which it was wrapped. The tiny baby, not minutes old, with tiny gasps and coughs, still startled and distressed with the sharp, frightful novelty of breathing air, never again to return to the shelter of its mother's body, lost in a chaos of sensation, its eyes not focused, unable scarcely to turn its head from side to side, lay before him. The cord had been cut and tied at its belly. Its tiny legs and arms moved. The blood, the membranes and fluids, had been wiped from its small, hot, red, firm body. Then it had been rubbed with animal fat. How tiny were its head and fingers. How startling and wonderful it seemed that such a thing should be alive. Genserix looked at it for a time, and then he turned it over, and examined it further. Then he put it again on its back. He then stood up, and looked down upon it.

The warriors about the fire, and the woman, and two other women, too, who had now come from the wagon, looked at him.

Then Genserix reached down and lifted up the child. The women cried out with pleasure and the men grunted with approval. Genserix held the child up now, happily, it almost lost in his large hands, and then he lifted it up high over his head.

"Ho!" called the warriors, standing up, rejoicing. The women beamed.

"It is a son!" cried one of the women.

"Yes," said Genserix. "It is a son!"

"Ho!" called the warriors. "Ho!"

"What is going on?" asked Feiqa.

"The child has been examined," I said. "It has been found sound. It will be permitted to live. It is now an Alar. Too, he has lifted the child up. In this he acknowledges it as his own."

Genserix then handed the child to one of the warriors. He then drew his knife.

"What is he going to do?" gasped Feiqa.

"Be quiet," I said.

Genserix then, carefully, made two incisions in the face of the infant, obliquely, one on each cheek. The infant began to cry. Blood ran down the sides of its face, about the sides of its neck and onto its tiny shoulders. "Let it be taken now," said Genserix, "to its mother."

The woman who had brought the child to the side of the fire now took up the blanket in which it had been wrapped, and, wrapping it again in its folds, took it then from the warrior, and made her way back to the wagon.

"These are a warrior people," I said to Feiqa, "and the child is an Alar. It must learn to endure wounds before it receives the nourishment of milk."

Feiqa shrank back, frightened to be among such men.

On the face of Genserix, and on the faces of those about us, the males, were the thin, white, knife-edge lines, the narrow scars, by which it might be known that each had, in his time, undergone the same ceremony. By such scars one may identify Alars.

"I rejoice in your happiness," I said to Genserix, who had now resumed his place by the fire.

Genserix declined his head briefly, smiling, and spread his hands, expansively.

"At a time of such happiness," said a fellow, his long dark hair bound back with a beaded leather talmit, "you need not even be killed for having come to our camp uninvited."

"Hold," I said, uneasily, "I was told in the camp of the wagoners, some of those in the supply trains of Cos, that there might be work here for me."

One or two of the men struck each other about the shoulders in amusement.

"I gather that it is not true," I said.

"Shall we kill him anyway?" asked a fellow.

"Surely folks come often to the wagons," I said.

"Do not mind Parthanx and Sorath," said a tall, broad-shouldered fellow sitting cross-legged beside me. He, too, like Genserix, had long braided hair and a yellow mustache. Too, like Genserix, he was blue-eyed. Many of the Alars are fair in complexion, blond-haired and blue-eyed. "They jest. They are the camp wits," he explained. "Many folks come to the wagons, as you know, informers, slavers, tradesmen, metal workers, craftsmen, peasants who will barter produce for skins and trinkets, and so on. If this were not so we could not as easily have the goods we have, nor could we keep up as well with the news. If it were not so, we would be too cut off from the world. We would consequently be unable to conduct our affairs as judiciously as we do."

I nodded. Folk like the Alars tended to move in, and about, settled territories. They were not isolated in vast plains areas, for example, as were certain subequatorial Wagon Peoples, such as Tuchuks and Kassars.

The fellows identified as Parthanx and Sorath shoved at one another good-naturedly, pleased with their joke.

"Let rings be brought!" called out Genserix.

"I am Hurtha," said the blond fellow beside me. "You must not think of us as barbarians. Tell us about the cities."

"What would you like to know?" I asked. He would be interested, I assumed, in such matters as the nature of their walls, the number of gates, their defenses, the strength of garrisons, and such.

"Is Ar as beautiful as they say?" he asked. "And what is it like to live there?"

"It is very beautiful," I said. "And although I am not a citizen of Ar, nor of Telnus, the capital of Cos, it is doubtless easier to live in such places than among the wagons. Why do you ask?"

"Hurtha is a weakling, and a poet!" laughed Sorath.

"I am a warrior, and an Alar," said Hurtha, "but it is true that I am fond of songs."

"There is no incompatibility between letters and arms," I said. "The greatest soldiers are often gifted men."

"I have considered going abroad, to seek my fortune," he said.

"What would you do?" I asked.

"My arm is strong," he said, "and I can ride."

"You would seek service then with some captain?" I said.

"Yes," he said, "and if possible with the finest."

"Many are the causes on Gor," I said, "and so, too, many are the captains."

"My first appointments," he said, "might be with anyone."

"Many captains," I said, "choose their causes on the scales of merchants, weighing their iron against gold. They fight, I fear, only for the Ubar with the deepest purse."

"I am an Alar," said Hurtha. "The cities are always at war with us. It is always the fields against the walls. No matter then which way I face, nor whom I strike, it would be a blow against enemies."

"I am a mercenary, of sorts," I said, "but I have usually selected my causes with care."

"And one should," agreed Hurtha, "for otherwise one might not improve one's fortunes."

I looked at him.

"Right," said Hurtha, "if that is what you are interested in, seems to me a very hard thing to understand. I am not sure there is really any such thing, at all. I have never tasted it, nor seen it, nor felt it. If it does exist, it seems likely to me that it would be on both sides, like sunlight and air. Surely no war has been fought in which both sides have not sincerely claimed, and presumably believed, for one reason or another, that they were right. Thus, if right is always on both sides, one cannot help but fight for it. If that then is the case, why should one not be paid as well as possible for the risks he takes?"

"Have you ever tasted, or seen, or felt honor?" I asked.

"Yes," said Hurtha. "I have tasted honor, and seen it, and felt it, but it is not like tasting bread, or seeing a rock, or feeling a woman. It is different."

"Perhaps right is like that," I said.

"Perhaps," said Hurtha. "But the matter seems very complex and difficult to me."

"It seems so to me, too," I said. "I am often surprised why it seems so easy to so many others."

"Yes," said Hurtha.

"Perhaps they are more gifted than we in detecting its presence," I speculated.

"Perhaps," said Hurtha, "but why, then, is there so much disagreement among them?"

"I do not know," I admitted.

Rings were then brought, heavy rings of silver and gold, large enough for a wrist or arm, and Genserix distributed these to high retainers. From the same box he then distributed coins among the others. Even I received a silver tarsk. There were treasures among the wagons, it seemed. The tarsk was one of Telnus. In this small detail I suspected there might be found evidence of the possible relationship between the movements of Cos and the coming of the Alar wagons to the Genesian road.

"Are there such women as these in the cities?" asked Hurtha, indicating Feiqa.

"Thousands," I informed him.

"Surely we should study siege work," smiled Hurtha.

Feiqa shrank back a bit.

"Such women may be bought in the cities," I said, "in slave markets, from the houses of slavers, from private dealers. Surely you could have such among the wagons, if you wished. You could have strings brought out to be examined, or accepted, on approval. I see no problem in the matter." Interestingly, I had noted few, if any, slaves among the wagons. This was quite different from the Wagon Peoples of the far south. There beautiful slaves, in the scandalously revealing chatka and curla, the kalmak and koora, tiny rings in their noses, were common among the wagons. "You mentioned, as I recall, that slavers, among others, came occasionally to the wagons."

"Yes," he said, "but usually to buy our captures, picked up generally in raids or fighting."

"Why are there so few slaves among the wagons?" I asked.

"The free women kill them," said Hurtha.

Feiqa gasped. I decided that perhaps I had best be soon on my way. She was a beauty, and was extremely sexually exciting, sometimes almost maddeningly so, to men. I had no wish to risk her in this place. She was exactly the sort of female which, in her helplessness and collar, in her vulnerability and brief tunic, tends to inspire jealous hatred, sometimes bordering almost on madness, in free women, particularly homely and sexually frustrated ones.

"Oh!" said Feiqa, as he called Sorath closed his hand about her upper arm. His grip was tight. There was no mistaking its nature. He had her in mind.

"Hold," I said to him, putting my hand on his arm.

"Hold?" he asked.

"Yes," I said. "Hold."

"You are not an Alar," he said. "I will take her."

"No," I said.

"This is our camp," he said.

"It is my slave," I said.

"Give her to me," he said. "I will give her back to you happier, and with only a few bruises."

"No," I said.

"In the camp I do what I wish," he said.

"I doubt that that is always the case," I said.

He stood up. I, too, stood up. He was a bit shorter than I, but was extremely broad and powerful. It is a not uncommon build among Alars.

"You have taken food here," said Sorath.

"And I have been pleased to have done so," I said. "Thank you."

"You are a guest here," said Sorath.

"And I expect to receive the respect and courtesy due a guest," I said.

"Let him have her for a few Ehn," suggested Hurtha.

"He has not asked," I said.

"Ask," suggested a fellow to Sorath.

"No," said Sorath.

I shrugged.

"Let axes be brought," said Sorath.

"He will not know the ax," said Hurtha. "He is not of the wagons."

"Let them then be blades!" roared Sorath.

"The ax will be fine," I said. I had learned its use in Torvaldsland. I had little doubt that the Torvaldslanders could stand up to any folk in the use of the ax.

"Let the axes be headless," said Genserix. This proposal surprised me somewhat, but I welcomed it. It seemed a decent and generous gesture on the part of Genserix. Not every chieftain of the Alars, I supposed, would have been so thoughtful. In this fashion the worse that was likely to happen was that the loser would have his head broken open. The men about the fire grunted their agreement. They all seemed rather decent fellows. Sorath, too, I was pleased to see, nodded. Apparently he, at least after a moment of choler, upon a more sober reflection, had no special wish to kill me. He would probably be satisfied to beat me unconscious. In the morning then I might awaken naked, tied to a stake outside the wagons. In a few days, then, which I might have spent ruminating on my ingratitude, while living on water poured into a hole near me, and on vegetables thrown to me, like a tarsk, when the wagons moved I might have been freed, a well-used Feiqa then returned to me, perhaps with a fresh Alar brand in her hide, that I might be reminded, from time to time, of the incident.

Two of the long heavy handles were brought.

I hefted one. It had good weight and balance.

"Beware, friend," said Hurtha. "Sorath well knows the ways of the ax."

"Thank you," I said.

Feiqa whimpered.

"Prepare yourself for the future," I said.

"Master?" she asked, puzzled.

"Shall the female be held?" asked a fellow.

"That will not be necessary," I said. "Stay, Feiqa."

"Yes, Master," she said. She would now keep her place, kneeling, as she was, until a free person might permit her to move.

Sorath spit upon his hands and gripped the handle. He cut the air with a stroke or two.

I went to an open place near the fire.

"See?" said one of the fellows. "He takes a position with the fire at his back." Some of the others nodded, too, seemingly having noted this.

When possible, of course, given considerations of the land, warriors like to have both the sun and the wind at their back. The glare from the sun, even if it is not blinding, can be wearing upon an enemy, particularly if the battle persists for

Ahn. The advantages of having the wind at one's back are obvious. It flights one's arrows, increasing their range; it gives additional impetus to one's movements and charges; and whatever dust or debris it might carry is more likely to effect the enemy than oneself.

Sorath struck fiercely down at me with the handle and I blocked the blow, smartly. His blow had been a simple, obvious one, and unless he had intended to use it in wearing down my strength or perhaps breaking the handle I carried, it made little sense. He stood back, considering matters.

"Surely you would not have struck at an Alar like that," I said. He must be clear that I had not brought my handle back, under the blow, slashing upward to his neck, a blow that can, with the Torvaldsland ax, at least, cut the head from a man.

"True, Stranger," said a woman's voice. I stepped back a little, sensing that there was momentary truce between Sorath and myself, but also keeping track of him. He could not change position without my detecting it. "I have seen tharlarion who could handle an ax better than that," she said. Sorath reddened, angrily. It was apparently a free woman of the Alars, only she was not dressed as were the other women of the camp, in their coarse, heavy, ankle-length woolen dresses. She wore rather the garmenture of a male, the furs and leather. At her belt there was even a knife. She was strikingly lovely, though, I supposed, given her mien and attitude, she would not have taken such an observation as a compliment. She was about the same size as Feiqa, though perhaps a tiny bit shorter, and, like Feiqa, was dark-haired and dark-eyed. I thought they might look well together, as a brace of slaves.

Sorath then, stung by her remark, flung himself wildly toward me and fought frenziedly, but rashly. I blocked blows, not wishing to take advantage of his recklessness. I refrained from striking him. Had we been using real axes, the handles armed with iron, I might have finished him several times. I do not know if he was fully aware of this, but I am sure some of the others were. Hurtha and Genserix, for example, judging from the alarm which I noted in their expressions, seemed to be under no misapprehensions in the matter. To be sure, had the handles been armed perhaps he would have addressed himself to our match with much greater circumspection. Panting, Sorath backed away.

"Fight, Sorath," taunted the woman. "He is an outsider. Are you not an Alar?"

"Be silent, woman," said Genserix, angrily.

"I am a free woman," she said. "I may speak as I please."

"Do not seek to interfere in the affairs of men." said Genserix.

She faced the group, standing on the other side of the fire. Her feet were spread. On her feet were boots of fur. Her arms were crossed insolently upon her chest. "Are there men here?" she asked. "I wonder."

There was a rumble of angry sounds from the gathered warriors. But none did anything to discipline the girl. She was, of course, free. Free women, among the Alars, have high standing.

"Do you think you are a man?" inquired one of the warriors.

"I am a female," she said, "but I am not different from you, not in the least."

There were angry murmurs from the men.

"Indeed," she said, "I am probably more a man than any of you here."

"Give her an ax," said Genserix.

An ax, a typical Alar ax, long-handled, armed with its heavy iron blade, was handed to the girl. She took it, holding it with difficulty. It was clear it was too heavy for her. She could scarcely lift it, let alone wield it.

"You could not use that blade, even for chopping wood," said Genserix.

"What is your name?" I asked her.

"Tenseric," she said.

"That is a male's name," I said.

"I chose it myself," she said. "I wear it proudly."

"Have you always been called that?" I asked.

"I was called Boabissia," she said, "until I came of age, and chose my own name."

"You are still Boabissia," said one of the warriors.

"No!" she said. "I am Tenseric."

"You are a female, are you not?" I asked.

"I suppose so," she said, angrily. "But what is that supposed to mean?"

"Does it mean nothing?" I asked.

"No," she said. "It means nothing."

"Are you the same as a man?" I asked.

"Yes!" she said.

There was laughter from the warriors about the fire.

"It takes more than fur and leather, and a dagger worn pretentiously at one's belt, to make a man," I said.

She looked at me with fury.

"You are a female," called one of the men. "Be one!"

"No!" she cried.

"Put on a dress!" called another of the men.

"Never!" she cried. "I do not want to be one of those pathetic creatures who must wait on you and serve you!"

"Are you an Alar?" I asked.

"Yes!" she said.

"No," said Genserix. "She is not an Alar. We found her, years ago, when she was an infant, beside the road, abandoned in blankets, amidst the wreckage of a raided caravan."

"One which had fallen to the Alars?" I inquired.

"No," said a fellow, chuckling.

"I wished it had fallen to us," said another. "From the size of the caravan, we conjecture the loot must have been considerable."

"There was little left when we arrived," commented another.

"Do not be misled," said Hurtha, smiling. "We do not really do much raiding. "It does not make for good relations with the city dwellers."

His remark made sense to me. The Alars, and such folk, can be aggressive and warlike in seeking their grazing grounds, but, if left alone, they are seldom practitioners of unrestricted or wholesale raiding.

"We took the child in, and raised it," said Genserix. "We named it Boabissia, a good Alar name."

"You are not then really of the wagons," I said to the girl. "Indeed, you are quite possibly a female of the cities."

"No!" said the girl. "I am truly of the wagons! I have lived among them all my life!"

"She is not of the wagons, by blood," said a man.

She looked at him angrily.

"Slash my face!" she cried.

"We do not slash the faces of our females," said a man.

"Slash mine!" she said.

"No," said Genserix.

"Then I shall do it myself!" she said.

"Do not," said Genserix, sternly.

"Very well," she said. "I shall not. I shall do as my chieftain asks."

I saw that she did not wish, truly, to disfigure herself in the mode of the Alar warriors. I found that of interest. From the point of view of the men, too, of course, they did not desire this. For one thing she was not of the warriors and was thus not entitled to this badge of station; indeed, her wearing it, as she was a mere female, would be a joke to outsiders and an embarrassment to the men; it would belittle its significance for them, making it shameful and meaningless. The insignia of men, like male garments, become empty mockeries when permitted to women. This type of thing leads eventually both to the demasculinization of men and the defeminization of females, a perversion of nature disapproved of generally, correctly or incorrectly, by Goreans. For another thing she was a beautiful woman and they had no desire to see her disfigured in this fashion.

"Your chieftain is grateful," said Genserix, ironically.

"Thank you, my chieftain," she said, reddening, inclining her head. She had little alternative, it seemed, in her anger, other than to pretend to accept his remark at face value. I wondered why Genserix did not strip her and have her tied under a wagon for a few days. She looked at me, in fury. "I am an Alar," she said.

Some of the warriors laughed.

"It seems more probable to me that you are a woman of the cities," I said.

"No!" she said. "No!"

"Consider your coloring," I said, "and your shortness,

and the darkness of your hair and eyes. Consider, too, the suggestion of interesting female curvatures beneath your leather and fur.'' Most the Alar women are rather large, plain, cold, blond, blue-eyed women. ''You remind me of many women I have seen chained naked in slave markets.''

There was much laughter from the men.

''No!'' she cried to them. ''No!'' she cried to me.

''It is true,'' I said.

''No!'' she cried.

There was more laughter.

''I am an Alar!'' she cried.

''No,'' said more than one man.

''Are you a man?'' asked a fellow.

''I am the same as a man!'' she cried.

''Are you a man?'' asked a fellow.

''No,'' she said. ''I am a woman!''

''It is true,'' laughed a man.

''But I am a free woman!'' she cried, with a look of hatred cast at Feiqa, who shrank back, trembling, beneath her fierce gaze.

''Lift up the ax you carry,'' said Genserix, ''high, over your head, as though to strike one with it. Hold it near the end of the handle.''

She, standing across from us, on the other side of the fire, tried to do this. But in a moment, struggling, unable to manage the weight, she twisted her body and the ax fell. Its head struck the dirt. The warriors were not pleased with this. Some murmured in anger. ''I cannot,'' she said. I myself would have had her kneel down and clean the blade with her hair. It can be a capital offense on Gor, incidentally, for a slave to so much as touch a weapon.

''Brandish it, wield it,'' said Genserix to her, sternly.

She tried again to lift the ax, and then, again, lowered it, until she held it before her, as she had before, with difficulty, with both hands, her hands separated well on the handle. ''I cannot,'' she said.

''Then put it down, and leave,'' said Genserix.

''Yes, my chieftain,'' she said. She put down the ax, and then hurried away, angrily, into the darkness. I supposed that

she, in her upbringing, had felt a little affinity with the Alar
women. Certainly it seemed she had not cared to identify
with them. Perhaps, too, as she was not an Alar by blood,
they had never truly accepted her. Yet it seemed she had
been, as is often the case with Alar children, raised with
much permissiveness. Not identifying with the women, or
being accepted by them, and perhaps coming to bitterly envy
the men, their position and status, their nature and power, it
seemed she may have turned toward trying to prove herself
the same as them, turning then to mannish customs and garb,
attempting thusly, desperately, angrily, to find some sort of
place for herself among the wagons. As a result, it seemed
she would be accepted by neither sex. She seemed to me
confused and terribly unhappy. I did not think she knew her
own identity. I do not think she knew who she was. Some of
the men, perhaps, knew better than she herself did.

"Now," said Genserix, "let us resume the contest."

There were grunts of approval by the men.

Once again Sorath and I squared off against one another.
This time, not mocked and taunted by the female, he fought
extremely well. As Hurtha had warned me earlier, Sorath
well knew the ways of the ax. Now that his temper had
cooled he fought with agility and precision. The reckless and
sometimes irrational temper of folks like Sorath, and it was a
temper not unusual among the proud Alar herders, was something that they would be well advised to guard against. Too
often it proves the undoing of such folks. Hundreds of times
calculated defenses and responsible tactics have proved their
worth in the face of brawn and wrath. The braveries of
barbarism are seldom of little avail against a rational,
determined, prepared foe. But let those of the cities tremble
that among the hordes there might one day arise one who can
unify storms and harness lightning.

I slipped to the side and, swinging the ax handle inward,
caught Sorath in the solar plexus, that network of nerves and
ganglia high in the abdominal cavity, lying behind the stomach and in front of the upper part of the abdominal aorta. I
did not strike deeply enough to injure him, to rupture or tear
open his body, slashing the stomach or crushing the aortal

tube, only enough to stop him, definitely. For good measure I then, with the left side of the handle, swinging it upward, and then down, brought it down on the back of his neck as he, helpfully, expectantly, grunting, doubled over. I did not strike him hard enough to break the vertebrae. He slipped to his knees, vomiting, and then, stunned, half paralyzed, fell forward. I then stood behind him, the handle grasped at the ready, near its end. From such a position one can, rather with impunity, with an unarmed handle, break the neck to the side or crush the head. Had the handle been armed, of course, one might, from such a position, sever the backbone or remove the head. Sorath was fast. I was faster.

"Do not kill him!" said Genserix.

"Of course not," I said. "He is one of my hosts." I stepped back from Sorath.

"You fought very well," said Genserix.

"Sorath is very good, don't you think?" asked Hurtha.

"Yes," I said. "He is quite good."

"Your prowess proves you well worthy to be a guest of the Alars," said Genserix. "Welcome to our camp. Welcome to the light and heat of our fire.

"Thank you," I said, tossing aside the handle.

"Are you still alive?" Parthanx inquired solicitously of Sorath, his friend.

"Yes," reported Sorath.

"Do not be so lazy, then," said Parthanx encouragingly. "Get up." Parthanx, like the others, seemed to have enjoyed the fight.

"Let me help you," I said. I gave Sorath a hand, and half pulled him to his place by the fire. He looked up at me, shaking his head. "Well done," he said.

"Thank you," I said. "You did splendidly yourself."

"Thank you," he said.

I looked about myself. "I gather that I am now welcome here," I said.

"Yes," said Genserix.

"Yes," said Sorath.

"Yes," said the others.

"Thank you," I said. "I am grateful for your welcome. I

thank you, too, for the food and drink I have received here, for the heat and light of your fire, and for your fellowship. I thank you for your hospitality. It is worthy of the best things I have heard of Alars. I would now like, if I may, in my own way, and of my own free will, as it will now be clearly understood, to do something for you, something that will help, in a small way, to express my appreciation.''

Genserix and his warriors looked at one another, puzzled.

I turned to Feiqa. "Strip," I said.

"Master?" she asked.

"Must a command be repeated?" I inquired.

"No, Master!" she cried. In an instant she was bared.

"Stand," I said. "Lift your arms over your head." Instantly she complied. She was then very beautiful, standing thusly in the light of the fire, before the barbaric warriors of Genserix, in the Alar camp.

"Such women," I said, "may be purchased in the cities."

There were appreciative murmurs as the men drank in the fire-illuminated beauty of the naked slave.

"Dance," I told Feiqa.

"I do not know how to dance, Master," she moaned.

"In every female there is a dancer," I said.

"Master," she protested.

"I know you are not trained," I said.

"Master," she said.

"There are many forms of dance," I said. "Music is not even necessary. It need not even be more than beautiful movement. Move before the men, and about them. Move as seductively and beautifully as you can, and as a slave, swaying, crawling, kneeling, rolling, supine, prone, begging, pleading, piteous, caressing, kissing, licking, rubbing against them.''

"Do I have a choice, Master?" she asked.

"No," I said, "absolutely not."

"Yes, Master," she said.

"Would you prefer for your pretty flesh to be lashed from your bones?" I asked.

"No, Master!" she said.

"And as the evening progresses, and as men might desire you," I said, "you will please them, and fully."

"Yes, Master," she said.

"You are a slave, an absolute and total slave," I reminded her.

"Yes, Master," she said.

One of the fellows, then, began to sing, "Hei, Hei," and clap his hands.

Feiqa danced.

The men cried out with pleasure, many of them joining in the song, and keeping time with their hands. I was incredibly proud of her. How joyful it is to own females and have absolute power over them! Seldom, indeed, I imagined, did the rude herders of the Alars have such a vision of imbonded loveliness in their camp, and in their arms. Such delicious females were not allowed in their camps, I gathered. The free women did not permit them. They probably had them hidden in wagons, until they could be sold off, or killed. How beautiful Feiqa was! What incredible power she exercised, though only a helpless slave, over men! How she pleased them and made them scream with pleasure! How incredibly basic, how fundamental, how real she was! I then felt a sudden, poignant sorrow for the women of Earth. How different Feiqa was from them. How far removed delicious, exquisite Feiqa was from the motivated artifices, the lies and fabrications, the propaganda, the demeaning, sterile, unsatisfying, reductive, negative superficialities of antibiological roles, the prescriptions of an unnatural and pathological politics, the manipulative instrumentations of monsters and freaks. I wondered how many of the women of Earth wished they might find themselves in a collar, dancing naked in the firelight before warriors in an Alar camp.

"Disgusting! Disguisting!" cried the free woman, Boabissia, in her leather and furs, having returned to the fire, and she rushed forward, a stout, thick, short, supple, single-bladed quirtlike whip in her hand. She began to lash Feiqa, who fell to her knees, howling with misery, a whipped slave. "We do not allow such as you in an Alar camp!" cried the free woman. Feiqa put her head down. Again the lash fell on her.

I leaped to the free woman and tore the whip from her hand, hurling it angrily to the side. She looked at me, wildly, in fury, not believing I had dared to interfere. "What right have you to interfere?" she demanded. "The right of a man who is not pleased with your behavior, female," I said. "Female!" she cried, in fury. "Yes," I said.

Her hand darted to the hilt of the dagger she wore at her belt. I regarded her evenly. She, frightened, quickly removed her hand from the hilt of the dagger, crying out in frustration, in rage. Then she lifted her fists and, with the sides of them, together, struck towards me. "Oh!" she cried, in misery, in frustration. I had caught both her small wrists. She could not begin to free them. "Oh!" she cried in misery, in protest, as, inexorably, slowly, I forced her down. Then she was kneeling before me, her wrists in my grip. I turned her about and flung her to her belly, and then knelt across her thighs. I removed her dagger from its sheath. "No!" she cried. I then, with her own dagger, cut her clothing from her body.

"Binding fiber," I said, not even looking, just putting out my hand. Some was fetched, a length of some five feet, or so, and, in a moment, with one end of the fiber, with a few loops and a knot, her wrists crossed, her hands were secured behind her back. I had tied her tightly, utterly helplessly, as I might have a slave. "Help!" she cried out to the warriors. "Help!" But none stirred to render her assistance. I then reversed my position on her body, kneeling now facing her feet, across the small of her back. I pulled her ankles up, behind her body, at an angle of about fifty degrees, and crossed them. I then, with the free end of the binding fiber, extending back from her wrists, tied them together, tightly, fastening them to her wrists. "Please!" she cried to the warriors but none leapt to accord her succor. I then lifted her up, in effect kneeling her, and then bent her back, her head back to the dirt, that the warriors might assess the bow of her beauty.

"She is pretty," said a fellow. "Yes," said another. It was true. She had a lovely figure. It had been hitherto muchly concealed from detection by the leather and furs she had worn, though even beneath them its subtle and tantalizing lineaments had been clearly suggested. "Come, see Boabissia," called a fellow, "trussed like a tarsk!" Some more fellows, and even some free women, came over to look. Boabissia, now permitted to kneel upright, squirmed, fighting the fiber. She was helpless. "Fieqa will now again dance," I said. "If you wish, you may be hooded or blindfolded." She looked down, sullenly, angrily, and shook her head. "If you cry out," I said, "you will be gagged. Do you understand?" "Yes," she said.

I looked at Boabissia's throat. About it, tied on a leather thong, was a small, punched, copper disk. "What is that?" I asked, pointing to it. She did not respond. I then put her to her back, her knees drawn up, her wrists behind her, under the small of her back. I then bent over her and lifted up the disk, examining it in the firelight. She did not resist. Bound as she was, there was little she could do. Too, resistance might have earned her perfunctory, disciplinary cuffs. The punched copper disk, threaded on its thong, was not large. It was about an inch or so in diameter. On it was the letter "Tau" and a number. "What is this?" I asked Genserix, indicating the disk. "We do not know," he said. "It was tied about her throat when we found her, years ago, a tiny infant, wrapped in a blanket, in the wreckage of the caravan."

"Surely you must have wondered about this," I said to Boabissia.

She looked away, not responding.

"It must be a key to your identity," I said.

She did not respond.

I let the disk fall back, just below her neck. It, on its thong, was now all she wore, except her bonds.

I looked to Feiqa, still kneeling, her back bright with the memory of the free woman's attentions.

"You may now continue to dance, Feiqa," I said.

"Yes, Master," she said.

The men then cried out with approval, and smote their left shoulders with pleasure. In a moment Feiqa, vital and sensuous, liberated now from the fear of the free woman, and having felt the whip, in that perhaps being reminded of what might be the consequences of failing to please free persons, addressed herself once more, eagerly and joyously, marvelously and subserviently, to the pleasures of masters. I was so aroused I was in pain. I could hardly wait to get her back to the camp of the wagoners. From time to time I glanced at Boabissia. She was on her side, trussed, watching Feiqa. In her eyes there was awe, understanding what a woman could be.

After some Ahn, in the neighborhood of dawn, I returned to the camp of the wagoners. Feiqa walked behind me, slowly, weary, heeling me, her body sore, her tiny tunic held over her left shoulder. Near the wagoners' camp I turned to face her. "Before you retire," I said, "I have business for you in my blankets. After that I will tether you for the night."

"Yes, Master," she smiled.

In a few moments we had come to the wagon of the fellow who had given us a ride earlier. Near the wagon, naked, chained by the neck to the back, right wheel, was the peasant girl, Tula. In the moonlight I examined her. Under her neck chain was a slave collar.

5: We Are on the Genesian Road

"What are you doing here?" I asked Hurtha.

"I am coming with you," he said. "I am interested in seeing the world, and will seek my fortune."

"You have no mount," I observed.

"Nor do you," he observed.

"That is true," I smiled.

"I sold it, in the camp," he said, "for some coins. It did not seem practical to bring it. There seem to be few such mounts with the wagons. Too, I do not know where we are going, nor what we will do."

"The road I project is a difficult one," I said, "and it may be dangerous."

"Splendid," he said.

I looked at him.

"I am easily bored," he explained.

"Oh," I said.

"You do not mind if I accompany you, do you?" he asked.

"No," I said.

"The matter is then fully settled," he announced.

"But you must feel free to part company from me at any time," I said. I had no wish to bring him into danger.

"If you insist," he said.

"I fear I must," I said.

"I accept your condition," he said.

"Good," I said.

"You drive a fierce bargain," he observed.

"Thank you," I said.

"Half of my coins are yours," he said. "You are welcome to them."

"That is very generous," I said.

"Just as half of yours are mine," he said.

"What?" I asked.

"As we will be traveling together," he said.

"How many coins do you have?" I asked.

"About seventeen copper tarsks," he said, "and two tarsk bits."

"That is all?" I inquired.

"Yes," he said.

"But you sold your tharlarion," I said, "and last night Genserix gave you, as he did me, a silver tarsk."

"True," he said, "but I used most of that to pay off a few old debts. You would not wish for me to have left the wagons owing debts, would you?"

"Of course not," I said.

"Too," he said, "I purchased this splendid sword." He unsheathed it and swung it about. He handled it lightly. It nearly decapitated a passing wagoner. It was a long, cutting sword, of the sort called a *spatha* among the wagons. It is more useful than the *gladius*, from the back of a tharlarion, because of its reach. He also carried among his things the short, stabbing sword, similar to the *gladius*, and doubtless related to it, called by his people the *sacramasax*. It is much more useful on foot, particularly in close combat. "Accordingly," he said, sheathing the sword, "I have with me only some seventeen, two. How much do you have?"

"Somewhat more than that," I said.

"Splendid," he said. "We may need every tarsk bit."

"What?" I asked.

"I have expensive tastes," he explained. "Further, I am an Alar, and we Alars are a generous, noble folk."

"That is a known fact," I granted him.

"We have a reputation to uphold," he said.

"Doubtless," I said.

"If we run short," he said, "I may always strike some good fellow on the head and take his purse."

"Surely you do not behave so in your own camp," I said.

"No, of course not," he said, rather surprised. "But they are Alars."

"I see," I said.

"Not outsiders, not city folks," he said.

"I must warn you," I said, "that even outside the wagons striking fellows on the head and taking their purses is often frowned upon."

"Oh?" he asked.

"Yes," I said, "Many folks have strong opinions about such matters."

"Interesting," he said.

"You would not like to be struck on the head, would you?" I asked.

"Of course not," he said.

"There you are," I said.

"But I am an Alar," he said.

"What difference does that make?" I asked.

"It makes all the difference in the world," he said. "Can you prove it does not?"

"No," I admitted.

"There you are," he said.

"I assure you," I said, "folks would not like it, and you might find yourself impaled, or cut to pieces."

"I am not impervious to such considerations," he said, "but I thought we were discussing purely moral issues."

"You should not behave in such a manner," I said.

"But it is not unseemly for me to do so, I assure you," he said. "Besides, such behavior lies well within my entitlements."

"How is that?" I asked.

"I am an Alar," he said.

"While we are traveling together," I said, "mainly because I do not wish to be impaled, or fed in bits to sleen, I would appreciate it if, as a favor to me, if nothing else, you would consider refraining from the exercise of certain of your Alar rights."

"Surely you would have no objection if fellows wished to make me loans, or bestow gifts upon me?" he asked.

"Of course not," I said. "No one could possibly object to that."

"Splendid," he said.

I relaxed.

"I was afraid you might be prone to eccentric reservations," he said.

"Not me," I said.

"Splendid!" he said, warmly.

We were in the camp of the wagoners, one of those associated with the supply trains of the soldiers of Cos and the Cosian mercenaries. It was in the neighborhood of dawn and now, after their breakfasts, wagoners were readying their wagons and harnessing their tharlarion and, indeed, some had already taken to the road. There seemed no numbering to their vehicles nor camp marshals in attendance. The trains, in spite of their length and numbers, and their diverse cargoes, seemed to me most casually organized. This differed considerably from the disciplines I would have expected to attend arrangements pertaining to the transportation and protection of such stores. I could not understand the apparent reluctance on the part of Ar to exploit these weaknesses.

"Are you ready?" inquired Mincon, our wagoner, he with whom Feiqa and I had traveled yesterday, jerking tight the harness of his tharlarion.

"In a moment," I said. "Hold still, Feiqa."

Quite near to him, as he worked, knelt Tula. She tried to put her cheek against his left thigh. He brushed her away. Properly handled, women become as subservient and affectionate as dogs. They all desire to be totally prisoners of love, and they will never be fully content until they become so.

"Would you make me so much a slave, Master?" inquired Feiqa.

"Yes," I said.

"Then do so," she said.

Tula now wore a tunic. Mincon had fashioned it for her from her former garments, those she had worn yesterday as a free woman. It was brief and sleeveless, and of white wool. She had excellent legs. Another part of her former garments he had cut into a sort of shawl which she might clutch about her when the winds blew chill. Some other bits of them he had cut up and she had fashioned them into a form of footwear, which she had tied on her small feet. The stones of the Genesian Road, in Se'Kara, would be cold. I considered again Tula's legs. They were well bared by her new tunic, as was appropriate for a slave.

On Gor it is commonly only slaves, incidentally, who bare their legs, and although they usually do so eagerly, proudly and beautifully, they realize that, in the final analysis, whether they wish it or not, they will generally have little, if any, choice in the matter. Such things are up to the master. One need not speculate overly long, either, on the usual decision of the master, for most Gorean masters are vital, strong, dominant males. It is thus common for the enslaved females, and it is usually implicit in the only modes of garmenture most masters will permit them, that their legs, with all the delicious excitements of their thighs, calves and ankles, will be exposed to the gaze of free persons.

Contrariwise, almost no free woman would bare her legs. They would not dare to do so. They would be horrified even to think of it. The scandal of such an act could ruin a reputation. It is said on Gor that any woman who bares her legs is a slave. Indeed, in some cities a free woman who might be found with bared legs is taken in hand by magistrates, tried and sentenced to bondage. After the judge's decision has been enacted, its effect carried out upon her, reducing her to the status of goods, sometimes publicly, that she may be suitably disgraced, sometimes privately, by a contract slaver, that the sensitivities of free women in the city not be offended, she is hooded and transported, stripped and chained, freshly branded and collared, a property female, slave cargo, to a distant market where, once sold, she will begin her life anew, fearfully, as a purchased girl, tremulously as the helpless and lowly slave she now is.

"Oh," said Feiqa.

"Steady," I said to her. I wiped the needle.

"Oh!" she said. I again wiped the needle. I then returned it to my sewing kit.

"Do not touch the wounds," I said.

She looked up at me. Her eyes were moist, and she seemed slightly afraid. In her eyes there was a sort of wonder, and awe. It seemed she found it hard to understand, truly, what had been done to her, from the Gorean point of view, the enormity of it.

"Does it hurt?" I asked.

"No," she said.

I wiped the tiny drops of blood away. I then fastened the tiny objects upon her.

"They are beautiful," said Hurtha, admiringly.

"They are cheap," I said.

"That is all right," he said.

I did not want free women attacking the girl in rage, and perhaps tearing the objects free.

I turned Feiqa's head from side to side. Yes, they were lovely. She looked up at me. She now wore earrings.

I again regarded Tula's legs. True, the baring of the legs in that fashion, by so short a tunic, was truly an indication of slavery. Only a slave would go so bared. Mincon, of course, was proud of her. He owned her. He enjoyed showing her off. Such an exposure of a girl's beauty surely marked her unmistakably as a slave. To be sure, it was not of the same degree of momentousness as certain other indications of slavery, irrefutable, irreversible, unmistakable indications, indications and degradations so fundamental that they would be likely to be inflicted only upon the most delicious and lowest of all slaves. It did not begin to compare, for example, with such things as the piercing of the ears.

"We are ready now," I told Mincon. "You may rise, Feiqa," I said.

"Go, stand behind the back of the wagon," said Mincon to Tula.

I put the rope on Feiqa's neck and then tied it to the side of the wagon, as I had before.

"Will it be necessary to chain you?" Mincon asked Tula.

"No, Master," she said.

"That is for me to decide," he said. He then took a length of chain from the wagon, that with which he had chained her to the wagon wheel last night, and, with a heavy padlock, fastened it on her neck. He then padlocked the other end of the chain to a stout ring, the central ring, at the rear of the wagon. She would walk behind the wagon, fastened to it by the neck.

"Yes, Master," she said, smiling, putting her head down.

Hurtha threw his things into the wagon. Among them was the heavy, single-bladed Alar war ax. In the dialect of the Alars, if it is of interest, this particular type of ax is called the *francisca*. Among those, too, who have learned to fear it, it is also often referred to by that name.

I decided that I would walk beside the wagon for a time. There did not seem room for both Hurtha and myself on the wagon box, beside Mincon.

"Ho!" called Mincon to his beast, shaking the reins with his left hand and cracking the tharlarion whip over its back with his right. Tula cried out, inadvertently, at the sharp crack of the whip, and Feiqa winced. Both were slaves and had some comprehension of the whip. To be sure, only Tula had felt the tharlarion whip, and I did not envy her her knowledge. Feiqa, on the other hand, had felt the five-bladed Gorean slave whip, used for the punishment and the correction of the behavior of females. Both, thus, were aware of what a whip could mean, from the slave's point of view. The wagon lurched and, moving unevenly, the wheels going over rocks and traversing ruts left from the passage of other wagons, began its climb to the road.

"Hold!" I said, suddenly, to Mincon, as we came to the edge of the road. He pulled back on the reins.

The free woman hurried forward. "I did not know where to find you," she said. "I knew you would come this way. I have been waiting by the side of the road."

"Do you know this woman?" inquired Mincon.

"Yes," I said.

Mincon was eager to be on his way. His hand had tightened on the tharlarion whip. If this woman were merely another begger he was ready, clearly, to strike her from his path.

"You are wearing a dress," said Hurtha.

"Yes," she said.

"Did you manage to free yourself?" he asked.

"No," she said, reddening. "I could not free myself. I was absolutely helpless."

Hurtha regarded her.

"I was cut loose by Genserix this morning," she said.

"A free woman is present," I said to Feiqa. Immediately she knelt. "Head to the ground," I whispered to her. Immediately she complied. Behind the wagon Tula, frightened, immediately followed her example. Both, in a sense, particularly Tula, were new to the collar. Both must learn that they were nothing in the sight of free persons.

"You are wearing a dress," said Hurtha.

"Yes," she said.

He continued to regard her.

"What are you staring at?" she asked.

"You," he said.

"I?" she asked.

"I have never seen you in a dress before," he said.

"So?" she asked.

"It is nothing," he said. "It is only that I am surprised to see you thusly." Boabissia was not in furs and leather. She now wore one of the simple, corded, belted, woolen, plain, widely sleeved, ankle-length dresses of the Alar women. It was brown. She had belted it snugly, and had, too, drawn its adjustment cording snugly from its loop about the back of her neck down to her breasts where she had crossed it and then taken it back, both cords, between and under her breasts, again to her belt, tying it closely at the sides of her body. This is not uncommon among Alar women. Even though they are free they are apparently not above reminding their men that they are females. It is a simple arrangement, but not unattractive. It covers almost everything, with seeming modesty, but in such a way, that it is likely to lead a man to think in terms of removing it. Boabissia, however, was presumably unaware of these things. From her point of view, she had probably done nothing more than to garb herself in the accustomed manner of the Alar woman. Even so, however, putting herself in a dress, in itself, seemed to represent some sort of considerable change in her. She wore, too, as she had last night, her dagger at her belt.

"I am entitled to dress in this fashion," she said defensively.

"Then you are a woman," he said.

She did not deign to respond.

"Are you a woman?" he asked.

"Yes," she said, angrily. "I am a woman!"

"Then it is appropriate that you should wear a dress," he said.

"Perhaps!" she said. She looked at him angrily.

"When did you discover that you were a woman," he asked. "Last night?"

She did not deign to answer.

"Yes," he speculated, "it was doubtless last night."

Her small fists clenched.

"Why are you here?" he asked.

"I want to come with you," she said. She put down her head.

"We must be on our way," said Mincon. Other wagons were emerging from the camp, coming up the small slope, and trundling onto the stones of the Genesian Road. The two slaves still knelt in their places, their heads down to the dirt. They had not yet been given permission to change their position.

"You had best remain within the safety of the wagons," said Hurtha. "This is the great outside world. You do not know what might become of you out here."

"I am not afraid," she said.

"You might be killed," said Hurtha.

"I am not afraid," she said.

"You might be caught, and put in chains," said Hurtha. He did not even mention, explicitly, the horrifying word "bondage." In this he was tactful. She was a free woman.

"That I fear most," she said. "That would be a fate a thousand times worse than death."

Feiqa, kneeling near my feet, her head down to the dirt, stifled a sound of amusement. I kicked her, gently, with the side of my foot, to silence her.

"Remain with the wagons," said Hurtha.

"No," said Boabissia.

"You are rather pretty," he said.

"Do not insult me," she said.

"I wonder what you would look like, stripped, and branded and collared, as a slave," he said.

"Please, Hurtha," she said.

"Do you think you could please a man?" he asked.

"I have no interest in pleasing men," she said.

"But do you think you could do so?" he asked.

"I am sure I do not know," she said.

"In a collar," he said, "subject to the whip, you would doubtless attempt desperately to learn to do so, and quickly and well."

"Perhaps," she said, angrily.

"Remain with the wagons," he said.

She looked at Hurtha, and then at me, and then again at Hurtha. She fingered the small copper disk, on its thong, tied about her throat, that disk which had been found on her in infancy, when she had been found by Alars in the wreckage of a burned, raided caravan, that disk on which a "Tau" and a number had been inscribed. "No," she said.

Another wagon climbed to the road, and rolled by.

Hurtha looked at me. I shrugged. She was pretty, and she was free. I supposed she could do much what she wished. It was not as though she were naught but a banded chattel, like Feiqa and Tula.

"Do you have any money?" asked Hurtha.

"No," she said.

"Are you wearing that dress in the manner of the Alar woman?" he asked.

"Yes," she said, reddening.

It was not winter now, but only Se'Kara. Accordingly all she now wore would be the dress. Beneath it she would be naked.

He then went to her and untied the strings which held the dagger sheath, with its small, narrow, sheathed weapon, with its ornamented, enameled handle, at her belt.

"What are you doing?" she asked.

"I am taking the dagger," he said. "I am going to throw it away, here, along the side of the road. Have no fear. It will not go unused. Someone will surely find it."

"But then I will be defenseless!" she protested.

"Such a weapon," he said, "might get you killed. It is better that you do not have it."

"But I will be defenseless without it," she insisted.

"You were defenseless with it," he said, "only you did not know it. Do you truly think that anyone who intended to take you, or harm you, would be dissuaded from doing so by that tiny weapon? Do not deceive yourself. Indeed, if he were not amused, he might even find it irritating, and see fit to turn it into your own heart. At the least, you would be likely to be punished severely for the pretensions of carrying it."

"What then are my defenses?" she asked.

"Those of the female," he said.

"Of the female!" she said.

"For that is what you are, Boabissia," he said.

"I see," she said.

"Docility, and total obedience," he said.

"I see," she said.

"Return to the wagons," he said.

"No," she said.

He looked at her.

"I want to come with you," she said.

"If you come with us," he said, "you come with us as a woman."

"I would then be helpless," she said, "with a woman's helplessness."

"You have always been such, Boabissia," he said, "though perhaps, among the wagons, you did not realize it."

"I would have to depend upon you, upon men, for my total protection," she said.

"Yes," said Hurtha. "And such protection extends to you, of course, only in so far as you are a free woman."

"Of course," she said.

Slaves are goods. Thus, whether they are protected, or defended, or not, depends on the decisions of free persons, like the defense or protection of other goods, whatever they might be, for example, sacks of gold, crates of sandals, tethered thalarion, caged vulos, and strings of fish. Many a caravan has saved itself by leaving lovely slaves behind in the desert, to slow the pursuit of marauders. So, too, more than one merchantman has saved itself by jettisoning beauties too luscious to be left behind by lustful pursuers. Better to lose part of a cargo, they reason, than all of it.

"Do you wish to come with us?" asked Hurtha.

"Yes," she said.

"Do you come with us as a woman?" he asked.

"Yes," she said. "I will come with you—as a woman."

He threw the dagger, with its sheath, to the side of the road.

She looked at it. I took her by the arm and conducted her to where Tula knelt, her head to the dirt. "This is a free woman," I told Tula. "She will be traveling with us." Tula, scarcely lifting her head, pressed her lips to the sandals of Boabissia, kissing them. "Mistress," she said. I then conducted Boabissia to the vicinity of Feiqa. Feiqa had once been the Lady Charlotte, of Samnium, a high lady in that city, one of aristocratic birth and upbringing, from one of her finest families, one prominent on her Street of Coins. Feiqa pressed her lips to the sandals of Boabissia, kissing them. "Mistress," she whispered. "What?" inquired Boabissia, imperiously. Feiqa again pressed her lips to Boabissia's sandals, kissing them. "Mistress," she said, trembling.

"These slaves," I said to Boabissia, "as you are a free woman, are at your disposal. On the other hand, you do not own them. Accordingly you are not to mutilate them or cause them permanent or serious injury unless they prove themselves to be, in some small way, at least, disobedient or displeasing."

"I understand," said Boabissia.

"Even then," I said, "it will be expected that you would first obtain the permission of their master."

"That is a common courtesy," said Boabissia.

"You may count, of course," I said, "on his understanding and sympathy, and his respect for your wishes, as those of a free woman."

"Of course," said Boabissia.

"In lesser matters, of course," I said, "where lesser exactitudes and punishments might be in order, you may, as any free person, at your whim, and without consulting the master, subject them to typical disciplines, things useful in helping them to keep in mind what they are."

"I understand," said Boabissia.

The slaves trembled. She was a free woman. The slave has some defense against a vital powerful male, female submission behaviors, indeed, the piteous and desperate prostration of her beauty and service at the feet of his authority and lust. This defense, however, minimal and uncertain as it may be, seldom avails her against the displeasure of the hostile free female.

"Oh!" said Boabissia.

Hurtha had taken her under the arms and swung her up to the wagon box.

"Good," said Mincon. "We must be our way."

To be sure, the other wagons from this camp were now more than a pasang or two down the road.

"We will never catch up," said Mincon.

"On your feet, imbonded sluts," I said.

Tula and Feiqa leapt up, Tula in her neck chain, Feiqa with the rope on her neck.

"May I speak, Master?" asked Feiqa.

"Yes," I said.

She touched her earrings. I saw that she was incredibly pleased to have them. Not only were they beautiful, though, indeed, they were not expensive, but, in Gorean eyes, they much confirmed, deeply and positively, her status upon her. I could see she was thrilled to wear them. What a slave they made her! "Master," she said, "may I sometimes be given slave silk?"

I smiled. None but a slave would put on slave silk. It is so tantalizingly beautiful and diaphanous that it seems to make a woman almost more naked than naked, and yet in such a way, driving a man almost mad with passion, that he can scarcely control himself, that he can scarcely rest, or think, having seen her in such a way, until he can put his hands on her, and part it, and thus reveal her as wholly bared, and helpless, and his. "Perhaps," I said.

"Thank you, Master," she whispered, happily. I was pleased

with Feiqa. She was now beginning to get in touch with her sexuality, indeed, with the deepest sexuality in the human female, that of the slave.

I saw the fists of Boabissia clench.

"Is anything wrong?" I asked.

"Put that slut back, behind the wagon," said Boabissia, "where she, like the animal she is, led, may follow with the other."

"Please?" I asked.

"Yes, please," said Boabissia, angrily.

"Very well," I said. I decided I would do this, at least this time, in deference to the wishes of Boabissia. She was after all, a free woman. I gathered she did not wish to glance to the side and see the beautiful, collared, scantily clad slave. She preferred, for whatever reason, it seemed, but one apparently not unusual for free women, to have her behind the wagon, out of sight. I myself, on the other hand, would have preferred keeping Feiqa at the side of the wagon. Indeed, I would rather have enjoyed, from time to time, looking down approvingly on the helplessness and seminudity of my nearby, neck-roped chattel. Surely, too, I had a right to do this if, and whenever, I pleased. It was merely another of the many, unlimited prerogatives attaching to my relationship to her, that of master to slave. I considered keeping her where she was. Still, Boabissia did not want her there, and Boabissia was, after all, a free woman. I supposed I should respect her wishes, at least once in a while. Too, I had earlier decided to move Feiqa. There did not seem much point in changing my mind, now. Too, there was much to be said objectively for putting Feiqa back of the wagon. Perhaps in indulging my own pleasure in seeing her I had been, inadvertently, too permissive with her. Surely I did not wish her to grow arrogant. Too, considering what she was, it was fitting that she was behind the wagon, attached to it by her neck rope.

"Master?" asked Feiqa.

"Be silent," I said.

Yes, Master," she said.

I untied her tether and led her to the back of the wagon. There were three rings there, the central ring, to which Tula had been chained, generally used for tethering, and two smaller, side rings, auxiliary rings, sometimes used for tethering, sometimes used for drawing a second wagon or cart. I tied her tether to the side ring on the right. She was smiling. I think she enjoyed being disturbing to Boabissia. To be sure, she should watch her step in such matters. I did tie her hands behind her back. I heard Boabissia gasp, and then she turned away. Such a tying makes a woman so helpless.

"We are ready," I called.

"Ho!" cried Mincon to his beast. He shook the reins and cracked the whip. The wagon moved forward, and rolled up onto the stones of the Genesian Road. In a bit we were moving forward. Hurtha and I walked beside the wagon. Boabissia, moving with the motion of the wagon, swaying with its motion, rode on the wagon box. Tula and Feiqa, her hands tied behind her, followed behind. I looked back, and they looked down, not meeting my eyes. Both were lovely. It was fitting, of course, that they followed on their tethers. Both were domestic animals.

"We will never catch up," said Mincon, grumbling. Then he cracked the whip again.

6: Hurtha's Feast

"Hurtha," said I, "what have you there?"

"Fruits, dried and fresh, candies, nuts, four sorts of meats, choice, all of them, fresh-baked bread, selected pastries," responded he, his arms full, "and some superb paga and delicate ka-la-na."

"Where did you get such things?" I asked.

"They were intended for the mess of the high officers, up the road," he said.

"They did not arrive there, apparently," I said.

"Have no fear," he said. "I purchased them honestly."

"You bought them surreptitiously from sutlers," I speculated.

"To be sure," he said, "the negotiations were conducted behind a wagon. On the other hand, it is surely not up to me to criticize the discretion of such fellows, nor how and where they conduct their business."

"I see," I said. I hoped earnestly that if these dealings were found out that any penalties which might be involved, in particular, such things as torturings and impalements, would be visited upon the sutlers and not on their customers, and particularly not on folks who might be traveling with their customers. To be sure, the rigors sometimes technically contingent upon such discoveries and exposures seldom actually resulted in the enactment of dismal sanctions, maimings, executions, and such, bribes instead, gifts and so on, usually changing hands on such occasions.

"Feast heartily," said Hurtha, unloading, half spilling, his acquisitions near the fire at our campsite.

"You should not have done this," I said to him.

"Nonsense," he said, depreciatingly, smiling, letting me

know that lavish gratitude on my part, however justified, was not even necessary.

"This is the food of generals," I said.

"It is excellent," agreed Hurtha.

"It is the food of *generals*," I said.

"There is plenty left for them," Hurtha assured me.

"You should not have done this," I said.

"It is time that I paid my share of the expenses," he said.

"I see," I said. It was difficult to argue with that.

"These are Ta grapes, I am told," he said, "from the terraces of Cos."

"Yes, they are," I said. "Or at least they are Ta grapes."

"Cos is an island," he said.

"I have heard that," I said. "These various things must have been terribly expensive."

"Yes," said Hurtha. "But money is no object."

"That is fortunate," I said.

"I am an Alar," Hurtha explained. "Have a stuffed mushroom."

I pondered the likely prices of a stuffed mushroom in a black-market transaction in a war-torn district, one turned into a near desert by the predations of organized foragers, in particular, the price of such a mushroom perhaps diverted at great hazard from the tables of Cosian generals.

"Have two," said Hurtha.

My heart suddenly began to beat with great alarm. "This is a great deal of food," I said, "to have been purchased by seventeen copper tarsks, and two tarsk bits." That was, as I recalled, the sum total of the monetary wealth which Hurtha had brought with him to the supply train, that or something much in its neighborhood.

"Oh," said Hurtha, "it cost more than that."

"I had thought it might," I said.

"Have a mushroom," said Hurtha. "They are quite good."

"What did all this cost?" I asked.

"I do not recall," said Hurtha. "But half of the change is yours."

"How much change do you have?" I asked.

"Fourteen copper tarsks," he said.

"You may keep them," I said.

"Very well," he said.

"I am quite hungry, Hurtha," said Boabissia. "May I have some food?"

"Would you like to beg?" he asked.

"No," she said.

"Oh, very well," said Hurtha. He then held out to her the plate of mushrooms. It did not seem to me that she needed to take that many. "Ah, Mincon, my friend, my dear fellow," said Hurtha. "Come, join us!"

I supposed he, too, would dive into the mushrooms. Still, one could not begrudge dear Mincon some greed in this matter, for he was a fine driver, and a splendid fellow. We had been with him now four days on the road. To be sure, we had received a late start on each of these days, and each day later than the preceding. It was difficult to get an early start with slaves such as Tula and Feiqa in the blankets. Boabissia, a free woman, must wait for us, of course, while we pleasured ourselves with the slaves. I think she did not much enjoy this. At any rate, she occasionally seemed somewhat impatient. Too, her irritability suggested that her own needs, and rather cruelly, might quite possibly be upon her.

Feiqa and Tula, those lovely properties, hovered in the background. I supposed that they, too, would want to be fed. I dared not speculate at what time we might be leaving in the morning. I hoped we could arouse Mincon and Hurtha at least by noon. There was even paga and ka-la-na. Mincon began to pick mushrooms off the plate and feed them to Tula. Did he not know she was a slave? "Thank you, Master," she said, being fed by hand. Sometimes slaves are not permitted to touch food with their own hands. Sometimes, in such a case, they are fed by hand; at other times their food might be thrown to them or put out for them in pans, and such, from which then, not using their hands, on all fours, head down, they must feed, in the manner of she-quadrupeds, or slaves, if it be the master's pleasure. Another mushroom disappeared. Had Tula not had some bread earlier?

"Have a mushroom." said Hurtha.

Mincon even gave a mushroom to Feiqa. I was watching. He was certainly a generous fellow with those mushrooms.

"No, thank you," I said. I wondered if, in the eating of such a mushroom, one became an inadvertent accomplice in some heinous misadventure.

"They are good," Hurtha insisted.

"I am sure they are," I said. I was particularly fond of stuffed mushrooms.

There was no problem for the slaves, of course. No one would blame them, any more than one would blame a pet sleen for eating something thrown his way.

Mincon and Boabissia might get off, I thought, watching them eat. After all, they did not know where the food came from. Mincon was a trusted driver, and a well-known good fellow. Boabissia was fresh from the wagons. She might be forgiven. Too, she was pretty. Hurtha, of course, might be impaled. I wondered if I counted as being guilty in this business whether I ate a mushroom or not. I knew where they came from, for example. It would be too bad to be impaled, I thought, and not have had a mushroom, at all. "What are they stuffed with?" I asked Hurtha.

"Sausage," he said.

"Tarsk?" I asked.

"Of course," he said.

"My favorite," I said. "I shall have one."

"Alas," said Hurtha. "They are all gone."

"Oh," I said. "Say," I said, "there seems to be a fellow lurking over there, by the wagons."

Hurtha turned about, looking.

It was undoubtedly a supply officer. I supposed it would be wrong to put a knife between his ribs. I did, however, for at least a moment, feverishly consider the practicalities that might be involved in doing so.

"Ho!" cried Hurtha, cheerfully, to the fellow.

The fellow, who was a bit portly, shrank back, as though in alarm, near one of the wagons. Perhaps he was not a supply officer. He did not have a dozen guardsmen at his back, for instance.

"Do you know him?" I asked.

"Of course," said Hurtha. "He is my benefactor!"

I looked again.

"Come," called Hurtha, cheerily. "Join us! Welcome!"

I feared the fellow was about to take to his heels.

"I am sorry the mushrooms are all gone," said Hurtha to me.

"That is all right," I said.

"Try a spiced verr cube," he suggested.

"Perhaps later," I said, uneasily. The portly fellow near the wagon had not approached, nor either had he left. He seemed to be signaling me, or attempting to attract my attention. But perhaps that was my imagination. When Hurtha glanced about he did not, certainly, seem to be doing so. I did not know him, as far as I knew.

"They are very good," said Hurtha, "though, to be sure, they are not a match for the stuffed mushrooms."

"Excuse me," said Mincon, "but I think that fellow over there would like to speak to you."

"Excuse me," I said to Hurtha.

"Certainly," he said.

In a moment I had approached the portly fellow by the wagon. "Sir?" I asked.

"I do not mean to intrude," he said, "but, by any chance, do you know the fellow sitting over there by the fire?"

"Why, yes," I said. "He is Mincon, a wagoner."

"Not him," said the fellow. "The other one."

"What other one?" I asked.

"The only other one," he said, "the big fellow, with yellow, braided hair, and the mustache."

"That one," I said.

"Yes," said he.

"He is called Hurtha," I said.

"Are you traveling with him?" he asked.

"I may have been," I speculated. "One sees many folks on the road. You know how it is."

"Are you responsible for him?" he asked.

"I hope not," I said. "Why?"

"Not an Ahn ago," he said, "he leaped out at me from

behind a wagon in the darkness, brandishing an ax. 'The Alars, at least one, are upon you!' he cried.''

"That sounds like Hurtha," I admitted.

"It was he," averred the fellow.

"You might be mistaken," I said.

"There are not many like him with the wagons," said the fellow.

"Perhaps there is at least one other," I said.

"It was he," said the fellow.

"You can't be sure," I said.

"I am sure," he said.

"Oh," I said.

"He then, brandishing his ax, importuned me for a loan. I was speechless with terror. I feared he might mistake my reticence for hesitation."

"I understand," I said, sympathetically.

" 'Take it,' " I cried. " 'Take my purse, my gold, all of it!' "

" 'As a gift,' he asked, seemingly delighted, though perhaps somewhat puzzled. 'Yes,' I cried. 'Yes!' "

"I see," I said. To be sure, when Hurtha had seen this fellow a few moments ago, he had referred to him not as his "creditor," but rather, now that I recalled it, warmly, as his "benefactor."

"That was very nice of you, to make him such a gift," I said.

"Shall I summon guardsmen from down the road?" he asked.

"I do not think that will be necessary," I said.

"In that purse," he said, "there were eighteen golden staters, from Tyros, three golden tarn disks, one from Port Kar, and two from Ar, sixteen silver tarsks from Tabor, twenty copper tarsks, and some fifteen tarsk bits."

"You keep very careful records," I said.

"I am from Tabor," he said.

"Probably you are a merchant, too," I said.

"Yes," he said.

I had feared as much. The merchants of Tabor are famed for the accuracy their accounts.

"Well?" he said.

"Would you care to join us?" I asked.

"No," he said.

"There is plenty to eat," I said.

"I am not surprised," he said.

"It is not my fault," I said, "if you, of your own free will, decided to make my friend a generous gift."

"Shall I summon guardsmen?" he asked.

"No," I said.

"Well?" said he.

"Do you have a witnessed, certified document attesting to the alleged contents of your purse?" I asked. "Too, was the purse closed with an imprinted seal, its number corresponding to the registration number of the certification document?"

"Yes," he said.

"Oh," I said.

"Here," he said. "I think you will find everything in order."

I had forgotten the fellow was from Tabor.

"This document seems a bit old," I said. "Doubtless it is no longer current, no longer an effective legal instrument. As you can see, it is dated two weeks ago. Where are you going?"

"To fetch guardsmen," he said.

"It will do," I said.

I then, without great pleasure, restored to the determined, inflexible fellow the amount in full which he had earlier, and of his own free will, as I did not fail to remind him, bestowed on my friend, Hurtha.

"I would also like something for my trouble," he said. "A silver tarsk will be sufficient."

"Of course," I said. He then, now seemingly content, left. How little it takes to please some people. I decided I must speak with Hurtha. I returned to the campfire.

"I will take some of the spiced verr cubes," I said.

"Alas," said Hurtha. "we have finished them. You should have invited my friend to sup with us."

"I did," I said. "But he did not agree to do so."

"It is perhaps just as well," said Hurtha, "as there is not much left. What did he want?"

"Oh, nothing," I said.

"Interesting," mused Hurtha.

"He just wanted to make certain that you were enjoying yourself," I said.

"A splendid fellow," said Hurtha.

"Hereafter," I said, "before you decide to apply for a loan or consider accepting an unusually generous gift, particularly while carrying an ax, at least while we are traveling together, I would appreciate it if you would take me into your confidence, if you would consult with me about it first."

"Of course, my dear friend," said Hurtha, "anything you like."

I regarded him.

"Did I do anything wrong?" he asked.

"No," I said.

"That is a relief," he said. "One must be so careful in one's dealings with civilized folks."

"Hurtha—" I said.

"Yes?" he said.

"Nothing," I said.

"You told me, or led me to believe, as I recall, that there could be no possible objection to fellows making me loans or bestowing gifts upon me," he said.

"That is true," I said.

"It is not my fault," he said, "if a complete stranger takes a liking to me and instantaneously decides to make me a fine gift."

"Of course not," I said.

"You see," he said.

"Just consult with me first, hereafter, if you would," I said.

"Of course, my dear fellow," he said.

"I am now nearly destitute," I said.

"Have no fear," he said. "Half of what I have is yours!"

"That would come to about seven copper tarsks, as I recall," I said.

"Precisely," said Hurtha.

"What is left to eat?" I asked.

"Not much, I am afraid," said Hurtha.

"Is there paga?" I asked.

"Yes," he said.

"Give it to me," I said.

7: We Get a Late Start; Boabissia Is Encouraged to Silence

"So at last we are upon our way, you lazy sleen," said Boabissia, lurching on the wagon box. "I thought it would never come about!"

"Please," said Mincon. "My head."

"It is well past noon!" said Boabissia.

"How do you feel?" I asked Mincon.

"I am sober now," said Mincon. "At least I see but one road ahead."

"You did very well," Hurtha congratulated me. "I had not known those of the cities could drink so much."

"We can do many remarkable things," I said, "when we are properly motivated." If one kept one's eyes closed it was easier to avoid the glare from the light on the stones. One could hold onto the edge of the wagon bed with one hand. To be sure, it increased the likelihood of stepping into potholes.

Hurtha fell against the side of the wagon. "Are you all right?" I asked.

"Certainly," he said.

"You are all monsters, and lazy sleen," said Boabissia. "I am sure, now, we will never catch up with the others, surely not until after dark!"

"That is my concern," said Mincon, blinking, shaking his head.

"Then I suggest you attend to it," said Boabissia.

"Please," begged Mincon.

"I think I shall see that you are reported to the wagon

89

officer," she said. "Surely he would have something to say about your broad-minded attitudes toward schedules, your unconscionable delays, your neglect of your duties. Do you think you are being paid to take your time? You have stores to deliver!"

"Please," said Mincon. "Please!"

Boabissia had been a pain all morning. Scarcely had we been permitted to sleep. Even before dawn, when others were having their breakfasts, and later, in the vicinity of dawn, when the other wagons were preparing to leave camp, we had been urged to bestir ourselves.

"We are alone on the road," said Boabissia. "You have deprived us of the safety of numbers. This could well be dangerous! Why did you not listen to me? What if we should be set upon by brigands?"

I hoped that would not happen, as I was not certain I could find my sword. Ah, yes, there it was, somehow in its sheath, over my left shoulder. The only problem, then, would be in attempting to dislodge it from its housing.

"Brigands might only slay you," said Boabissia, "but I am free woman! I have much more to fear! I might be put in a collar, and made a slave! Like those sluts in the back! You could have thought of me! You never think of me!"

How is it, I wondered, that each time I put my food down, my head hurts. That was interesting. Could it be normal? There was nothing in the codes of the warriors, as I recalled, that explicitly demanded resistance to brigands, though perhaps it was presupposed. It was an interesting interpretative question, probably one calling for the attention of high councils. If I were beheaded by a brigand's sword, I mused, I would be ridded of this headache. To be sure, such a remedy can be used but once. That is a count against it. Too, it was not true that we never thought of Boabissia. We often thought of her. In fact, I was thinking of her now.

"Men are beasts," she said, "tarsks, miserable drunken sleen!"

Tula and Feiqa, too, however, if it had to be known, had not been feeling too well. They were now both sleeping in the back of the wagon. It had been with difficulty that Hurtha and

I had managed to put them there. We would not have left them, of course. We were far too alert for that. Too, one does not leave Tulas and Feiqas simply lying about. They are far too desirable, far too luscious. To be sure, we had forgotten to chain them up last night, or rather, this morning, but neither, it seemed, as far as we could tell, had pondered escape.

"Oh!" cried Hurtha.

"Wait!" I said to Mincon.

"Here," I said to Hurtha, going to where he had stumbled off the road. I drew him up, with two hands, from the ditch. Fortunately it was not deep. "Hold to the side of the wagon," I advised him. He clutched it with both hands. In a moment we were again on our way.

"Drunken tarsks, all of you!" said Boabissia.

We were not drunk, of course. Last night, perhaps, we might have been a little drunk.

"Would you like some paga?" asked Hurtha, hospitably, clinging grimly to the wagon.

"No," I said.

"There is none left," said Boabissia.

"It is all gone?" asked Hurtha, in dismay.

"Yes," said Boabissia.

"All of it?" he pressed.

"Yes," she said.

I did not find this report disquieting.

"It is possible, of course," said Hurtha. "I am an Alar."

I heard Tula twist in the wagon, and groan. They had been lovely last night, in the firelight, naked, in their collars. More than once we had put down some ka-la-na for them, in pans. Too, particularly when they had licked and begged, and with sufficient fervor and skill, and prettiness, we had put dishes on the ground for them. It was only the first time, I think, that Tula was genuinely surprised when she found herself caught at her dish by Mincon. How incredibly beautiful and desirable are women. How marvelous are slaves!

"If you had listened to me," said Boabissia to Mincon, "we would have been on the road more than four Ahn ago!"

I swung up to the wagon box. I looked about in the wagon bed.

"We would then not be so far behind the others," she said. "Oh!" she said.

Boabissia looked at me, angrily.

"Good," said Mincon.

With my thumb I pressed the small sack more deeply into her mouth, until her lovely, sometimes irritating oral orifice was well stuffed with it. The small sack had drawstrings. These I took to the sides and yanked back, drawing them deeply back between her teeth, and then knotted them tightly behind the back of her neck. I could not make out what she was saying.

"Be silent," I said to her.

She stopped saying whatever it was she was saying.

"You will leave this as it is," I said, "until one of the men with the wagon sees fit to remove it."

She looked at me.

"If you should remove it yourself, or attempt to do so," I said, "it will be promptly replaced, or resecured, and you will be stripped and put in slave bracelets, your hands behind your back. Furthermore, you will then be put on a rope and will follow the wagon, naked, and so braceleted and gagged, as might a slave. Do you understand? If so, nod, Yes."

Boabissia looked at me in fury. And then, tears in her eyes, she nodded. I then returned to the road.

"It is more peaceful now," said Hurtha.

Boabissia struck down at the lid of the wagon box, serving as her bench, with her small fists. But she did not attempt to dislodge the device by means of which, in accordance with the will of men, she had been silenced.

"Yes," I said.

8: Evidence of a Disquieting Event Is Found

"There is smoke ahead," said Mincon, pulling back on the reins, halting the wagon. He and Boabissia rose to their feet, looking ahead. I climbed on the spokes of the front wheel, near Boabissia. It was now late in the afternoon. The gag which I had fixed on her somewhat after the noon hour, shortly after we had begun our day's journey, I had, after an Ahn or two, loosened and pulled free. She was then somewhat subdued, knowing that it could be instantly replaced at our least irritation. It now, if only as a reminder, on its strings, still wet, hung loosely about her neck.

"What is it?" asked Hurtha.

"I do not know," I said.

Feiqa and Tula, kneeling on sacks in the back of the wagon, moved about a little. They had been very quiet all afternoon. I think they had not wished to call attention to themselves. After all, they were there, riding in the wagon, and not afoot, on their tethers, behind it. Was this not almost like being a privileged free woman? To be sure, they were in the back of the wagon, where cargo is kept, in collars and slave tunics, and were kneeling. Slave girls can be very clever in such ways. Mincon and I, of course, indulgently, pretended not to notice this.

"What is it?" asked Boabissia.

"I do not know," I said.

Feiqa and Tula, frightened, kneeling in the back of the wagon, looked at one another. They were goods.

"Remain here," I said. "I will investigate."

"I am coming with you," said Hurtha.

I nodded. I would welcome the company of the Alar.

"I think there is trouble," said Mincon.

"Watch for our signal," I said.

I stepped down from the wheel and unsheathed my sword. I began then to advance down the road. Hurtha took his ax from the wagon and followed me.

The man lifted his hand, weakly, as though to fend a blow.

"Do not fear," I told him.

"Are you not with them?" he asked.

"No," I said.

"They came," he said, "as though from nowhere."

"They emerged from covered pits," I said, "dug near the road."

"They were suddenly everywhere, all about us, crying out, with reddened blades," he said, "and merciless. They were swift. We could not resist them. We are not soldiers. Then they were gone."

"Are there any other survivors?" I asked.

"I do not know," he said.

"There are others," I said, looking over the road.

"Yes," he said.

Free women had come to the road. They were now poking through the wreckage and ashes, moving bodies about, hunting for loot, or food. I did not think there would be much left for them.

The smell of smoke hung heavy in the still air.

"When did this happen?" I asked.

"An Ahn, perhaps two Ahn ago," he said. "I do not know." He sat wearily beside the road, his head in his hands.

"It was more likely two Ahn," I said. There was little active fire now. Stalks of veminium broken beside the road had now dried.

Hurtha looked about, uneasily.

"I do not think any would be about now," I said. "Their work here has been finished."

"There are only the women now," he said, bitterly.

"Yes," I said. "Now there are only the women."

I looked about myself. Had the terrain been properly scouted, had the wagons been properly guarded, this thing presumably could not have happened, or, surely, not in as devastating a fashion as this.

"Ar has struck," said Hurtha, grimly.

"I do not think this is the work of the troops of Ar," I said.

"But who else?" he asked.

"I do not know," I said.

"But what troops?" he asked.

"This does not look to me like the work of regular troops," I said. "Consider the wagons, the bodies."

The wagons had not merely been burned, that their cargos might be destroyed, but, clearly, had been ransacked. Wrappings, sackings and broken vessels lay strewn about. Several bodies, it seemed, had been hastily examined. Some had been stripped of articles of clothing. I had found none with their wallets intact. In some cases digits had been cut away, presumably to free rings.

"Mercenaries," said Hurtha.

"It would seem so," I said. It is difficult to control such men. Most commanders, in certain situations, will give them their head. Indeed, in certain circumstances the attempt to impose discipline upon them can be extremely dangerous. It is something like informing the hunting sleen, eager, hot from the chase, his jaws red with blood, that he should now relinquish his kill. It must be understood, of course, that the average mercenary looks upon loot as his perquisite. He regards it, so to speak, as a part of his pay. Indeed, the promise of loot is almost always one of the recruiter's major inducements.

"Cosian mercenaries?" asked Hurtha.

"Who knows?" I said. It did not seem to me impossible that some of the mercenary troops with the Cosian army might have doubled back to strike at one of their own supply columns. Surely the paucity of protection provided for such columns would not have escaped their notice.

I looked at the women, poking about amidst the wreckage. It had not taken them long to arrive. I could see some others, too, coming just now, from between the hills. Perhaps they had camps nearby. The wagons were in a long line, about a pasang long. Some, too, were off the road. Some were overturned. Most showed signs of fire. There were few tharlarion in evidence. Harnesses had been cut and they, it seems, had either been driven away or had wandered off. In one place there was a dead tharlarion, and the women, some crouching on it, were cutting it into pieces with knives, putting pieces of meat in their mouths, and hiding other pieces in their dresses.

"Jards," said Hurtha, in disgust.

I shrugged. These women were of the peasants. They were not given to the niceties of civilized women. Too, they were doubtless starving.

"Jards!" said Hurtha.

"Even the jard desires to live," I said.

"It is not unknown that such women come to the fields," he said, "and even when not hungry."

"That is true," I said. Perhaps all women belonged in collars.

"We could probably follow the raiders," he said.

"Probably," I said. The trail was doubtless still fresh enough to permit this. One man, who knows what he is doing, can be extremely difficult to follow. It is extremely difficult, on the other hand, for a large group of men to cover their traces.

"Shall we do so?" asked Hurtha.

"Do you really wish to catch up with them?" I asked.

"I suppose not," he said.

"It is not our business," I said. "It is the business of those of Cos."

Hurtha nodded.

"Perhaps you should signal Mincon," I said.

Hurtha walked back to the top of a small rise in the road. From there he could look back to where we had left the wagon. I saw him standing there, on the crest. He lifted his ax and beckoned that the others might now join us.

"Are you all right?" I asked the fellow by the side of the road.

"Yes," he said.

"Are you not hurt?" I asked.

"I hid," he said. "I think no one saw me. I am sick. That is all. I am all right."

"We have a wagon," I told him. "You are welcome to ride with us to the next camp."

"Thank you," he said.

"You do not know who did this?" I asked.

"No," he said.

I saw the head of Mincon's tharlarion come over the rise, moving about, on its long neck, scanning the road, and then, in a moment, the wagon. I advanced to meet it.

Boabissia sat white-faced on the wagon box. I recalled that she was not Alar by blood. Her makeshift gag still hung about her neck. "It is not necessary to look," I told her.

"What went on here?" said Mincon.

"War," said Hurtha.

"Who did this?" asked Mincon. "Those of Ar?"

"We do not know," said Hurtha.

Feiqa looked sick. Even Tula, of the peasants, was pale.

"Slaves," I said, "lie on your bellies in the wagon." This would bring their heads below the sides of the wagon.

Boabissia looked at me.

"There is nothing we can do," I said.

She nodded.

"Are you all right?" I asked.

"If we had left this morning, with the others," she whispered, "we would have been here."

"Yes," I said. "But we might have survived. Doubtless some have survived. There are usually survivors. Even now word has probably been brought to the contingents ahead on the road."

"We would have been here," she said.

"That is true," I said.

I then went to the fellow whom we had found by the road and helped him to his feet.

"I would like for this fellow to sit on the wagon box, Boabissia," I said. "Please sit in the back."

Boabissia, saying nothing, crawled into the back of the wagon. She sat with her back against one side of the wagon bed. She said nothing.

I helped the fellow up to the wagon box. He was unsteady. I think he was in shock. I put a blanket about him.

"Shall we go?" asked Mincon.

"Yes," I said.

We then began to thread our way among the burned wagons. Free women, now and then, as we passed, stopped to look up, and watch us. Twice Mincon, in rage, cracked his whip at them, and they fled back. But, in a moment, as I ascertained, looking back, they had returned to their labors.

9: Torcodino

"Riders," said Mincon.

Hurtha and I, on foot beside the wagon, could not yet see them.

"It will be more Cosian cavalry," said Hurtha.

I thought this was probably true. Raiders would not be likely to move so openly. Nonetheless, I loosened the blade in my sheath. Too, several contingents of cavalry had swept by us earlier in the evening.

Boabissia, now again on the wagon box, beside Mincon, looked down at Hurtha, frightened. He did not notice this, however. He was looking ahead, gripping his ax.

"Get under the blanket," I said to Feiqa and Tula.

The wagons in our line slowed, and then stopped. A guard, nearby, on his tharlarion, stood in the stirrups.

"Who are they?" I asked Mincon.

"Cosian cavalry, I think," he said.

We heard trumpet calls ahead of us. These calls, like passwords, are frequently changed.

"Yes," said Mincon. "It seems they have the signs."

We were now two days past the scene of the massacre. Last night we had drawn into our assigned wagon space in a fortified camp. It was the first in this march the Cosians had prepared, as far as I knew. Such camps, of course, are common with Gorean armed forces, set at march intervals. They are usually constructed rather along the following lines. A surrounding ditch, or perimeter ditch, is dug about the campsite. The earth from this ditch is piled behind the ditch, thus forming, with the ditch, a primitive wall. Sometimes, materials permitting, a palisade is erected at the height of this wall. More commonly, in temporary camps, it may be surmounted with brush or archers' hurdles. The tents of commanders are usually placed on high ground near the center of the camp. This facilitates observation, defense and communication.

I stood on the wheel of the wagon, my left foot on one of the spokes. "Yes," I said. "I think so." Hurtha was close to the side of the wagon. In a moment he would go behind it, or press himself against its side. I could now see the approaching riders. Too, one could now hear clearly the drumming of the approaching beasts. The force approaching us, it seemed, wore the blue of Cos. Too, it seemed their point riders flew the pennons of Cos on their lances. In a moment they would be sweeping past us, divided by the wagons like a stream in flight. I looked back into the wagon. Feiqa and Tula were on the floor of the wagon bed, their soft bodies on coarse sacking, which would leave its temporary print in their flesh, affording them some protection from the harsh planks of the wagon bed. They lay between sacks of grain, not moving, scarcely daring to breathe. They had drawn the dark blanket drawn over them. It would not do, I did not think, to display such goods to strong men. The female slave, sometimes considered nothing, supposedly, is yet in actuality valued commonly more highly than even gold, which, in its turn, is often valued for its capacity to buy such women, to bring them into your chains. No, I did not think it would do to display them. Both were the most excruciatingly desirable type of female in existence, both were the sort of female for which men might kill, female slaves. I pulled at an edge of the blanket. It would not do for the curve of that delicious, branded flank, that of Feiqa, I believe, to suggest itself beneath the dark concealment of the heavy blanket.

In a moment, in a rush of bodies and blue, with the sound of weapons, the Cosian contingent had swept by. To one side, off the road, a Cosian guard, mounted, lifted his lance in salute. We had had such guards with the train within Ahn of the massacre. The wagons now, again, began to move.

"Tonight," said Mincon, "we will be safe. Tonight we will be in Torcodino."

Torcodino, on the flats of Serpeto, is a crossroads city. It is located at the intersection of various routes, the Genesian, connecting Brundisium and other coastal cities with the south, the Northern Salt Line and the Northern Silk Road, leading respectively west and north from the east and south, the Pilgrims' Road, leading to the Sardar, and the Eastern Way, sometimes called the Treasure Road, which links the western cities with Ar. Supposedly Torcodino, with its strategic location, was an ally of Ar. I gathered, however, that it had, in recent weeks, shifted its allegiances. It is sometimes said that any city can fall behind the walls of which can be placed a tharlarion laden with gold. Perhaps, too, the councils of Torcodino, did not care to dispute their gates with forces as considerable as those which now surrounded them. The choice between riches and death is one that few men will ponder at length. Still I was surprised that Ar had not moved swiftly on behalf of her ally. Torcodino, as far as I knew, had been left at the mercy of the Cosian armies. The city was now used as a Cosian stronghold and staging area. Mincon, for example, after delivering his goods in Torcodino, was to return northward on the Genesian to Brundisium, where he was scheduled to pick up a new cargo. Certainly the movements of Cos seemed quite leisurely, particularly as it was late in the season. Mercenaries, as I may have mentioned, are often mustered out in the fall, to be recruited anew in the spring. To be sure, in these latitudes, cold though it might become, the red games of war need seldom be canceled.

"There are the aqueducts of Torcodino!" said Mincon.

"I see them," I said. The natural wells of Torcodino, originally sufficing for a small population, had, more than a century ago, proved inadequate to furnish sufficient water for an expanding city. Two aqueducts now brought fresh water to Torcodino from more than a hundred pasangs away, one from the Issus, a northwestwardly flowing tributary to the Vosk and the other from springs in the Hills of Eteocles, southwest of Corcyrus. The remote termini of both aqueducts were defended by guard stations. The vicinities of the aqueducts themselves are usually patrolled and, of course, engineers and workmen attend regularly to their inspection and repair.

These aqueducts are marvelous constructions, actually, having a pitch of as little as a hort for every pasang.

I pulled the blanket from the slaves. If there were to be inspections or halts before entering the gates of Torcodino it would be impossible to conceal them. Besides I enjoyed seeing them.

"How long will it take to reach the city?" asked Boabissia.

"The first wagons are doubtless near the gates now," said Mincon.

In something like a half of an Ahn we had come to Torcadino's Sun Gate. Many cities have a "Sun Gate." It is called that because it is commonly opened at dawn and closed at dusk. Once a Gorean city closes its gates it is usually difficult to leave the city. They are seldom opened and closed to suit the convenience of private persons. Sometimes rogues and brigands, and even slavers, hang about the gates, seeking to trap late comers against the walls. Many a lovely woman has fallen to the slaver's noose in just such a fashion. To be sure, a given gate, the "night gate," is usually maintained somewhere, through which bona fide citizens, known in the city, or capable of identifying themselves, may be admitted.

Two of the gate guards crawled into the wagon. Mincon presented his papers to the gate captain. "Mercenaries, from the north," said Mincon to the captain, indicating Hurtha and myself. The captain nodded. "More come in each day," he said. "They smell loot."

"Who is this?" asked the captain, indicating Boabissia. He returned the papers to Mincon. They were apparently in order.

"I am an Alar woman," said Boabissia.

"No," said Hurtha. "She is only a woman who has been with the wagons of the Alars."

Boabissia's small hands clenched.

The captain removed a whip from his belt. He held it up for Boabissia to regard. "Do you know what this is?" he asked.

"Of course," she said, uneasily. "It is a slave whip."

"Is she a free woman?" asked the captain.

"Yes," said Mincon.

"Yes," said Hurtha.

In the back of the wagon Feiqa and Tula knelt small, trembling, their heads down to the coarse sacking covering the boards of the wagon bed. One of the guards took Feiqa's head and pulled it up, and then bent her painfully backward, exposing brazenly, as is fully appropriate for slaves, the luscious bow of her owned beauty. He then did the same for blond Tula. "Not bad," he said.

"There are many such in Torcodino," said the captain.

"Oh!" said Boabissia. He had, with the coiled whip, brushing it under her long skirt, lifted it up, over her knees, so that one could see the beginning of her thighs. "But there are not so many such as these," he said.

"Oh!" suddenly said Feiqa, squirming helplessly. "Oh!" wept Tula, startled, her body helplessly leaping.

"Yes," laughed one of the guards. "These are slaves."

Boabissia looked in fear at the captain. But he replaced the whip at his belt. Swiftly she pulled down her skirt.

"No," said the captain, regarding Boabissia, who looked straight ahead, terrified, the tiny metal disk on its thong about her throat, "there are not so many such as these, these days, free females, in Torcodino." His men left the wagon. He then motioned that we might proceed. In a moment or two we had passed under the gate. Feiqa and Tula looked at one another, frightened. They had been handled as the slaves and goods they were.

"Why did you not protect me?" Boabissia asked Hurtha.

"Did you see how he looked at her?" Hurtha said to me.

"Certainly," I said.

"Why did you not protect me from his insolence, Hurtha?" she demanded.

"Does Boabissia need protection?" asked Hurtha.

"Of course not!" she said.

"What are our finances?" asked Hurtha.

"We have very little," I said.

"What are we to do?" asked Hurtha, concerned.

"I am sure I do not know," I said.

"We can strip Boabissia and sell her," said Hurtha.

"Hurtha!" cried Boabissia. It was indeed an idea, I thought.

"You saw the interest of the captain," he said.

"Yes," I said.

"She is not worth so much as the slaves," said Hurtha, "but doubtless she would bring something."

"We cannot sell her," I said, upon reflection. "She is a free woman."

"But if we sell her," said Hurtha, "she would no longer be a free woman."

"That is true," I granted him.

"But still you have reservations?" he asked.

"She is a free woman *now*," I said. "Perhaps that is worth some consideration."

"Not at all," said Hurtha.

"Oh?" I asked, interested.

"Come now," said Hurtha. "Be realistic. Free women are often sold. No one expects you to give them away."

"That is true," I said.

"Where do slaves come from?" asked Hurtha. "Surely only a small percentage of them are bred."

"That is true," I granted him.

"If it were not for the bringing of free females into the toils of bondage, capturing them, getting them properly marked, seeing to the legal details, putting them up for sale, and so forth, there would be few slaves."

"True," I said.

"I shall not listen to such things!" said Boabissia. "Oh!" Hurtha's hand was on her ankle.

"What are you doing?" she demanded.

"I am tying your ankles together," he said.

"Untie me!" she said.

"Do not touch the cords," he said.

I observed her ankles. They looked well, lashed tightly together.

"Why have you done this!" she asked.

"I do not want you running away, while we are thinking about such things," he said.

"I am an Alar woman!" she said.

"No," he said. "You are only a woman who has been with the Alar wagons."

She cried out in rage, her fists clenched.

"But she might not bring much," said Hurtha, disconsolately. "She is only a free female, and is not trained."

"True," I said.

"I gather," said Hurtha, "that you do not wish for me to accept spontaneous gifts from total strangers, or apply to them for loans."

I recalled the portly little fellow from Tabor. "I think I would prefer that you do not do so," I said. That time we had narrowly missed tangling with guardsmen.

"How then can we make some money?" asked Hurtha.

"I suppose we could do some work," I said.

"Work?" asked Hurtha, in horror. He was an Alar warrior. To be sure, manual labor was not exactly prescribed by my own caste codes either.

"It is a possibility," I said. After all, desperate men will resort to desperate measures.

"Rule it out," said Hurtha.

"How then do you propose, within the limits of legality, that we obtain our supper?" I asked.

"You may sup with me," said Mincon.

"Thank you," I said. "But imposing on your hospitality could be at best a temporary expedient."

"I, personally, on the other hand," said Hurtha, "would not consider one or two meals thrust as a wedge between myself and starvation to be beneath contempt."

"Besides, in the morning," I said, "I expect you will be returning to Brundisium."

"Yes," admitted Mincon.

"That would clear supper and breakfast," said Hurtha.

"I have a few coins left," I informed Hurtha.

"I thought you were merely being noble," said Hurtha.

"I am," I said. "It is always easier to be noble when one has the price of supper."

"That is almost poetic," said Hurtha, impressed.

"Thank you," I said. I had forgotten that Hurtha was a poet. This came then, I conjectured, as high praise. To be sure, he had hedged his declaration with the modification, 'almost'. Still, when all was said and done, what could that matter?

"Aha!" said Hurtha.

"What is it?" I asked.

"I have an idea!" said Hurtha.

My blood turned momentarily cold.

"Selling Boabissia?" asked Mincon. Boabissia's ankles squirmed in the thongs. She could probably not stand upright as she had been bound. We would probably have to help her down from the wagon box, and carry her to where we decided to put her.

"No," said Hurtha. "It is a different idea."

"I am glad to hear that," said Boabissia.

"But it may be every bit as good, or better, than that one," said Hurtha.

"I am eager to hear it, I assure you," said Boabissia.

"Would you like to hear it?" asked Hurtha of me.

"Certainly," I said, uncertainly. I felt a vague pang of anxiety.

"Surely you would have no objection to our selling a few things," said Hurtha.

"What?" asked Boabissia. "Me?"

"Not yet, at least," said Hurtha.

"What could you sell?" I asked. "You do not have much clothing with you, or many possessions, it seems."

"True," he said, his eyes shining with excitement.

"Would you sell your ax?" I asked. It was an excellent one.

"Of course not," he said.

"What then?" I asked.

"Trust me," he said.

"Must I?" I asked.

"All I wish from you," he said, "as you are more experienced in the strange ways of civilization than I, is that you would have no objection to my selling a few things to raise money."

"No one could have any possible objection to that," I said.

"Wonderful," he said, warmly. "I will then see you at the wagon yards!" He then turned about and disappeared.

"He is a good fellow," I said.

"Yes," said Mincon. "I wonder what it is that he intends to sell."

"I do not know," I said.

"As far as I could tell," said Mincon, "he did not take anything with him."

"That is true," I said. Hurtha's bag was still in the wagon.

"Maybe he will sell the ax," said Mincon. "He took that."

"I doubt that he would sell that," I said.

"What then?" asked Mincon.

"Perhaps he has precious stones, rare gems, sewn in his clothing, for an emergency," I said.

"That must be it," said Mincon.

"Yes," I said.

"At any rate," said Mincon. "Hurtha is a clever, splendid fellow. Doubtless he knows exactly what he is doing."

"Doubtless," I said.

"I have great confidence in him," said Mincon.

"So do I," I said.

"Untie me," said Boabissia.

"Not yet," I said.

"Ho!" called Mincon to his tharlarion. "Ho! Move!" We then drew again into the street and began to follow the rough signs painted on the sides of buildings to the wagon yards.

10: We Proceed
to the Wagon Yards

"It is not necessary to look at those things," I said to Boabissia.

She had already put her head down.

Judging from the condition of the bodies, the effects of the predations of birds, some still about, jards primarily, and the tattering of the winds and rains, they had been there for several weeks. The ropes on the necks had been tarred to protect them from the weather, an indication that it had been intended they should remain in place for some time. These inert, suspended, dessicated weights, now little more than skulls and the bones of men, with some bits of cloth, fluttering in the air's stirrings, and threads and patches of dried flesh clinging about them, had been arranged in a line along the Avenue of Adminius, the main thoroughfare of Torcadino, near the Semnium, the hall of the high council, doubtless as some sort of mnemonic and admonitory display. They swung creaking, a few feet off the ground, some turning slowly, backward and forward, at the ropes' terminations. A child reached up and struck the feet of one, to set it into motion.

"They are still up," said Mincon, angrily.

"I gather you have seen them before," I said.

"Twice," he said.

"I see," I said.

"There is no need, to reach the wagon yards, to pass this place," said Mincon, angrily.

"You know Torcadino then?" I said.

"To some extent," he said.

"We have followed the signs," I said.

"Of course," he said, bitterly.

I nodded. Clearly it had been intended that those coming and going in Torcadino would take this route.

"Who are they?" I asked.

"Members of the high council, and lesser councils, and certain of their supporters," he said, "who favored the cause of Ar."

"I had thought they might be," I said.

"Have you counted them?" he asked.

"No," I said.

"There are more than two hundred," he said.

"That is a large number," I said.

"Others perished, too," he said, "but were not regarded as prominent enough, I suppose, to serve as warnings."

"I see," I said.

We then continued on our way.

"There must, by now, given the past weeks, be a great amount of supplies in Torcadino," I said.

"Yes," said Mincon.

"It is interesting that Ar has not struck," I said.

"Perhaps," he said.

"If Torcadino were to be stormed, and fired, and these supplies captured or destroyed, the Cosian movements would surely be hampered, if not altogether arrested. Such an action would frustrate and stall the invasion. This could give Ar the time she might require to deploy and arm for extensive action, what time she might need to meet the enemy in detail and force."

"The Cosian armies are in the vicinity," said Mincon. "It would require armies to cut through them."

"Perhaps there are other ways," I said.

"Not tarnsmen," said Mincon.

"Perhaps not," I said.

"It is hard to see at this time of day," said Mincon. "But the sky over the city is crisscrossed with thousands of strands of tarn wire. Even in the daytime it can be hard to see. It is there, however, I assure you."

I did not doubt him. I could see mountings for it on several of the buildings.

"The gates of Torcadino are firm," he said. "Her walls are high and strong."

"Doubtless," I said.

"Torcadino is impregnable," he said. "It cannot be taken."

"I know how I would take it," I said.

Boabissia was quiet. Feiqa and Tula, too, in the back, were quiet. I looked at some people in the streets. The streets were not too crowded. I saw a vendor with a cart. I saw a slave girl, in a brief tunic. She looked at me, and looked away. Beneath the tiny, brief skirt of that tunic it was almost certain that there would be only girl. In such a way do Gorean masters commonly keep their women. Certainly we kept Feiqa and Tula that way. It helps the girls to keep clearly in mind that they are slaves. I glanced at Boabissia. Her head was still down. She had her long skirt pulled down, and closely, about her ankles. Its thus hid the fact that they were lashed together.

"We will be in the wagon yards in a quarter of an Ahn," said Mincon.

"Good," I said.

11: We Decide Boabissia Will Help Out with our Finances

"Perhaps you remember me," said the fellow.

"No, not at all," I said, hastily.

"From several nights ago," he said, "on the Genesian Road, at one of the camps."

"Oh?" I said.

"I am a merchant, from Tabor," he said.

"Ah, yes," I said. Indeed, it was the merchant from Tabor, that portly fellow who had been so inflexibly and boorishly determined to retrieve a gift, one which he had bestowed, of his own free will, as I had pointed out to him, on one of the fellows traveling with me, Hurtha, as I recalled. "How are you?" I asked. I feared the answer would not be reassuring.

"Fine," he said, somewhat bitterly I thought.

"That is good to hear," I said. But his demeanor suggested, and rather clearly, that it might actually be his intention to broach some new grievance. I had some suspicion, also, as to what it might be. It is good, in such situations, to be friendly, and smile a good deal.

"I see very little to smile about," he said.

"Sorry," I said.

He looked about himself. "That giant lout with the mustache and braided hair, and ax, is not about, is he?" he asked.

"To whom might you be referring?" I asked.

"To one who is called Hurtha," said the fellow.

"Oh," I said.

"That is, at any rate, what you told me his name was, the last time we spoke of him."

"Yes," I said, "of course." Perhaps I had made a mistake, earlier, several nights before, in revealing the Alar's name. Still I did not think he would be a difficult fellow to locate, even if his name were not known. There were not too many like him with the wagons. It did not seem to me a very complimentary way, incidentally, in which to refer to Hurtha. He was, after all, even if perhaps a giant lout, from some points of view, a poet, and was entitled to some respect on that account, particularly if one had not read his poems. Too, he prided himself on his sensitivity. "No," I said. "He is not about."

"Here!" said the fellow, firmly, thrusting a piece of paper toward me. There was some writing on it.

"Whose writing is this?" I asked.

"Mine," he said.

"Oh," I said. To be sure, Hurtha was illiterate, like most Alars. Boabissia, too, incidentally, was illiterate. Illiteracy, however, has seldom deterred poets. Indeed, some of the greatest poets of all times were illiterate. Among folks as different as Tuchuks and Torvaldslanders, for example, poetry is seldom written down. It is memorized and sung about the fires, and in the halls, and thus is carried on the literary tradition. And poets such as Hurtha, it seemed to me, were even less likely to be deterred by illiteracy than many others.

"He leaped out at me, from behind a wagon, with his ax!" said the fellow. " 'I am a poet,' he announced, his ax at the ready. 'Would you care to purchase a poem?' 'Yes!' cried I. 'Write,' he then said, and dictated to me this poem, which I, for my very life, hastily scribbled on this slip of parchment."

"You did so, of your own free will," I noted, thinking it important to emphasize this fact.

"I want my silver tarsk back!" he said.

"It is a very fine poem," I said.

"You have not read it," he pointed out.

"I have read others of his," I said. "I am sure it is every bit as good." Indeed, I had already read three others this very night. The Tabor merchant was the fourth fellow who had come by to look me up. Too, coincidentally, he was the fourth fellow who was demanding his silver tarsk back.

"To me," said the merchant, "it seems merely strange, or perhaps, at best, unmitigated trash, but then I am a simple man of business, and not a scribe. Doubtless such things come more within their jurisdiction than mine."

"That is true," I said, encouraging him.

"Would you care to interpret this line?" he asked, pointing to a line.

"No," I said.

"What about this one?" he asked.

"I do not think so," I said.

"What about this?" he asked. " 'Her eyes were like green moons.' "

"That is an easy one," I said. "Doubtless moons are supposed to suggest romance, and green the vitality and promise of life."

"It is addressed to a wounded tharlarion," he said.

"Oh," I said.

"I want my silver tarsk back," he said.

"Of course," I said, emptying my wallet into the palm of my hand. It was not hard to do. "Perhaps that tarsk is it," I said.

"I suspect so," he said. "You have only one there, and that is stamped with the mark of the mint of Tabor."

"So it is," I said, handing it back to him. One thing about Hurtha. He thought highly of his poems. He did not let them go for nothing. They were not cheap. He maintained his standards. Still, it seemed that a silver tarsk was a high price to pay for a poem, even if it were as good as one of Hurtha's, particularly one one had to copy oneself. Indeed, many lovely women on Gor do not bring as much as a silver tarsk on the slave block.

"Thank you," said the merchant.

"Yes?" I said. He was still there.

"I am surely entitled to something for my trouble," he said.

The other fellows had not taken this attitude. Still, they had not been merchants.

"Here," I said, giving him a copper tarsk. That left me with two.

"Thank you," he said, after scrutinizing the change in my palm.

"You're welcome," I said. He then left.

"Alas," said Hurtha, coming up to me, disconsolately, "I fear I have made a terrible mistake."

"How could that be?" I asked.

"In my good-hearted enthusiasm to assuage our needs," he said, "I fear I may have suffered dishonor, if not ruination."

"How is that?" I asked. That was certainly an interesting thing to hear.

"I have been selling my poems," he said, collapsing near Mincon's fire, by the wagon. He sat there, with his head in his hands.

"Oh?" I said.

"Yes," he said. "Surely you recall the four silver tarsks I gave you earlier in the evening."

"Of course," I said.

"I received them from the sale of poems, my poems!" he said, shaking with emotion.

"No!" I cried.

"Yes," he said, miserably.

"I had thought it must be from the sale of numerous rich gems, doubtless sewn in your jacket," I said.

"No," he said. "I looked about the yards, and when I found fine-looking, sensitive-looking chaps, splendid-seeming fellows, of apparent refinement and taste, those of a sort I thought might be capable of appreciating my work, I offered them one of my poems, and for no more than a mere token of appreciation, a silver tarsk."

"That was incredibly generous," I said.

"It was a terrible mistake," said Hurtha.

"I am glad you realize that," I said.

"What?" he asked.

"Nothing," I said.

"My poems are priceless," he said.

"You think you should have asked for more than a silver tarsk?" I asked, alarmed.

"No," he said. "I should not have sold them at all."

"I see," I said, relieved. "But they are probably not really all that bad."

"What?" he asked.

"Nothing," I said.

"I realized it with the last poem," he said, miserably. "I looked down at the silver tarsk in my hand, and at the poem in the fellow's hand, and it all became clear to me. I saw then how terrible was the thing I had done, selling my poems, my own poems, my precious, priceless poems! They now belonged to another! Better I had torn my heart out and sold it for a tarsk bit!"

"Perhaps," I said.

"I then begged the fellow to take back his worthless tarsk, and return the poem to me."

"And did he do so?" I asked.

"Yes," said Hurtha, looking up at me.

"Well," I said, "it all ended well then."

"No," he said, tears in his eyes. "You do not understand."

"We are now short a tarsk?" I said.

"No!" cried Hurtha. "There were four other poems sold! I shall never be able to recover those poems! They are gone, gone!" He put his head again in his hands, sobbing. "I shall never be able to find all those fellows again. Scarcely had I sold them the poems than they all hastened away, covetous, lucky, greedy fellows, lest I change my mind. Now I shall never be able to find them again and appeal earnestly, fervently, to their better selves, and higher natures, to take back their filthy money. What a fool I was! My poems, gone! Sold for a mere four silver tarsks! Waste! Dishonor! Misery! Ruin! Tragedy! What if this story should ever get back to the wagons? I am unworthy of my scars!"

"Hurtha, old fellow," I said, gently.

"Yes," he said.

I placed my hand on his shoulder.

"Yes?" he asked.

"Look," I said.

He lifted his head and looked up.

"Here," I said, softly. I held forth to him the four copies of poems which had been given to me earlier by his four customers, or patrons.

"It is they!" he cried, wonderingly, tears in his eyes.

"Yes," I said.

"You knew!" he cried.

I shrugged.

"You could not let me go through with it!" he wept. "You sought them out! You purchased them back! You have saved me from myself, from my own folly!"

"It is little enough to do for a friend," I said.

He leaped to his feet and embraced me, weeping, tears in his eyes. I struggled for breath, clutching the four poems. I speculated that this must be much like the grip of the dreaded, constricting hith. Surely that, capable of pulverizing a fellow, crushing his bones and popping him like a grape, could scarcely be worse.

"How can I ever thank you?" he cried, stepping back, holding me, proudly, looking at me.

"Between friends," I said, "thanks are neither needed, nor possible."

"You, too, are overcome with emotion!" he cried, sympathetically.

"I am trying to breathe," I told him.

"Let me have those poems," he said. He took them and put them with the one he had kept, that retrieved from his last transaction, the one in which, happily, I had had no part. "I have them back, thanks to you!" he said.

I had now caught my breath, nearly.

"There they are," he said, blissfully, regarding them, "written down, in little marks."

"That is the way most things are written down," I said.

"Are they well transcribed?" he asked.

"I think so," I said. I took a deep breath.

"Are you all right?" asked Hurtha.

"Yes," I said. "Occasionally there is a line which is difficult to make out, and there seems to be a misspelled word here and there." That was to be expected, I supposed, given the fact that they had presumably been written in a condition of some agitation, under a condition of some stress. There was an occasional spot on the parchment. Perhaps sweat had dropped from someone's brow there.

"You are sure you are all right?" he said.

"Yes, I am all right now," I said.

"I am not surprised that a small mistake, perhaps a poorly formed letter, an irregular margin, or such, might have been made," said Hurtha. "Some of the fellows transcribing the poems were actually shaking. They seemed almost overwhelmed."

"I am not surprised," I said. "It was all part of the impact of the experience of hearing them for the first time, I suppose," I added.

"Yes," said Hurtha. "It would seem so."

"You do not know your own power as a poet," I said.

"Few of us do," said Hurtha.

"Well," I said, "fortunately, we have the five poems back. It would be too bad to have lost them."

"A tragedy, yes," said Hurtha, "but I have others."

"Oh?" I said.

"Yes, more than two thousand," he said.

"That is a great many," I said.

"Not really, considering their quality," he said.

"You are prolific," I said.

"All great poets are prolific," he said. "Would you care to hear them?"

"Not at the moment," I said. "You see, I have just, this evening, read some of them. I do not know if I could take more, just now."

"I understand," said Hurtha. "I am one well aware of the complexities of coping with grandeur, of the exquisite agonies attendant upon wrestling with nigh ineffable sublimities, with the excruciating intensities of the authentic aesthetic experience, with the travails of poignant significance, with the exhausting consequences of confronting sudden and startling distillations of meaning. No, old friend, I understand these things full well. I shall not force you beyond your strength."

"Thank you," I said.

He looked down at the poems in his hand. "Can you believe," he asked, "that these saw light only this evening, that I dictated them upon the spot?"

"Yes," I said.

He stood there, looking down at them, in awe of his own power.

"I wonder if poems should be written down," he said.

"I have a very poor handwriting," I said, "and I am particularly bad at the lines that go from right to left."

"I am illiterate," said Tula, quickly, in the crisis of the moment forgetting even to request permission to speak.

"So am I," said Mincon, happily.

Boabissia, of course, was also illiterate. She sat on the ground with her back against the right, rear wagon wheel, her ankles still bound together.

Hurtha looked at Feiqa. She could read and write. She was highly intelligent, and had been well educated. She was of a well-known city. She had even been of high station, before being enslaved, before becoming only an animal subject to her masters. She turned white.

"She is a slave," I said.

"Oh, yes," said Hurtha, dismissing her then from his mind.

Feiqa threw me a wild look of gratitude. To be sure, much of the copy work, lower-order clerical work, trivial account keeping, and such, on Gor, was done by slaves. Hurtha, however, I thought, apparently correctly, might prefer having his poems transcribed by free folks. It had been a close call for Feiqa.

"I am starving," I said.

Hurtha consulted his internal states. "So, too, am I," he reported. "But I remain firm in my resolve not to sell my poems. Better starvation."

"Certainly," I said.

"What are our resources?" he inquired.

"Something like two copper tarsks, and some four or five tarsk bits," I said.

"Not enough," he said.

"I agree," I said.

"What are we to do?" asked Hurtha.

"Work?" I speculated.

"Be serious," he admonished me. "We are in desperate straits. This is no joking matter."

"Untie my ankles," said Boabissia.

Hurtha and I looked at one another.

"You take her left hand and I will take her right," said Hurtha.

Boabissia tried to scramble to her feet but, bound as she was, she fell. Then we had her wrists, and pulled her back, by them, to the wagon wheel.

"What are you doing?" cried Boabissia.

I tied her left wrist back to one of the spokes, and Hurtha, similarly, fastened her right wrist back, to another spoke.

"What are you doing?" asked Boabissia.

"You have seen several of the fellows about looking at Boabissia, haven't you?" asked Hurtha of me.

"Of course," I said. "Though there are many slaves in Torcadino, and lovely ones, apparently there is a dearth of free women here, particularly of ones not veiled."

"Veil me then!" she begged.

"It is time you earned your keep, Boabissia," said Hurtha.

"What do you mean?" she cried. "I am a free woman!"

"I think I can round up a few interested fellows," said Hurtha.

"What are you thinking of!" she cried. She struggled, helplessly.

"She wanted her ankles untied," said Hurtha.

"Yes," I said.

"No, no!" she cried. "Do not untie my ankles!

Hurtha dropped the ankle cords to one side. She clenched her ankles tightly together. She pulled desperately, futilely, against the thongs that held her wrists to the spokes. Hurtha left the vicinity of the wagon.

"Relax, Boabissia," I encouraged her. "You have serious sexual needs, which you have been frustrating for too long. This has been evident in your temper, and in your demeanor and attitudes. This will do you a great deal of good."

"I am not a slave!" she said, weeping, struggling. "I am a free woman! I do not have sexual needs!"

"Perhaps not," I said. To be sure, it was difficult, and probably fruitless, to argue with a free woman about such matters. Too, I might have misread what seemed to be numerous and obvious signs of need in her. Perhaps free women neither needed nor wanted sexual experience. That, I supposed, was their business. On the other hand, if they did not want or need sex, the transformation between the free woman and the slave becomes difficult to understand. To be sure, perhaps it is merely the collar, and the uncompromising male domination, which so unlocks, and calls forth, the passion, service and love of a female.

"What are you doing?" she asked, weeping.

"Doubtless men will be here soon," I said.

"What are you doing?" she wept.

I put the opaque sack over her head and tied it, with its own strings, under her chin, close about her neck, rather like a slave hood. "This will make it easier for you," I said. "I am veiling you. Too, this will enable you, by shutting out certain extraneous factors, to concentrate more closely on the exact nature of your sensations."

"Release me!" she wept.

"No," I said.

I heard a fellow near me. I looked about. "She is certified free?" he asked.

"Yes," I said. "Examine her."

He thrust Boabissia's dress up, high, over her breasts. He examined her thighs, and the usual brand sites on a Gorean female slave.

"How much?" he asked.

"She is only a free woman," I said. I put a copper bowl on the ground, beside her, at her left. "She is not trained. Only a tarsk bit." It was the smallest, least significant Gorean coin, at least in common circulation.

"In advance," I said. Men are commonly disappointed in free women, and almost certainly if they have experienced the alternative. They are not slaves, trained in the giving of pleasure to men. Some free women believe that their role in lovemaking consists primarily in lying down. Should they become slaves the whip soon teaches them differently.

"Of course," he said. The coin rattled into the copper bowl.

"No!" wept Boabissia. She clenched her ankles tightly together. Then her ankles, one in each hand of the fellow, were parted.

It was now late in the evening.

Hurtha happily shook the copper bowl. In it were several coins. I had not kept track. We were now, at any rate, once again solvent.

"How do you feel?" I asked Boabissia.

She twisted in the thongs and turned to the side. She whimpered, softly.

We had kept Tula and Feiqa under the blanket in the back of the wagon. We had not wanted them to distract our visitors.

I looked at Boabissia. She made another small, soft, whimpering noise. Some of the men, in their intense excitement, I feared, had been somewhat stronger, or ruder, with her than might have been appropriate for a free woman. Indeed, some had handled her almost as though she might have been a slave. We had not cautioned them to gentleness, however. After all, they had paid their tarsk bits.

"Are you all right?" I asked.

"Yes," she whispered.

I put my ear down close to her. Her head in the sack, it tied on her, fastened under her chin, she did not know my nearness. I listened to the tiny, soft noises she made. It was like a soft moaning or tiny whimpering. It was almost inaudible. I knew such sounds. I smiled. She was still feeling, even now, wonderingly perhaps, the results of her havings. Perhaps she was trying, even now, in her depth of her femininity, to understand what had been done to her, to come to grips with her feelings, with those sensations which men had seen fit to induce in her.

I leaned back. "You are sure you are all right?" I asked.

"Yes," she said.

I pulled down her dress, and freed her wrists. They were ringed with thong marks.

She, her palms on the dirt, half knelt, half lay, by the wheel. Her head, still in the sack, was down.

"Did you take me?" she asked.

"No," I said.

"Did Hurtha have me?" she asked.

"No," I said.

"Why not?" she asked.

"You are a free woman," I told her. I then removed the sack from her head. Her face was red, and broken out. Her hair was damp. I turned the sack inside out, that it might dry and air. Boabissia turned away from me, apparently not wanting to meet my eyes. I do not think she wanted us to see her face. She was afraid, I think, of what we might see there. We would respect this. She was, after all, a free woman. We would, similarly, in deference to her feelings, keep Feiqa and Tula under the blanket for a time, lest their eyes suddenly, inadvertently, meet hers, and women read in one another's eyes truths which might be deeper than speech.

"Good night," I said to her.

"Good night," she said.

I watched her pull her blanket about her. She suddenly shuddered. "Oh!" she said. Then she pulled the blanket more tightly about her shoulders. We would not chain her. She was not a slave. She was a free woman. She might leave, if she wished.

12: It Is a Standard, That of a Silver Tarn

"The city is taken!" I heard. "The city is taken!"

I lay absolutely still for an instant. I heard no clash of weapons. There were no sounds of rushing feet, of flight. No cries of pain, of men cut in their blankets.

I did hear the ringing of an alarm bar in the distance.

My eyes might have appeared closed to a careless observer. They were open. Peripheral vision is important at such times. In that first instant, every sense suddenly alert, I appeared to be still asleep. There was the wagon. There were the remains of the fire. I detected no movement in my immediate vicinity.

No longer now did I even hear the cry of the man.

The first object that moves is often that which attracts the immediate attention of the predator. Too, the swiftest moving object, particularly that which moves silently, and with obvious menace or purpose, is often construed, and generally correctly, by the attacker as the most dangerous, that to be dealt with first. Those overcome with surprise, those expostulating or cursing, those stunned, may be left for the instants later. There is a dark mathematics in such matters, in the subtle equations balancing reaction times against the movements of blades. One gambles. Is the instant one waits, that instant of fearful reconnoitering, that instant in which one hopes to convince a foe that one is temporarily harmless, an instant of loss, or of gain? Does it grant him his opportunity, or does it obtain you yours? Much depends on the actual situation. If one is roused by known voices, one generally rises quickly. The defensive is being assumed. If one does not know what is occurring, it is sometimes wise to find out before leaping up, perhaps into the weapons of enemies who might be as close as one's elbow. My right hand was on the hilt of my sword, my left on the sheath, its straps wrapped about it, to steady the draw. Doubtless I appeared to be still asleep. But no sounds of carnage rang about me.

I sat up quickly, freeing myself from the blankets. I did not draw the weapon. I saw no immediate need to do so. I slung it, on its strap, over my left shoulder. The scabbard can be discarded more quickly in this suspension than in one which crosses the body.

"Hurtha," I said, "wake up." I moved his shoulder.

"What is it?" he said. "Is it not early?"

"Something strange is going on," I said. "Get up. There was an alarm bar ringing."

"I hear nothing," he said, sitting up.

To be sure, the bar had now stopped ringing.

"I do not understand it," I said. "A fellow was crying out that the city had been taken. I do not hear him now. Too, the alarm bar was ringing. I heard it."

"It is very early," said Hurtha.

"Get up," I said.

I looked over to Boabissia. Her eyes were open. She was looking at me, frightened.

"Did you hear the alarm bar?" I asked.

"Yes," she said.

"Get up, Hurtha," I said. He had once again returned to his blankets.

"It is too early," he said. Actually it was not all that early. Some other folks were now up, too, about the camp.

"You may be in jeopardy of your life," I informed him.

"At this hour?" he asked, horrified.

"Yes," I said. "The enemy may be near."

"What enemy?" he asked.

"I do not know," I said.

"Report to me when you learn," he said, rolling over.

"I am not joking," I said.

"I feared not," he grumbled.

"Get up," I said.

"One cannot begin to fight until the fight has begun, can one?" he asked.

"I hope it does not follow from that that fighting is impossible," I said.

"Of course not," he said. I began to sense and dread a lesson in Alar logic.

"Well, in a sense," I said, "maybe not."

"Has the fight begun?" he inquired.

"No," I said.

"Then you cannot expect me to begin fighting," he said.

"Of course not," I said, hesitantly.

"When the fray begins," said he, "awaken me."

"Do you wish to be murdered in your bed?" I asked.

"I had never thought much about it," said Hurtha, "but now that I reflect actively upon the matter, no. Why? Who is going to murder me in my bed?"

"I am considering it," I said.

"You will not do so," he informed me.

"Why?" I asked, genuinely interested.

"Among other things," he said, "your respect for poetry is too great."

"You must be prepared for combat," I told him.

"I am preparing even now," he said, rolling over.

"How is that?" I asked.

"I am pacing myself," he said. "I am conserving my strength. Surely you are aware that a well-rested body and a clear mind are two among several of the soldier's best friends."

"Perhaps," I granted him.

"They are important, too, to poetry," he said, "of the sturdy, manly sort, that is, not to the neurasthenic drivel of mere poetasters and versifiers."

"Doubtless," I said. He was then again asleep. Hurtha was one of the few folks I had ever known who had the capacity to fall asleep like lightning. Doubtless this was connected with a clear conscience. Alars, incidentally, are renowned for their capacity to wreak havoc, conduct massacres, chop off heads, and such, and then get a good night's sleep afterwards. They just do not worry about such things. I hoped that the enemy, if there was one, would not now fall upon the camp like a storm. Still, if they did, Hurtha might have escaped, sleeping through the slaughter.

"Did you hear the alarm bar?" asked Mincon, coming over to me, his blanket over his arm.

"Yes," I said.

"I thought I might have dreamed it," he said.

"Boabissia heard it, too," I said.

"It is not now ringing," he said.

"No," I said.

"The camp is pretty quiet," he said.

"Yes," I said. We could see folks going about their business, folding their blankets, seeking out the latrines, starting up their morning fires.

"It was a false alarm," he said.

"Apparently," I said.

"You are not certain?" he asked.

"No," I said.

"What could have happened?" he asked.

"I heard a fellow crying out that the city had fallen," I said.

"That is impossible," he said. "No enemy is within hundreds of pasangs. Torcadino is garrisoned. It is impregnable. It lies even, in these times, in the midst of allied armies."

"It could be done," I said.

"You would have to move an army through armies to take the city," he said.

"Or over armies," I said.

"You would have to smuggle an army into the city," he said.

"Yes," I said.

"Impossible," he said.

"With some modest collusion, not really," I said.

"You're joking," he said.

"No," I said.

"If there was such a thing," he said, "we would hear of it. There would be great fighting."

"It is quiet here," I said. "That does not mean, however, that somewhere else in the city, even now, there might not be fighting. A few blocks away, unknown to us, men may be dying. The streets may be running with blood."

"I see no smoke," he said. "There seem no signs of flames."

"That could mean little," I said. "Perhaps it is desired to keep the city intact, to maintain the integrity of its walls, to preserve its resources."

"Perhaps," he smiled.

I looked at him, suddenly, surprised.

"There is one way to find out," he said.

"How?" I asked.

"Climb up here," he said, "to the wagon box."

I joined him on the height of the wagon box. He pointed over the wagons, over the camp, over the buildings about the camp.

"Do you see the cylinder there?" he asked.

"Yes," I said.

"That is the central cylinder of Torcadino," he said, "the administrative headquarters of her first executive, whether it be Adminstrator or Ubar."

"Yes?" I said.

"Look to its summit," he said.

I did so.

"Do you know the flag of Torcadino?" he asked.

"No," I said.

"It does not matter," he said, "for of recent months what has flown there has not been the flag of Torcadino, but another flag, that of Cos."

"There is no flag there," I said. "I know the flag of Cos. I have seen it frequently. But there is no flag whatsoever there."

"Do you not find that interesting?" he asked.

"You are not a simple wagoner," I said.

"What do you see there?" he asked.

"I see a standard," I said.

"What sort of standard?" he asked.

"A military standard, I suppose," I said.

"Describe it," he said.

"It is silver," I said. "It is far off. It is hard to make out. The sun is glinting on it."

"It is the standard of the silver tarn," he said. "It is

mounted on a silvered pole. Near the top of the pole there is a rectangular plate on which there is writing. Surmounting this plate, clutching it in its talons, is a tarn, done in silver, its wings outstretched.''

''You can see that,'' I asked, ''at this distance?''

''No,'' he said. ''But I know the standard. I have seen it before.''

I regarded him.

''Do you know the standard?'' he asked.

''No,'' I said.

''You are an astute fellow,'' he said. ''The city has indeed fallen. Furthermore, if I am not mistaken, you understand how this could have taken place.''

''Through the aqueducts,'' I said.

''Of course,'' he said. ''They were entered, one near the Issus, the other in the Hills of Eteocles, more than a hundred pasangs away. Soldiers, in double file, wading, moving sometimes even over the heads of Cosian troops, traversed them.''

''Brilliant,'' I said.

''Guards of one watch were purchased by gold,'' he said. ''Those of another had their throats cut by partisans within the city.''

''Whose standard is it?'' I asked.

''It is the standard of my captain,'' he said, ''Dietrich of Tarnburg.''

13: We Proceed
to the Semnium

I heard the crying of confused, frightened children, the lamentations of women.

"That way, go that way," said a soldier, closing off a street.

In the streets there was much movement, much of it between soldiers, directed movement, movement toward the great gate of Torcadino. Many folks had packs on their backs.

"Look out, fellow!" said a voice.

I moved aside, to let a two-wheeled cart, laden with baggage, drawn by a fellow, pass. The streets were crowded, filled with refugees.

"Follow me," had said Mincon. "You will be safe. Keep closely together."

"I want my ax," said Hurtha.

"Keep closely together," I said. "Do not get separated."

A number of dwellings along the way had been roped off. We could catch occasional glimpses within them, through opened doors, and, sometimes, through windows. Too, we could hear shouts, and other sounds, such as furniture being broken. Within these buildings, soldiers were looting. From the high, opened window of another building, some four or five feet below the sill, some forty feet or so above the street, its back against the stuccoed surface of the wall, there hung a body.

"What is that?" I asked Mincon.

"I cannot read," said Mincon. "There is a sign on its neck. What does it say?"

" 'Looter,' " I said.

"Then that is what it was," said Mincon.

"There is much looting going on," I said. "In more than a dozen buildings we have seen it."

"That was a civilian," said Mincon. "It is illegal for such to loot. They are not authorized to do so."

"I see," I said.

"There must be order in Torcadino," said Mincon.

"Of course," I said.

"I want my ax," said Hurtha.

"Just keep close to us," I said.

We had surrendered our weapons at the entrance to the wagon camp, as, in the company of Mincon, we had left it a few Ehn ago. A strict weapons control had been instituted in Torcadino. Possession of an unauthorized weapon could be construed as a capital offense, the penalty for which, at the discretion of any soldier, could be exacted in place, instantly and without recourse or appeal. The talons of the silver tarn did not grasp weakly. Yet this had been done in a legalistic fashion. In my wallet was a scrap of paper with a number on it, a number which matched another, that left with my weapons, left behind near the weapons table, that set up at the entrance of the camp.

We were jostled in the throngs.

"That way," said a soldier, gesturing. "That way."

In the streets there was no smell of smoke. Smoke, like stifling clouds, did not block the sun, turning the day to choking dusk. Our eyes did not sting and water. One could breathe without difficulty. Sometimes, when a town is taken, you can feel the heat of burning buildings even blocks away. But Torcadino was not aflame.

"That way," said another soldier.

We hurried along in the crowds, following Mincon.

We passed a slave girl, kneeling, chained by the neck to a slave ring. It was fixed in the side of a building, fastened to its bolted plate, about a yard above the level of the street. Her face was stained with tears. She had her hands clutched desperately on the chain, near the ring. I did not know if her master had put her there, intending to return for her, or if she had been abandoned. She was naked. She would remain where she was. She was chained there.

"Come along," said Mincon. We continued on, through the throngs. "Keep together," he said. We did so, as best we could. I was behind him, closely, and then came Hurtha, and then, close behind him, Boabissia. Behind Boabissia, ropes on their necks, the captor's termini of these hempen confinements in the grip of Hurtha, came Feiqa and Tula. How fearful they had been this morning to learn that the city had now a new master. How frightened they had been, exchanging glances. So, too, I supposed, might have been tharlarion and sleen, other forms of animals, if they, too, were aware of such things, or saw fit to consider them. Yet Feiqa and Tula, objectively, had far less to fear in the fall of a city than a free person. They had, objectively, little more to fear than other domestic animals. They presumably, like them, would merely find themselves with new masters. We had not put the tethers on Feiqa and Tula because we feared they might try to slip away from us in the crowds, but to keep them with us, to make certain that they were not swept from us, or perhaps seized and pulled away into the crowd. Near us we heard the bleating of a pair of domestic verr. A woman was pulling them along beside her in the throng. They, too, like Feiqa and Tula, had ropes on their necks.

"It seems hard to make headway now," I said to Mincon.

"The press is being held," he said. "There are several barriers. Then there are separated lines, leading to the great gate. There searches are made, lest it be attempted to carry valuables from the city."

"The civilian population is being ejected from the city," I said.

"Yes," he said. "Let us move ahead. One side, one side!"

We moved slowly, single file, through the crowds.

"Move aside," said Mincon.

"Where are you taking us?" I asked.

"To the Semnium," he said.

"Why?" I asked.

"It is my intention to obtain for you letters of safety," he said.

"I would welcome such," I said.

"You need not accept them," he said, turning about.

"Why would I not desire such letters?" I asked.

"The decision will be yours," he said.

"I do not understand," I said.

"Follow me," he said, turning about, pressing once again through the crowd.

We came then to a barrier, several poles on tripods, set across the main way in Torcadino. The crowd was arrested at this barrier. Some pressed back, against those behind them, to keep from being forced against it.

"Hold," said a soldier, his spear held across his body, behind the barrier.

Mincon uttered a password. The barrier was opened. It was a relief to walk freely. Some two hundred yards down the street we could see another segment of the crowd, it, too, doubtless, waiting behind some barrier. We then, in a few Ehn, passed that barrier, and then another.

To one side, when we crossed the first of these second two barriers, there was a great pile of objects. In it were such things as furniture, cushions, rugs, wall hangings, tapestries, bolts of cloth, robes, clothes, chests, coffers, utensils, vessels, and plates. A soldier went to the pile and emptied a pillow-case out at its foot. I supposed that its spillage, a short, clattering rain of goblets, would scarcely be noticed in such an accumulation. Yet, doubtless, in just such a way had that mountain of artifacts been constructed. It was more than ten feet high. It was cheap booty, probably on the whole to be sold by contract to dealers.

"Look!" said Boabissia, pointing ahead and to our left, as we crossed an intersection, that beyond the third barrier.

There, some fifty yards away, kneeling, huddled together against the brick wall of a public building, the wall composed of the flat, narrow bricks common in southern Gorean architecture, was a group of some one hundred to one hundred and fifty females. They were naked. They were chained together by the neck. They were in the keeping of two soldiers, with whips.

"More booty," said Mincon.

"Slaves!" said Boabissia disparagingly, in disgust.

"Or to be slaves," said Mincon.

"Oh," said Boabissia, frightened.

"Surely they are slaves," I said.

"Many," said Mincon, "are the women, and daughters, of those who were adherents of Cos in Torcadino. They, thus, have been apprehended for branding and bondage."

"I see," I said.

"Their seizure lists were prepared weeks ago," he said.

"Of course," I said. An action of the sort now accomplished in Torcadino, in which judicious selections and discriminations are to be made among the civilian populace, necessitates a sensitive preparation.

We were now closer to the women.

One of them stood but, immediately, the lash fell upon her, and she returned to her knees, sobbing. "Hands on thighs," called the soldier, "spread your knees, back straight, chin up!" He pushed up her chin with the coiled whip. She looked straight ahead, tears streaming down her face. "You will be struck twice more," he said. She cried out in misery, twice, each time shaken, each time almost thrown forward on her belly to the pavement. The blows were perfunctory, but, I suppose, to the one who receives them, they seemed intensely personal and meaningful. "Position," said the soldier. She resumed the position to which she had been earlier commanded, promptly and exactly. In her eyes now, with their tears, there was also fear and contrition. Now that we were closer I could see that the women were all on a single chain, fastened on it by side-loops, of the same chain, secured with sturdy padlocks. It is a simple, practical, inexpensive arrangement. On the upper portion of their left breasts there were numbers written.

"Oh!" said a bound girl, being brought to the group.

"Oh!" said Boabissia, at the same time. She had turned about, from watching the disciplining of the neck-chained girl, and struck against the new girl. "Clumsy slave!" cried Boabissia, angrily. Twice then, angrily, she struck the new girl with the sides of her small fists. The new girl was, by the soldier in whose custody she was, thrust rudely to the pavement before Boabissia, his hand in her hair, forcing her head down to Boabissia's sandals. "Beg forgiveness!" he said.

"Forgive me! Forgive me!" wept the new girl.

" 'Forgive me,' what?" asked the soldier, tightening his grip in her hair.

"Forgive me, *Mistress*!" wept the new girl, her head down, her back bent forward, her small hands twisting helplessly in the cords that held them behind her back.

"Clumsy slave!" scolded Boabissia.

"Forgive me, Mistress," wept the girl. As far as I could see the new girl was not a slave. She was, at least, neither branded nor collared. On the other hand, doubtless she was destined to soon receive those lovely adornments proclamatory of the uncompromising condition of Gorean bondage, those adornments which so enhance the beauty of a woman, those adornments significatory that all the institutional niceties pertinent to her bondage have been properly and legally completed. Accordingly, the fellow was doubtless being quite merciful, and helpful, to the female. He was preparing her, in a small way, not for what would be her role in her new life, but for what in her new life would be her total and uncompromising actuality.

"Kiss her feet," said the soldier.

Obediently the frightened girl kissed Boabissia's feet, desperately, fervently.

"Clumsy slave," said Boabissia, angrily.

"Please forgive me, Mistress," wept the girl.

The soldier drew up her head and bent her backwards, before Boabissia. "Shall I kill her for you?" he asked. I saw the girl had a number, like the others, written on the upper portion of her left breast. I gathered that he had been sent to pick her up, and to mark her with that number. It had to do with records.

"No," said Boabissia. "That will not be necessary."

The soldier pulled the girl up straight, and released her hair. She remained kneeling before us, her head down. "Thank you, Mistress," she whispered.

"Sir," said the soldier, suddenly straightening his body.

"Lift your head and thrown your hair behind your back, girl," said the officer, newly arrived, come up from the side, with a backing board and sheaf of papers. "Put your head back as far as it will go." Immediately the girl complied. The officer then, there being no impediments now to his vision, checked the number on her left breast. He then referred to his papers, turning some over. "Name, female?" he asked the girl.

She began to shudder.

"Speak up, quickly, while you still have one," he said.

The soldier kicked her.

"Euphrosyne, Lady of Torcadino," she gasped.

"Family, and caste?" he inquired.

"Daughter of the matron Aglaia, Lady of Torcadino," she said, "of the Myrtos lineage, she high in the trade of spices, Confirmation Treasurer of the Spice Council of Torcadino, she of the Merchants."

"Ah, yes," said the officer. "I believe your mother is already on the chain."

The girl looked about, wildly. Doubtless she would have covered her breasts, and nakedness, if she could have. What a foolish gesture in one who was soon to be a slave.

"I do not know if you will see her again, or not," he said, "except perhaps at a distance. Too, fraternization may not be permitted between slaves."

"I am not a slave," she moaned.

"Now," he said, "for a moment or two more you may think of yourself as Euphrosyne, as your mother was hitherto permitted for a time to think of herself as Aglaia. In a time, of course, you may receive new names. 'Euphrosyne' is a a name a bit too fine, I think, for a slave. You will probably soon become something else, perhaps a "Puta" or a "Sita." In the meantime, you are, for our purposes, and for your own purposes, Four-three-seven. That is your capture name, and you will think of yourself only as that. You may not inquire as to the former names of others nor reveal to them, even if they should ask, your own. Similarly, you may not make inquiries pertaining to such things as their families, stations and castes, nor reveal to others, even if asked, any such information pertaining to yourself. You are merely, and simply, the captive Four-three-seven. Your mother, incidentally, is Two-six-one. You are now to think of her, as she is now to think of herself, as only that. She was more important than you, and thus has an earlier number.''

Four-three-seven, of course, was the number written on the girl's left breast. As her number was 437 and there were only some one hundred or one hundred and fifty or so females in the chain, near the wall, I assumed there was probably one or more collection points elsewhere, perhaps nearer the Semnium, the Council Hall. On the other hand perhaps there were merely more females to come in. The numbers, it seemed, were prearranged numbers, and not merely numbers indicating the order of capture. The officer, for example, already had had her number on his list, probably with her name. In this fashion, the girls being added to the chain as captured, this chain, or any others, might have diverse numbers upon it. I had gathered, for example, from what the officer had said, that the girl's mother, number 261 on the list, was somewhere in this very chain, which would have been unlikely if its prisoners were being added to it in a strict numerical sequence. A strict numerical order, if desired, of course, could always be set up later, at the leisure of the captors. In the meantime, it was the list that was crucial.

The officer looked down at the girl. ''You may bring your head forward,'' he said.

Gratefully, she did so.

''Who are you?'' he asked.

''Euphrosyne, Lady of Torcadino,'' she sobbed.

He looked at her, reprovingly.

''Four-three-seven!'' she said quickly.

''Anything else?'' he inquired.

''No,'' she said, shaking her head. ''No!''

The soldier then pulled her to her feet by the hair and thrust her before him, toward the chain. In a moment she was on the chain, kneeling, her throat snugly enclosed in a side-loop of the same chain, it fastened shut on her by a padlock.

"Do you expect to find all the women on your seizure lists?" I asked the officer.

"Most of them," he said. "Doubtless some will elude us, at least for a time."

"Many," said Mincon, "will be apprehended at the gates. They will not know they were on the lists. They will then be stripped, bound, marked with their number and brought to a collection point."

"After tomorrow, too," said the officer, "unauthorized civilians will not be permitted within the walls. The penalty for the unauthorized male will be swift and honorable execution, that for the unauthorized female being fed to sleen, or, if she is comely enough, and zealous enough to please, perhaps bondage."

"There is little point in trying to hide the city," said Mincon. "Eventually all the houses will be searched. Too, when they are hungry enough they will creep out at night to seek food. They may then, sooner or later, with the aid of tracking sleen, be taken."

"I see," I said.

"With the nature of Torcadino," said the officer, "the walls, and our control of the city, it is highly likely, sooner or later, that we will have every one of the women on our list."

I nodded. The listed females, under the particular circumstances currently prevailing in Torcadino, had little chance of escape. To be sure, many were not yet female slaves. For most practical purposes, for the Gorean female slave, properly identified, branded and collared, there is no escape. If she escapes from one master, which is exceedingly unlikely, she will doubtless soon find herself in the chains of another, and one who is perhaps worse. Certainly the new master will know that she is an escaped slave and will be likely to treat her with great harshness and keep her under the strictest confinements. He will probably make certain, as well, that sleen have her scent. Too, the penalties for running away can be severe, in the second case generally involving being fed to sleen or being hamstrung, to be used perhaps thereafter as a begging slave.

"What is to be done with these women?" I asked the officer.

"Most of them will be sold in lots to contractors," he said.

"Like much of the other loot?" I asked.

"Yes," he said. "The general contracts, for pickups of loot, projected quantities, and such, were let weeks ago."

"Of course," I said.

I noted one of the soldiers. He moved about, here and there within the chain lines, among the women. Occasionally he would put his whip before the lips of one of them. She would then kiss it.

"But some of these females are quite beautiful," I said. "For example, 437 is extremely lovely."

"Her mother, 261, is also quite lovely," he said. "Certain of these women, of course, the better ones, like the more expensive loot, will not go to the contractors, but will be kept for distribution, the less beautiful ones to the troops, the more beautiful ones to the officers."

I nodded. These arrangements were typical.

"I have already made notations with respect to several of them," he said, indicating his papers, "including 437 and 261. In advance, of course, when one enters them upon the lists as free women, and one has seen them, if at all, only in the robes of concealment, one does not know which are the most beautiful."

"Such determinations now, of course," I said, "may be easily made."

"Yes," he said.

I regarded the women. For the past weeks, they had been going about their business, ignorantly, naively, unsuspectingly, totally unaware of how they might be included as humble objects in the plans of masters. Doubtless they had given much attention to the matters of their day, to their various competitions, pursuits, vanities, occupations and concerns. All that time they did not know that already, in dried, indelible ink, their names were recorded on seizure lists. I observed them. They knelt, chained. On the upper portion of the left breast of each was a number. It was the number which had followed their name on the seizure lists. That number was theirs. It had been theirs for weeks. But only now, to their horror, did they learn so, and find it literally inscribed on their bodies.

I saw the soldier hold the whip before 437. She bent forward and kissed it.

"Come along," said Mincon. "We must go to the Semnium."

We then followed him, Hurtha and I, and Boabissia, the hempen leashes of Tula and Feiqa in the grasp of Hurtha.

14: The Semnium;
The Outer Office

"These are new bodies, fresh bodies," I said.

"Of course," said Mincon.

We were at the foot of the low, broad steps of the Semnium, the hall of the high council, which building, it seemed, might now serve as the headquarters of the new masters of Torcadino. These steps extended before the building, for the entire length of its portico.

"Who are they?" I asked.

There were some two to three hundred new bodies hung now from tarred ropes along the Avenue of Adminius, in the vicinity of the Semnium.

"Collaborators, traitors, men who were of the party of Cos, betrayers of the alliance with Ar, and such," said Mincon.

"As those earlier were similarly adherents of Ar?" I asked.

"Perhaps," said Mincon.

"Some of those here," I said, regarding the dismal lines of bodies, dangling in the tarred halters, "are perhaps the same as those who had been active in bringing about the downfall of those who hung here formerly."

"Of course," said Mincon.

"The winds have shifted in Torcadino," I said.

"Yes," said Mincon.

"It seems your captain is in the pay of Ar," I said.

"Of that you may judge yourself," he said, "shortly."

"I?" I asked.

"Yes," he said.

"I do not understand," I said.

"Follow me," he said. I then, and the others, followed

him up the steps of the Semnium. I stopped once, at the entrance, to look back, at the bodies. I briefly recalled the girl at the chain, 437, and her mother, 261. Her mother, before her capture, I had gathered, had been important, having been the confirmation treasurer of one of Torcadino's commercial councils, the Spice Council. She had also, in her position, I had gathered, and doubtless by her influence and acts, supported the cause of Cos. This inclination, incidentally, is not all that uncommon among individuals whose fortunes tend to be intimately involved in such matters as importation and exportation, the location and exploitation of foreign markets, and, in general, the overseas trade, the Thassa and island trade. This is understandable. The navies of Tyros and Cos, for most practical purposes, command the green waves of gleaming Thassa. They control many of the most familiar and practical oceanic trade corridors. Few coasts are free from their patrols. Few ports could scorn their blockades. 261, however, aside from all such considerations, was a citizeness of Torcadino, and Torcadino had been sworn to the cause of Ar. She had, it seemed, for whatever reason, presumably opportunism or greed, betrayed the pledge of her Home Stone. In the case of a man this can be a capital offense. She was not a man, however, but a female. It was thus, doubtless, that she had not been placed on a proscription list, but only on a seizure list. It was her sex which had saved her. Had she been a man she would have been hung.

Within the entrance to the Semnium was a marble-floored, lofty hall. Passageways and stairways led variously from this broad vestibule. The walls were adorned with mosaics, scenes generally of civic life, prominent among them scenes of public gatherings, conferences and processions. One depicted the laying of the first stone in Torcadino's walls, an act which presumably would have taken place more than seven hundred years ago, when, according to the legends, the first wall, only a dozen feet high, was built to encircle and protect a great, sprawling encampment at the joining of trade routes. Within the hall were several soldiers, and several officers, at tables, conducting various sorts of business. To one side, permanent fixtures, immovable and sturdy, their supports fixed in the floor, were several rows of long, low, marble benches. It was on these that clients and claimants, with their various causes, grievances and petitions, would wait until their turn came to be called for their appointments or hearings. It was here, too, that witnesses, and such, might wait, before being summoned to give testimony on various matters before the courts.

"It is in here, I gather," I said, "that these letters of safety may be obtained." I eyed the various tables.

"Yes," said Mincon, making his way toward a guard station at the opening to one of the long corridors leading from the vaulted vestibule.

"Are we not to petition for these letters at one of the tables?" I asked, looking back.

"No," he said.

We were then following him down the corridor. He was known, it seemed.

"Is the city being administered from this building?" I asked.

"Yes," he said, "in most things, in most ways."

"The city is under martial law," I said. "Why is it not being administered from the central cylinder, or its arsenal?"

"This building supplies an appearance of civic normality," he said. "Thus it is more as though one form of municipal administration had merely succeeded another."

"I see," I said. "Your captain, however," I said, "is doubtless reigning in the central cylinder."

"No, he is conducting business in this building," said Mincon, continuing down the hall.

I said nothing. This seemed to me, however, politically astute, particularly since the city was not currently under attack. I had realized for years, of course, that Dietrich of Tarnburg was a capable mercenary, and one of Gor's finest commanders. I had not found mention, however, in the annals, or diaries, which had been generally concerned with marches and campaigns, a sufficient appreciation of this other side of his character. He was apparently not only a military genius but perhaps also a political one. Or, perhaps they are not really so separate as they are often considered to be. Territory must be held as well as won.

"Civilians are being ejected from the city," I said. "Surely they are not being given letters of safety."

"No," said Mincon.

"You think, however, that we might need them?" I asked.

"It seems very likely," said Mincon, "considering where you are going."

"I do not understand," I said.

"I have gathered that you are familiar with the sword," he said, "and that you are from Port Kar."

"I know something of the sword," I said. "And I have a holding in Port Kar."

"Perhaps you are even of the scarlet caste," he said.

"Perhaps," I said.

"Port Kar is at war with Cos," he said.

"Yes," I said.

"We are here," he said. We stopped before a large door. He ushered us between guards. We found ourselves in a reception room. An officer was at a table at one end of the room, with two more guards. Behind him and to his right was another door. In this fashion, to pass him, as is common, one would have to pass him on his sword-arm side.

"Anything so simple as letters of safety could have been issued in the main hall," I said.

Mincon spoke to the officer at the table, who, it seemed, recognized him.

"I would think so," said Hurtha, righteously, adding "whatever a letter of safety might be." He looked about, with his Alar distrust of bureaucracy and enclosed spaces. "I trust there will be no necessity for me to read such a letter," he said, "as this would be difficult, as I cannot read."

"You could learn," I said, somewhat snappishly.

"Between now and when we receive the letters?" asked Hurtha, incredulously.

"Alars do not read," said Boabissia, proudly. "And we are Alars."

"I am an Alar," said Hurtha.

"Doubtless we will get the letters from that fellow," I said, indicating the officer to whom Mincon was speaking.

"My letter of safety would be my ax," said Hurtha, "if I had it."

Mincon, however, to my surprise, went through the door behind the officer.

"I frankly do not understand what is going on," I said.

"I have sometimes had that experience," said Hurtha.

"Mincon is behaving strangely," I said.

"What can you expect?" said Hurtha. "He is not an Alar."

"Neither am I," I said.

"I know," said Hurtha.

"This whole business makes little sense to me," I said.

"Civilization is bizarre," said Hurtha.

"Perhaps you can get a poem out of this," I said.

"I already have," he said, "two. Would you care to hear them?"

"There is no time now," I said.

"They are quite short," he said. "One is a mere fifty liner."

"By all means, then," I said.

" 'In the halls of Torcadino,' " he began. " ' 'neath sacks of noosed bones—' "

"You have composed more than one hundred lines of poetry while we have been standing here?" I asked.

"Many more," he said, "but I have eliminated many lines which did not meet my standards. 'In the streets of Torcadino, 'neath bundles of brittle bones—' "

"Wait," I said. "That is not the same line."

"I have revised it," said Hurtha.

At this moment, Mincon, naively, his timing, from his point of view, tragically awry, emerged from the inner office. "What news, good fellow?" I called to him.

"Please go in," he said to me. "The rest of you please remain here."

We looked at one another.

"Please," he said.

"Very well," I said, resigned.

"Would you care to hear two poems?" asked Hurtha.

"Of course," said Mincon. He was a fine fellow.

"Bara," said Mincon to Tula. "Bara," said I to Feiqa. Both slaves went immediately to their bellies, their heads to the left, their wrists crossed behind their backs, their ankles also crossed. It is a common binding position. We did not bother to bind them, however. It was enough that they lay there in this position. Hurtha dropped their leashes to the tiles beside them. His hands were now freed for gestures, an important contributory element in oral poetry.

"Would you care to hear two poems?" Hurtha asked the officer at the table.

"What?" he asked.

Then I had entered the inner office.

15: The Semnium; What Transpired in the Inner Offices

I whipped my head to the side. The blade moved past me and with a solid sound, followed by a sturdy vibration, lodged itself in the heavy wood of the door.

"Excellent," said a voice. "You have had training."

I looked down the room. At the end of the room, standing behind a functionary's desk, some forty feet away, there stood a soldier.

"Perhaps you are of the scarlet caste?" he asked.

"Perhaps," I said. I removed the blade from the wood behind me, over my shoulder, not taking my eyes off the fellow behind the desk.

"You are quick," he said. "Excellent. It is doubtless as Mincon has suspected. His judgment is good. You are a soldier."

"I have fought," I said. "I am not now in fee."

"Tal, Rarius," said he to me then. "Greetings, Warrior."

I regarded him. He did not seem to me the sort of fellow from whom one might expect letters of safety, licenses of passage, or bureaucratic services. He wore no insignia. His men, I gathered, must know him by sight. His presence, I suspected, whether in the camp or in the march, in the mines, on the walls, in the trenches or fields, would not be unfamiliar among them. They would know him. He would know them. He was a tall, spare man. He had high cheekbones and gray eyes. His dark hair was graying at the temples, unusual among Goreans. He reminded me something of Centius of Cos, though he had not the latter's gentleness. In him I sensed practicality, and mercilessness, and intelligence and power. On the table, before him, resting on what appeared to be state papers, was a sword.

"Tal, Rarius," I whispered.

"Come forward," he said. "It was only a test. I even favored you, to your left. Do not be afraid."

I approached the fellow, who then took his place behind the desk.

At the side of the desk, to its right, as you faced it, on the bare tiles, there lay a chained, naked woman. She was dark-haired, and beautiful. It was not surprising to me that such a woman should lie at the side of his desk. He was obviously a man of great strength. Many Goreans believe that woman is nature's gift to man, that nature has designed her for his stimulation, pleasure and service. Accordingly, they seldom hesitate to avail themselves of this gift. Too, they are sensitive to the pleasures of power. They know the pleasures of power, and they honestly and candidly seek, appreciate and relish them. They know there is no thrill in the world comparable to having absolute power over a female. These feelings, like those of glory and victory, to which they are akin, are their own reward. Goreans do not apologize for such natural and biologically validated urges. Too, they do not feel guilty over them. Indeed, to feel guilty over such natural, profound, deep, and common urges would be, from the Gorean point of view, madness. The male is dominant, unless crippled. Without the mastery there can be no complete male fulfillment, and, interestingly, without complete male fulfillment there can be no complete female fulfillment.

"How do you call yourself?" he asked.

"Tarl," I said.

"You are from Port Kar?" he said.

"I have a holding there," I said.

"Are you a spy for Ar?" he asked.

"No," I said.

"Perhaps for Cos?" he asked.

"No," I said. I put the knife on the desk, before him.

"Your sympathies, I assume, are with Ar," he said.

"I have no special love for Ar," I said. Once I had been

banished from that city, being denied there bread, salt and fire.

"Good," he said. "That way it will be easier for you to retain your objectivity."

"You are no simple officer," I said, "from whom may be obtained letters of safety."

"And you are no simple man-at-arms," he said.

"Oh?" I said.

"These days," he said, "dozens of captains are buying swords. Yet you do not seem to be in fee. Further, I gather from Mincon, my friend, that your financial resources are quite limited."

I said nothing.

"It was clever of you to use the free woman with you in the manner of a rent slave. Some men will pay higher use rents for a free prisoner."

I shrugged.

"But you would make only a handful of copper coins in that sort of thing," he said. "It is not like receiving the weight of your sword in gold coin."

"True," I said.

"You may also, of course, have ruined her for freedom," he said.

"Possibly," I said.

He rose from the desk and went to its side. He kicked the woman who lay there. She recoiled and whimpered, with a rattle of chain.

"What do you think, Lady Cara?" he asked.

"Yes, Master," she said. "I think possibly, Master."

I saw, interestingly enough, that he seemed to be genuinely interested in her opinion. This did not, of course, in any way alter the categorical relation in which they obviously stood to one another.

"Have you been spoiled for freedom?" he asked her.

"What you have done to me!" she wept. "I beg the brand! I beg it! Put the mark on me! Collar me! Confirm it on my body! Confirm it on me with fire and iron, and with the circlet of locked steel, for all the world to see, what you have done to me, what you have made me!"

"She is still free," I observed.

"Yes," he said.

"Do not shame me by keeping me free," she said. "Mark and collar me, so that I may at last be free to be what I now know I am!"

"Do you wish to feel the lash again, Lady Cara?" he asked.

"No, Master," she said, shuddering.

It seemed to me that the woman, obviously, was now ready for enslavement. To be sure, whether it was to be granted to her or not was up to her captor. At any rate, whether she was to be put legally into slavery or not she was now clearly bond, psychologically, intellectually and emotionally. She would now never be anything else.

"This is the Lady Cara, of Venna," he said. "Once she was overheard making remarks disparaging of Tarnburg. Perhaps I shall take her there one day, and keep her there as a house slave."

The prone woman groaned. Her chains slid a little on the tiles.

"Or would you prefer, Lady Cara," he asked, "to serve there only as a cleaning prisoner, simply as a confined servant, a mere housekeeper in captivity?"

"No," she sobbed. "as a slave, a full slave."

"Why?" he asked.

"It is what I am," she sobbed.

I regarded her. She looked luscious at our feet, in her chains. Clearly, too, she had been "ruined for freedom." I wondered about Boabissia. I wondered if she, too, had been ruined for freedom. To be sure, she still spoke much like a proud free woman. Still, too, she often seemed bitter, selfish, frustrated, haughty and arrogant. Too, she had never been put under slave discipline. I had noticed, however, unless it were only my imagination, that she now seemed to move her body somewhat differently under her dress than she had before, before we had prostituted her to replenish our resources.

"And so," asked the fellow, "what of your free tart? Did her rent uses spoil her for freedom?"

"Perhaps," I said. "I do not know."

"Well, if so," he said, "you may always sell her and be done with it."

"True," I said. I thought it might be fun to sell Boabissia. She occasionally got on one's nerves. Too, as a free woman, she could be something of a nuisance. Too, I thought she might make a fine slave. Too, like any other woman, she would look lovely in a collar.

"If you have a holding in Port Kar," he said, "I gather you have no fondness for Cos."

"No," I said. "I have no fondness for Cos." I had fought against her, and Tyros, at sea. I had once served on a Cosian galley. Once, in last carnival time in Port Kar, before the Waiting Hand, her Ubar, gross Lurius of Jad, had sent an assassin against me. His dagger I had thrust into his own heart.

"Yet," said he, "you were traveling with a Cosian supply train, using the cover of the train to move southward in troubled times. This is an act of audacity, of inventiveness, of courage."

I said nothing.

"I respect such things," he said.

I had little doubt he did. I also had little doubt who it must be, he with whom I spoke. I had stood in awe of this man for years. I had studied his campaigns, his tactics and strategems. Yet nothing had prepared me for the presence I felt in this room, a simple room, a bare room, with a large window behind, suitable for a minor functionary in the bureaucracy of Torcadino. How odd it seemed that I should meet this man here, in such a place, rather than in a feast of state, in the corridors of a conference, or on a bloodstained field. The power of this man seemed to radiate forth from him. This is a difficult thing to explain, unless one has felt it. Perhaps in another situation, or in another time I would not have felt this. I do not know. Certainly it had nothing to do with pretentiousness or any obvious demonstrations of authority on his part. If anything, he seemed on the surface little more than a simple soldier, perhaps no more than merely another unpretentious, candid, efficient officer. It was beneath the surface that I sensed more. This was perhaps a matter of subliminal cues. I had little doubt that when he chose he could be warm and charming. Too, I supposed he could be hearty and convivial. Perhaps he was fond of jokes. Perhaps one might enjoy drinking with him. His men would die for him. I thought he must be much alone. I suspected it might be death to cross his will.

"I suspect," he said, "that you were heading toward Ar."

"I have business in Ar," I said.

"Do you know the delta of the Vosk?" he asked.

"I once traversed it," I said.

"Tell me about it," he said.

"It is treacherous, and trackless," I said. "It covers thousands of square pasangs. It is infested with insects, snakes and tharlarion. Marsh sharks even swim among its reeds. In it there is little solid ground. Its waters are usually shallow, seldom rising above the chest of a tall man. The footing is unreliable. There is much quicksand. It protects Port Kar from the east. Few but rencers can find their way about in it. Too, for most practical purposes, they keep it closed to traffic and trade."

"That, too, is my impression," he said.

"Why do you ask?" I asked.

"Do you understand much of military matters?" he asked.

"A little," I said.

"Do you know who I am?" he asked.

"I think so," I said.

"Do you know why I have brought you here?" he asked.

"No," I said.

"Why do you think Torcadino has been taken?" he asked.

"To stall the invasion," I said. "To give Ar time to arm. It is a powerful and decisive stroke. Torcadino is Cos's major depot for supplies and siege equipment. You have now seized these things. They are now yours. You may remain indefinitely in Torcadino with these vast quantities of supplies. Too, though you will doubtless be invested, Cos now lacks the equipment to dislodge you. Similarly, because of their new shortage of supplies, they will have to withdraw many of their troops from this area. Presumably they will also have to be divided, marched into diverse areas to facilitate the acquisition of new supplies. You have thus scattered and disrupted your enemy. Too, I suspect your ejection of the civilian population from Torcadino is not merely political, to appear to show concern, generosity, and mercy, nor merely expedient, to remove them from the city, thus conserving supplies and removing possible Cosian sympathizers from behind your back, but to increase the intensity of Cos's supply problems."

"Very good," he said.

"Cos will not dare let these refugees starve," I said, "as they are citizens of a city which had declared for them, which had gone over to them. If they did not care for them, this would be a dark lesson, and one favoring Ar, to every wavering or uncommitted village, town and city within a dozen horizons."

"Quite," he agreed.

"What was done with the garrison of Torcadino?" I asked.

"Most were surprised in their beds," he said. "Their weapons were seized. Resistance was useless. We then expelled them, disarmed, from the city."

"So that they, too, like the civilians, would aggravate the problems of Cos."

"Yes," he said.

"Did you march them beneath a yoke?" I asked. This is usually formed of three spears, two upright and the third bound horizontally across the first two. The prisoners are then usually marched in a long line, two abreast, between the uprights. They cannot pass under the horizontal spear, a weapon of their enemy, without lowering their heads and bending their backs. Some warriors choose to die rather than do this. A similar yoke is sometimes used for the captive women of a city, but it is set much lower, usually such that they must pass under it on their belly. After all, they are not men; they are women. Too, it is usually formed not of spears but of brooms, brought from the conquering city, and the horizontal bar is hung with dangling slave beads. In this, although the original meanings are perhaps lost in antiquity, most commentators see symbolized the servility and sensuousness which, as they are to be slaves, is henceforth, upon pain of death, to be required of them. It is an impressive sight to see the women of a captive city, single file, stripped and on their bellies, in a long line winding through the streets and across the piazza, moving between soldiers with whips, crawling toward the yoke. As they crawl beneath it, the slave beads touch their back. On the other side of the yoke, while they are still on their bellies, they generally feel a collar locked on their neck. It is one of many, and it, like the others, has been attached in its turn, and at its interval, to a long chain. They are now in coffle. They will probably not be removed from this coffle until, in one way or another, they have been sold.

"No," said the fellow with me.

I nodded.

"They are good fellows," he said. "Too, perhaps one day some of them will bear arms in my company."

"I understand," I said.

He turned about and looked through the window. We could see the walls of Torcadino from the window and one of the aqueducts. He then turned about and faced me, again. "You did not try to kill me," he commented.

"Another test?" I asked.

"Yes," he said.

"I thought so," I said. "Else you would not have been likely to turn your back on an unknown stranger."

"True," he smiled.

"I considered it," I said.

"It would have been difficult to cross the table," he said. "Too, it would be difficult, in the time I gave you, to pick up the knife, or sword, without rustling papers."

"Also you were anticipating the possibility of an attack," I said. "It is difficult to move surreptitiously on a person under such circumstances. Also the female here, at the side of the desk, would presumably have moved, or gasped or cried out."

"Would you have cried out, Lady Cara?" he asked.

"Yes!" she said.

"In spite of all I have done to you?" he asked.

"Because of what you have done to me!" she wept. "I would die for you!"

"Why?" he asked.

"A slave girl owes all to her master, her passion, her being, her life, everything. It is yours, my Master!"

"Belly," said he to her, and she lay then on her belly, beside the desk, in her chains.

"But I did not think you would attack me," he said to me. "You are too rational, I think. Too, you would have, at least now, no adequate motivation for such an attack. Also, you suspect, or are not sure, but what we may share certain common objectives."

"There are other reasons, too," I said. "For one, even if I succeeded in such an attack, I would not be likely to escape from the Semnium alive."

"The window is a possibility," he said.

"Yes," I said.

"But you had not examined it for ledges, and such," he said.

"No," I said.

"There is no extended ledge," he said.

I nodded.

"You said there were 'reasons,' " he said.

"Another would be," I said, "my respect for you, as a commander, as a soldier."

"In many men," he said, "emotion functions to the detriment of policy. Perhaps it is so with you."

"Perhaps, sometimes," I said.

"I shall remember that about you," he said. "I may be able to use it sometime."

"Your entrance through the aqueducts, and using both, rather than one, as an insurance attack, was brilliant," I said.

"It is an obvious strategem," he said. "I have considered it for years, but I did not use it until now."

"Had you used it earlier," I said, "it would now be a part of military history, of the lore associated with your name, something which all garrisons in appropriate cities would now anticipate and take steps to prevent."

"Of course," he said.

"You saved it," I smiled, "for an occasion worthy of it."

"For a Torcadino," he said.

"Of course," I said.

"The aqueducts have now been closed by the Cosians, and their flows diverted," he said.

"There is no shortage of water in the city," I said. "You are now depending on the original wells, dating from before the aqueducts, which, with the ejection of the civilian population, are now more than ample for your needs."

He smiled.

"But I fear that you may not have anticipated all things," I said.

"It is seldom possible to do so," he said.

"I am troubled by certain obvious problems," I said.

"Speak," he said.

"There is no road from Torcadino," I said. "It would seem that you have trapped yourself here. The walls are surrounded. Your army is small. Cos will maintain a considerable force in the area, at least compared to what is at your disposal. I do not think you will be able to fight your way out. I am sure you do not have enough tarns to evacuate your men."

"Interesting," he said.

"Obviously you have made strict arrangements with Ar," I said.

"No," he said. "I have no understanding with Ar."

"You must have!" I said.

"No," he said.

"Are you not in the pay of Ar?" I asked, astonished.

"No," he said.

"You have done this of your own initiative?" I asked.

"Yes," he said. "The powers of Ar and Cos must be balanced. The victory of either means the end of the free companies."

"But you are depending on Ar to raise the siege, surely," I said.

"Of course," he said.

"What if she does not do so?" I asked.

"I think that would be quite unfortunate," he said.

"You could negotiate with the Cosians," I said. "I am sure they would agree to almost any terms, offering suitable inducements for withdrawal, guarantees of safety for yourself and your troops, and such, in order to regain Torcadino.''

''Do you think, after what we have done here, and the considerable delays we have caused them, they would just let us walk out of Torcadino?'' he asked.

''No,'' I said.

''Nor do I,'' he smiled.

''Everything depends on Ar,'' I said.

''Yes,'' he said.

''You have taken great risks for Ar,'' I said.

''For myself, and the free companies,'' he said.

''Ar would seem to have no choice but to act as you expect,'' I said.

''It would seem so,'' he said.

''Yet you seem troubled,'' I said.

''I am,'' he said. ''Come with me.''

We then went out through a side door, into another room. I looked back, once. I saw Lady Cara, in her chains, beside his desk. She was still on her belly. She had not been given permission to rise. She looked after us.

''What do you think of this little bird on her perch?'' he asked me.

''It is hard to say,'' I said.

He pulled up her head with his fist in her hair. He was not gentle with her. She cried out, whimpering, her head bent back.

''Lovely,'' I said. Her neck was encircled by a collar. She was branded. As he had her head pulled back her back was pulled back against the short, horizontal wooden post behind which her arms were hooked. This horizontal post was mounted on a short vertical post, in the manner of a ''T.'' She was kneeling on the platform, about a yard high, on which this ''T'' was fixed. Her ankles were chained together, behind and about the vertical post. Manacles, and a length of chain, running across her belly, completed the closure that kept her arms in place, holding her wrists back, at her sides. ''Perhaps she is a captain's woman.''

''More than that,'' he said. ''She was a general's woman.''

She whimpered. Her eyes were almost glassy with terror.

He released her hair. Her head fell forward, her long, dark hair before her body. I pulled the chain out a bit from her belly. There were marks in her flesh, from where it had been tight on her. She whimpered.

I regarded her. Jewels did not bedeck her. Her silks were now gone. No cosmetics now adorned her, begging to be licked and kissed from her lips. No scent of perfume now clung to her. There were smells which were perhaps those of sweat and fear. Too, she had soiled the platform. She had been beaten, doubtless quite a rare experience for a high slave. If she had once worn a golden, bejeweled collar it was now gone. On her neck now was a simple iron collar, hammered shut, such as might be put on the neck of any slut picked up by any soldier in a flaming city.

"What is your name, my dear?" he inquired.

"I have no name, no name!" she said, quickly.

"How do you know?" he asked. "Perhaps I have given you one."

"I have no name that I know," she said, terrified, jerking in her metal bonds, fearing that she might be being tricked into earning herself punishment. "I do not yet know my name, if I have one. If Master has named me, he has not yet informed me! If I have a name, it will be as Master pleases! I am a slave! I am his, only his! If I have a name, I beg to know it, that I may answer to it obediently and promptly!"

"You have no name," he said.

"Yes, Master," she said, weakly, putting down her head again.

"What was your name?" he asked.

"Lucilina," she said.

The fellow regarded me. "Do you know the name of the high officer of the Cosian forces in the south?" he asked.

"Myron, Polemarkos of Temos, cousin to Lurius of Jad, Ubar of Cos," I said.

"And what do you think might have been the name of his preferred slave?" he asked.

"I gather it was Lucilina," I said.

"She was as greedy as she is beautiful," said the officer. "She had much freedom in the Cosian camp, given even her own quarters, in which the Polemarkos could call upon her. In these quarters, amidst her cushions and silks, surrounded by her jewel boxes, attended by female slaves assigned to her for her own use, to whom she was as absolute mistress, she held sway almost as might have a Ubara. Comfortably secure in the favor of her powerful and highborn master, esteemed and pampered, she, though only a slave, gathered power about herself.''

I became angry hearing this. A female slave is not to have power. Rather she is to be subjected to it, totally.

"Her influence with the Polemarkos became well known. She had his ear. A word from her, for or against a fellow, as she pleased, could promote or ruin a career. In her tents she would receive visitors, callers and petitioners. Dozens, coming to understand her power, came soon to sue for her favor. There were gifts for her, naturally. Surely that was only fitting. Her jewel boxes began to brim with precious stones. Rings were brought to her worth the ransom of a Ubar. Her cosmetic cases could boast perfumes that might have been the envy of a Ubara.''

"Better chains of iron and a whip for her," I said, bitterly.

"Among these petitioners came one fellow bringing with him the promise of a gift of wine, a wine supposedly secret, the rare Falarian, a wine only rumored among collectors to exist, a wine supposedly so rare and precious that its cost might purchase a city. She, of course, would test this. She, though only a slave, would choose to sip it.''

"Arrogant slave," I said. The woman put down her head even more, whimpering, trembling. No slave takes wine without the permission of the master. And even then, as often as not, she takes it only on his command, and under his eye, usually kneeling before him. Sometimes, even, he puts his hand in her hair, bends her head back, and pours it down her throat. It is done by his will.

"The wine, of course," he said, "was too precious to have been brought with him, but it is in his tent. She summons her palanquin and bearers, male slaves, and is to be carried to this place. Too, in this fashion the matter may best be kept secret from her attendants. She is often carried about the

Cosian camp in her closed palanquin by bearers. This excites little curiosity. In his tent she will taste the wine, demanding even that he pour it for her. It is done. She looks at him, startled. Can this wine, which seems like a cheap ka-la-na, be the rare Falarian? But in a moment she is unconscious. Arrangements have already been made with the bearers, of course. They will receive their freedom. It could have been done otherwise but this is best. They were known. Had we substituted others for them we would have increased our risks. Too, left behind they might well have been killed, absurdly enough, by the Cosians, an unnecessary and foolish waste of able men, in my opinion, whereas I now have four more grateful, loyal fellows in my ranks, any one of whom I think would willingly die for me."

"Of course," I said.

"The palanquin is then brought within the walls of the outer tent. Meanwhile the female is stripped. She is placed, unconscious, in the palanquin. Binding thongs, about her ankles, her legs spread, about her wrists, they tied down at her sides, and about her thighs, belly, above her breasts and below her arms, and about her throat, fasten her to it, securing her tightly in place. When she awakens she will discover she can scarcely move a muscle. She is then gagged. Lastly the curtains of the palanquin are closed. She is now ready to be transported."

"She has been drugged, of course," I said.

"Not heavily," he said. "She will remain unconscious, by our intent, for only a few Ehn, for little longer than it takes to strip, bind and gag her. We want her to awaken quite soon, while still in the Cosian camp, and, awakening, to be fully appreciative of her predicament. We want her to lie there, helpless, fully conscious of what is being done to her."

"Excellent," I said.

"My man checked in on her once," he said. "Her eyes were wild, frantic, over her gag. He then, again, closed the curtains."

"It is a splendid coup," I said, "to have stolen the preferred slave of the Polemarkos of Temos."

"Had it not been for your arrogance and greed, it would

not have been so easy, would it, my dear?'' he said to the woman.

"No, Master," she said.

"But you are not arrogant and greedy anymore, are you, my dear?" he asked.

"No, Master!" she said.

"We brought her to Torcadino," he said. "As you may remember, she had had my man, though she was a slave, pour wine for her."

"I remember," I said.

"Her first beating, thus," he said, "she received from him."

"Naturally," I said.

"Her next four beatings, at given intervals, she received from the four fellows who had been her bearers formerly, now free men."

"Naturally," I said.

"At times we had to caution them, and restrain them," he said, "that they not kill her."

"I understand," I said.

"She was then ready to be interrogated," he said.

"Interrogated?" I said.

"Certainly," he said. "Do you think I find this slut of any personal interest or worth?"

"I can see how some men might," I said.

"She is vain, and shallow," he said. "Aren't you, my dear?"

"Yes, Master," she said.

"But we are going to work hard to overcome those flaws, aren't we, my dear?" he inquired.

"Yes, Master!" she said.

He put his hand on her.

She cried out, startled. She jerked back against the stout post. Her hands jerked in the metal fastenings. She regarded him with disbelief, with horror.

"You are no longer a high slave," he said. "You are going to have to get used to being touched like this."

She looked at him, wildly. Her hands twisted. She could not close her legs.

"I thought you might have had her stolen," I said, "in order to do insult to Myron, the Polemarkos."

"Please, no!" she cried.

"No," he said. "I would not risk men in such an unnecessary and gratuitous enterprise. My major concern is with the expeditious and efficient attainment of certain ultimate objectives. I seldom indulge in the gratifications of such transient vanities unless they lead to these objectives, or, at the least, are not inimical to their attainment. Such an insult, stinging as it would be, would not serve any particular purpose at the moment, for example, stirring a foe to a fury of vengeance which might lead to miscalculation on his part. In this particular situation it would presumably only make it more difficult to deal with the Polemarkos, to whom I must soon give the appearance of inviting bona fide negotiation."

"No, no, no," whispered the girl.

"In that way you will delay attacks and buy time," I said.

"Yes," he said.

"No, no," whimpered the girl. "No!"

"Besides," he said, "I bear the Polemarkos no ill will. He is a clever, if weak, officer."

"No, no!" said the girl. "Oh, yes," she cried, suddenly, "Yes!" Her eyes were wild. "Yes, please!" she said. She squirmed. She closed her eyes. Her knees moved piteously. "Yes, please!" she said.

"She is vital," I observed.

"Yes," agreed the officer.

"Perhaps the Polemarkos would not be pleased to observe how you have her leaping under your touch."

"Perhaps not," he said. "But he would presumably understand I mean no insult by it. She is, after all, only a slave."

"True," I said.

"Please, do not stop," she said. "Please do not stop!"

"Do you move like this under the touch of the Polemarkos?" he asked her.

"No," she said. "No, never. I did not know it could be like this!"

The officer stepped back. Her eyes opened. They were wild. There were tears in them. "Please," she said. "Please!"

She thrust her body forward, toward him, piteously begging the continuation of his attentions.

"How is that you would have had her stolen, not for her own beauty, for she is prize collar meat, which I would think would have been a sufficient reason for doing so, nor as an insult to the Polemarkos, but merely to interrogate?" I asked.

"What do you mean?" he asked.

"Yes, yes!" she cried, gratefully. "Thank you, Master! Thank you, Master!"

"She is only a slave," I said.

"Now, she is only a slave," he said.

"Yes," she whimpered. "Oh, yes!"

"But before," he continued, "she was also the confidante of the Polemarkos. By means of her wiles and beauty she had ingratiated herself with him and there were few secrets of state to which she, in one way or another, was not privy. She even attended certain meetings of war, though concealed in her silks behind a modesty screen. Her presence there, as you might imagine, even concealed behind the screen, considerably discomfited several of the officers. It was partly as a result of their resentful, guarded comments, overheard by certain spies, that I came to realize her importance." He paused for a moment. "Are you important now, my dear?" he asked.

"No, Master!" she said.

"What are you now?" he asked.

"A slave, only a slave, your slave!" she said.

He then renewed his attentions to her body.

"Yes, yes, yes!" she said.

"What was your name?" he said.

"Lucilina!" she gasped.

"You are not responding like a Lucilina," he said. She moaned, and squirmed. "You are responding more like a Luchita," he said.

"Yes, Master," she said. "Yes, Master!"

"You are Luchita," he said.

"Yes, Master," she said, named. I thought this a good name for her. It was a good name for a hot, helpless, dominated slave.

"Are you a high slave, Luchita?" he asked.

"I do not know," she said.

"No," he said. "You are not. You are now among the lowest of low slaves."

"Yes, Master," she said.

"And I will give you, accordingly," he said, "to one of my lowest soldiers, to a rude and common fellow, one of the lowest rank."

"Yes, Master," she said.

"You will serve him well," he said.

"Yes, Master," she said.

"You will be treated as the slave you are."

"Yes, Master," she said.

"But have no fear," he said. "You will receive, I assure you, in this sort of bondage, low and common, and absolutely uncompromising, your complete fulfillment, both as a female and a slave."

"Yes, Master," she said.

She then licked and kissed his hands, cleaning them. He then wiped his hands on her sweat-dampened hair. He then left the room, I following him. I glanced back. The slave on the perch was looking after him, her dark, wet hair much before her chained body, her eyes filled with awe. She was pretty I thought, the slave, Luchita.

"What did you learn from her?" I asked, once the door was closed.

"You may kneel, Lady Cara," he said.

The woman from Venna, with a movement of chains, rose from her belly to kneel beside his desk. She knelt in the position of the pleasure slave, back on her heels, back straight, head up, knees spread, palms of her hands on her thighs.

"We learned a great deal, in a sense," he said, "but most of it we already knew, or suspected, from various other sources. Two things, however, came as a surprise to us."

"May I inquire?" I asked.

"Of course," he said. "Otherwise I would not have brought you here in the first place. It is because of these things I had you brought here."

"Speak, please," I encouraged him.

"Should I be fetched from the room, Master?" asked Lady Cara. Because of the nature of her ankle chaining, it would have been difficult for her to walk.

Suddenly cuffed, she fell to her side, blood at her mouth. "Did you ask permission to speak?" he asked. In a situation of this sort it was common, though not always required, that a slave request permission to speak. Apparently this officer, in this sort of situation, did require his women to request such permission. Lady Cara, after this, would be in no doubt about this.

"No, Master," she said. "Forgive me, Master."

He snapped his fingers. Immediately she resumed her former position.

"The main forces of Cos are here," he said, "in the vicinity of Torcadino, now, at the moment, investing it."

"I am sure that is common knowledge," I said.

"One would think so," he said, "but two things which disturb and puzzle me we have learned recently, only this morning, from our little informant in the other room. First, a movement of Cosian troops, originating in Brundisium, apparently several regiments, are moving eastward, parallel to the Vosk."

"Towards Ar's Station?" I speculated. This was Ar's stronghold on the Vosk. It was situated on the southern bank, east of Jort's Ferry and west of Forest Port, both on the northern bank.

"Presumably so," he said.

"It must be a diversion," I said.

"Presumably Ar's Station, if subjected to attack, could be relieved by a small force," he said, "and a countermarch to the coast could cut off the Cosians from their base in Brundisium."

"I would think so," I said.

"Why then, according to our information, and this is the second item of interest here, is Ar preparing, if this is correct, to launch its main forces northward toward Ar's Station?"

"That would be madness," I said.

"That is the information which the spies of Cos in Ar have transmitted to the Polemarkos," he said.

"They must be mistaken," I said.

"Perhaps," said the officer, moodily.

"The main forces of Cos are here, by Torcadino," I said. "If the main might of Ar is sent northward there would be a free road from the trenches about Torcadino almost to the gates of Ar themselves. The land between here and Ar, and the city itself, would be in effect without defense."

"I think there can be only one plausible explanation for this," said the officer. "—That the councils of Ar do not know that the main force of Cos is here."

"That seems incredible," I said.

"What other explanation could there be?" he asked.

"That the spies of the Polemarkos are simply mistaken," I said.

"Perhaps," he said.

"There is, of course, another," I said.

"What is that?" he asked.

"Treachery in Ar," I said.

"Of this enormity?" he asked.

I shrugged.

"Unthinkable," he said.

"Surely you have thought it," I said.

"Yes," he said, "I have considered it."

"Why did you ask me about the delta of the Vosk?" I asked.

"Because I think the move toward Ar's Station is a diversion," he said. "And because the Cosians could be too easily cut off from Brundisium."

"You think they will withdraw into the delta?" I asked.

"I would," he said.

"So, too, would I," I said.

"And the main forces of Ar may be marching toward Ar's Station," he said, grimly.

The hair on the back of my neck rose.

"They could not be lured into that area," I said.

"I would think not," he said.

"No sane commander in such a situation could issue orders to enter the delta in force," I said, "certainly not without obtaining guides, accumulating transportation, organizing supplies and support, treating with the natives of the area, and so on.''

"In such a place an army might disappear," he said.

"Never will Ar march northward in force," I said, "not with Cos entrenched outside Torcadino."

"Why has Ar not yet moved?" he asked.

"I do not know," I said.

"I can hold Cos here for the winter," said the officer. "That is probably all."

"What would you like of me?" I asked.

"Gnieus Lelius," said he, "high councilor, first minister to Ar, is regent in the absence of Marlenus. I have here letters to be delivered to him. They outline the dispositions of the main forces of Cos and the situation in Torcadino. Too, I have letters here for Seremides, high general of Ar. They bear the seal of the silver tarn. I do not think you will have difficulty obtaining an audience with him." I had once known a Seremides in Ar. To be sure, such names are common.

"I understand," I said.

"With these letters, of course," he said, "I shall include letters of safety."

"How shall we pass through the forces of Cos?" I asked. "Such letters may have their weight with those of Ar but would scarcely seem designed to impress Cosians."

"You and your party will seem to be ejected from the city with other civilians," he said, "some thousand or so who will be held until tomorrow. I do not think you will attract much attention. Indeed, Cos encourages the dispersion of these refugees, as it has little inclination to care for them."

"I see," I said.

"You were intending to Ar anyway, were you not?" he asked.

"Yes," I admitted.

"You will, of course, be well paid for your trouble," he said. He threw a weighty purse upon the table.

I looked at it.

"It is mostly silver," he said, "and some copper. Gold would provoke suspicion."

"I would suppose I am not the first you have entrusted with such a mission," I said.

"No," he said. "You are the fifth. I have sent others with such letters, warnings, and such, as long ago as Tarnburg, and as recently as the banks of the Issus."

"Your messages then must have been already received," I said.

"Apparently not," he said. "I have, at any rate, as yet, received no responses."

"This could be dangerous," I speculated.

"I think that is quite possible," he said. "I would exercise great caution, if I were you."

"What if I do not wish to do this?" I asked.

"You need not do it, of course," he said. "Beyond that, for your trouble, and with no hard feelings, I shall give you letters of safety which will conduct you and your party safely through my men."

"That is very generous," I said.

"I place you under no pressure whatsoever," he said.

"I shall do it," I said.

"I knew you would," he said.

"And that is why you placed me under no pressure?" I asked.

"Of course," he said.

"I share your general views on these matters," I said.

"I gathered that," he said.

"Do you wish me to take an oath, to pledge my sword?" I asked.

"No," he said, "that will not be necessary."

"I see;" I said.

"If you succeed in this matter, of course, I will be grateful," he said.

"Of course," I said.

"Whereas I have a reputation of being merciless to enemies, at least when it suits my purpose," he said, "I, too, have a reputation of being generous to my friends."

"I have heard such," I said.

"Some expression of my gratitude would be in order," he

said. "Perhaps a bag of gold, perhaps a hundred prize Cosian women?"

"No," I said. "I shall do this labor of my own will, and for my own purposes."

"Warrior," said he.

"Warrior," I, in turn, saluted him.

I eyed the papers on the desk.

"Sleep this night in the Semnium," he said.

"Why?" I asked.

"It will be safer," he said.

"My weapons, and goods," I asked, "and those of my party?"

"Give the receipts, yours and those of your friends, to the officer outside," he said. "They will be delivered in the morning."

"Why will it be safer to sleep in the Semnium?" I asked.

"Who knows whom one can trust?" he asked.

He sat behind the desk. He began to sign various documents. The signature was forward-slanting, ascendant and bold.

"Shall I wait for the letters?" I asked.

"No, Captain," he said.

"Captain?" I asked.

"Surely you have served, in some capacity or another, in one place or another, with that rank or one at least equivalent to it," he said.

"How did you know?" I asked.

"You carry yourself like a captain," he said.

There was no reason for me to receive the letters, of course, until I was ready to leave. I now sensed, however, more than before, the security in which he wished to hold them, and how important they might be. To be sure, developments might occur during the night, events to which pertinent references might be judiciously included.

"It has been my experience," he said, looking up, "that a judgment too hastily entered upon is sometimes, in the light of cooler reflection, regretted."

"Sir?" I asked.

"Consider carefully, tonight," he said, "in repose, and at length, whether or not you wish, truly, to carry these letters."

"I have agreed to do so," I said. I felt sweat about the back of my neck, and on my back, and in my palms. There was apparently more danger in being the bearer of these messages than I had hitherto realized.

"I shall wait upon your considered decision in the morning," he said.

"And if I then do not choose to carry them?" I asked.

"You may keep the coins," he said. "Too, you and your party will still receive letters of safety."

"You are incredibly generous," I said.

"Not really," he said. "What is the cost, really, of some scraps of parchment and a few drops of ink?"

"The coins," I said.

"A contribution from the treasury of Torcadino," he said.

"If I do not accept the commission," I said, "I shall return ₋em to you."

"As you wish," he smiled.

I thrust the coins in my wallet.

They were more than enough, I had gathered, to get myself, and the others, too, if they wished to accompany me, to Ar.

He finished signing the papers before him, and stood up. He regarded me. "Captain?" he asked.

I found myself reluctant to leave the presence of this man. I stood in awe of him.

"Captain?" he asked.

"Nothing," I said.

He looked down at the free woman, Lady Cara, of Venna, kneeling beside the desk.

"I need contentment," he said.

She straightened herself, with a tiny sound of chain.

"You may leave, Captain," he said.

"Sir," I said.

"Yes?" he said.

"Recently, on the Genesian Road, north of Torcadino, there was an attack on a portion of the Cosian supply trains, a massacre. Were your men responsible for that?"

"No," he said.

"Do you know what party, or parties, were?" I asked.

"No," he said.

"But it was done by mercenaries," I said.

"Doubtless," he said.

I then turned about and went toward the door. "Oh!" said Lady Cara. I heard the sounds of her chains. At the door, turning, I saw her on her feet, naked, in her chains, being held closely against him, looking up into his eyes. Then he threw her on her belly on the desk, on the papers, and the various documents of state. I then took my leave.

16: A Night in the Semnium

I turned in the blankets, brought by soldiers, on the tiles of the vestibule of the Semnium. There were perhaps two hundred people, many of them civilians, being housed there this night. Near me, a free female, one of those to be counted among the spoils of Torcadino, was chained on one of the clients' marble benches, one of several serving on such benches, women who, one after the other, in turn, were replaced with others.

I was troubled. I wished to go to Ar, but I had my own business there. I did not think I needed a mercenary's coins to buy my way there. Too, as an unknown fellow, it seemed I might be able to enter her gates without great difficulty. Letters of safety, aside from the difficulties they might involve me in with Cosian sentries or outposts, which might be considerable, would presumably not be needed by everyone entering Ar. To be sure, if I wished to enter the presence of the first minister, or the high general, they might be of some use, but the letters for them, sealed with the sign of the silver tarn, might do as well. Besides, if I chose not to deliver these letters, who would know the difference. Others may have defaulted, for some reason or another, in this, or a similar mission. The officer, at any rate, seemed not, as yet, at least, to have received replies to such missives.

The woman on the bench, groaning and ravished, on her belly on it, clutching it, her legs chained on either side of it, was now alone. She lay on the cool marble, clutching it. "Master, Master!" she had wept. Nearby, to her right, and my right, only feet away, almost at our elbows, some sitting, some lying down, crowded together, chained, huddled, in the half darkness, illuminated by a tiny lamp on the wall, against one wall of the Semnium, was a large group of choice free women, probably gathered here as the cream of Torcadino's free flesh loot, doubtless to be distributed as gifts in the near future. Most would doubtless go to high officers and agents. Some, on the other hand, I supposed, perhaps lesser beauties, might receive a different disposition, being bestowed perhaps on local civilian supporters or given as good-will emoluments to suppliers and contractors.

Nearby, Hurtha and Boabissia were asleep. Mincon, apparently a trusted agent of his captain, had quarters, or business, elsewhere. His Tula he had taken with him. Feiqa was now far to the left, against the far wall, chained there by the ankle with a number of other slaves. They did not wish to mix the slaves and the free females. From her collar there was suspended a small rectangle of cardboard. This was attached to the collar by a small, closed-loop string. This is first put through a hole in the cardboard and drawn through itself, fastening it to the cardboard; it is then passed under or over the collar, the cardboard thrust through it, and then pulled down, snugly, about the collar, the cardboard now dangling from it. On the cardboard there was a number, matching a number on a similar piece of cardboard now in my wallet. By means of this tag I would claim her in the morning.

I wondered why the officer had not, as yet, received any replies to his messages. Perhaps, of course, the messages had gotten through. Perhaps it was only that the recipients did not deign to reply, or that their replies, perhaps, had been intercepted.

The woman on the bench moaned, holding it. Elsewhere I saw another woman being removed from a similar bench, and being returned to the common chain.

I wondered if some of these women had been here before, perhaps as clients, or petitioners or even witnesses. I supposed so. It seemed likely.

A new female was brought to the further bench. She was sat upon it, straddling it. Her ankles were chained together beneath it. Her wrists were similarly secured, the length of chain running under the heavy, fixed-position marble bench.

She was then, by the hair, drawn forward, to lie upon her belly on the cool marble.

All of these women, I suspected, had been in the Semnium before, in one fashion or another, or for one purpose or another, if only to meet friends or to examine and admire the interior appointments and mosaics. It is, after all, one of Torcadino's great buildings. But doubtless none of them had ever before been here in their present capacity, casual love meat set forth for the delectation of passers-by, or even of the idle or curious.

A new woman was being brought to the common chain now, to a place quite near me. She was a dark-haired, sweetly bodied beauty. On her neck was a hempen leash. Her hands were tied behind her back. In a moment she wore a heavy collar, and was on the chain. Her leash was then unknotted, and, with a quick, whiplike motion, as she winced, jerked away from her. Her hands, too, then, were freed. She was now on the chain, no different from the others.

The woman on the bench near to me whimpered. She moved her body a little on the cool marble, piteously, clutching it with her hands, her legs chained on either side of the smooth, inflexible expanse.

The woman who had just been added to the chain rubbed her wrists. Apparently she had not been tied gently. I wondered if she, a free woman, not yet a slave, had dared to express less than total deference before a man, or if she were important.

"Mother," whispered a voice, from among the other captives, "is it you?"

"Is it you?" whispered the new woman, startled, wildly, turning about.

"Yes," said the other. "Yes!"

"Daughter!" she whispered.

The other, with a movement of chain, crawling, emerged from the other captives. They embraced, on their knees, weeping.

"Be quiet," said another woman, whispering. "Do you want us to be beaten?"

"Mother! Mother!" wept the girl.

"Daughter!" wept the woman.

"Be quiet," said the other woman.

"Are we permitted to speak?" asked the daughter, fearfully.

"We have not been told we may not speak," said another woman. "But I would not be too loud about it. Do not draw attention to yourselves."

"I do not even know if I may speak to you or not," sobbed the girl.

"We are women," said her mother. "If men do not wish us to speak, they will tell us, with their whips."

"Mother, mother," wept the girl, holding her.

"I had thought you might have escaped," said the older woman.

"No," said the girl. "The collar is on my neck."

"Who are you?" asked the mother.

"437," whispered the girl. "Who are you?"

"I am 261," she said. She then drew back, holding her daughter at arm's length. "You see?" she said. "You may read it upon my breast."

"As you may read mine upon mine," said the daughter.

They then again embraced, sobbing, on their knees.

"What has become of us?" sobbed the girl.

"It is a common fate for women," she said.

"What will become of us?" asked the girl.

"Doubtless the collar, and the service of a man," she said.

"I do not want to serve men!" said the girl.

"As a slave you will have no choice but to do so, and perfectly," said the woman.

"I do not want to serve them!" wept the girl. "I am afraid of men! They are brutes! I hate them!"

"Surely, from time to time," said the woman, "you have considered what it would be like to be their slave and serve them, fully, in all things."

"Mother!" said the girl. "You are my mother! How can you dare to even think of speaking to me like that!"

"You are not a little girl any longer," said the woman, gently. "You are now old enough to begin to understand such matters. Indeed, I think you do, or begin to, but do not admit this to me."

"Mother!" said the girl, reproachfully.

"You are no longer a child," she said. "The years have passed. Are you not clear as to what has happened to you? Do you not understand the meaning of the wondrous changes which have transformed you into what you now are, the meaning of your new sensibilities, and feelings, and desires and instincts, and curves."

"Do not speak to me like this!" said the girl.

'You are no longer a child," she said. "You are now a grown woman, indeed, a beautiful young woman, a desirable young woman."

" 'Desirable'!" she said, scandalized. But I could tell she was thrilled to hear this.

"That at any rate, whatever you may personally think about it, is the judgment of men, who are the arbiters and masters in these matters," she said. "Indeed, that much is attested to by your presence on this chain."

"Am I desirable," she asked, "*truly* desirable—as a *female*?"

"I believe so," said the mother. "And I am sure, sweet and dear daughter, that when you find yourself helpless in the arms of men, kicking and crying out, and squirming, their lust will make it quite clear to you."

"You needn't put it just that way," said the girl. She shrank back in the collar and chain. She put her hand to the collar. It was closed with a padlock. The collars these women wore had rings. It was by means of these rings, one to each collar, at the right side of the collar, and a second padlock, the bolt of which passed through the ring and a link of the chain, that the collars were attached to the common chain. In this fashion, a woman could be removed from the chain and yet be kept in a closed, padlocked collar. This was a different arrangement than had held the larger groups of women earlier, outside, at various points on the Avenue of Adminius. To be sure these were choice wenches. It was not surprising, then, that they should now find themselves the captives of a somewhat more refined constraint system. Additional security can be achieved, and often is, particularly when moving women, or when they are to be kept on the chain for a longer time, by riveting the collars shut. Needless to say, there is a large number of collar types, chaining arrangements, and security devices, the choices among them largely dictated by the motives and tastes of the master, and sometimes by his cultural background, all of which serve to keep women in perfect custody.

"True," said the woman.

"But you do think I am desirable?"

"Yes," said the woman.

"Oh," said the girl pleased.

"You are now ready for the collar," said the woman.

"No!" said the girl.

"You will find you have little choice in the matter," she said.

"I will resist!" said the girl. "I will be strong!"

"And doubtless, after a test period, if they are so kind as to give you one, you will simply be killed."

"Killed?" she gasped.

"Yes," said the woman. "Men are only human. They do not, nor should they have, endless patience, particularly with the sort of animal which you will then be. It is not like having a foolish free companion, one who knows no better, who will patiently work with you for years, trying to help you become a woman."

"I will try to be strong!" she wept.

"Such expressions often constitute but transparent conceal-ments for envy and resentment," she said. "Consider whether or not this might be true in your case. Similarly, even worse, do not use them to disguise your fear of men and of your own true nature. Too, they are but ill used when put forth to praise what may be actually only sexual inertness, neurotic rigidity or false pride. Do not concern yourself in this matter, sweet daughter, with the values of others, and particularly of men, or of those who desire to be imitative of men, but seek to find your own female values, the deepest and most feminine values in your being, those of your deepest self. Try to find out who you are, in the depths of your most complete femaleness, and then dare to be what, truly, you are."

"You are my mother," she said. "You must not talk to me in this way!"

"Perhaps you are right," said the woman. "And perhaps I would not myself even dare to do so if I were not here with you, naked, in a collar, too, with a number on my breast."

"It is shameful for you to speak so!" said the girl, angrily.

"I want you to live," said the woman. "And I want you to be happy, truly happy."

"Shame!" scolded the girl.

"It is my love that prompts me to speak so," said the woman.

"I hate you!" said the girl.

"Have I truly touched something so deep in you, so familiar, so recurrent, yet so frightening, that you dare not face it," she asked, "that you would lash out so at me?"

"You are a terrible person!" said the daughter.

"I am one who loves you, more deeply than you can ever know," said the woman.

"Liar!" wept the girl.

"No," she said. "I am trying to tell you an end to lies."

"Naked female!" said the girl.

"You said, earlier, when first we discovered one another here, both stripped prisoners, the loot of soldiers, on a common chain, when I said that I had thought you might have escaped, that you had not, that the collar was on your neck."

"Yes," said the girl.

"Is it on your neck?" she asked.

"Yes, of course," said the girl. Almost inadvertently, lifting both hands, she touched it.

"Then there is no escape for you," she said.

"I know," whispered the girl. "Nor for you."

"I know," said the woman.

The girl sobbed.

"Surely you understand what this means," she said. "Soon, my lovely daughter, you will learn the delicate, lascivious draping of slave garments and the tying of slave girdles, in such a way as to accentuate your beauty for the pleasure of a master. You will be taught to kneel, and caress, and do things you have not now dreamed of. You will learn to wear chains attractively and to move in them in such a way as to drive men wild with passion. You will be taught to cook and sew, and to polish boots and scrub floors. You will learn to bring a whip to a man in your teeth, on your hands and knees, head down. You will learn to love, and to serve. You will learn to be a slave.''

"No! No!" said the girl.

"Soon your lovely thigh will feel the kiss of the blazing iron, and you will be sold," she said. "You will then have entered upon your new reality. You will then have begun your new life."

"Mother," protested the girl.

"Beware of free women," said the woman, "for you will be altogether different from them."

"Do not speak to me in this fashion!" begged the girl.

"I must speak to you," she said. "I do not know how long we might have to speak together."

"What do you mean?" asked the girl.

"At any moment a man might put a whip between us, and stop our talking," she said. "Too, soon we may never see one another again."

"Mother," she said, frightened.

"Surely you do not think we will be kept together," she said. "Soon we will both be evaluated, not as mother and daughter, but merely as women, and be taken on our diverse ways."

"You," asked the daughter, skeptically, "being evaluated as a woman."

"Yes, my dear," she said, "the same as you."

"That seems absurd," said the girl.

"I am nonetheless a woman," she said.

The girl looked down, angrily.

"Does it disturb you to think of me in that fashion?" asked the woman.

"Yes," said the girl, angrily.

"That is the way men will think of me, and look at me, I assure you," she said.

"Absurd," said the girl. "What are you even doing here? Why are you here?"

"I am here," she said, "for the same reason you are."

"Why is that?" asked the girl.

"Surely you can guess," she said.

"Why?" asked the girl.

"I was not brought here, and put here among these women, because I was your mother, I assure you," she said.

"Why, then?" asked the girl.

"I do not wish to speak," she said, "before you."

"Speak," demanded the girl.

"I have been found attractive by men," she said.

"You?" asked the girl, scornfully.

"Yes," she said. "Is it so hard to understand, or accept, that men might find your mother an attractive female, a desirable property, a lovely animal, a sex slut of interest, one whom they might think worth taking, or buying, or stealing, one they might think worth owning, one whom they might not mind having on their chain?"

"You, too, then might have to crawl to men," said the girl, "and serve them."

"Yes," said the woman, "and with the same perfection as you, my dear."

"Absurd," said the girl.

"I will doubtless be taken my way, and you yours," she said, "as no more than separate females. I see the thought offends you."

"Yes," said the girl.

"I am sorry," she said. "But I will be owned, as much as you."

"You would have to please a master, as I!" said the girl.

"Yes," she said.

"I cannot believe that," said the girl. "It makes no sense to me."

"Do you think it will be only your fair self, with all its beauty, which will soon be at the bidding of a master?" she asked.

"But you are my mother," she said.

"Surely you must understand that I must have been attractive to at least one man, at least once," she said and smiled. "Your presence would seem to attest to that."

"Not necessarily," said the girl.

"True," smiled the woman.

"You are my mother," said the girl.

"Do you think that means my body is now like ice or wood," she asked, "that I am not a human female, that I do not have feelings, that I do not have needs?"

"You cannot have needs," wept the girl. "It is improper. You are my mother!"

"Your father did not much care for me," she said. "Too, I think you, too, took me too much for granted, as little more than an object in your environment. I have been terribly lonely."

"You are my mother!" said the girl.

"I am many things," she said, "or have been many things."

"You cannot have needs," said the girl.

"Look at me," said the woman. "Do you think a woman so bared and chained, so exposed and dominated, cannot have needs? These things free me to have needs. They free me to be myself."

"Disgusting!" said the girl.

"All my life," she said, "I have wanted to kiss, and lick, and serve a man, and make him happy."

"Disgusting!" said the girl.

"Now, perhaps," she said, "I shall have the opportunity to do so."

"I cannot believe you are speaking in this fashion," said the girl.

"Look at me," she said. "I have a collar on my neck. I cannot remove it. It attaches me to a chain, with others. I am naked. Men may look upon me as they please. There is a number on my breast. I am 261, among the catches of mercenaries. I will be sold. Do not tell me how I can speak. I am, like you, a woman on a chain!"

"I am afraid, Mother," said the girl, suddenly. "I am so afraid!"

"We are all afraid," she said, holding her.

"I do not know what will happen to me," said the girl.

"None of us do," said the woman.

"I do not want to be owned," wept the girl.

"Think of it from the man's point of view," she said. "You are quite beautiful. Think of what pleasure men will take in owning you. Think how happy it will make them."

"I would then have value?" asked the girl.

"Yes," said the mother. "In time you might even become a treasure."

"No, no," said the girl, suddenly. "We must never think of things from the man's point of view!"

"Why?" asked the woman.

"I do not know!" she said. "But what pleases them, what fulfills them, what makes them so masculine, so powerful and strong, so different from us, must be denied to them!"

"Why?" asked the woman.

"I do not know," wept the girl.

"To make them piteous and weak, so that we may dominate them?" asked the mother.

"I do not know," said the girl.

"So that we can pretend we are more like them?"

"I do not know," said the girl.

"As a free female you might, if you wished, for whatever purposes, hatred or envy, the seeking of power, or whatever it might be, attempt do them such hurt, such insidious and grievous injury, but such terrible and grotesque crimes, for which legal penalties are not even prescribed, my lovely daughter, when you are a slave, will not be permitted to you."

"I am afraid to be a slave," she said.

"We all are," said the mother.

"I do not understand slaves," said the girl.

"You understand them only too well," said the mother.

"Why is it that so many of them, owning not even a bowl for their food, or their rags and collars, seem to be among the happiest of women, so radiant and fulfilled?"

"They have masters," she said.

"Mother," said the girl, timorously.

"Yes, my daughter," said the mother, encouragingly.

"This morning, near noon, on the Avenue of Adminius, I was forced to call a man Master."

"So, too, were we all," said the mother, soothingly. "It is

just their way of accustoming us to obedience, and what lies before us.''

"There was something else," she whispered.

"Yes?" asked the mother.

"I had to kiss a man's whip," she whispered.

"So, too, did we all, I am sure," said the mother, kindly.

"But it is worse," she whispered. "I fear to speak."

"Tell me," said the mother, soothingly, taking the girl's head upon her breast.

"I had feelings," said the girl. "I had never felt just those feelings before."

"I understand," said the mother.

"When I felt the stout leather thrust against my lips, I trembled," she said. "Then, as bidden, I kissed, and licked it, lingeringly. I looked up at him. I saw the ferocity, and the strength, and the uncompromising determination, in his eyes. Then, again, I bent to my work. I felt thrilled to the quick. My belly became hot. My thighs flamed. I felt wet.''

The mother kissed her, and caressed her hair, softly, soothingly.

"I am a terrible person," said the girl.

"Such feelings are perfectly natural," said the mother. "Do not be ashamed of them. They tell you what you are. It is not wrong to be what you are. It is good to be what you are, exactly what you are, whatever it may be.''

"Have you ever had such feelings?" asked the girl.

"Yes," said the mother.

"What can possibly be their meaning?" asked the girl, frightened.

"It is simple," said the mother.

"What?" asked the girl.

"That we are females," said the mother.

"Females?" said the daughter.

"Yes," said the mother. "Such feelings, of need and helplessness, are natural for us. Do not be afraid of them. They tell us what we are.''

"Are we—are we slaves, Mother?" asked the girl.

"Hush," said the mother, quickly. "One approaches; a guard.''

Quickly they separated, each looking down. The mother rested now on her right thigh and hip, her hands on the floor of the Semnium, the girl on her left thigh and hip, her hands, too, on the Semnium's floor. They did not lift their heads. They did not wish to risk meeting the eyes of the guard, calling attention to themselves. They looked well in the collars, both affixed to the chain.

The woman near me, on the marble bench, grasped it more tightly. The padlock on her collar moved on the marble. The guard was removing her ankle shackles. He then sat her upright, and unchained her wrists. The ankle chain and wrist chain he left lying over the bench, in front of her. He then took her by the hair and drew her from the bench. He walked her, bent over, to a place on the chain. A second padlock was there, marking what had been her place. He knelt her there, and then opened the padlock on the chain. Without removing it from the chain he pushed its bolt through the ring on her collar and snapped it shut. She was again a part of the chain. She lay down on the floor, in her place. The guard looked over the nearby women. None met his eyes. He was the same fellow who, earlier, had brought in the newest arrival, bound and leashed, in the Semnium.

"261," he said.

"Please, no," she said.

He regarded her.

"Master," she said, putting her head down.

A young girl, near her, gasped, hearing her mother use this word to a man.

261 was freed from the chain. He sat her on the bench, straddling it.

"Please," she said, "do not. My daughter is near." Then her ankles were shackled, the chain running under the heavy fixed-position bench. Then her wrists were enclosed in the wrist rings, the chain from them, too, running under the bench. He then put her down on the bench. She lay on it, on her stomach, her legs on either side of it. Her throat still wore the padlocked collar. The other padlock, that which had held the collar to the chain, he left on the chain. It marked the place to which she would be returned. He then left her.

In a few Ahn it would be dawn. I had not slept well. I must make the decision soon, whether or not to carry certain letters. I gathered this couriership might be not without its dangers. I glanced at the female on the bench. She was lusciously desirable. I put her from my mind.

I had reservations about taking Hurtha and Boabissia into danger. Even if they were willing, and informed, at least to the extent I was, I did not think I should permit them to accompany me. It might be too perilous for them, how perilous, of course, I did not know.

The female stirred on the bench. There was a tiny sound of chain. I forced the thought of her from my mind. She was excitingly desirable.

I had little doubt, however, that Hurtha would cheerfully come along, if asked, and perhaps if not asked, abounding with his customary indefatiguable optimism whatever might be the odds. He had already complained, more than once, that his ax was getting rusty. This is an Alar way, I took it, of saying that it had not been used lately. That was perhaps just as well. If Hurtha came with me, however, it seemed that Boabissia should be left behind. If she were left behind, however, I did not doubt but what she would soon find herself in a collar. She was that attractive. I put the woman on the bench again from my mind. I wondered what Boabissia would look like on a bench, in such a predicament. Rather well, I supposed. I might slip from the city, without them, I thought. In that way I would not carry them into danger. That would be thoughtful on my part. If I did that, of course, I might miss out on some of Hurtha's new poems. That, of course, could not be helped. I put the woman again from my mind. I wondered if I should carry the letters. I wondered if I should speak to Hurtha and Boabissia. I wondered if I should slip from the city. I did not know what to do. It was hard to sleep.

"Oh!" said the woman on the bench, stiffening, my hand on her.

"Do not relax your body," I said. "Keep it tight against my hand."

She moaned.

"You are a free woman, are you not?" I said.

"Yes," she said.

"You may relax your body," I said.

Quickly she drew herself forward on the bench, frightened, an inch or so.

"Move back," I said.

She moaned, and slid back a tiny bit.

"More," I said.

She complied, fearfully.

"More," I said.

She was now back where she had been before. "I do not now where your hand is," she said.

"It is here," I said, lifting a finger, touching her.

"Oh!" she said.

"You look well in a collar, and chains," I said.

"Please," she said. "Do not touch me."

"Why?" I asked.

"My daughter is near," she said.

"What is that to me?" I asked.

"She can see, she can hear!" she whispered. "Ohh!" She shuddered, caressed.

"You are a lusciously bodied female," I said. "Doubtless you will bring your seller a good price."

"Ohh," she said.

"When you were brought in," I said, "it seems your wrists were quite tightly bound behind you, more than with the customary tightness ample to keep a female in perfect custody."

"Sir?" she asked.

"You may call me Master," I said.

"Master?" she said.

"The way you rubbed your wrists, that suggests you were not merely bound with customary tightness, but punishment bound."

"Perhaps," she said.

"Perhaps you had showed less than absolutely perfect reference to men?" I speculated.

"No, Master," she said. "I am not a fool."

"I would guess then," I said, caressing her, "that the tie was intended to be an informative, or admonitory one, one from which you were to gather something of the meaning of your reduction in station."

"Yes," she said.

"Doubtless, then, you were formerly of some importance."

"Yes," she said. "I was important."

"Are you important now?" I asked.

"No!" she gasped.

"Are you sure?" I asked.

"Yes, yes!" she gasped.

"Who are you?" I asked.

"I am—I am 261!" she said.

I pulled her to a sitting position, before me, and then bent her backward and turned her body. "Yes," I said, "you are 261." I then put her back on her stomach. "And who is your daughter?" I asked.

"437," she said.

"Are you more beautiful than your daughter?" I asked.

"I do not know," she wept, clutching the bench.

I heard a gasp from the side, from our right, from among the other women.

I stepped from the bench, looking at the other women. "You," I said to a girl there. "Kneel, straighten your back, put your chin up, throw your hair behind your back." She did these things. "You are 437," I said, reading her number.

"Yes," she said.

"Yes, what?" I asked.

"Yes, Master," she said, quickly.

"Yes," I said to the woman on the bench, "she has something of your beauty."

"Something!" gasped the girl.

"You are both quite beautiful," I said to the woman on the bench, returning to her. "I suppose it would be difficult to say who, ultimately, under proper slave disciplines, will prove the most beautiful, but, clearly, now, at the moment, if these things are pertinent to the issue, you would bring the highest price."

"I?" asked the woman before me, wonderingly.

"Yes," I said. "But she has something of your coloring and characteristics, and is quite beautiful, and I think it likely, in time, with more experience in life and love, she might aspire to equal your beauty."

The girl gasped.

"Please," said the woman. "We are mother and daughter."

"You are only two women," I said, "two women in collars, and, at this time, you, my chained beauty, would bring a higher price on the auction block, a price she could not hope, for perhaps years, to equal or excel. To be sure, I think you are both excellent collar meat."

The woman moaned. I then renewed my attentions to her body.

"I gather it has been a long time since you have been touched," I said.

"Yes," she said. "Are you disappointed in me? Do I take too long to respond?"

"Mother!" cried the girl, scandalized.

"You are not a slave," I said. "You do not have trained, honed reflexes. Smoldering fires have not been set in your belly, never far from the surface, ready to leap into flame at the smallest touch. You are a free woman. I do not expect much of you."

"Oh!" she cried, suddenly.

"Still," I said, "you seem to have in you the promise of vitality."

"Oh!" she said.

"Interesting," I said.

"Oh!" she said. "Oh!"

"Perhaps, as in all women," I mused, "there is a slave in you."

She moaned.

"Or perhaps it is not so much that there is a slave in you," I mused, "as that you are simply a slave."

"Please do not make me yield!" she begged, suddenly. I continued to caress her.

"Do not yield, Mother!" cried the girl.

"Be silent!" she said. "Be silent! Can't you see I am in the hands of a man!"

"Mother!" cried the girl.

"Oh!" cried the woman.

"You squirm like a slut!" cried the girl.

"What you are doing to me!" cried the woman, half rearing up on the palms of her hands, the chains on her wrists.

"Lie down," I instructed her.

She then lay there, on the cool marble, clutching it, tensely, her eyes wild, her head to the left.

"Is anything wrong?" I asked.

She lay extremely still, almost rigid, tensely, on the bench. She gripped the marble tightly. It seemed she did not dare to move.

"Yes?" I asked.

"Do not make me yield," she begged. She was very beautiful, and very helpless. Such a female would indeed, I thought, bring a high price.

"Why?" I asked.

She moaned.

"Why?" I pressed. It was not necessary to beat her for not having responded promptly to my question. She was a free woman. Such tardiness in a slave, of course, is not acceptable. It can mean the whip for her.

"Please," she said.

"You want to yield, do you not?" I asked.

"No, no," she said.

"I think it has been a long time since you have yielded, if ever before you have truly yielded to a man."

"Yes," she whispered.

"Did you ever before, truly, yield to a man?" I asked.

"No," she whispered.

"I think you now suspect what it might be like to do so," I said.

"Yes, yes," she whispered, tensely.

I touched her, slightly. "Oh!" she said, grasping the marble even more tightly.

"Be strong, Mother," called the girl.

Tears fell from the woman's eyes, falling to the marble. The padlock, holding her in the close-fitting metal collar, moved a little on the smooth marble. It made a small sound. She had long, dark hair.

"I think you want to yield," I said.

"No, no," she said.

I touched her, gently. "Ohhh," she said.

"I think you want to yield," I said.

"No, no!" she said.

I again caressed her, this time with an exquisite delicacy, a brief, sweet touch that brought her, in her present condition, to the brink of an uncontrollable response. If I should continue I had little doubt but what she would, in a moment or two, be jerking on her belly, crying out in a rattle of chain, writhing helplessly on the marble, then bruising and marking the soft interiors of her lovely thighs against it, so tightly gripping it.

"No man can make you yield, Mother!" cried the girl.

I gathered she was a mere virgin. Doubtless in the next few weeks she would learn better.

"Be silent, you stupid girl!" wept the mother.

"Mother!" protested the girl.

"Why do you not wish to yield?" I asked the woman.

"My daughter," she gasped. "My daughter is here!"

"But you would be willing to yield if she were not present," I asked.

"Yes, yes!" said the woman.

"Interesting," I said.

"Mother!" protested the girl, horrified.

"Do you think I would have her removed from the room?" I asked.

"Please!" said the woman.

"No," I said.

She moaned.

"Do you not want her to know what a pleasure and a joy you can be to a man?" I asked.

"I am her mother!" she wept.

"You are only another woman in a collar," I said. "And, soon, you will be going your different ways. Besides, I do not think she is your equal in these things. Perhaps sometime she might possibly be your equal. I do not know. Perhaps you, in your love, could hope that for her, and even give her training, and advice. At present, however, dear lady, it is you, I assure you, who are the prize, you whom strong men would relish most on her belly before them. Who knows? Perhaps you will both find yourselves eventually in the same household. It might be interesting to see you competing for the favor of the same master. I have little doubt it would be you, properly enslaved, my dear, and not she, who would be most often drawn by the hair to the master's couch."

The woman sobbed.

"What has been the relationship between you and your daughter?" I asked.

The woman did not respond.

"I gather it has been distant," I said. "I gather that your love for her has been little reciprocated, that your sacrifices, your concerns and efforts in her behalf, have been little understood or appreciated. I gather that she, in the customary, unquestioning self-centeredness and vanity of her youth, seemingly so inevitable in the young, has given little concern to your feelings, to your reality as an independent woman and human being, that she has scarcely thought of you, or understood you, in these ways, that she has, typically, much taken you for granted, considering you often as little more than a convenience, a tool and fixture, in her world, as little more than her servant and satellite."

"No, no!" said the daughter.

The woman was silent.

"But such things are over now," I said.

"Yes," whispered the woman.

"You are now only two women," I said, "each in the custody of impartial iron, each destined to stand by herself on the sawdust of the slave block, each, separately, to helplessly submit to, and endure, the objective scrutiny of buyers. There it will not matter that you are mother and daughter. Probably you will not even be sold in proximity to one another, but in the order of your numbers, or in some order deemed aesthetically or commercially appropriate by professional slavers. There you will be evaluated, bid upon and purchased, as different animals, as separate properties, merely as independent items up for sale, solely on your own merits. Then you will go your own ways, doubtless never to see one another again, doubtless each to the chains of a separate master. I wonder who will make the better slave?"

I then touched her, gently, again.

"Ohhh," she said, softly.

"Who would be best?" I asked.

"I do not know," said the woman.

"Mother!" scolded the girl.

"Doubtless, in the end, under the suitable tutelage of strong men, you will both become superb," I speculated.

"Yes," whispered the woman.

"Mother!" said the girl.

"Perhaps, in the end, when you are both marvelous, there will be little to choose from between you," I speculated.

The woman said nothing.

"But now," I said, "there is a great deal to choose from, between you."

The girl cried out, in anger.

The woman groaned, clutching the bench.

"Can you imagine your daughter in slave silk?" I asked the woman. "Can you imagine her in a collar, kneeling and obeying?"

"Yes," whispered the woman.

"Do not speak so," begged the daughter.

"Can you imagine her naked, kicking in her chains," I asked, "crying out, begging for a man's touch?"

"Yes," said the woman.

The daughter put her head in her hands, sobbing.

"Hush, dear," said the woman. "It will be so."

"Men are horrid," wept the girl.

"No," she said, "they are the masters. They are as they are, as we are as we are."

"I will never yield to them," wept the girl.

"Then you will be killed," said the woman.

The girl gasped, shrinking back in the chains. "I could pretend to yield," she whispered.

"That is the crime of false yielding," said the mother. "It

is easy to detect, by infalliable physiological signs. It is punishable by death.''

"What, then, can I do?'' she wept.

"Yield truly, or die,'' she said.

"What chance have I, then?'' asked the girl.

"None,'' said the mother. "You will be a slave.''

"If you like,'' I said to the woman, "I can go over there and, in moments, one hand on the back of her neck, my other hand free, have her leaping like a child's toy.''

"No,'' said the woman. "It will be soon enough done to her, such things. She will learn, soon enough, what it is, a bond maid, to be owned by men.''

"Do not worry so much about her,'' I said.

"I am her mother,'' she said.

"I would worry more about myself, if I were you,'' I said. "I think you will find that you will prove to be a much more frequent object of male aggression than she. Merely to see you is to want to strip you and put you in a collar.''

"No!'' gasped the woman.

"I am a man, and I can vouch for it,'' I said. I gave her an intimate, friendly pat.

"Please!'' she said.

"Be silent,'' I said.

"Yes, Master,'' she said.

"I assure you,'' I said, "you are at present much more likely to excite the predations of men, to be viewed as a mere imbonded lust object, than your daughter. You are much more likely than she, at least at present, in my opinion, to discover that you have, perhaps to your terror and distress, and with predictable consequences to yourself, then a slave, occasioned their interest.

"No!'' said the girl.

"Be silent, low slave,'' I said to her.

"Low slave!'' she cried.

"I am now attending to this other woman,'' I said. "I find her of interest.''

"You are a free woman, Mother,'' said the girl. "You are not a slave. You do not have to yield to him. Resist him. Do not yield to him.''

"Do not fret, daughter," said the woman. "Can you not see? Even though he is a man, he consents to speak kindly to us. Appreciate such things, for you do not know when you will hear such words again."

"He is a brute!" said the daughter.

"The master is merciful to me," said the mother. "Can you not see? In virtue of your presence, and in respect for the delicacy of our situation, he has permitted me to almost entirely subside."

" 'Subside'!" said the daughter, scandalized.

"Yes," said the woman. "Thank you, Master."

"Oh!" said the woman.

"Do you think I am merciful?" I asked her. I feared she had misunderstood my intent.

"He is touching me again!" said the woman. She clutched the marble bench again.

"Do you truly think I am merciful?" I asked.

"No, no!" she said.

"Do you think any true man would let a curvaceous, luscious beauty like you, a mere prisoner set out for pleasure, a future slave, off the hook in a situation like this, that he would not press home his advantage, so to speak," I said.

"Tell him that that is exactly what a true man would do!" said the daughter.

"Do not be stupid," said the woman. "We are not talking here about weaklings who call themselves 'true men,' trying to disguise their weakness under false titles, but true men." Then she suddenly moaned. I found that of interest. She had not, apparently, subsided to the extent that either of us had thought. The coals of slave heat, it seemed, had not ceased to glow in her belly.

"I ask mercy," she said.

"It is denied," I informed her.

"Resist him!" said the daughter.

"His hands are strong and powerful," said the woman. "He knows what he is doing! I am soft, and female!"

"You wish to yield," I told her. "It is not difficult to tell."

"I must not, Master," she said. "My daughter is here. She would never again respect me! Ohh!"

"Is it so wrong for her to know that her mother is a hot slut?" I asked.

"Please," she begged.

"You are, you know," I said, commending her.

"I can't help it!" she wept.

"You are like a she-sleen in heat," I said. "You squirm well. You are almost as hot as a slave. It is interesting to consider what you might be like when truly in bondage."

"Please," she wept.

"You belong in a collar," I said.

"I must try to resist," she whispered tensely.

"You could, instead, of course," I said, "provide your daughter with an instructive exhibition of how a female can give incredible rapture to a man. She might profit from this lesson, carrying it to her advantage into slavery with her. You might even give her your impression, as far as your current understandings of such things might go, of such things as will soon be expected of her, of how a slave might respond to a master."

"If you take me," she said, "I will remain inert. I will not participate in your pleasure."

"You do not seem very inert to me," I said.

She squirmed.

"Was that a threat?" I asked. I lifted her head up by the hair, with both hands. The padlock on the collar swung free. I could dash her brains out on the marble bench.

"No," she said. "No, Master!"

I let her put her head down. The padlock again lay on the marble bench. There was a sound from the chains on her wrists. Beneath the bench the chain linking her ankles moved on the floor of the Semnium.

"There are many ways to take a woman," I said. "All of them are pleasurable. Much depends on the situation, and the time of day, and the preferences and tastes of the master. If you think that the pleasure of the man is inextricably linked with the pleasure of the woman you are naive. That is a common misunderstanding of the free woman. That is much like thinking that the fruit cannot be enjoyed if it has not first begged to be plucked from the tree. That is simply not true. One can simply take it and enjoy it. Indeed, there is something to be said for such takings. In them one simply imposes one's will upon the helpless other. In them one senses imperiousness and power. Those who have felt such things know their value."

"I am yours to do with as you wish," she said, "and you know it well."

"I wonder if I should force you to yield," I mused.

She lay quietly now, tense, muchly aroused, not knowing what my decision would be. Whatever it was, helpless as she was, she would abide it.

Her wrists suddenly jerked up, and were then stopped by the chain. The chain under the bench, on her ankles, moved, too, as her feet moved under the bench.

"Lie still," I told her.

I then began, with care, and exquisite delicacy, not hurrying, to exploit her profound needs, and the remarkable vitality of her body. I thought she would, in time, make a splendid slave. It would be a lucky fellow, who would have her in his collar.

"He is making me yield!" she said.

I continued to draw her gently, and as implacably as though she were bound and on a leash, up the long stairwell of her need and helplessness. It was as though, then, that I had brought her, whimpering and needful, with me, again in the Gorean fashion, down a long, patient, narrow-walled, heavily carpeted corridor, one in which her bare feet could feel the deep, soft piling of the carpeting, and through a heavy, barred door, one which I had locked behind me, showing her that there was no escape for her, and had then put her, mine, to her place at the foot of my couch.

"Take me!" she cried. "I beg you to take me!"

"I wonder if I should force you to yield," I said.

"I beg to yield!" she wept.

"Mother!" cried the girl.

"But your daughter is present," I reminded her.

"I beg to yield!" she wept. "I beg to yield!"

"No, Mother!" cried the girl. "Do not permit him to so degrade you!"

"Be silent," wept the mother. "He has put me in his power."

"When you are instructed to do so," I said, "you will yield."

"Yes, Master," she said.

"Do not yield, Mother!" cried the girl.

"You will now yield," I told her.

"Yes, Master," she said.

I now rolled again in my blankets. It was an Ahn or so until dawn. I must try to catch a bit of sleep. I felt content. I felt good. The female on the bench had now been returned to the common chain. She had been the last placed on that bench this night. When I had finished with her I had sat for a few Ehn on the bench, beside her, and had put my hand down before her. She had licked and kissed it, in gratitude, the padlock on her collar moving gently on the marble. I gathered that she had desperately needed what I had done to her. This was particularly interesting, as she was not even, as yet, a slave.

"What a slut you are!" the daughter whispered chidingly, angrily, to her mother. Her mother now lay near her, on her side, her legs drawn up.

"Yes, my daughter," said the mother.

"You were like a slave!" said the daughter.

"I will soon be a slave, truly," said the mother, "and so, too, do not forget, will you, my darling daughter."

"I do not respect you any longer," said the daughter. "You do not deserve respect any longer."

"I do not ask for your respect," said the woman. "Neither do I need it, nor any longer want it. There are things better and deeper than respect. That I have now learned. Too, when we are both enslaved, neither of us will be entitled to that commodity. Our conditions then, I assure you, will be far deeper and more biological than respect. I ask, rather, your understanding, and a little love."

"I hate you!" cried the girl.

"As you will," said the woman.

Suddenly the daughter lashed out and struck her. The mother cried out, softly, and drew her legs up more, but did not attempt to defend herself, nor to return the blow.

"Hateful slut!" hissed the daughter.

"Is it so hard for you to understand that I, like you, am a female" asked the mother, "only that, and one now, like you, naked, and in a collar?"

"Slut!" hissed the daughter.

"Are you angry," asked the woman, "that some men might prefer me to you?"

"No!" said the daughter, intensely.

"Did you wish it was you, and not I, who was chained on your belly on the bench, helplessly put out for the pleasure of strangers?"

"No!" she said, angrily.

"Are you truly so jealous of me?" asked the woman.

"No, no!" said the daughter, almost crying out, wildly.

"Be silent," said another woman on the chain. "You will get us all whipped."

"Mother," whispered the girl. "I am chained, and naked, and afraid."

"Of course you are, my dear," said the woman. She then sat up. "Come here, sweet," she said. She took her daughter gently in her arms, and held her head against her shoulder.

"What is to become of us?" asked the girl.

"We are to become slaves," said the woman softly, kissing her gently on the side of the head.

"Men will have their way with us, fully," whispered the girl.

"Of course," said the mother.

"We will exist merely for their service and pleasure," said the girl.

"Yes," said the mother, kissing her.

"I want it, Mother," whispered the girl.

"I know," said the mother, soothingly.

"How terrible I am," whispered the girl.

"No, no, you are not," smiled the mother, caressing the girl's head.

"Are we slaves, Mother?" asked the girl.

"Yes," said the mother, kissing her. "Now, rest."

"I love you, Mother," said the girl.

"I love you, too, very much," said the mother.

"Good night, Mother," whispered the girl, "261."

"Good night, 437," said the woman gently, "my daughter."

I awakened to the hand of Mincon on my shoulder. "It is time to rise," he said.

I sat up in the blankets. I glanced over to where the fair prisoners had been kept. They were gone now. They had been moved out.

Mincon handed me a packet of letters. "Here," he said. "They are all here."

"How do you know I am going to carry them?" I asked.

"Aren't you?" he asked.

"Yes," I said, and thrust them into my tunic.

"I have had your weapons, and other things, brought," he said. "Do you have the claim ticket for Feiqa?"

"Yes," I said. "It is in my wallet."

"Most of the other girls have already been picked up," he said.

"Surely it is still early," I said.

"Not really, my friend," he said. "Even Hurtha is up."

"That late?" I marveled. It was well known that Hurtha often slept past dawn. To be sure I occasionally permitted myself a similar indulgence, particularly after a pleasant evening with drink and slaves.

"Yes," said Mincon. "He and Boabissia are waiting for you, outside."

"I must speak to them," I said. "It is necessary to inform them of the dangers we might face. They might not wish to accompany me."

"I have already spoken to them," said Mincon. "Boabissia is determined to go to Ar. It seems she seeks there the answer to some mystery pertaining to her past. Hurtha, too, naturally, is undeterred."

"Naturally," I said.

"He seeks adventure," said Mincon.

"Wonderful," I said.

"He likes you," said Mincon.

"Oh?" I asked.

"Yes," said Mincon. "He appreciates finding someone who listens gladly to his poetry."

"Gladly?" I asked.

"He has already composed a poem this morning," said Mincon. "He considers it a humorous poem. It is a jolly teasing of folks who sleep late."

"*Hurtha* is composing such a poem?" I asked.

"Yes," said Mincon. "Too, aside from adventure, and such, I think he regards himself as being on Alar business."

"What is that?" I asked.

"He plans on scouting out the territories of Ar, to see if they are worth seizing by Alars."

"I think he does not quite understand what is involved," I said.

"True," said Mincon.

"I will pick up Feiqa," I said.

"Your things are over there," said Mincon.

In a few moments I was descending the outside steps of the Semnium, Feiqa heeling me, carrying my pack.

"Tal, Rarius!" called Hurtha, heartily.

"Tal, Rarius," I said to him.

"Greetings," said Boabissia.

"Greetings," I said to her. She seemed to me very pretty this morning, smiling, in the long Alar dress. I think she was wearing it a little differently. I think she had corded it a bit more snugly. Clearly the delights of her figure were more evident now within it. Perhaps I should speak to her about that. She might not realize what that sort of thing might do to men, how it might stimulate and effect them, particularly strong men. Ever since we had set her out for the fellows at the wagon camp, making some coppers on her, a subtle change had seemed to come over her, indeed, a sort of transformation was becoming more and more evident every day. She seemed to be becoming more radiant, and female. I noted she even wore the yellow metal disk on her neck, on its thong, a bit more snugly than she had before. The thong was looped twice about her neck now.

"I wish you well, all of you," said Mincon.

We bade him farewell.

"Even you, pretty, enslaved Feiqa," he said.

"Thank you, Master," she said. "And, I, too, wish you well."

Mincon then motioned to a guard. The man approached. Mincon spoke to him as though we might be strangers, unknown to him, just emerged from the Semium. "Put these civilians with the others," he said. "Usher them forth, with the others, from the city."

"Move," said the guard, going behind us, prodding us with his spear. "Over there. Get over there, with the others."

"Do not resist," I said to Hurtha.

"Very well," he said, agreeably.

"Oh!" said Feiqa, suddenly. The guard had apparently, for his amusement, touched her with the spear blade, probably putting it between her legs and moving it upward, brushing it against the interior of her thigh.

As we passed another guard she cried out, again, softly. He had apparently lifted her brief skirt with the blade of his sword, considering her. Then we were with the larger group.

"Master," said Feiqa.

"Yes?" I said.

"Let it be you," she said.

I regarded her. I saw that the attentions she had received had much aroused her, the merciless weapon metal of men about her legs and belly. Her needs were much upon her. She had passed the night alone, a checked item, awaiting a morning pickup, on a holding chain. Such attentions as she had received, particularly when they literally touch the body, are sometimes called the caresses of the master's steel.

She shuddered, facing away from me, hearing the draw of my steel. She stood very straight. She was quite pretty. I waited for a few moments, and then touched her, and then, after a time, lifted her skirt, that she could feel the air upon her, and then, after a longer time, when I was pleased to do so, let it fall. "Please, Master," she begged. "Perhaps tonight," I said. "All right," said a voice. "Now, move, all of you!" I resheathed the steel and, with Hurtha and Boabissia, now again followed by Feiqa, moved with the throng down the Avenue of Adminius toward the great gate of Torcadino.

"How terrible it must be to be a slave," said Boabissia, "and have to submit to whatever men choose to do to you."

I did not respond.

"Don't you think so?" she asked.

"What do you have in mind?" I asked.

"Like having your body touched with their steel," she said, "as poor, dear little Feiqa."

"I did not realize you were so solicitous for her," I said.

"She is a sweet little slave," said Boabissia, condescendingly.

Feiqa, behind us, made a tiny, angry noise. She had been, of course, at one time, before being collared, a free woman of high station, of the city of Samnium. This word, incidentally, is, in effect, the same word as 'Semnium', although in the western coastal dialects it is commonly pronounced as I have given the spelling here. Its original meaning is apparently "Meeting Place," and its application to a building, or a hall for the meeting of councils, is, it seems, a later development. In Feiqa's opinion, of course, Boabissia, having come from the Alar camp, was little better, if any better, than a simple barbarian.

"Did you say something, Feiqa?" I asked.

"No, Master," she said, quickly, humbly. She did not want to be beaten.

"The touching of the naked body of the slave with steel," I said, "helps her to understand that she is subject to the master in all things, totally."

"I suppose you are right," said Boabissia.

"Conceive of it touching your body," I said, "particularly as you might have to wait for it, expecting it, and knowing it was to come, and that you had to submit to it, the cool, cruel touch of it, the caress of it, and as you might be bound, or chained."

"Yes, perhaps," said Boabissia, uneasily.

"Sometimes slaves oil much more quickly after such a touch," I said.

" 'Oil'?" she asked.

"Yes," I said.

"What a horrid expression," she said.

"Not at all," I said. "It is an intimate, wonderful, exciting, succulent expression. Her body is being prepared for use."

" 'Use'!" she said.

"Of course," I said. "She is a slave."

"That is true," granted Boabissia.

"And the intimate and exciting odors attendant upon such oilings, those of the helplessly aroused female, prepared for the master's use, are quite stimulatory to a male."

"Doubtless," she said.

"And so," I said, "it is not uncommon that after such a touch, the caress of the master's steel, that the slave, cognizant then of her utter helplessness and the master's power, and her complete dependence upon his mercies, that she is totally and absolutely under his domination, yields to him quickly and lusciously."

"I see," she said. Momentarily she trembled.

We continued to move along the Avenue of Adminius. There were some two or three hundred of us. We were some two-thirds of the way, or so, back in the group. This seemed to me a good position. I thought it possible that any guards who might have the duty of supervising our exit from the city, or perhaps the duties of inspecting or searching us, might, given the numbers involved, be somewhat lax or a bit less diligent in their efforts by the time we reached them, and we were not so far back that, the guards perhaps perking up, the end of the group in sight, we might find ourselves the target of some burst of compensatory ardor. We were now beyond the lines of suspended bodies outside the Semnium. I was not sorry to leave them behind me.

We continued to move slowly along the avenue, toward the great gate.

I saw a naked slave girl kneeling to one side, at the side of a building, on the stones, her hands chained behind her to a slave ring. About her neck hung a sign on which was written,

"Free for Use." As our eyes met she swiftly lowered her head.

"Keep moving," said a guard.

Such women had apparently been put out as a municipal convenience, and to help keep order in the city. She might also, of course, have been put out for punishment, but, given the current conditions in the city, that seemed unlikely.

"What a slut," said Boabissia.

"A pretty one," I said. "And free for use, too."

"I wish they would not put them out like that," she said.

"Do you object to public drinking fountains?" I asked.

"No," she said. "But that is different."

"Oh?" I asked.

"Yes," she said. "Men are beasts, and seeing such women may get ideas. Perhaps free women would be less safe."

"The existence of such women on Gorean streets, particularly in times of stress," I said, "tends to keep free women safer."

She was silent.

"It is true," I said.

"Perhaps," she said.

"Few men will will trouble themselves to steal a dried crust of bread, perhaps even at great personal risk, if a free banquet is set forth for them. To be sure, some men are unusual."

"I am not a dried crust of bread," she said, irritably.

"It is only a figure of speech," I said.

"I am not a dried crust of bread," she said.

"You are a free woman," I said.

"If I chose to be, if I were in the least interested in that sort of thing," she said, "I could prove to be a quite tasty pudding for a man."

" 'Tasty pudding'?" I asked, pleased to hear her speak in this way.

"Yes," she said.

"That is a common misconception of untrained free women," I said. "They think themselves attractive and skilled, when they know little of attractiveness and almost nothing of skill."

"Skill?" she asked.

"Yes," I said. "There is more in pleasing a man than taking off your clothes and lying down."

"Perhaps," she said, irritably.

"Indeed," I said, "sometimes you do not take off your clothes, and you do not lie down."

"I see," she said, angrily.

"Perhaps you could get lessons from Feiqa," I said.

"Oh, no, please, Master!" cried Feiqa, fearfully. "Please, no!"

I smiled. I did not think, under the circumstances, it would be necessary to beat her. It had, after all, been a joke on my part, a capital one. To be sure, not everyone appreciates my splendid sense of humor. Boots Tarsk-Bit had not always done so, as I recalled.

"That would be absurd," said Boabissia, angrily.

"Yes, Mistress!" said Feiqa, quickly.

"To be sure," I said to Boabissia, "you are in somewhat greater danger than many free women for you have not chosen to veil yourself."

"Alar women do not wear veils," she said. "They are an artifice of civilization, fit rather for perfumed girls who would be better off in collars."

"You are not an Alar woman," said Hurtha.

"I grew up with the wagons," she said, angrily.

"That is true," he admitted, it seemed almost reluctantly. I supposed if Hurtha had encountered Boabissia under somewhat different circumstances his relationship to her would have been considerably different, for example, if he had bought her in a slave market. Her background with the wagons had perhaps, rightly or wrongly, inhibited him somewhat, I feared, keeping him from viewing her as what she essentially was, a rather juicy possibility for a female.

"You do want to be safe, don't you?" I asked Boabissia.

"Of course, of course," she said, irritably.

"Then perhaps you should not object to the occasional chaining out of slaves," I said.

"Perhaps," she said.

"And perhaps you should veil yourself."

"Nonsense," she said.

"But you do want to be safe?" I asked.

"Of course," she said.

"Then veil yourself," I said.

"No," she said.

"Well, perhaps it does not matter," I said.

"Why is that?" she asked.

"You are probably right," I said.

"What do you mean?" she asked.

"You are probably not pretty enough to interest anyone," I said.

"Nonsense," she said. "I am beautiful. And men would pay a high price for me."

Hurtha roared with laughter.

Boabissia turned about and glared at him. I was pleased she no longer possessed her dagger.

"Do not laugh," I laughed.

I, too, then, I fear, had she been armed, might have had to defend myself.

"You are stupid, both of you," she said, "like all men. You simply do not know what to make of free women."

"I am an Alar," said Hurtha. "I know what to make of free women."

"What?" she asked.

"Slaves," he roared.

"I am pretty, aren't I?" asked Boabissia.

"Yes," I said. "You are. We are teasing you."

"And I would bring a high price, would I not?" asked Boabissia.

"I would think so," I said, "at least for a new, untrained slave, for slave meat a master has not yet seasoned and prepared to his taste."

"You see?" she asked Hurtha.

Hurtha snorted with derision.

"Am I not attractive, Hurtha?" she asked.

"You?" he asked.

"I," she said, angrily.

"You are of no more interest than a she-tharlarion," he said, and if you were a she-tharlarion, I do not even think a male tharlarion would be interested in you.'' He threw back his head, laughing.

''If you saw me all soft and naked, at your feet, and perfumed and painted, and in a collar and chains, you would want me,'' she said, angrily.

Hurtha stopped laughing. Suddenly he seemed angry. His hand closed on the ax handle over his shoulder. His other hand clenched into a fist.

''Do not fear, Hurtha,'' she said, ''you big simple beast, that pleasure will never be yours.''

Hurtha did not respond, but glared angrily, fixedly ahead.

We continued on our way.

''He does think I am attractive, doesn't he?'' she asked.

''Of course,'' I said.

''And you would like to have me, too, wouldn't you?'' she asked.

''Under certain conditions, perhaps,'' I said.

''If I were a slave?'' she asked.

''Of course,'' I said.

''Of course!'' she laughed.

''Move along,'' said a guard, one of several along our route.

Boabissia began to hum an Alar tune. She seemed in fine spirits. I glanced over at her. A great transformation had come over her since the night before last, since she had been put on her back, her wrists tied to the spokes, a copper bowl resting on the dirt beside her. I wondered if she might make a suitable slave. It seemed possible. I imagined what she might look like with a collar on her neck, instead of the familiar thong and disk. I supposed it might be nice to have her. It was not too late, really, I supposed, to enslave her. One could then have her when and as one pleased.

''What is wrong?'' she asked.

''Nothing,'' I said.

''Move, move along,'' said another guard.

''Ah,'' said another, regarding Boabissia. She was, of course, not veiled.

''Move,'' said another.

''You, too, free wench,'' said another, irritably.

Boabissia would walk straightly by these fellows, regally, her head high, seemingly ignoring them, apparently not even deigning to glance at them. To be sure, I was confident she was only too keenly and pleasurably aware of their scrutiny, their appraisal and appreciation. She was now, after her experiences of the night before last, too much of an awakened female not to be aware of, and pleased at, the effects she could exercise upon men.

"Do you think it wise to behave in such fashion?" I asked her.

"In what fashion?" she asked, innocently, smiling.

"Never mind," I said.

She laughed.

To be sure, what had she to fear from them? She was a free woman. She had nothing to fear from them, absolutely nothing to fear from them, unless perhaps, one day, she should become a slave. Then she might have much to fear from them. In the distance I could see the great gate of Torcadino.

"Slut," said one of the soldiers.

Boabissia laughed, not looking at him.

"Collar meat," he called out.

She laughed again, giving him no other notice.

How well, if haughtily, she now walked. I considered the walks of free women, and of slaves. How few free women really walk their beauty. Perhaps they are ashamed of it, or fear it. Few free women walk in such a way as to display their beauty, as, for example, a slave must. I considered the length of garments. The long garments, usually worn by free women, such as that now worn by Boabissia, might cover certain defects of gait perhaps, but when one's legs are bared, as a slave's commonly are, one must walk with beauty and grace. Too, given the scantiness of many slave garments, it is sometimes necessary to walk in them with exquisite care.

The slave, for example, and this is commonly included in her training, seldom bends over to retrieve a fallen object. Rather she flexes her knees, lowering the body beautifully, and retrieves the object from a graceful and humble crouch. Sometimes, to be sure, commonly in serving at the parties of young men, certain objects, sometimes as part of a game, objects with prearranged significances among the young men, are thrown to the floor, and she must pick them up in a less graceful fashion. Whichever object she first touches determines to whose lusty abuse she must then submit. This game is sometimes played several times in the evening. I considered Boabissia. Her walk now seemed something between that of a free woman and a slave. It was, if haughty, quite good, and it showed, I thought, definite signs of slave promise. There seemed little doubt that, with some tutelage, and perhaps a collar on her neck, the beauty could be kept in it, and considerably improved, and the sullying haughtiness removed. I glanced again at her. Yes, it seemed to me that Boabissia might even be ready to walk in a slave tunic. I had little doubt but what several of the fellows she had passed, her nose in the air, would, with whips, have been more than willing to give her instruction in the matter, with or without the tunic.

"Are you sure you want to go to Ar?" I asked her. "It might be dangerous."

She touched the copper disk at her neck. "Yes," she said. "I will learn who I am."

"And who do you think you are?" I asked.

"I do not know," she said. "But I was found, as I understand it, in the remains of what had apparently been a large and wealthy caravan. Perhaps it was the caravan of my father."

"Perhaps," I said.

"At the least, passage in such a caravan would doubtless have to have been purchased, and that suggests affluence."

"That is true," I said.

"Presumably no drover, or low person, a mere employee, say, would have had a baby with him," she said.

"Probably not," I said.

"It seems likely to me, then," she said, "that I am of wealthy family."

"I suppose that is possible," I granted her. Indeed, it seemed to me to be quite possible. I was uneasy, however. The letter "Tau" on the disk, for some reason I could not place, seemed vaguely familiar to me. I wondered if, somewhere, someplace, I might have seen that particular "Tau," that is, that particular design of a Tau. "Why is there a number on the disk?" I asked.

"I do not know," she said, "but it must be some sort of an identificatory device, perhaps indexed to an address or a passenger list."

"Or a wagon number," I said, "if it was a large caravan, or, more likely, that of a merchant or company with many wagons."

"Yes," she said. "I never thought of that. That is perhaps it."

"Perhaps," I said.

"They would want to have some way of knowing where the baby belonged, I suppose," she said.

"I would suppose so," I said.

"That must be it," she said.

"Perhaps," I said.

"Would you care to hear my latest poem now," asked Hurtha, "that which lightly chides those lazy fellows who choose upon occasion to sleep late?"

"Of course," I said, grimly.

"It is a jolly poem," Hurtha informed me.

"I am certain of it," I said.

" 'Awake, abominable sluggards!' " quoth Hurtha. "That is a strong first line, isn't it?"

"Catchy," I admitted.

" 'Arise, loathsome miscreants!' " said Hurtha.

"Already you have revised the first line?" I asked.

"Certainly not," said Hurtha. "One does not tamper with that which is already perfect. That is the second line."

"You are certain that this is a humorous poem?" I asked.

"Definitely," said Hurtha, chuckling.

"I did not know you wrote humorous poems," I said.

"I am versatile," Hurtha reminded me. "I suppose you thought I spent all my time composing tragic odes."

"I had not given it that much thought," I admitted.

"I have a lighter side," said Hurtha, "though doubtless only those who know me well have detected it. Too, it is not, in my opinion, salutary for poetic growth to be too fixedly despondent.''

"I suppose not," I said.

"You may believe me in the matter," said Hurtha.

"Very well," I said.

"A little despair goes a long way," he said.

"I am sure of it," I said.

"I shall begin again," said Hurtha. " 'Get up, you odious, foul, stinking, dawdling sleen!' " said Hurtha.

"I thought you said you were going to begin again," I said.

"I am beginning with the third line," he said. He then turned to the fellow near him, an innocent fellow with a pack on his back. "This poem," he told the fellow, "is dedicated to my friend, Tarl, there. Indeed, it was he who inspired me to compose it."

"I see," said the fellow, looking at me narrowly. He then moved a bit further away.

" 'Up, up, I say, inert tarsks, vile, loathsome, somnolent slimy urts!' " cried Hurtha.

Several folks were looking at me in a strange way. I quickened my pace, staring ahead.

" 'It is noon!' " called out Hurtha. Then he stopped, and began to laugh. Tears rolled down his cheeks.

"What is wrong?" I asked.

Some folks passed us.

"I told you it was funny," laughed Hurtha, bent over.

"Yes?" I said.

"Surely the humor is not too subtle for you?" he asked suddenly, startled.

"I am not an Alar," I admitted.

Boabissia laughed merrily, but, I thought, a bit uneasily, uncertainly.

"You see," explained Hurtha, patiently, "I did not say it was morning. I said it was noon."

"Yes?" I said.

"So you would expect me to say *morning*, but, you see, it is already *past* morning. It is then *noon*."

"Oh, yes," I said, thinking that perhaps I had a glimmer

of his point, "excellent, excellent." Many Goreans arise quite early. Perhaps it is well to keep that in mind. It may help somewhat, though perhaps not significantly. Boabissia made a noise, one I think intended to desperately simulate a laugh. She was, I am sure, merely attempting to improve her claim as to being an Alar. Feiqa, happily, laboring under no such onus, looked aghast.

"We are here," I said, happily, "at the gate!"

Certain of the folks passed through the great gate of Torcadino were searched rather thoroughly. Some of the women, probably because the guards were interested in seeing them, were stripped stark naked, standing on the stones before the portal and, to their dismay, examined with Gorean efficiency. Certain coins and rings were found. After such a search a woman is sometimes good for nothing more than being a slave. But they were thrust through the gate, their clothes then clutched in their hands. Boabissia, interestingly, though quite comely, was spared this indignity. Some objects were confiscated from various folks, men and women, but little, really, was taken. I began to suspect that the treatment this group was receiving was, on the whole, little more than *pro forma*.

I also suspected, after a few Ehn, that Boabissia's immunity from Gorean Strip Search, in spite of the promise of pleasure to the guards of such a search, might be due to her party, that she was with us. The letters of the officer were now within my sheath. This tightened the draw, but the hiding place, considering the few options at my disposal, seemed a sensible one. Papers can be easily detected within tunic or cloak linings. To be sure, if one has time, the messages can be written on cloth within the linings, and then should elude search, unless the garment be torn open. There are many possible hiding places for messages or valuables, of course. A few that might be mentioned are false heels or divided soles in sandals, tiny secret compartments in rings, brooches, ornate hair pins, hollow combs, fibulae, studs and clasps. The pommels of some swords are made, too, in such a way as to unscrew, revealing such a compartment. Similarly walking sticks and staffs often have one or more such compartments in them, reached by unscrewing various sections of the stick or staff. Needless to say, some of these, too, contain, daggers or thrusting swords. Such concealed compartments and weapons, and sometimes even builders' glasses, sun chronometers, and compasses, and such, are found in such objects. It is cultural for white-clad pilgrims from certain cities to carry such staffs, often entwined with flowers, in pilgrimages to the Sardar. Such folks are not as harmless as they might seem, as various brigands have learned to their sorrow.

"You are together, all of you?" asked a guard.

"Yes," I said.

"Pass," he said.

In moments were were past the great gate, and blinking against the sun, outside the walls of Torcadino. I looked back. The walls, from this close to them, the fall sun bright on them, seemed very high and formidable. No common scaling ladders could ascend them. Too, numerous, low, horizontal wall slots, some three or four inches in height, through which metal-shod poles, stout metal crescents at their tips, could be thrust, and maneuvered, marked their bleakness. Such poles, with little danger to the defenders, at sufficient heights, where sufficient leverages can be exerted, address themselves to the enemy's ladders. Their effects are often devastating. The slots through which the poles are thrust may serve also, of course, as arrow ports. Individuals behind us were still coming through the gate. I then turned my eyes forward. I could see, some two hundred yards or so away, pennons of Cos, marking presumably the first row of siege trenches.

My hand I put inadvertently against the sheath of my sword. It was there that I had concealed the documents I carried.

"You were not searched," said a small fellow, near me. He had a mustache, like string, and narrow eyes. He had a pack on his back.

"Many were not searched," I said.

He then continued on his way, toward the pennons in the distance.

"What are we to do?" asked Boabissia, uneasily.

"Keep moving," said a soldier, outside the gate, pointing toward the pennons.

Boabissia and I, then, followed by Hurtha and Feiqa, she bearing my pack, set out, with others, toward the pennons. "I think there will be little difficulty in clearing the lines of Cos," I said. "Refugees, I suspect, will be sped on their way. I am not sure what would be the best way to approach Ar. We might reach the Argentum Road and take it east to the Viktel Aria. We would then trek south to Ar.

"That is a longer route, is it not?" asked Boabissia.

"Yes," I said.

"Why take it?" she asked.

"It is not the route we might be expected to take," I said.

"Are you afraid?" she asked.

"I am uneasy," I said.

"Could we not trek directly to Ar, across country?" she asked.

"If I were alone, I would," I said.

"I am not afraid," she said.

"In the open country, there may be sleen," I said, "particularly after dark."

"Oh," she said.

"Too," I said, "you are pretty."

"What has that to do with it?" she asked.

"Would you like to be a naked slave of peasants, a community slave, in a peasant village," I asked, "and wear a rope collar, and be taught to hoe weeds and pull a plow, and spend your nights in a sunken cage?"

"No!" she said.

"To be sure, they would probably sell you in a town, sooner or later, when they needed drinking money," I said.

She shuddered.

"I think, however," I said, "we shall take the most direct civilized route from here to Ar."

"Why?" she asked.

"To save time," I said. "Time, I think, is important."

"As you say," she said.

"We will take, then, that route called the Eastern Road, or Eastern Way," I said.

"That is the route called the Treasure Road, is it not?" she asked.

"Yes," I said.

"Why is it called that?" she asked.

"Because of the riches, and slaves, and such, often transported upon it," I said.

"I see," she said, uneasily.

"Doubtless you will see many slave caravans," I said, "and, too, perhaps, the girls of poorer merchants, many women being marched on foot, chained in coffle, sometimes gagged and blindfolded."

"Oh," she said, uneasily.

"Splendid!" said Hurtha.

I glanced back at Feiqa, who, bearing my pack, looked quickly down.

I had letters of safety. It seemed to me probably best, all things considered, to take the Treasure Road.

"Single file here," called a soldier of Cos, near the pennons. "Watch your step."

A long plank had been laid across the first of the siege ditches.

The small fellow with the narrow eyes and the mustache like string was ahead of us. He went across the plank. I then crossed it, too, the plank bending under my weight, and was followed by Boabissia, and Hurtha, and Feiqa.

"That way," said the soldier, pointing.

We were, in a few Ehn, over other entrenchments, and were then near the hurdles commanding the interior ditches. Interspersed among these was an occasional lookout tower, composed of poles and planks, the lashed poles supporting a horizontal platform of planks, from which a watch could be kept on the gate of Torcadino. At night fires would be set and lanterns hung at various points about the siegeworks.

"That way," said a soldier, directing us.

We were then within the perimeters of the Cosian camp. Most of the tents were circular, with low, sloping tops. Many were brightly colored, and set with bold stripes, and various striking designs and patterns. Goreans tend to be fond of such things. A Gorean camp is often a spectacular sight, with its arrays of silks and flags, even from a distance. They also tend to be fond of fabrics stimulatory to the touch, spices tantalizing to their taste, strong, powerful melodies, and beautiful females. In this they make clear their primitiveness, and their vitality and health. The streets were laid out geometrically. This is usually done by engineers, with surveying cords.

"Look," said Boabissia.

"I see," I said.

Seeing herself the object of our attention the girl lying on her side in the mud shrank back, pressing her back against the heavy stake, some eight inches in diameter, it sunk deeply in the mud. She did not meet our eyes. She was naked, and dirty. She was chained to the stake by a heavy chain, it looped three times about the stake, tight in a groove, and bolted in place, then looped twice about her neck and fastened there by a padlock. She could not move more than four feet from the stake.

"Girl," I said to her.

She, addressed, scrambled to her knees. She kept her head down. She whimpered.

"She does not speak," said Boabissia.

"She is perhaps under the discipline of the she-quadruped," I said.

The girl whimpered, looking at us, nodding her head affirmatively. Then she put down her head, again.

"Oh," said Boabissia. In this discipline the female is forbidden human speech. She is also forbidden human posture, in the sense that she is not allowed to rise to her feet. Her locomotion, unless commanded to roll, or put under similar commands, suitable for a pet, will be on all fours. Her food will be thrown to her, or put in pans on the ground. In either case, she must feed without the use of her hands. She may also, of course, be fed by hand, but, again, will not be permitted to touch the food with her hands. She may be taught tricks. Sometimes these are taught as functions of arbitrary sounds, so that she must learn them as any animal might, without the benefit of an earlier understanding of the words used. If she is slow to learn, of course, she is punished, as would be any other animal. When used, too, it will commonly be in the modality of the she-quadruped. This discipline is often used as a punishment, but it may also figure in the training of a new girl. It helps her to understand what she now is, an animal totally subject to her master. After some time, sometimes as little as a few Ahn, in this discipline, she begs mutely, pleadingly, as eloquently as she can, to be permitted to serve her master in fashions more typical of the normal female slave, fashions in which her bondage, because of the greater complexities and latitudes of dutifulness and subservience possible with human activity, speech and posture, for example, dance, beginning at least on her feet, and song, may be even more deliciously complete and pleasing to him. To make certain that there are no possible confusions or misunderstandings involved in such cases the master usually gives the female a brief opportunity to speak, usually only a few Ihn, in which she must make her pleas, hoping to win his favor. If he is not satisfied with her pleas, of course, she is returned promptly to the former discipline. Too, for wasting his time, she might be exposed to other disciplines, as well, usually the lash.

We continued on, through the camp. In a few Ehn, as we were making our way through a corner of the camp, we would presumably encounter some contravallation, some outer lines or ditches, set up to protect the besiegers against possible attack by an outside, relieving force.

"There," said Hurtha, pointing, "there are the pens for camp girls."

He had indicated a fenced enclosure, within which were various smaller enclosures, and some cages. In such areas, there was probably more than one in a camp of this size, public girls are kept, slaves for the pleasures of the soldiers. The Gorean seldom does without women. Such girls are usually supplied in groups by contract slavers, for the course of given campaigns. They may be used in their enclosures or, more commonly, they are sent to the tents of the men who rent them, usually for the night. In the morning they return to their masters. Outside the entrance to this enclosure, where the girls could see it, coming and going, was a simple structure of three heavy, squared timbers, two of which were upright, and the third fixed upon them, crosswise, in the manner of a lintel. In the underside of the horizontal beam there was fixed a stout ring, from which cords dangled. In these cords, her wrists crossed and bound over her head, there was now a fair prisoner. On the outside surface of the horizontal beam, the side facing us, there were two hooks, over which there hung a sign. The hooks are permanent fixtures, the signs may be changed, if one wishes to use them at all, depending on the error, deficiency or offense. This sign read, "I was not fully pleasing to my master of the night. Punish me. Use whip at left." To the girl's left, on the vertical beam there, suspended from a hook, was a five-stranded Gorean slave lash.

"Wait," said Boabissia.

"Yes?" I said.

"She was not fully pleasing," said Boabissia.

The girl tensed in the cords, hearing us behind her.

"It would seem not," I said.

"Are you not going to strike her?" asked Boabissia.

"I think she has already been well punished," I said. Certainly the girl's back suggested that. To be sure, most of those stripes had probably been put on her earlier by her master, that he might assure himself that no matter what happened later in the day, the girl would be brought to understand that anything less than perfect performance was not to be tolerated in a female slave. The female slave is not permitted flaws in her service. She is not purchased for that. They will not escape notice, or correction.

"Men are weak," said Boabissia. She went to the hook and removed the lash. "Girl," she said.

"Yes, Mistress," said the girl, frightened.

"You were not fully pleasing to your master of the night," said Boabissia, sternly.

"Yes, Mistress," said the girl, trembling.

"Let her go," I said. "You can see she has been liberally whipped."

"What are you?" asked Boabissia.

"A slave, Mistress," said the girl, trembling in the confining cords. Her small hands twisted above the tight loops.

"Then it is up to you to be pleasing," said Boabissia.

"Yes, Mistress," said the girl.

"Fully pleasing," said Boabissia.

"Yes, Mistress," said the girl.

"But you were not," said Boabissia.

"No, Mistress," said the girl, trembling.

"You must then be punished," said Boabissia.

"Yes, Mistress," moaned the girl.

"She has already been punished," I said to Boabissia. "Show her mercy."

"No," said Boabissia.

"Girl," I said to the bound slave.

"Yes, Master!" she cried, eagerly.

"Is it your intention to improve your service in the future?" I asked.

"Yes, Master!" she said.

"And will you strive to be a dream of perfection to your masters hereafter, no matter how brief your term of service may be to them, or whoever they might be?"

"Yes, Master! Yes, Master!" she said.

"You see, Boabissia?" I asked.

"She is lying," said Boabissia. "I am a female. I can tell."

"No, Mistress!" wept the girl.

"Are you lying?" I asked the girl.

"No, no, Master!" she wept.

"I believe her," I said. "Let us be on our way."

"You are apparently more tolerant than I of inadequacies in a slave," said Boabissia.

"Let us go," I said.

"Not yet," she said.

"Come along," said Hurtha.

"I know females," said Boabissia. "I am one of them. If you are weak with them, they will take away your manhood and destroy you. If you are strong with them, they will lick your feet with gratitude."

She touched the body of the female slave with the whip. "Is it not so?" she asked the girl.

"Yes, Mistress," wept the girl.

"If you are not strict with slaves," said Boabissia, "they will grow lax, and then arrogant, and then begin to assume the airs of free persons."

"I suppose that is true," I said.

"They must be kept under perfect discipline," said Boabissia, "absolutely uncompromising and perfect discipline."

"Of course," I said.

Boabissia drew back the whip. How she hated the female slave. It is sometimes hard to understand the hatred of the free female for her imbonded sister. It has to do, I suppose, with the venomous jealousy of a woman who has taken an unhappy path, a road commended to her by many but one which she has discovered leads only to her ultimate frustration, misery and lack of fulfillment. No woman is truly happy until she occupies her place in the order of nature.

"Do not strike her," I said.

"I am a free woman," said Boabissia, "and I shall do as I please."

"Do not strike her," said Hurtha. "Come along."

"Men are weak," said Boabissia. "I will teach you what women deserve, and need."

"Please, no, Mistress!" wept the girl.

Boabissia then, holding to the butt of the whip with two hands, swung it back, the lashes separated, free.

"Please, no, Mistress!" cried the girl.

Boabissia then, taking her time, struck her five times. She did not spare the wench. Then the girl, punished, hung in the cords, gasping, weeping.

"Now will you be pleasing to your masters?" asked Boabissia.

"Yes, Mistress," wept the girl.

"Now have you learned your lesson?" asked Boabissia.

"Yes, Mistress. Yes, Mistress," wept the girl.

"She is now telling the truth," said Boabissia. She then hung the whip again on its hook.

I looked into the eyes of the slave. Swiftly she put down

her head. But in that instant I saw that what Boabissia had said was true. She would now be pleasing. She had now learned her lesson.

"Now," said Boabissia, "let us go."

"Interesting," I said.

"You must learn how to handle women," said Boabissia. "That is all."

"You are a woman," I said.

"Do not be clever," she said. "I am a free woman."

"This way, this way," said a Cosian soldier. "Do not straggle."

We then again set out on our way, following others. In my wallet there was a sack of coins, a plentiful supply of coins, though mostly of small denomination, such as would not be likely to attract attention. They had been given to me by the officer in Torcadino. I had kept them. I would attempt to discharge his commission. They would be more than enough, it seemed, to get us to Ar. In my sheath were his letters, and my letters of safety. I did not know what lay before me.

"That way," said a soldier.

"You have not yet heard my entire poem," said Hurtha.

"True," I admitted, reluctantly.

Then, for several Ehn, he altering lines here and there, with a liberal abandon, subjecting the piece, it seemed, to immediate and amazing revisions, rampant and wholesale, doubtless justified by certain disputable if not heinous exploitations of poetic license, generously construed, I was regaled by Hurtha's latest creation.

"What do you think?" he asked.

"I have never heard anything just like it," I admitted.

"Really?" he asked, eagerly.

"Yes," I said, "except, of course, certain of your other poems."

"Of course," he said. "Do you think it will become immortal?"

"It is hard to say," I said. "Are you worried about it?"

"Somewhat," he said.

"Why?" I inquired.

"Because it is dedicated to you, my friend," he said.

"I do not understand," I said.

"Suppose it becomes immortal," he said.

"Yes?" I said.

"It well might do so," he said, "for it is a genuine Hurtha."

"Yes?" I said.

"Then you might be remembered in history as being no more than a despicable, loathsome, notorious sleepyhead."

"I see your point," I admitted.

"And even if that should be true," he said, "you are still my dear friend, in spite of all, and I simply could not bring myself to do that to you. What am I to do?"

"Dedicate it to some mythical fellow," I said, "someone you just made up."

"A splendid suggestion!" cried Hurtha. He then turned to one of our fellow refugees. "Excuse me, Sir," he said, "but what is your name?"

"Gnieus Sorissius, of Brundisium," he said.

"Thank you, Sir," said Hurtha. He then turned back to me. "I shall dedicate the poem to Gnieus Sorissius, of Brundisium."

"What?" asked Gnieus Sorissius, of that coastal city.

"Rejoice," said Hurtha to him. "You may now die, for you have just become immortal."

"What?" asked Gnieus Sorissius, somewhat alarmed. Hurtha was, after all, carrying a large ax.

"But what if you discard your poem," I asked, "feeling as you often do, that it may not be up to your incredible standards, or what if you should be struck heavily upon the head, as I could conceive happening, sometimes more readily than others, and simply forget it?"

"I see your point," said Hurtha, gravely. "I would then be denying poor Gnieus his place in history."

"Of course," I said. "It is not fair to make him so dependent on you."

"Yes," said Hurtha.

"Suppose, thinking himself immortal," I said, "he then lives recklessly, fearing nothing, takes unwise risks gleefully and perhaps suffers unfortunate and grievous consequences?"

"I had not thought of that," admitted Hurtha.

"You might feel terribly responsible," I said.

"Yes," said Hurtha. "I am a sensitive fellow."

"Too, he might then go through life uneasily, not knowing whether you had kept the poem not, and thus not knowing whether he was still immortal or not."

"True," moaned Hurtha. "What am I to do?"

"Is this that poem about fellows who sleep late," asked Gnieus, "that one you have been carrying on about for the past ten Ehn?"

"Yes," said Hurtha.

"Well," said Gnieus, "it is my habit to arise each morning by the fourth Ahn."

"The fourth Ahn?" cried Hurtha, aghast. "That is rather early."

"In my opinion," snapped the fellow, who seemed in a rather disagreeable mood, perhaps still somewhat disgruntled at having been turned out of Torcadino with little more than the clothes on his back, "folks who remain longer in the furs are no better than lazy sleen."

"Oh," said Hurtha. He shuddered.

"Yes," said the fellow.

"I am afraid I cannot dedicate my poem to you," said Hurtha. "You get up just too early."

"It is just as well," said Gnieus, "for I charge a fee for having poems dedicated to me."

"What?" cried Hurtha.

I decided I liked Gnieus. He was not a bad fellow, even for coming from Brundisium.

"A silver tarsk," snapped Gnieus.

"That is very expensive," said Hurtha.

"That is what I charge," said the fellow.

"Do we have a silver tarsk?" asked Hurtha.

"You would sell your priceless dedications, for mere money?" I asked.

"Never!" cried Hurtha, resolved.

That was a close one. I had saved a silver tarsk, or its equivalent in smaller coins.

Gnieus Sorissius had now taken his leave.

"What a scroundrel," growled Hurtha, looking after him.

"Indeed," I admitted. I wished that I had managed to handle my large friend as neatly as Gnieus Sorissius, even if he was from Brundisium. Perhaps he had had dealings with Alar poets before. Could that be?

"Perhaps I shall have to dedicate the poem to you, after all," said Hurtha.

"We have now come to the edge of the camp," I said.

We paused, to look back. We were on a slight slope.

"How beautiful it is," said Boabissia.

The camp was a splendid sight. Torcadino was in the distance.

"I think," said Hurtha, looking back, "I shall compose a poem, a mood piece."

"What about the poem about fellows who sleep late?" I asked.

"I think I shall discard it," he said. "The subject is trivial, and perhaps unworthy of my powers. Do you mind, much?"

"No," I said.

"Good fellow," said Hurtha.

"That also solves your problem about the dedication," I said.

"It does, doesn't it?" he said.

"Yes," I said.

"Since I have saved us a silver tarsk then," he said, "perhaps you would be so good as to divide a tarsk with me, sharing and sharing alike, as always."

"Very well," I said. Alars are not always adept at mathematics, but many of them are large, fearsome fellows.

"Thank you," said Hurtha.

"Think nothing of it," I said. "How often can one save a tarsk so adroitly? Had there been two fellows we might have saved two tarsks."

"No," said Hurtha. "For there was only one dedication."

"You are right, of course," I said.

"Let us go," said Hurtha.

"Wait, just a moment," I said.

"Yes?" he said.

"Do you notice anything unusual about the camp?" I asked.

"It is very beautiful," said Hurtha, "as was observed even by Boabissia, who is only a female."

"Something else," I said.

"What?" he asked.

"We are beyond the camp," I said.

"Yes?" he said.

"There is no contravallation here," I said, "no defending, outer ditches, nothing to protect the camp against outside attack."

"Interesting," said Hurtha.

"The Cosians," I said, "apparently do not fear the arrival of a relieving force from Ar."

"That seems very strange, does it not?" asked Hurtha.

"I find it very troubling," I said. "I do not understand it. It is simply, if nothing else, a matter of routine military precaution."

"How can they be so sure that Ar will not come to the relief of Torcadino?" asked Hurtha.

"I do not know," I said. I found this detail, however, the absence of external contravallation, like many others in the past weeks, disturbing. It seemed to be a new military anomaly. It, like several of the other things, such as the absence of fortified camps and defended supply trains, seemed inexplicable, and, cumulatively now, alarmingly so.

"What can explain such things?" asked Hurtha.

"I do not know," I said. "I am uneasy."

"I think we should go on," said a man, another refugee with us. "If we are caught here we may be taken for loiterers, or spies."

"That is true," I granted him.

I then looked back at Feiqa, the former Lady Charlotte of Samnium. She wore a brief slave tunic, with a neckline that plunged to her belly. The soft, interior curvatures of her breasts could be seen within the opening of the garment. This is suitable for women who are only slaves. I considered her. She was lovely. I went to stand near her, the camp and the walls of Torcadino behind her. I put my hands within her garment. She looked up at me. My touch was gentle. The straps of my pack, which she bore for me, were wet and hot on her shoulders. There were bands of sweat beneath the straps, and beneath them, too, the tunic was wet and wrinkled. Some of the wrinkles would leave a mark on her skin for a time. Her breasts felt interesting, warm, full, moist with sweat. She had a collar locked on her neck. She was mine.

"Let us go," said Boabissia.

"Tonight," I said, "we will have to get you cleaned up. Your body is sweaty. Your feet are dirty."

"Yes, Master," she said, pressing herself softly, purring, like the small, sweet, owned beast she was, against my hands. I put down my head and let her lift her lips to mine, where they briefly met. "Ah," she said, softly. Then I lifted my head away from her. I removed my hands from her. I drew then the sides of her tunic back to their original position. I held her then by the upper arms. My grip was tight. She could not think of freeing herself. "You are a slave, are you not?" I asked.

"Yes, Master," she said, "totally, and yours, completely!"

I turned her about, facing the camp, with Torcadino in the distance.

"Do you think you have the favor of your master?" I asked.

"It is my fervent hope that I do," she said.

"Do you see that area?" I asked, pointing.

"Yes, Master," she said.

"Speak," I said.

"It is the enclosure of camp girls," she said.

"Yes," I said. "Do you recall a girl there," I asked, "one who had not been fully pleasing last night to a rent master?"

"Yes, Master," she said.

"What was done to her?" I asked.

"She was whipped, mercilessly," she said.

"Tonight," I said, "you will serve me."

"Yes, Master," she said.

"What will be done to you, if you are not fully pleasing?" I asked.

"I will be whipped, mercilessly," she said.

"Do you object?" I asked.

"No, Master," she said. "I would have it no other way."

I then stepped away from her, and rejoined the others. "That is the Treasure Road," I said, indicating a narrow road in the distance. "At its end lies Ar."

"Let us be on our way," said Boabissia. "I am eager to reach Ar."

I glanced back once at Feiqa. She smiled. She was very beautiful. I would look forward to having her tonight. I was confident she would prove to be fully pleasing. If she were not, of course, I would whip her, and well. One cannot compromise with female slaves. They are women.

We then began to descend from the crest of the slope, making our way slowly toward the road. Most of the refugees were already there, or in its vicinity. In my sheath were the letters of safety, and, below them, thrust down beneath them, the letters given to me by the officer, he who was now the master of Torcadino. These letters, all, bore his signature. The signature was written in an ascendant, bold script. It was not difficult to read. It was "Dietrich of Tarnburg." I noticed the small fellow with narrow eyes, he with the mustache like string, nearby. He had apparently lagged behind. I did not give this much thought at the time.

17: Slavery Agrees with Feiqa

"Papers, papers?" inquired the soldier. "Have you papers?"

"No," I said. I did not think it would be wise to advertise my possession of letters of safety until it should prove impossible to proceed further without them.

He then went to others, making the same inquiry. None of the refugees, of course, carried such papers.

We were in a roadside camp, eleven days from Torcadino. It was not a bad camp. There was shade, and a spring nearby. Peasants came there to sell produce. In a few Ehn Boabissia, Hurtha and I, and Feiqa, would be again on our way. I had purchased passage on a fee cart.

"It is good to see a uniform of Ar," said a man.

"Yes," I said.

"Does one need papers?" the small fellow with the mustache like string was asking the soldier.

The soldier did not respond to him.

"Can one enter Ar without them?" he asked.

But the soldier had then continued on his way.

Boabissia came up to me. "I have spoken to the driver," she said. "He is ready to leave." Many of the refugees, afoot, had already left the camp.

I nodded.

"You are looking pretty, Feiqa," observed Boabissia, somewhat critically.

Feiqa looked up smiling from where she knelt, packing my things. "Thank you, beautiful Mistress," she said, and then put down her head.

"Slavery apparently agrees with you, slut," said Boabissia.

"Yes, Mistress. Thank you, Mistress," said Feiqa, smiling, looking down.

"Cart Seventeen will leave in two Ehn!" called a fellow.

"That is our cart," said Boabissia.

"We had better get Hurtha," I said.

"He is still asleep," she said.

"Awaken him," I said. "He can sleep on the cart."

"Finish that packing, slut," said Boabissia to Feiqa.

"Yes, Mistress!" she said.

Boabissia then went to awaken Hurtha. I did not envy her this task. It was not always easy to awaken the Alar giant.

"I am ready, Master," said Feiqa, smiling, shouldering my pack.

I went to Feiqa and put my hands on the collar on her throat. She looked up at me, eagerly.

"Apparently slavery does agree with you," I said, looking into her eyes.

"Oh, yes, Master," she whispered. "Yes, yes!"

18: The Treasure Road

"Way! Make way!" called the driver. He sat on the wagon box, some yard or so below, and separated from, the high railed wagon bed, serving, with its benches, as the passenger area. The wheels of the cart were narrow, and some seven feet in height. There were two of them. They were treaded with strips of metal. The cart was drawn by a bipedalian tharlarion, a slighter breed than, but related to, and swifter than, the common shock tharlarion used generally by the lancers of Gorean heavy cavalry.

"Rich tarsks," snarled a fellow on the road, moving to the side.

"Make way!" called the driver, cracking his whip. The arrival of the cart was announced as well by the jangling of two bells, affixed to projections on its sides, before the wheels. Then we were through the group of refugees, and moving swiftly again.

"I think little treasure moves these days upon this road," said Hurtha.

"You are doubtless right," I said, "and the traffic, it seems, flows toward Ar."

"Will the Cosians take this route?" asked Hurtha.

"Probably," I said. "It is the most direct route between Torcadino and Ar."

I glanced at Boabissia. She was standing at the front of the cart, grasping the front rail, looking forward. Her hair and dress were blown backward in the wind.

"Look," I said to Hurtha. "See the soldier by the road, there?"

"Yes," he said, turning about to get a better look.

"That is another uniform of Ar," I said.

"That is comforting news," said the fellow to my right. We had seen few such uniforms lately.

"Are you going to Ar?" asked the small fellow sitting across from me. It was he who had the thin mustache.

"Yes," I said.

"Do you have papers?" he asked.

"No," I said.

"Oh," he said, smiling.

"Why?" I asked.

"I assume Ar will not accommodate all the refugees who may seek asylum there," he said. "It is hard to see how she could. Doubtless papers, or letters, might be needed."

"Perhaps," I said.

"Such might be worth their weight in gold," he speculated.

"Perhaps," I said.

He leaned forward, confidentially. "Are you carrying valuables?" he whispered.

"No," I said. My left hand, I fear, moved, as though to touch the sheath beside me. Then I checked the movement.

"It is just as well," he said.

"Why?" I asked.

"Do you see the fellow at the end of your bench?" he asked.

"Yes," I said. "Why?"

He covered the right side of his mouth with his open hand. "That is Ephialtes," he whispered, "the notorious thief of Torcadino. Beware of him."

"My thanks," I said. It is always good to have such warnings.

The fellow nodded, and sat back on his bench, leaning back against the railing.

I resolved that I must watch out for the fellow at the end of the bench, Ephialtes. I was grateful to the fellow across the way for pointing this out to me.

In the back of the cart there was a place for baggage. It was there, in that section, behind that railing, that I had put Feiqa. This was appropriate, as she was property. She was in chains. I did not fear that she would attempt to escape. But it is good, from time to time, to so secure your girls. Just as they are subject to the whip, so, too, are they subject to chains.

I rose to my feet and went to stand beside Boabissia.

"Greetings," she said.

"Greetings," I said to her.

"I cannot wait to see Ar," she said.

"If you are standing here, hoping for a first glimpse of Ar," I said, "you are a few days too early."

"I cannot wait to get to Ar," she said.

"Look," I said, gesturing to the side of the road with my head.

"Female slaves," she said, noting them, as we sped past. They were off the road, on the grass, in various attitudes of rest.

"They could give them clothing," she said.

"The day is warm," I said. "Too, such women are often marched naked to save their tunics, that they may not be soiled with dirt and sweat."

The girls were chained together by the neck. Some of them watched us as we passed. Then they were behind us.

"Normally, many more slaves are transported on this road," I said. "We have actually seen very few."

"What will I find in Ar?" asked Boabissia. She fingered the copper disk at her neck.

"I do not know," I said.

"I think I may have a great inheritance," she said. "Perhaps I shall find I own vast estates, that funds in trust have been left for me, that I am of noble family, that I am one of the richest and most powerful women in Ar!"

"Why should you think such things?" I asked.

"Do you think them impossible?" she asked, turning to me.

"No," I said. "I do not think they would be impossible."

"I was traveling, though only a baby, with a great caravan," she said. "Does that not bespeak station and wealth?"

I shrugged. "I do not know," I said.

"I think it possible," she said.

"Yes," I said. "It is possible, surely."

"Look at those poor women," said Boabissia. We were now passing, they had been coming towards us, three sturdy lasses under the herd stick of a brawny male. They were bent almost double under towering burdens of branches and sticks, bound together in fagots. They were moving single file. They were tied together, a rope on their necks. They looked up as the fee cart passed them. The male waved to our driver, who returned the salute.

"Such a fate might have been yours," I said, "had we attempted to reach Ar across country."

"They are slaves?" she asked.

"Of course," I said.

"Oh," she said, "then it does not matter."

"I had not anticipated the possibility of buying passage on a fee cart," I said. "I did not know any would still be running. Else I would not even have considered traveling across country, at least with a free woman."

"We are making excellent time," she said.

"Yes," I said. "In a few days we should reach Ar."

"Is it a beautiful city?" she asked.

"Yes," I told her.

"I am certain," said Boabissia, happily, fingering the small copper disk at her neck, "that I am of lofty birth, and high station. I cannot wait until I get to Ar, to claim my glory and wealth!"

I did not respond.

"There is no telling, what with interest rates on the Street of Coins, the maturation of notes, and such, to what heights my fortune, in these several years, may have soared."

I did not respond.

"I may be one of the noblest, richest and most powerful women in Ar," she said.

"Perhaps," I said.

We then passed a cage wagon. There were some five female slaves within it, in rag tunics. Two of them held the bars of the cage, watching us, as we passed.

"They are probably on their way to a market, somewhere," I said.

"Feiqa is looking well lately," said Boabissia, somewhat critically.

"Yes, I think so," I said.

"What are you doing with her at night?" asked Boabissia.

"I do not know," I said. "I suppose the usual things masters do with slaves."

"I see," said Boabissia. "I spoke to her this morning."

"Oh?" I said.

"Yes," said Boabissia. "She seems frightened of me."

"You are a free woman," I told her.

"She did not dare even to look into my eyes," she said.

"Perhaps she feared to be thought too forward or bold, looking into the eyes of a free woman," I said.

"Perhaps," said Boabissia. "Is she so timid with you?"

"Sometimes," I said.

"I do not think you have beaten her much lately," said Boabissia.

"No," I said.

"Why not?" asked Boabissia.

"She is now pretty well trained," I said.

" 'Trained,' " said Boabissia.

"Yes," I said, "ideally, once a girl is trained, suitably trained, of course, there is not likely to be much call for beating her. She may also, of course," I said, "be beaten at the master's pleasure, for any reason or for no reason."

"Of course," said Boabissia. "She is a slave."

"Too, some masters feel that a girl should be whipped once in a while, if only to help her keep clearly in mind that she is still a slave. Such whippings, occasionally administered, are thought by many to have a salutary effect on her."

"Of course," said Boabissia. "One must be strict with slaves."

"To be sure," I said, "a skilled, diligent slave is seldom beaten."

"Perhaps," said Boabissia, "but I think it is still good for them to feel the whip once in a while."

"Perhaps you are right," I said.

"If I were a man," she said, "I would be merciless with them."

I was silent.

"I would teach them their sex, and quickly, and no two ways about it," she said.

"It is perhaps fortunate for them that you are not a man," I said.

"Perhaps," she laughed.

"You are not a man," I said.

"I know," she said.

"Do you?" I asked.

"Of course," she said.

"You are a beautiful young woman," I said.

She blushed, even with the wind against her face.

"Perhaps you should hope, and desperately," I said, "that you never fall slave."

"Why?" she asked.

"Because perhaps you might fall into the hands of a fellow who might be as rigorous and strict with you, as you would be, or as you seem to claim you would be, had you a female such as yourself in your power, and you were a man."

"But I am a free woman."

"Feiqa was once free," I said.

"Not really," she said.

"Oh?" I asked.

"No," she said. "I spoke to Feiqa the other day. I asked her if she was a natural slave. Do you know what she said?"

"No," I said.

"She said, " 'Yes.' "

"I think it is true," I said.

"Is it true that she begged bondage," asked Boabissia, "that she chose slavery of her own free will?"

"Yes," I said.

"What a fool," said Boabissia.

"Perhaps," I said. To be sure, such a decision should not be made lightly. Such a decision may be made of one's own free will, but it cannot be revoked by one's own free will, for, after it is made, one is then helpless to alter or influence one's new condition in any way.

"You do not think so?" asked Boabissia.

"No," I said.

"Why not?" asked Boabissia.

"Suppose some women were natural slaves," I said.

"Some wicked, low women?" asked Boabissia.

"If you like," I said.

"Continue," she said.

"If some women are natural slaves, and know this in their hearts," I said, "would you prefer that they conceal this from the world? Do such lies please you? Do you commend them, truly? Would you advise these women to indulge in deceit, to rejoice in the practice of hypocrisy? What do you say to their needs? Are these of no importance, because they may not appeal to you, personally? Do you encourage them to deprivation? Do you really prescribe for them in their tumult and yearning larger and larger, and more and more bitter, doses of frustration? Must everyone be as you think perhaps you yourself should be, as you desperately command yourself to be? What do you fear? What accounts for your hostility, your venomous resentment? Would you truly keep them from their natural fulfillment?"

"I suppose not," said Boabissia, "if they are truly such things."

"Yet, there are some I have heard of," I said, "who might deny a natural slave her bondage, even by law, no matter what might be the mental, emotional and physical damage of this."

"That is absurd," said Boabissia. "Slavery is fitting, morally and legally, for the natural slave, of course. No one in their right mind could conceive of denying that."

"For natural slaves?" I said.

"Yes," she said.

"A wench such as Feiqa?" I said.

"Of course," said Boabissia.

"In such a case then," I said, "if Feiqa is a natural slave, it might be fitting, don't you think, that she acknowledged this, and then entered humbly upon her authentic reality."

"Yes," said Boabissia, "as she is such a slut."

"Perhaps you think it was even morally incumbent upon her, given what she was, to have done so?" I asked.

"I think it was fitting, that it was fully appropriate," said

Boabissia, uneasily, "but I do not think it was her actual duty to have done so."

"Then you might see her act, considering all that is involved, the bold confession, the loss of status, the stern nature of bondage, the now belonging helplessly and totally to a master, how free women will now treat her and look upon her, as the act of a very brave woman," I said.

"Or of a very desperate one," said Boabissia, "perhaps one who has fought with herself for so long and so painfully that at last she can stand it no longer, and in piteous surrender and relief flings herself to the feet of a man, where she belongs."

"Perhaps," I said.

"Such a fate is appropriate for natural slaves," said Boabissia scornfully. "The sooner they get the collars on their necks the better."

"The better?" I asked.

"The better for themselves, the better for men, the beasts, and the better for noble free women, whom they can then no longer pretend to be like."

"I am glad to hear you say that," I said.

"Oh?" asked Boabissia.

"Yes," I said, "for all women are natural slaves."

"No!" cried Boabissia. "No!"

"And no woman," I said, "can be completely fulfilled unless she understands this, accepts it and behaves accordingly."

"No!" said Boabissia. "No! No!"

"It is just a theory," I said.

Boabissia clung to the rail, gasping. Her hands were white on the rail. She was trembling.

"Are you all right?" I asked.

"Yes," she whispered, her head down, clinging to the rail. I could not help thinking how lovely a collar would look on her throat.

She looked up. "It is only a theory, is it not?" she asked.

"Yes," I said.

She shook, clinging to the rail.

"To be sure," I said, "it may be a true theory."

She did not respond. I then, seeing that she was distressed, returned to my seat. After a time, she returned, too, to her place on the bench. She did not meet my eyes, then, nor those of Hurtha, nor, I think, of any of the other men in the cart.

19: The Checkpoint

"They are gone!" I whispered, tensely.

"What are gone?" asked Hurtha, sitting up in the furs, a few feet from me.

The camp had been stirring now for better than an Ahn.

"The letters of safety," I said, "those of safe conduct for our party."

"What is wrong?" asked Boabissia, her hair wet and loose, come from the nearby stream, where she had washed it.

"Our letters of safety," I said, "are gone. I had them here, in the sheath."

"Perhaps they have fallen out," she said.

"No," I said. "They were firmly lodged within. They could be withdrawn only purposefully."

"There is supposedly a checkpoint down the road," said Boabissia. "I heard of it last night."

"So, too, doubtless," said I, "did the thief."

"We were all about," said Boabissia. "How could anyone have done it?"

"Presumably it could have been done only by one practiced in stealth, who knew for what he was searching, and where it might be found. He might even have had a tool for the extraction of the papers."

"The blade was in the sheath, was it not," asked Boabissia, "and the sheath beside you?"

"Yes," I said, "and the sheath was on its strap, slung about my shoulder. The blade would have had to be removed, I assume, and then replaced, after the extraction of the papers."

"Why would it be replaced?" asked Hurtha.

"That the absence of the papers not be immediately noticed,"
I said. "I would not have noticed the matter had I not, as a
matter of habit, this morning, tested the draw of the blade."
This habit, unnecessary and trivial though it may seem, is one
inculcated in warriors, in many cities. The theory is not only
that it is well to practice the draw frequently, as the first to
draw may be the first to strike, but also to be familiar with it
on a daily basis lest its parameters alter from time to time, due
to such things as contractions and swellings of the leather,
these having to do with temperature and moisture. Less
obviously, but more deviously, the blade could be tightened,
or even fastened, in the sheath by an enemy, by such means
as a tiny wooden shim or plug, or a fine wire looped below
the hilt. The practicing of the draw, and the associated testing
of sheath resistance, is a small, but seldom neglected detail,
in the practice of arms.

"Such skill seems impossible," said Boabissia. "Who is
there who could have done such a thing?"

"Some warriors could have done it," I said. "Many red
savages could have done it."

"But who is about here?" asked Boabissia.

"Some thief," I said, "one who is highly skillful, one
worthy even of the thief's scar of Port Kar, though I doubt he
wears it." The thief's scar in Port Kar is a tiny, three-
pronged brand, burned into the face over the right cheekbone.
It marks the members of the Caste of Thieves in Port Kar.
That is the only city in which, as far as I know, there is a
recognized caste for thieves. They tend to be quite proud of
their calling, it being handed down often from father to son.
There are various perquisites connected with membership in
this caste, among them, if one is a professional thief, protection from being hunted down and killed by caste members,
who tend to be quite jealous of their various territories and
prerogatives. Because of the caste of thieves there is probably
much less thievery in Port Kar than in most cities of comparable size. They regulate their numbers and craft in much the
same way that, in many cities, the various castes, such as
those of the metal workers or cloth workers, do theirs.

"Feiqa," said Boabissia.

"Yes, Mistress?" said Feiqa, frightened. The lovely slave had knelt immediately, being addressed by a free person.

"Did you see anything?" asked Boabissia.

"No, Mistress," said Feiqa, putting her head down.

"Stupid slave," said Boabissia.

"Yes, Mistress," whispered Feiqa, not looking up.

"Are such papers needed at the checkpoint?" asked Hurtha.

"Quite possibly," I said. "We are near Ar. I do not know."

"In this camp," said Boabissia, "it seems unlikely that there could have been so skilled a thief."

"Not necessarily," I said.

"I think Feiqa took them," said Boabissia.

"No, Mistress!" cried Feiqa.

"Let her be tortured for the truth," said Boabissia. It is legal in Gorean courts for the testimony of slaves to be taken under torture. Indeed, it is commonly done.

"Please, no, Mistress," wept Feiqa.

"It would have been difficult for her to have done so," I told Boabissia, "for last night her hands were chained behind her, that she might awaken me intimately, not using her hands, at dawn."

"Disgusting," said Boabissia.

"I then put her to her back and caressed her, while recovering, until she begged to be put to further use, to which plea I acceded. I then, when pleased to do so, a time or so later, released her."

"Disgusting," said Boabissia.

"But she is only a slave," I said.

"True," said Boabissia. Then she looked at Feiqa. "Slut," she said.

"Yes, Mistress," said Feiqa, not meeting her eyes.

How Boabissia hated Feiqa! Did she really think it was wrong, or improper, for Feiqa to give her master such incredible pleasure? I did not think so. Feiqa, after all, was a slave. It was one of her purposes. I think it was rather that she was intensely jealous of Feiqa, that she keenly resented that she, the proud Boabissia, being free, was not subject to the same imperious enforcements.

"No thief so skilled, surely," said Boabissia, "would be with the refugees." She continued to regard the trembling Feiqa balefully. "It must have been the slave. Let her be tortured."

Feiqa moaned.

"It could not have been Feiqa," I said to Boabissia. "Last night her hands were secured," I reminded her, "chained behind her back."

"Then who?" asked Boabissia.

"Perhaps you," said Hurtha, coming up behind Boabissia and holding her by the upper arms, from behind. His grasp, I gathered, was not gentle.

"No," said Boabissia. "No!" She squirmed. She was as helpless as a slave in Hurtha's grip.

"Perhaps it is you who should be put under torture," growled Hurtha.

"No, no!" said Boabissia. "I am free!"

"It would not be impossible for a skilled thief to be with the refugees," I said. "It would be necessary only that he, or she, had been turned out of Torcadino with other citizens."

"Do you know of such a person?" asked Hurtha.

"Yes," I said.

"Who?" asked Hurtha.

"Wait here," I said.

"Who?" asked Hurta.

"One called Ephialtes, of Torcadino," I said. "I was warned about him."

"Let me come with you," he said. "I shall break his neck."

"That will not recover the letters," I said. "Wait here."

"Some of the carts, and many of the refugees, have already left," said Boabissia, pulling free of Hurtha's hands, he loosening his grip. She was shaking. She was not accustomed to having been so helplessly in the power of a man, as helplessly, it might seem, as might have been a slave.

"Please, Mistress," wept Feiqa. "I did not steal the letters. I could not have done so, even if I had dared to do so, which I would not in my life have dared to do. Do not ask to have Feiqa tortured. Please be kind to Feiqa."

"You are a slave," snapped Boabissia, "and, as such, are subject to torture, or to whatever free persons desire to do to you."

"Yes, Mistress," wept Feiqa, shuddering.

"Wait here," I said.

Boabissia made as though to accompany me, but Hurtha's hand on her arm stayed her.

"Aii!" cried the fellow, startled, in pain. My hand had closed on the back of his neck. I then forced him to his knees, and then to his belly. He squirmed. I thrust his nose and mouth into the soft earth. Instantly he was quiet. I permitted him to lift his head a little. He coughed and gasped.

"Where are they?" I asked him.

"What?" he said, wildly, spitting out dirt.

"The letters, three of them," I said.

"You cannot rob me here," he said. "There are too many about!"

To be sure, some of the refugees had gathered about us. "Do not interfere," I warned them.

"Where are the letters?" I demanded.

"What letters?" he asked.

I again thrust his face into the dirt. He coughed and spit, and twisted his head to the side, gasping.

"Where are they?" I demanded.

"I know nothing of letters," he gasped.

"Do not interfere," I warned those about. More than one of them carried heavy clubs.

I then, with a length of binding fiber, extracted from my pouch, tied his ankles together, and then fastened his hands to his ankles. He turned to his side. I then, methodically, began to go through his belongings.

"What are you doing?" he asked. "Stop him," he called to those about. A man or two took a step forward, but none challenged me.

"He is armed," said one of the fellows to the trussed captive.

"I do not find them here," I said to the crowd.

"What is he looking for?" asked a fellow, just come up to the group.

"Letters of some sort," said a fellow to the newcomer.

"Where are they?" I asked the captive, again.

"I know nothing of your letters, or whatever they are," he said. "Let me go!"

"Let him go," suggested a fellow in the crowd. To be sure he did not step boldly forth.

"What do you think you are doing?" asked another fellow.

"Let him go," said another man. That one I saw.

"This fellow," I said to the crowd, "is a thief. He stole three letters from me. I mean to have them back."

"I am not a thief," said the fellow.

"Did you see him steal the letters?" asked a fellow.

"No," I said.

"Did someone else, then?" asked another.

"No," I said, irritably.

"How do you know he took them then?" asked a fellow. It seemed a fair question.

"You have not recovered the letters from him," said another. "Does that not suggest that you might be mistaken?"

I opened the fellow's pouch. It contained coins, but there were no letters within it.

I poured the coins back into the pouch, and pulled shut its drawstrings.

"Where have you hidden the letters?" I asked the fellow. My voice was not pleasant.

"I do not know anything about your letters," he whispered. I think he had little doubt that I was in earnest. He was frightened.

"Have you sold them already?" I asked.

"I do not know anything about them," he said. "Are you not a thief?"

"No," I said.

"Release him," said a man.

"You have no proof," said another.

"He has a sword," said a man. "He does not need proof."

"Let the fellow go," said another man.

"He is a thief," I said, angrily.

"I am not a thief," said the fellow.

"He is not a thief," said another man.

"He is a well-known thief from Torcadino," I said.

"Nonsense," said a man.

"Who do you think he is?" asked another fellow.

"Ephialtes, of Torcadino," I said.

"I am not Ephialtes," said the man.

"He is not Ephialtes," said another fellow.

"He has been so identified for me, days ago," I said.

"And who made this identification?" asked a fellow.

"I do not now see him about," I said.

"That is not Ephialtes," said a man.

"Even if it were," said another fellow, "you apparently did not see the theft, and do not have clear evidence, even of a circumstantial nature, that he is the culprit." The fellow who had said this wore the blue of the scribes. He may even have been a scribe of the law.

"Release him," suggested another fellow.

"I am Philebus, a vintner, of Torcadino," said the man.

"He is lying," I said.

"That is Philebus," said a man. "I have dealt with him."

"Release him," said a man.

I untied the fellow. "Put your things back in your pack," I said. I watched him do this. The pack might have had a false lining. Still I had not felt the resistance of letters, nor heard the sound of paper from it, when I had tested it.

"Cart Seventeen is ready to leave!" I heard called.

"That is my cart," said the fellow, thrusting the last of his various articles, strewn about, into the pack.

"It is mine, too, as well you know," I said. "Do not fear. I shall accompany you to the cart and see that you board safely." I had no intention of letting him out of my sight. Although I had no proof of the sort which might convince a praetor I was confident that it was Ephialtes of Torcadino who had stolen the letters. It was ironic. I had ridden in the very cart with him.

"We are ready to go," said Boabissia coming up to me. "The cart is going to leave."

"I know," I said. "I heard. Go along, you." I thrust the fellow before me, toward the carts.

I stood near the front railing of the cart. I did look back to make sure the fellow was still on the bench where I had placed him. "That is the checkpoint ahead?" I asked the driver, as I leaned over the railing.

"Yes," he said, lifting his head and speaking back over his shoulder. "You will all get out here, and those who pass will board again, on the other side. There are no refunds, if you do not pass. Such failures are not the responsibility of the company."

"We are only a day from Ar," said a fellow.

"There is the barrier," said another, coming to stand beside me at the railing.

"Look," said another, joining us. "Look at that poor sleen." He indicated a small figure near the checkpoint, impaled on a high pole, lifted some twenty feet above the heads of the refugees.

"Among the crowds there," I said, suddenly, pointing, "there are soldiers with purple cloaks and helmets." I had not seen such things in years, since the time of the usurper, Cernus, in Ar, dethroned long ago in the restoration of Marlenus, ubar of ubars.

"Those are Taurentians, members of the elite palace guard," said a man.

"The Taurentians were disbanded in 10,119," I said.

"They have been restored to favor," said a man.

"Had you not heard?" asked another.

"No," I said. The sight of Taurentians made me uneasy. Such men, with their internal esprit de corps, their identification with their own units, their allegiance to their personal commanders, their status, privileges and skills, their proximity to the delicate fulcrums of power, hold in their hands the power to enthrone and dethrone ubars.

"It was done only this year," said a man.

"They are fine soldiers," said another.

"I know," I said. I had met them in combat, as long ago as the sands of the Stadium of Blades. There is a common myth, given their post in the city, that Taurentians are spoiled, and soft. This myth is false. They are elite troops, highly trained and devoted to their commanders. One does not gain admittance to their coveted ranks in virtue of mediocre skills or poor condition. The current year was 10,130 C.A. In the chronology of Port Kar, it was Year 11 in the Sovereignty of the Council of Captains. Their captain, when I had known them long ago, had been Saphronicus of Ar. Seremides of Tyros, in those days, had been high general of Ar. He, appointed through the influence of Cernus, who was soon to ascend the throne of Ar, had replaced the venerated hero, Maximus Hegesius Quintilius of Ar, who had earlier expressed reservations concerning the investiture of Cernus, a merchant and slaver, in the caste of warriors. Maximus Hegesius Quintilius was later found assassinated in his own pleasure gardens, slain there by the bite of a chemically prepared poison girl, one killed by Taurentians before she could be questioned. Such an appointment, of course, that of one of Tyros to such a post, later would have been unthinkable, given the developing frictions between Ar and Cos, and her mighty ally, Tyros, frictions largely consequent upon competitions in the valley of the Vosk. After the defeat and deposition of Cernus, so briefly a ubar, I had seen both Saphronicus and Seremides in chains before Marlenus, then again upon the throne. They had both, with other high traitorous officers, been ordered to Port Kar, in chains, to be sold to the galleys.

One of the figures in the purple cloak and helmet stood out from the others near the side of the road and lifted his hand.

The driver pulled back on the reins of his tharlarion and the beast slowed, grunting. The high-wheeled fee cart halted.

"Passengers alight and take your places in the line to the right," said the driver. "I am going in the wagon line. Rejoin me on the far side of the barrier, in the wagon line." He had been here before.

"How will we be able to pass?" whispered Boabissia, whom I helped down, through the cart gate. "You no longer have the letters."

"I am not sure," I said. "But surely most of the folks here do not have letters." I kept my eye on the fellow who had called himself Philebus, claiming to be a vintner of Torcadino. I had no intention of letting him out of my sight. If letters were required, and he presented those stolen from me, I would find that of interest. I would also, when the opportunity presented itself, an opportunity which I would see to it would present itself, break his arms and legs.

"Waiting, waiting," complained Hurtha. "I think that I shall compose a poem on the insolencies of bureaucracy."

"A good idea," I said.

"Done!" he said.

"Done?" I asked.

"It is a short poem," he said. "Would you care to hear it?"

"It must be quite short," I said.

"Yes," said Hurtha.

"I would be pleased to hear it," I said, keeping my eyes on the so-called Philebus.

"Lines, lines, lines, lines, lines, lines, lines," began Hurtha.

"Wait," I said. "There is only one word in the poem?" I began to suspect I had penetrated the secret of the poem's swift completion.

"No," said Hurtha, "already there are more than a half dozen. Count them. 'Lines, lines, lines, lines, lines, lines, lines.' "

"Yes," I said, "you are right."

The lines moved forward a few feet. I kept my eyes on the so-called Philebus.

"Lines, lines, lines, lines, lines, lines, lines, lines," said Hurtha.

"You are starting again?" I asked.

"No," he said, "I am picking up from where I left off. Do you really want to hear this poem?"

"Yes, of course," I said. I began to suspect that certain basic civilities, hitherto regarded as largely innocent, retained from my English upbringing, might not be wholly without occasional disadvantages.

"Then do not interrupt," said Hurtha.

"Sorry," I said.

" 'Those lines, lines, lines, lines, lines, lines, lines are very long, those long lines, lines, lines, lines, lines, lines, lines.''

"Yes, they are," I granted him.

"What?" asked Hurtha.

"Those lines," I said, "they are pretty long."

"Yes," agreed Hurtha, somewhat suspiciously. "Please do not interrupt."

"Sorry," I chuckled. After all, how often does a common fellow like myself get a chance to put one over on a poet.

"You are quite a wit," observed Boabissia.

"Thank you," I said. But, from the tone of her voice, I suspected her compliment was not to be taken at face value. I think she was prejudiced somewhat by her affection for the stocky larl, Hurtha. I did not think it was to be explained by her love of poetry. I did glance back at Feiqa. She was smiling. She was obviously of high intelligence. Then, observing herself the object of my scrutiny, she put down her head, quickly, even more humbly than was perhaps required under the circumstances. After all, her neck was in a collar.

"Be pleased that Hurtha does not strike you to the ground with a heavy blow," said Boabissia.

"I am pleased," I said. "I am pleased."

"If I may continue," said Hurtha.

"Please," I said.

" 'Those long lines, lines, lines, lines, lines, lines, lines, they make me tired, those long lines, lines, lines, lines, lines, lines, lines,' " said Hurtha.

I could believe it. But I refrained from comment.

" 'I do not like them, those long lines, those long lines, lines, lines, lines, lines, lines, lines,' " said Hurtha.

"Is that it?" I asked.

"That is the first verse," said Hurtha. "Also, I am catching my breath."

"I thought you said it was a short poem," I said.

"You needn't listen if you do not wish to," said Hurtha. "I can recite it to Boabissia."

"No, no," I said. "I just thought you said it was a short poem."

"It was, when I said that," he said. "But I have since

expanded it. Does the subject matter not seem worthy to you of a more substantial treatment?''

"Of course," I said.

Our own lines moved forward a few steps.

"You do not like it?'' asked Hurtha.

"It is wonderful," I said. "It is only that I am not sure that it is as wonderful as many of your other poems.''

"What is wrong with it?'' he asked.

"It seems to me perhaps a bit long," I said. "Also, it may be a bit repetitious.''

" 'Repetitious'?'' he asked, in disbelief.

"Yes," I said. For example, with respect to the word 'lines'.'' I kept my eye on the fellow before me, the so-called Philebus, he who claimed to be a vintner from Torcadino.

Hurtha burst out laughing and, tears in his eyes, seized me by the arms. I kept an eye on the so-called Philebus, lest he take this opportunity to take to his heels.

"My poor, dear sweet friend," said Hurtha. "How simple you are, dear friend! How little you know of poetry! The length is deliberate, of course, constituting an implicit allegory of interminability, manifesting and conveying in no uncertain manner, but in one which perhaps you have not as yet fully grasped, the withering tedium of the bureaucratic assault on the spirit and senses of man!''

"Oh," I said.

"Too, similarly pungent and subtle is the recurrent emphasis on the expression 'lines', which, on a level and in a dimension to which I have hopes you may yet attain, forcefully enunciates and clarifies not only the concept but more significantly the emotional significance of lines, those inevitable attributes, attaining in themselves an almost symbolic grandeur, of the perfidious bureaucratic infection.''

"I see," I said.

"May I now continue?'' he asked.

"Please, do," I said. I was so overawed by Hurtha's exposition that the so-called Philebus might then have slipped away unnoticed, but when I checked he had not done so. He did not wish to lose his place in line, it seemed. I decided that I, as a simple soldier, an unpretentious fellow devoted to the profession of arms, had best reserve judgment on such things as poets and poetry. It was dangerous, weighty stuff. I felt a sudden twinge of jealousy for Hurtha. He was both a warrior and a poet.

Hurtha then regaled us with his poem, which, truly, seemed to capture something of the inscrutability and ponderousness of the institution which had inspired it. I listened in awe, keeping my attention from time to time, and actually rather often, as my attention wandered, on the so-called Philebus. Boabissia, as I occasionally noted, with an admixture of skepticism and envy, seemed enraptured. Feiqa's countenance was cheerfully inscrutable. She would not meet my eyes. The so-called Philebus seemed as though he might desire to withdraw from our vicinity now and then, even giving up his place in line, particularly when Hurtha would come to an often-repeated, stirring refrain, but my hand on his collar kept him in his place. I will not attempt to give Hurtha's poem in its entirety, but I think I may have suggested something of its drift already. I might also mention that it is possible that it might lose something in the reading of it. Poetry, after all, or most poetry, is presumably meant to be heard, not read. It is intended for the ear, not the eye. And certainly the mere reading of it could scarcely convey the impact of hearing it proclaimed in the living voice, and particularly in a voice such as Hurtha's.

The line had been moving along rapidly enough, incongruous though this might have seemed, given the thesis of Hurtha's poem. We were now rather near the checkpoint.

"You are a Taurentian, are you not?" I asked a fellow in a purple helmet.

He did not answer me.

"You are a bit far from Ar, for Taurentians, are you not?" I inquired. We must be at least a day from Ar. It did not seem to make much sense to me that Taurentians, supposedly the palace guard, though they also patrol certain portions of the city, should be this far abroad, particularly in these troubled times.

He turned away from me, not answering me.

"A surly fellow," remarked Hurtha, somewhat offended.

We were now a few yards from the checkpoint. Only a few feet away, set off from the road a little, on our right, was the impaling pole we had seen from the cart. It was some six inches in diameter. On it was a small body. It had apparently been twisted and jerked until the point of the pole had emerged through the chest. It had then been drawn down the pole better than a yard. I could see some ribs erupted through the tunic. Its limbs were askew, hanging downward. The pole itself was red with blood. Nailed to it were some papers, fluttering in the wind.

"Wait," I said.

"What is it?" asked Boabissia.

"We know that fellow, do we not?" I asked, looking up to the impaled body.

Boabissia averted her eyes, sick. Feiqa did not raise her head.

"He seems familiar," admitted Hurtha.

"He should," I said. "He came with us from Torcadino. He was our fellow passenger for several days."

I looked up at the dangling head. The mouth was open. The roof of the mouth would be exposed. I could see the upper teeth. From the upper lip, on either side, the two ends of the mustache dangled back, as the head hung, on the sides of the neck, like two pieces of oiled string.

"So they have finally caught up with him," said the fellow before us.

"Yes," agreed a man a place or two behind us.

"Do you know him?" I asked the fellow before us.

"Of course," said the man. "He is well known to everyone in Torcadino."

"Hold my place," I said to Hurtha.

"I do not think any will strive to take it," said Hurtha, adjusting his ax on his shoulder, cheerfully looking about himself.

I walked to the side where the pole had been set up. I examined the papers nailed to the pole. They were partly ripped by the wind, and were stained with blood, where the blood had run down the pole.

"What are you doing there?" said a Taurentian.

"What was his crime?" I asked.

"Carrying false papers," he said.

"I see," I said.

"Return to your place," said the Taurentian.

I returned to my place.

"Do you know that fellow?" I asked the fellow before me, he whom I had treated so harshly.

"Of course," he said.

"It was he who identified you as Ephialtes of Torcadino, to me," I said.

"I am Philebus of Torcadino," said the man.

"Do you know who he is?" I asked.

"Of course," he said. "That is your man. That is Ephialtes of Torcadino."

"I am sorry for the way in which I treated you," I said.

"My bruises rejoice," said the fellow.

"I am really sorry," I said. "I hope I did not hurt your feelings."

"My feelings are fine," he said. "It is only my body which was damaged. It is only that which, as a whole, is in acute misery."

"I am really very sorry," I said.

"It could have been far worse," he said. "Think how sorry you would have had to have been, had you broken my neck before you discovered your error."

"That is right," said Hurtha. "There is much to be thankful for."

"What were the papers?" asked Boabissia.

"I shall tell you later," I said.

"Next," said a Taurentian. "You, there, what is your business in Ar?"

"I am a vintner," said the fellow before me. "I was put out of Torcadino. I have relatives in Ar. It is my intention to seek caste asylum in Ar."

"Have you papers?" asked the Taurentian.

"I have documents certifying my caste standing," he said. He then produced some papers from his pack.

The Taurentian then wrote a notation on the papers and motioned him ahead.

"I am called Tarl," I said, stepping forward. "I am from Port Kar, a city neutral to Ar. My friend is Hurtha, an Alar. The free woman is Boabissia, a woman from the Alar camp. The shapely collar slut bearing my pack is mine. I call her Feiqa. We are venturing to Ar on various errands, such as the seeking of our fortunes." The use of 'we' in the sentence, of course, was understood, as is common in Gorean, to refer only to free persons. The collar slut, Feiqa, my lovely slave, was along only as any other animal in such a situation might be along, because her master had brought her.

"Have you papers?" asked the man.

"No," I said.

"You have no papers, whatsoever?" asked the man.

"No," I said. "We have none whatsoever."

He looked at me for a moment, and then he waved us through. Boabissia was shuddering. In a few Ehn we had climbed up through the cart gate and, beyond the checkpoint, were again moving toward Ar.

As we left the checkpoint it was not toward Ar that I looked but back toward the checkpoint. There I could see people still waiting in line, and other carts coming up to the point. I could also see the twisted, bent body of Ephialtes of Torcadino on the impaling pole, and the flutter of papers nailed to it. I had been a fool. It had been Ephialtes of Torcadino himself who had cleverly directed my attention away from himself, focusing it on an innocent vintner. In a way I had to admire him. It seemed clear to me now that, in asking if I was carrying valuables, he had tricked me into inadvertently betraying their hiding place, by the incipient movement of my hand toward the sheath. Too, he had certainly removed the letters of safety from my sheath with great skill, even replacing the blade. Had I not checked the draw this morning, as is my wont, I might not have known the papers were missing until I had arrived at the checkpoint. I had determined, incidentally, that the deeper papers, the letters, some addressed to Ar's regent, Gnieus Lelius, and the others to her high general, Seremides, were still in the sheath. I now had strong, mixed feelings about them. I was now convinced more than ever of their importance, but also of the danger of carrying them.

The Taurentians were far from Ar. I suspected that it was their mission, on behalf of some high-placed power in Ar, to sift through refugees and travelers, seeking out those who might be inimical to their interests, or party, in Ar. I now understood more clearly than before why earlier messengers or agents might have failed to make contact with the regent and high general. I was, as I recalled, seemingly not the first to have been dispatched upon this delicate mission. Doubtless Ephialtes, in possession of the letters of safety, had been mistaken for an agent of Dietrich of Tarnburg. I shuddered. I was pleased that it had been Ephialtes, and not I, who had presented the letters at the checkpoint. Probably, at the demand of the officer, I would have surrendered them. And doubtless, if not there, then somewhere else I might have surrendered them, in some context, or upon some demand, somewhere or another.

I smiled bitterly. Letters of safety, indeed! They had not been letters of safety so much, it seemed, as death warrants, or orders for execution, laden with mortal peril for any so bold or foolish as to carry them. I saw the small figure of Ephialtes disappearing now in the distance. He had sought to steal protection but had purloined only death. He had been caught like some tiny insect in a dark and terrible web, one whose existence he had not even suspected.

"What were the papers nailed to the pole?" asked Boabissia.

"Our letters of safety," I told her. Then I turned about to look ahead, down the road. "We will be in Ar tomorrow morning," I told her. "Perhaps from the night's camp you will be able to see her lights."

"Is Ar a great city?" she asked.

"Yes," I said.

20: We See the City of Ar

"When we come over the crest of this hill," called the driver, "you will see Ar."

Boabissia rose from her seat to stand by the front railing of the fee cart. She clutched it with both her hands.

"Move, move aside," called the driver to some of the pedestrians on the road.

The sun was on our left. The hill was steep. There were few wagons drawn up along the road here. If they were halted, it seemed they had chosen to halt on the far side of the hill, where, at rest, they might see the city.

A woman, with a pack on her back, stumbled, and then regained her feet, hurrying along the side of the road.

"Ah!" cried Boabissia. "Ohh!"

More than one of the passengers rose to their feet, standing near the benches.

The driver halted the fee cart at the crest of the hill.

I had seen Ar at various times before. Such a sight I was accustomed to. It would not move me, as it might others, the first time to look upon it.

"Incredible!" said a man.

"Marvelous!" whispered another.

I smiled at their childish enthusiasm, at their lack of maturity. Then I rose, too, to my feet. I saw then, in the distance, some four or five pasangs away, the gleaming walls of glorious Ar.

"I had not realized how vast was the city," said one of the men.

"It is large," said another fellow.

"There is the Central Cylinder!" said a man, pointing.

The high, uprearing walls of the city, some hundred feet or

more in height, the sun bright upon them, stretched into the distance. They were now white. That had been done, apparently, since the time of Cernus, the usurper, and the restoration of Marlenus, ubar of ubars. It was hard to look at them, for the glare upon them. We could see the great gate, too, and the main road leading to it, the Viktel Aria. Indeed, we ourselves, soon, I thought, would transfer to the Viktel Aria. Within the gamut of those gleaming walls, so lofty and mighty, rose thousands of buildings, and a veritable forest of ascendant towers, of diverse heights and colors. Many of these towers, I knew, were joined by traceries of soaring bridges, set at different levels. These bridges, however, save for tiny glintings here and there, could not be well made out at this distance.

"I do not think I have ever seen anything so beautiful," said a man.

We were looking upon what was doubtless the greatest city of known Gor.

"I did not know it was like that," said another man.

I remembered the great gate. I remembered, long ago, the horde of Pa-Kur. I did not forget the house of Cernus, the Stadium of Tarns, the great tarn, Ubar of the Skies, the racing factions, the Stadium of Blades, the bloodied sands of the arena. I had not forgotten the streets, the baths, the shops, the broad, noble avenues, with their fountains, the narrow, twisting streets, little more than darkened corridors, shielded from the sun, of the lower districts.

"I have never seen anything like it," said a man.

"Nor I," said another, in awe.

I gazed down upon the city. In such places came together the complexities and the poverties, the elementalities and the richnesses of the worlds. In such places were to be found the rare, precious habitats of culture, the astonishing, moving delights of art and music, the truths of theater and literature, the glories and allegories of architecture, bespeaking the meanings of peoples, man-made symbols like mountain ranges; in them, too, were to be found iron and silver, and gold and steel, the chairs of finance and the thrones of power. I gazed at the shining city. How startling it seemed. Such places were like magnets to man; they call to him like gilded sirens; they lure him inward to their dazzling wonders, bewitching him with their often so meretricious whispered promises; they were symbols of races. In them were fortunes to be sought, and fortunes to be won, and fortunes to be lost; in them there were crowds, and loneliness; in them success trod the same pavements as failure; in their plazas hope jostled with despair, and meaning ate at the same table with meaninglessness. In such places were perhaps the best and worst that man could do, his past and future, his pain and pleasure, his darkness and light, come together in a single focus.

"Drinks, cool drinks!" called a woman, selling juices by the side of the road, coming up to the cart. There was a small crowd at the crest of the hill. It was a place where carts, and wagons, and travelers often stopped. In such a place there were coins to be made. She paid no attention to the sight below. Doubtless she had seen it a thousand times. Her eyes were on possible customers.

"Would you like a drink?" I asked Boabissia.

"Yes," she said.

I purchased her some larma juice for a tarsk bit.

"Is it cool?" I asked.

"Yes," she said. The morning was hot.

It would have been stored overnight, I assumed, in an amphora, buried to the neck in the cool earth. Sometimes Earth girls, first brought to Gor, do not understand why so many of these two-handled, narrow-necked vessels have such a narrow, usually pointed base, for they cannot stand upright on such a base. They have not yet learned that these vessels are not intended to stand upright. Rather they are commonly fitted into a storage hole, buried there to keep their contents cool, the necks above the earth. The pointed base, of course, presses into the soft earth at the bottom of the storage hole.

"Bread, meat!" called a fellow, coming up beside the cart. Several of us availed ourselves of his provender. I bought some wedges of Sa-Tarna bread and slices of dried tarsk meat, taking some and giving the rest to Boabissia and Hurtha. I also went to the back of the cart, to the baggage area where I kept Feiqa. I gave her some of my bread and meat. I did not permit her to touch it with her hands, but, reaching between the thick wooden bars, some six inches apart, to where she knelt among the packs and boxes at the back, fed her by hand. "Thank you, Master," she said.

I then returned to the front of the cart. Some of the passengers had alighted.

I regarded again the walls of glorious Ar, shining in the distance.

"I cannot wait," said Boabissia, "to claim my patrimony."

I nodded. I finished my food.

"Let us return to the cart!" the driver called to some of the fellows who had alighted. "Let us return to the cart!"

I looked again at the city in the distance. From here it looked very beautiful. Yet I knew that somewhere within it, perhaps within its crowded quarters, from which mobs might erupt like floods, or within its sheltered patios and gardens, where high ladies might exchange gossip, sip nectars and toy with dainty repasts, served to them by male silk slaves, or among its houses and towers, or on its streets or in the great baths, that somewhere there, somewhere behind those walls, was treason. Somewhere there, within those walls, coiled in the darkness of secrecy, corruption and sedition, like serpents, I was sure, awaited their hour to strike.

"It is a fine sight," said a fellow, climbing up through the cart gate, and standing beside me for a moment, to look down on the city.

"Yes," I said.

He returned to his place.

From where we were, of course, we could not see dirt and crime, or poverty or hunger. We could not detect pain, misery and greed. We could not feel loneliness and woe. And yet, for all these things, which so afflict so many of its own, how impressive is the city. How precious it must be, that so many men are willing to pay its price. I wondered why this was, I a voyager and soldier, more fond of the tumultuous sea and the wind-swept field than the street and plaza. Perhaps because it is alive, like drums and trumpets. To be near it or within it, to be stirred by its life, to call its cylinders their own, is for many reward enough.

The last fellow, climbing up and closing the cart gate behind him, took his seat.

I did not take my eyes from the city, so splendid before us. Yes, I thought, it is all there, the habitats of culture, the intricate poetries of stone, the incredible places where, their heads among clouds, common bricks have been taught to speak and sing, the meanings uttered scarcely understood by those who walk among them; yes, it is all there, in them, in the cities, I thought; in them were dirt and crime, iron and silver, gold and steel; in them were perfume and silk, and whips and chains; in them were love and lust; in them were mastery and submission, the owning and the helplessly being owned; in them were intrigue and greed, nobility and honor, deceit and treachery, the exalted and the base, the strong and the weak. In such places, filthy, and crowded and frail, are found the fortresses of man. They are castles and prisons, arenas and troves; they are cities; they are the citadels of civilization.

The driver called to his tharlarion and shook the reins. "Ahead!" he called to the beast. "Move!"

I returned to my seat, the cart beginning to move.

"You have seen Ar before?" said a man.

"Yes," I said.

"It is then an old thing for you," he said.

"Yes," I said.

"You will have to forgive me," he said. "But I found it quite astonishing, this first time."

"It often affects one that way, the first time," I said.

"I suppose so," he said.

The cart continued to move down the incline. I noted the sound of the narrow, metal-rimmed wheels on the stones. I watched the walls of Ar grow closer.

21: Within the Walls of Ar

"Are you come from Torcadino?" asked the man.

"Yes," I said.

"Thousands of you are in the city," he said, "from Torcadino and other places."

I nodded. I had never, myself, seen Ar so crowded.

"We need no more of you refugees here," snapped a woman, a seller of suls at the Teiban Market.

"We seek lodging in the city," I said to the man.

"Lodging is dear," he said. "It is difficult to know what to tell you." He glanced at Feiqa, who put down her head. She was kneeling behind me, to my left, my pack still on her back. She had knelt when we had stopped, and begun to speak to the free person. This was appropriate, of course, for she was a slave. Her location was approximately what it had been when she had been following me, in the heeling position.

"She," he said, "you could sleep in the street, chaining her by the neck to a ring, perhaps putting her in an iron belt, but that sort of thing will not do for free folks."

"No," I said.

"You could try the southern insulae," he said, "such as those below the Plaza of Tarns."

"The Anbar district?" I asked, skeptically.

"Or those of the Metellan Quarter," he said.

"What about east of the Avenue of the Central Cylinder?" I asked.

"There is the District of Trevelyan," he said.

"That sounds nice," said Boabissia.

"We would hope to survive the night," I said.

"You know the city?" he asked.

"I have been here before," I said.

"You are two big fellows," he said. "I doubt that anyone would bother you."

"If they do bother us," said Hurtha, "it is my hope that they are carrying coins."

"We do not have much to steal," I told the man.

"You have a free female there," he said. "Such can bring their prices in certain places."

"I am not afraid," said Boabissia.

"Brave and noble girl," he said.

"I can take care of myself," said Boabissia.

"To be sure," he said, "her price could be lowered for stupidity."

"I am not stupid," said Boabissia.

"Forgive me," he said. "From your remark I thought that perhaps you were."

Boabissia regarded him in fury.

The fellow regarded her. It was one of those looks which, in effect, undress a woman, exposing her lineaments, careless of her will, to his view.

"Do not look at me in that way," she said. "I am free."

He continued to consider her, perhaps now as she might look trembling, suing for his favor, in chains at his feet.

"You are not veiled," he said.

"I am an Alar woman," she said.

"No," said Hurtha. "She is not an Alar."

"I have been with the wagons," she said.

"That is true," said Hurtha.

Boabissia, as I have mentioned, did not much resemble the typical Alar women. She seemed of a much different type, that of the delicious, soft women of the cities, the sort which are generally put on slave blocks. Indeed, I suspected that her origin might be urban.

"What district do you think we might try?" I asked the fellow.

"Regardless of this free woman," he said, "you have something of value there." He indicated Feiqa. She put down her head, appraised.

"What district do you think we might try?" I asked.

"I have suggested several," he said.

"Ar is a large city," I said.

"Are you looking for decent lodging?" he asked.

"Yes," I said.

"Are you willing to pay a silver tarsk a night?" he asked.

"No," I said. We could not afford that.

"Then I do not think you will find any," he said.

"I thank you, Citizen," I said, "for your time."

"Is it true," he asked, "that there are considerable Cosian forces in the vicinity of Torcadino?"

"Yes," I said.

"They have taken the city?" he asked.

"I do not think so," I said.

"But the refugees," he said, "so many of them."

"They have been turned out of the city to make its defense more practical," I said.

"The main forces of Cos," he said, "are said to be advancing on Ar's Station."

"I doubt that," I said.

"That would make sense," he said. "The Cosians want the river, and the control of its basin. That is what the trouble is all about. That is why their major move will be there. Too, it is probably no more than a raid."

"Ar is in danger," I said.

"They would never dare to meet us in pitched battle," he said.

"Ar is in great danger," I said.

"Ar is invincible," he said.

"The main forces of Cos are as close as Torcadino," I said.

"Rumors are rampant," he said. "One does not know what to think."

"I trust the regent, your high councils, your military leaders, the general staff, and such, are well informed."

"Doubtless," he said.

"Where is Marlenus?" I asked.

"In the Voltai," said the fellow. "On a punitive expedition against Treve." That, too, had been my information.

"He has been absent for months, has he not?" I asked.

"Yes," he said.

"Does this not seem to you strange?" I asked.

"He does as he chooses," said the man. "He is Ubar."

"Is the city content that he should be absent in what may be perilous times?" I asked.

"If there were any true danger," said the man, "he would swiftly return. He has not returned. Thus there is no true danger."

"You do not think there is any real danger?" I asked.

"No," said the man. "Any one of our lads could best a dozen Cosians."

"It seems to me Marlenus should return," I said.

The man shrugged.

"Perhaps they have lost contact with him, in the reaches of the Voltai."

"Perhaps," said the man. "But the city does not need him."

"The Ubar is not popular?" I asked.

"He has held power in Ar for a long time," said the man. "Perhaps it is time for a change."

"Do many think so?" I asked.

"Such voices are heard here and there," he said, "in the taverns, the markets, the baths. Gnieus Lelius is an excellent regent. Marlenus is too bellicose. The city is sound. We are not threatened. The squabble with Cos is peripheral to our interests."

"Is Gnieus Lelius interested in being Ubar?" I asked.

"No," said the fellow. "He is far too modest, too humble and unpretentious for that sort of thing. The folds of the purple cloak, the weight of the Ubar's medallion, are of no interest to him. He cares only for excellent governance, and the peace and prosperity of the city."

"But you are sure he is interested in the welfare of Ar?" I asked.

"Of course," said the fellow. That answer was reassuring to me. This Gnieus Lelius, if truly interested in the welfare of Ar, must act. If he had flaws as a regent presumably they might be due to his lack of information, or perhaps to a certain unwarranted optimism, or untutored innocence or naivety. Such things are not uncommon among idealists, so tender and thoughtful, so loving and trusting, prisoners of verbalisms, dazzled by inventions and dreams, projecting their own benevolence unto the larl and the forests, skeptical of reality, construing the world in the metaphor of the flower. What consolation is it for others if they should eventually discover they live in a world of facts, if disillusioned they should eventually recognize their errors, living to see the harvests of their foolishness, living to see their civilization split asunder, to see their world fall bleeding under the knives of power and reality?

"What of Seremides, the high general?" I asked. "Might he not ascend the throne?"

"Unthinkable," said the man. "He is as loyal as the stones of the Central Cylinder itself."

"I see," I said. My question had not been prompted, of course, merely by the obvious consideration that the Ubar's cloak might seem an attractive prize to a strong, ambitious man, but by the sober understanding that Ar was in a situation of crisis, whether she knew it or not. In such times, of course, in the light of the failures and ineffectuality of an inept civilian administration, it is not unknown for military men, seeing what must be done, simply responding to the imperatives of survival, to take power and attempt to instill the will, the discipline and order without which catastrophe cannot be diverted.

"But surely it is not anticipated that the governance of Ar will long remain under a regency," I said.

"Marlenus is expected back soon," said the man.

"Suppose, however," I suggested, "he does not soon return?"

"Then there is another possibility," he said, "an interesting one."

"What is that?" I asked.

"A Ubara," he said.

"A Ubara?" I asked.

"She who was, until forsworn, the daughter of Marlenus," he said.

"Oh?" I asked.

"Talena," he said. "Have you heard of her?"

"Yes," I said.

"Marlenus was dissatisfied with her," said the fellow. "It had to do with some business in the Northern forests. He swore her from him, making her no longer his daughter. For years she has lived in obscurity, sequestered in the Central Cylinder. Now, with the absence of Marlenus, and the generosity of Gnieus Lelius, she is carried publicly, once again, in the streets of Ar."

"I gather that would not be in accord with the will of Marlenus," I said.

"Marlenus is not here," he said.

"Why would one think of her in the terms of a Ubara?" I asked. "Sworn from Marlenus, she is no longer his daughter."

"I am not a scribe of the law," he said. "I do not know."

"I do not think she has a Home Stone," I said.

"Gnieus Lelius permitted her to kiss the Home Stone," he said. "It was done in a public ceremony. She is once again a citizeness of Ar."

"Gnieus Lelius seems a generous, noble fellow," I said.

"He is a patron of the arts," said the fellow. "He has founded parks and museums. He has won the support of the elite in this fashion. I myself favor him for he has remitted certain classes of debts. This has considerably eased my financial burdens. The lower castes are fond of him for he frequently, at his own expense, distributes free bread and paga, and sponsors games and races. He has also declared new holidays. He has made life better and easier in Ar. He is much supported by the people."

"You are certain that he is concerned for the welfare of Ar?" I asked.

"Of course," he said.

"Is he difficult to see?" I asked.

"One does not simply walk up to the Central Cylinder and knock on the door," he said.

"I suppose not," I said.

"But Gnieus Lelius makes a point of being available to the people," he said. "That is one reason he is so much loved."

"Commoners, then, can look upon the regent," I asked,

"other than from afar, as in state processions or at official games?"

"Of course," said the man.

I was pleased to hear that. I had urgent letters for Gnieus Lelius and Seremides. I must somehow manage to deliver them. I had feared it might be difficult. I did not wish to deliver these missives into the hands of a subordinate. Who could one trust? Too, I surely had no wish to attempt to cut my way through the corridors of the Central Cylinder to effect a private audience with these fellows.

"Can they actually speak with him?" I asked.

"Surely," he said.

"When, next, do you think he might be holding public audiences?" I asked.

"Two days from now," said the fellow.

"It is a court day?" I asked.

"Better than that," he said. "It is one of the new holidays, the Day of Generosity and Petitions."

"Excellent," I said.

"The audiences are held near the Central Cylinder, on the Avenue of the Central Cylinder," he said.

"Thank you," I said.

"Did you wish to speak to him about something?" asked the man.

"I thought it might be nice," I said, "at least to look upon him."

"He is a charming fellow," said the man.

"I am sure of it," I said.

"Many minor petitions are granted," he said, "and some of the major ones. To be sure, it depends wholly, at least in the major cases, upon the justice of the petition."

"I understand," I said.

"Those wishing to present petitions must take a place on the rope," he said.

"What is that?" I asked.

"Obviously the regent cannot give an audience to everyone," he said. "Those who are granted audiences wear the Gnieus Lelius Generosity Ribbon which encircles them and is tied about the rope, actually a velvet cable, leading to the dais.

This helps to keep the line straight and, as the audiences are held out of doors, controls the number of petitioners.''

"I understand," I said. "How does one obtain a position on the rope?" I asked.

"Sometimes it is a nasty business," said the man.

"Good," said Hurtha, approvingly.

"I suppose it is a good idea to come early," I said.

"Some people are there from the fourteenth Ahn the day before," he said.

"I see," I said. "Thank you, Citizen."

"You might try the Alley of the Slave Brothels of Ludmilla. That is behind the Avenue of Turia."

"What?" I said.

"For lodging," he said.

"Oh," I said.

"Do you know where it is?" he asked.

"I know where the Avenue of Turia is," I said. It is named for the city in the southern hemisphere, incidentally, doubtless as a gesture of amicability on the part of Ar. Stately Tur trees, appropriately enough, line its walks. It is a broad avenue with fountains. It is well known for its exclusive shops. "It is in the vicinity of the Street of Brands."

"That is the one," he said. The Street of Brands, incidentally, can be a particular street, but, generally, as in Ar, it is a district, one which has received its name from its dealings in slaves, and articles having to do with slaves. In it, commonly, are located the major slave houses of a city. To it, slavers may take their catches. In it, on a wholesale or retail basis, one may purchase slaves. Similarly one may bid upon them in public auction. The major markets are there. For example, the Curulean is there. One may also rent and board slaves there. It is there, too, in the confines of the houses, that girls are often trained superbly and thoroughly in the intimate arts of giving exquisite pleasures to masters. Too, of course, in such a district, one may purchase such articles as appropriate cosmetics for slaves, suitable simple but attractive jewelry, fit for slaves, in particular, earrings which, in Gorean eyes, so fasten a woman's degradation helplessly upon her, appropriate perfumes, slave silk, and such. Too, it is in such a district that one will find a wide variety of other articles helpful in the identification, keeping, training and disciplining of females, such things as collars, of the fixed and lock variety, leashes, of metal and leather, neck, wrist and ankle, ranging from simple guide thongs to stern control devices, wrist belts and ankle belts, yokes and leg-stretchers, waist-and-wrist stocks, iron belts, to prevent her penetration without the master's permission, linked bracelets, with long chains and short chains, body chains, pleasure shackles, multicolored, silken binding cords, some cored with chain, and, of various types, for various purposes, whips.

"My thanks," I said. "We will try it."

"I wish you well," he said.

"I, too, wish you well," I said.

He then went about his business. The woman near us, sitting on a blanket on the stones, her basket of suls before her, looked up. "Do you want suls?" she asked.

"No," I said.

"Be gone, then," she said.

"Come along," I said to my party. I led them east on Venaticus, to the Avenue of the Central Cylinder. It was then my intention to go south on that avenue until I came to Wagon Street, taking it east to Turia. There is more than one "wagon Street" in Ar, incidentally, but the one I had in mind, that which led to the Street of Brands, was the one usually called Wagon Street. The "wagon streets" are generally east-west streets. They are called that, I suppose, because they are open to wagon traffic during the day, and wide enough for two wagons to pass on them. On many streets in Ar wagon traffic is discouraged during daylight hours because of their narrowness. There is little difficulty, of course, with the avenues and boulevards. They are generally wider. Many girls, incidentally, have been on Wagon Street, being brought down it on their first trip to Ar, though perhaps they did not see much of it, their ankles chained to the central bar in the blue-and-yellow slave wagons, those delivering them, according, say, to the disk numbers on their collars, or the addresses marked on their left breasts, to the various houses on the Street of Brands.

"Ah!" said Boabissia.

"The Avenue of the Central Cylinder," I said. "It is indeed beautiful. We will go right here."

"I am thirsty," said Hurtha, going toward a fountain. We followed him. There are many among this avenue.

Hurtha leaned his ax against the fountain and thrust his head half in the water and then pulled it out sputtering. He then splashed water on his face. Then, cupping his hands, he drank. I drank, too. And Boabissia, too, drank, lifting water delicately to her lips. I saw that in our company she had learned something of her femininity. It seemed that she was beginning, timidly and hopefully, to suspect and experience the true nature of her sexuality, that she might now be daring to think of fulfilling her softness and nature, daring to think of what it might be to be, fully and truly, what she actually was, a female. She, at any rate, was now no longer attempting, grotesquely, and laughably, to emulate the behavior of an Alar warrior.

"May I drink, Master?" asked Feiqa.

"Certainly," I said. Then, suddenly, angry, scandalized, I seized her by the hair. She cried out in pain, twisting.

"Are you not a beast?" I asked.

"Yes, Master!" she wept.

"And only that?" I inquired.

"Yes, Master!" she cried.

I then flung her to her knees at my feet, and with my foot spurned her to the stones. She lay there, startled, on her side, my pack awry on her back, near the fountain. "Master?" she asked, tears in her eyes.

"You are a beast," I said. "You drink from the lower bowl, like other animals, like sleen and tharlarion."

"Yes, Master," she said.

"What a stupid slave," said Boabissia.

"Forgive me, Master," wept Feiqa.

I regarded her. She was quite attractive, and she had good legs. There was little doubt of that the way she lay on the stones. She was terrified, the former Lady Charlotte, once a rich, high citizeness of Samnium, now the mere beast, mine and collared, Feiqa. She looked up at me in terror. She had grievously erred.

"That was good," said Hurtha, wiping his mouth.

"Master?" asked Feiqa.

"Tonight," I told her. "You will be whipped."

"Yes, Master," she said.

"A chair, with soldiers, is coming," said Boabissia.

We saw some folks gathering about to watch, but leaving a path for the movement of the chair and soldiers. It was an enclosed sedan chair, its silken curtains drawn. It was borne on long poles slung in tandem fashion between two tharlarion. The chair and soldiers were making their way north on the Avenue of the Central Cylinder, toward the Central Cylinder. The soldiers were Taurentians.

"It is a woman's chair, is it not?" asked Boabissia.

"Yes," I said.

"Those are palace guardsmen, aren't they?" asked Hurtha.

"Probably," I said. "They are, at least, of the same sort as the palace guardsmen."

"Taurentians, they are called," he said.

"Yes," I said.

"They look like capable fellows," he said.

"I am sure they are," I said. The eyes of the soldiers were mostly on the crowd. There seemed little doubt such men formed an efficient guard. The chair, I noted, was not borne by male draft slaves, but was supported by tharlarion. There might be various reasons for this. One might be ostentation, a simple display of wealth, for good tharlarion are generally more expensive than male slaves, particularly draft slaves. But perhaps, even more, the cargo might be regarded as too precious to be risked in the vicinity of male slaves. After all, they are men. Too, perhaps it was felt inappropriate, if the cargo was deemed of sufficient beauty, that it even be borne by male slaves. After all, might there not be some danger, as the fair occupant entered into, or descended gracefully from the sedan chair, that there might be the careless movement of a veil, revealing a bit of throat, or the inadvertent lifting of a robe of concealment, giving them the glimpse of a briefly exposed ankle?

"Drink," I said to Feiqa.

"Yes, Master," she said.

"Whose chair is that?" I asked a fellow near us, as the chair moved past.

"Do you not know?" he asked.

"No," I said. "We are but newly come to Ar "

"From Torcadino?" he asked.

"Yes," I said.

"That," he said, "is the chair of she who may become the Ubara of Ar."

"Talena," said another fellow.

"What is wrong?" asked Boabissia.

"Nothing," I said. I watched the chair move down the street, toward the Central Cylinder.

I looked at Feiqa. She knelt on all fours before the lower bowl of the fountain, her head down, drinking.

"How could this Talena become Ubara of Ar?" I asked. "I thought she was sworn from the line of Marlenus."

"She can be given legal entitlement to the succession," said a fellow. "I have heard it discussed."

"Not as of the line of Marlenus," I said.

"No," he said. "But one need not be of the line of Marlenus, surely, to rule in Ar."

"Minus Tentius Hinrabius and Cernus, both, ruled in Ar," said a man. "Neither was of his line."

"That is true," I said.

"She is a free citizen," said a man. "Accordingly, she could be given such entitlement."

"Why not Gnieus Lelius or Seremides?" I asked.

"Neither is ambitious, happily," said a fellow.

"But why her?" I asked. "Why not any one of thousands of others?"

"She was of royal family," said a man. "She was once the daughter of Marlenus."

"I see," I said. I looked down at Feiqa. "Are you watered?" asked her.

"Yes, Master," she said.

She looked lovely, on all fours, at the lower bowl of the

fountain, where, drinking, as a collared, briefly tunicked beast, she belonged. "Rise," I said.

"Yes, Master," she said.

I looked after the chair. But I could not now see it for the folks following it.

"Which way are we going?" asked Hurtha.

"This way," I said. We could go south on the Avenue of the Central Cylinder, some four or five pasangs, and then make a left on Wagon Street, taking it over to the Avenue of Turia. Somewhere in that vicinity, probably in the lower end of the avenue, somewhere in the Street of Brands district, was the Alley of the Slave Brothels of Ludmilla. I would have to ask directions once we were on the Avenue of Turia. I did not doubt but what we could quickly find such an area. It sounded as though it would not be unknown.

"What is the name of the place?" asked Boabissia.

"The Alley of the Slave Brothels of Ludmilla," I said.

"I do not like the sound of that," said Boabissia.

"I do not think it sounds bad," I said.

"No," said Hurtha.

I looked back at Feiqa. She put down her head. She had been careless. She had been thoughtless. Tonight she would be whipped.

22: The Insula of Achiates

"The stench is terrible," said Boabissia.

"Do not throw up," I told her. "You will get used to it."

"I have told them, time and time again," said the proprietor, testily, carrying the small lamp, "that they should keep the lid on. It is heavy, of course, and so it is too often left awry." With a grating sound, he shoved the heavy terracotta lid back in place, on the huge vat. It was at the foot of the stairs, where the slop pots could be emptied into it. Such vats are changed once or twice weekly, the old vats loaded in wagons and taken outside the city, where their contents are disposed of at one of the carnarii, or places of refuse pits. They are then rinsed out and ready to be delivered again, in their turn, to customers. This is done by one of several companies organized for the purpose. The work is commonly done by male slaves, supervised by free men.

"Follow me," said the proprietor, beginning to ascend the stairs.

I followed him. Behind me came Boabissia. Then came Hurtha. Feiqa came last. The staircase was narrow. It would be difficult for two people to pass on it. That would make it easy to defend, I thought. It was also steep. That was good. It did not have an open side but was set between two walls. That conserved space. It made possible extra rooms. Space is precious in a crowded insula. The stairwell boards were narrow. That was not so good, unless one were on the landing. That would be the place to make a stand. One could not get one's entire foot on them. They were old. Some were split. Several were loose. For a bit we could make our way in the light from the shallow vestibule below, where it filtered in through the shutters of the entrance gate, but in a moment or two, we became substantially dependent on the proprietor's tiny lamp. It cast odd shadows.

"I cannot stand the smell," said Boabissia.

"The room is a tarsk bit a night," said the proprietor. "You may take it or leave it. You are lucky we have one left. These are busy days in Ar."

"We could have had a better place were it not for something," said Boabissia, irritably.

That might have been true. I did not know. It was hard to say. Several of the insulae we had investigated did not allow animals, which meant, of course, that we could not keep Feiqa with us. Some of them did, however, have some provision for slaves, such as basement kennels or chaining posts in the yard. I preferred, however, to keep Feiqa with us. She was lovely. I did not wish to have her stolen.

"The insula of Achiates," said the proprietor, "is the finest insula in all Ar."

"It is dark," said Boabissia.

"How far is it now?" I asked.

"Not far," said the proprietor.

As we climbed, the landings were frequent. The ceilings on the various levels of insulae are generally very low. In most of the rooms a man cannot stand upright. This makes additional floors possible.

I put out my hands and touched the walls on the sides of the staircase. They were very close. They were chipped. In places there were long diagonal cracks in them, marking stress points in the structure where the plaster had broken. The insula of Achiates might be the finest insula in Ar, but I thought that it stood somewhat in a condition of at least minor disrepair. A bit of renovation might not have been entirely out of order. The walls, too, were frequently discolored, run with various stains, water stains and other stains.

"This place stinks," said Boabissia. "It stinks."

"It is those brats," said the proprietor. "They are too lazy to go downstairs."

"There are families here?" asked Boabissia.

"Of course," said the proprietor. "Most of my tenants are permanent residents."

We continued to climb. We had now come some seven or eight landings.

"It is stuffy," said Boabissia. "I can hardly breathe."

Insulae were not noted for their ventilation, no more than for the luxury of their appointments or their roominess. To be sure it conserves fuel.

"It is hot," said Boabissia.

"You complain a great deal," observed the proprietor.

"It is so dark," said Boabissia. "How can one find one's way around in this place?"

"One becomes familiar with it," said the proprietor.

"You should have lamps illuminating the stairs," said Boabissia. "I suppose that tharlarion oil is just too expensive."

"Yes," said the proprietor. "But it is also against the law."

"Why is that?" I asked.

"The danger of fire," he said.

"Oh," said Boabissia, sobered.

Insulae, incidentally, are famed for their proneness to fire. Sometimes entire districts of such dwellings are wiped out by a single fire.

"Can we have a lamp in the room?" I asked.

"Of course," said the fellow. "As long as it is tended. But you may not wish to have one much lit. It fouls the air."

"Do you have insurance on this building?" I asked.

"No," said the fellow.

I was pleased to hear that. He would then not be likely to have the building fired to collect on the policy. On the other hand, it was not unusual that such dwellings lacked insurance. This was not simply a matter of proprietary optimism, but also of the difficulty of obtaining it, at least at affordable rates. Most carriers would not accept the risks involved.

We came to another landing.

We heard a noise and the proprietor lifted his lamp. A slave girl was illuminated, on the landing. She was barefoot. She wore an extremely brief tunic, one which was divided to her navel. It was awry. Her hair was in disarray. In the light of the lamp her collar glinted. She flung herself to her belly before us, fearfully yielding slave obeisance.

"She belongs to Clitus, the Cloth Worker, on the floor above," said the proprietor.

The girl trembled on her belly before us.

I saw that if Achiates permitted slaves in his house they must exhibit suitable discipline. They must be well trained.

We continued up the stairs. The girl had had light brown hair, it seemed. When we had passed she continued on her way. We could hear her bare feet for a time on the stairs. She seemed to know them well. In time one can find one's way around on them in the dark. She was doubtless on an errand.

"Oh!" cried Boabissia, on the next landing. "An urt!"

"That is not an urt," said the proprietor. "They usually come out after dark. There is too much noise and movement for them during the day." The small animal skittered backward, with a sound of claws on the boards. Its eyes gleamed in the reflected light of the lamp. "Generally, too, they do not come this high," said the proprietor. "That is a frevet." The frevet is a small, quick, mammalian insectivore. "We have several in the house," he said. "They control the insects, the beetles and lice, and such."

Boabissia was silent.

"Not every insula furnishes frevets," said the proprietor. "They are charming as well as useful creatures. You will probably grow fond of them. You will probably wish to keep your door open at night, for coolness, and to give access to them. They cannot gnaw through walls like urts, you know."

"Is it far now?" I asked.

"No," said the proprietor. "We are almost there. It is just under the roof."

"It seems we have come a long way," I said.

"Not really," he said. "We are not really so high up. The flights are short."

We then climbed another flight, to the next landing.

"Oh!" said Boabissia, recoiling.

"You see," said the proprietor. "You will come to like the frevets." We watched a large, oblong, flat-bodied black object about a half hort in length, with long feelers, hurry toward crack at the base of the wall. "That is a roach," he said. "They are harmless, not like the gitches whose bites are rather painful. Some of them are big fellows, too. But there aren't many of them around. The frevets see to it. Achiates prides himself on a clean house."

"Ai!" said Feiqa, suddenly, startled, moving.

"Kneel, slave girl," said a young, imperious voice.

Swiftly Feiqa knelt.

"Kiss my feet, female slave," said the voice.

Feiqa was kneeling before a boy, perhaps some eleven or twelve years of age. His face was dirty. He was barefoot, and in rags. I assumed he must live in the rooms somewhere. Feiqa, a full-grown and beautiful female, but a slave, put down her head and, doing him obeisance, kissed his feet, and fearfully, and humbly. He was a free person, and a male.

"Go away, you disgusting child," said Boabissia.

"Be silent, woman," he said.

"I have a good mind to strike you," said Boabissia.

"Lift your head, slut," said the lad to Feiqa.

She obeyed.

He regarded her. "You are a pretty one," he said. "What do you say?" he demanded.

"Thank you, Master," she said.

He then stood close to her and ran his hands through her hair. He then took her collar by the sides in his small fingers and jerked it forward, towards him, against the back of her neck. He then, by the pressure on the collar, forced her head rudely from side to side. He then pressed it up, cruelly, under her chin, forcing her head up. He was exerting his force on her through her slave collar. She would have no doubt it was on her. He did these things, incidentally, with the typical awareness of men who know how to handle women in collars, in such a way as not to injure or threaten the windpipe. Such a thing is never done, unless it is intentional. "A good, solid collar," he said.

"I am pleased that master is pleased," whispered Feiqa, frightened.

"It is on you well, isn't it?" he said.

"Yes, Master," she said.

"What does it mean?" he asked.

"That I am a slave," she said.

"Go away," said Boabissia.

"Oh," said Feiqa.

The lad had put his hands rudely within her tunic and caressed her. Tears sprang to Feiqa's eyes.

"Go away," said Boabissia.

"Are you not grateful, slave?" asked the lad.

"Yes, Master," said Feiqa.

"You may kiss my feet in gratitude, slave," said the lad.

"Yes, Master. Thank you, Master," said Feiqa, and put her head down, kissing his feet.

"More lingeringly," he said.

"Yes, Master," she said.

The lad than turned about. "It is pleasant to master slaves," he said. "Perhaps when I am older, and rich, I shall buy myself one, much like this one, though perhaps younger, nearer my own age."

He then left.

"He lives in the building," said the proprietor. "He, and some of the others, sometimes in gangs, enjoy playing "Capture the Slave Girl.""

"I see," I said.

Feiqa, still kneeling, somewhat shaken, adjusted her tunic.

I smiled. I now had an excellent idea what had happened to the lovely, light-haired slave we had seen earlier on a lower landing, she whose tunic was opened and whose hair had been in such disorder. She had been "captured" earlier.

"It is an excellent game," said the proprietor. "It helps them to become men."

Many Gorean games, incidentally, have features which encourage the development of properties regarded as desirable in a Gorean youth, such as courage, discipline, and honor. Similarly, some of the games tend to encourage the development of audacity and leadership. Others, like the one referred to by the proprietor, encourage the young man to see the female in terms of her most basic and radical meaning, in the terms of her deepest and true nature, that nature which is most biologically fundamental to her, that nature which is that oι the inestimable prize, that of the most desirable prey, the most luscious quarry, that of she who is to be captured and mastered, absolutely, she to whose owning and domination all of nature inclines, and without which the ancient sexual equations of humanity cannot be resolved. Such games, in short, thus, encourage the lad, almost from infancy on, to reality and nature, to manhood and mastery.

"What a disgusting child," said Boabissia.

The lad had now disappeared.

She looked at Feiqa. "You, too, are disgusting," she said.

"Yes, Mistress," whispered Feiqa.

"It would be the same with you, Boabissia," I said, "if you were a slave. You, too, then, as much as Feiqa, would be at the mercy of free persons. You, too, then, would have to obey, and anyone, as much as she. You, too, as then a mere slave, would have to cringe, and perform, and kiss, even if it were only at the command of a child. You, too, then, as much as she, would have to obey, responding swiftly, hoping desperately to please, while being put through your paces."

"It is this way," said the proprietor. "Up this ladder, now."

"It is stifling," said Boabissia.

"Up the ladder," I said.

She went up the ladder, carefully. She held her skirt together, with one hand, as she could, about her legs. That, I thought, was a note of charming reserve, appropriate in a free woman. I followed her, into the dark opening above. Then I turned about and, on my hands and knees, looked down. Feiqa looked frightened. I do not think she wished to ascend into that darkness. To be sure, it did not seem a pleasant prospect. "Hand up the pack," I said to Hurtha. I was not sure Feiqa could manage it on the ladder. Hurtha removed it from her back, and stood on the lower rungs, lifting it up to me. I glanced at Feiqa. She had backed away. She was near the stairs. She was frightened. She did not wish to ascend the ladder. It frightened her, and that to which it might lead. Certainly it was not much of a ladder. It was narrow, and moved with one's weight. The rungs, of different sizes and unevenly spaced, were roped in place. Too, it would be dark, and hot, in the loft. What would await her there? She was a slave. Feiqa backed away another step. Her hand was before her mouth. I was afraid she might bolt.

"Slave," I said, sternly.

"Yes, Master," she said, and hurried to the ladder.

"Keep both your hands on the uprights," I told her.

"Yes, Master," she said.

Below, Hurtha grinned.

"Disgusting," said Boabissia.

I reached down and helped Feiqa to the loft.

"Here is the lamp," said the proprietor, handing it to Hurtha. He then, the lamp in hand, climbed up to join us.

"Be careful of the lamp," said the proprietor.

I took the lamp from Hurtha and lifted it up. There was a narrow corridor there, with some rooms on the left and right.

"It is the last room on the right," called the proprietor.

"Wait," I said to him. I then, bending down, carrying the lamp, led the way to the room.

I pushed open the door. It was small and low, but it was stout. It could doubtless be well secured from the inside. It would doubtless prove to be an effective barrier. The folks in insulae take their doors seriously. Such a door, plus his own dagger, is the poor man's best insurance against theft.

"Frightful," said Boabissia.

"It is furnished, as you can see," called the proprietor from below.

"It is too small, it is too dirty, I can hardly breathe up here," said Boabissia.

"It is my last vacancy," called the proprietor.

"I cannot stay here," said Boabissia.

"Go inside, and wait for me," I told my party. They bent down and entered the room.

"Is there no light?" asked Boabissia.

"There is a small shuttered aperture on the left," I said, holding up the lamp. "Some light will come through that in daylight hours."

"It is dirty here, and hot," said Boabissia. "I will not stay here."

It is a copper tarsk a night," called Achiates. "Take it or leave it. It is my last vacancy."

"I will not stay here," said Boabissia, firmly. I saw that Feiqa, too, regarded the room with horror.

"I feel faint," said Boabissia. "There is not enough air."

"Open the shutters," I said.

"It is too hot in here," said Boabissia.

"We are just under the roof," I said. "The hot air rises and gets trapped here."

"I think I will be sick," said Boabissia.

"Open the shutters," I said.

"This is a terrible place," said Boabissia.

"It is an insula," I said. "Thousands live in them."

"I will not stay here," she said.

"What do you think?" I asked Hurtha.

"It is splendid," said Hurtha. "To be sure, it would be even better if the temperature were more equable and if there were air to breathe."

"I came to Ar to claim my patrimony," said Boabissia, "not to suffocate and roast in a loft."

"Have no fear," I said. "When the temperature goes down these places, I am told, can be freezing."

"There, you see," said Hurtha.

"I will not stay here," repeated Boabissia.

I then retraced my steps to the opening to the upper level, where the loft had been converted into even more rooms. The proprietor was waiting below.

"We will take it," I told him. I dropped a copper tarsk into his palm. He then turned about and went down the steps, and I, with the lamp, returned to the room.

They had opened the shutters. There was a tiny falling of light, in a narrow, descendant shaft, into the room. In it there drifted particles of dust. They were rather pretty.

I blew out the lamp.

"Surely you did not pay a copper tarsk for this place," said Boabissia.

"Ar is packed with refugees," I said. "Many will not do so well as this."

"This is a terrible place," she said.

"It is furnished," I said. I looked about. Against one wall, there was a chest. There was some straw in a corner of the room. One could distribute it and sleep upon it. There were also some folded blankets. Too, there was a bucket with some water in it, with a dipper in it. That had probably not been changed recently. Then there was a slop pot as well, one for the wastes to be emptied into the vat on the ground floor. It was a long trip. It was not hard to understand how such wastes were occasionally cast from roofs and windows, usually with a warning cry to pedestrians below.

I looked about the room, in the dim light.

There, in one wall, was a long crack. The floor creaked, too, in places, as one trod upon it. I trusted this was merely from the disrepair and age of the boards. Insulae are seldom maintained well. They are cheap to build, and easily replaced. Their structure is primarily wood and brick. There are ordinances governing how high they may be built. Although we had come up several flights, we were probably not more than seventy or eighty feet Gorean from the street level. Without girders, frame steel and timber iron, as the Goreans say, wrought in the iron shops, such as are used in the towers, physics, even indexed to the Gorean gravity, is quick to impose its inexorable limits on heights. Such buildings tend to be vulnerable to structural stresses, and are sometimes weakened by slight movements of the earth. Sometimes walls give way; sometimes entire floors collapse.

I put the lamp down on the chest. I put my pack against a wall.

"This is a terrible place," said Boabissia. She knelt to one side, her knees together, in the position of the free woman. She did not sit cross-legged. No longer did she affect the posture of an Alar warrior. She had learned, I think, to some extent, in some sense or other, in a sense that she herself perhaps did not yet fully understood, in a sense that she had not yet herself fully plumbed, that she was a female.

The room was dusty, and dingy.

Hurtha was sitting to one side, cross-legged. He was examining his ax.

The room was hot. It was small. It was, at least, furnished.

To one side there was a slave ring. Near it were some chains. Too, among them, opened, I saw an iron collar, woman-size, with its lock ring. This permits it to be fastened on various chains, to be incorporated in a sirik, to be locked about the linkage of slave bracelets, and such. Too, there were some manacles there, of a size appropriate to confine perfectly and helplessly the small, lovely wrists of a female. Various keys hung on a hook near the door, well out of reach from the ring. On the wall, too, near the keys, an implement common in Gorean dwellings, hung a slave whip.

I removed the whip from the wall, and shook out the strands. There were five of them, pliant and broad.

I looked at Feiqa.

She knelt before me.

"This morning," I said, "you erred. It was a rather serious mistake. You were intending to drink from the upper bowl of the fountain, that reserved for free persons."

"Please do not punish me, Master," she begged. "I do not want to be whipped! Let me go this time! Just this time!"

I looked at her.

"I will not do it again!" she wept.

"I am sure you will not," I said. "Take off your clothes."

23: The Day of Generosity and Petitions

"Hurtha!" I protested. "No!" But it was too late. The fellow had already been struck with a thrust of the ax handle, to the back of the neck. He was having difficulty falling, however, unconscious though he might be, for the press of folks about the far end of the velvet rope, leading to the Central Cylinder, fighting for places on it.

"Here is his ribbon," said Hurtha cheerily, holding it above grasping hands. "Tie it about yourself and the rope."

"That fellow may have been waiting in line since yesterday," I said.

"Perhaps," admitted Hurtha, thrusting the ribbon to me. I seized it, and looped it about my shoulder and body, and about the velvet rope, and tied it. This would keep me on the rope. Hurtha's elbow, with a lateral stroke of great force, discouraged a fellow from snatching at the ribbon. I do not think he knew what hit him. Two other fellows backed away. I waved to them. "Move forward," said a Taurentian. We shuffled forward.

"The ribbons are all gone," moaned a man.

"Gone!" wept a woman.

"Are you a citizen of Ar?" inquired a fellow.

"Why?" I asked, warily.

"Only citizens of Ar, on the Day of Generosity and Petitions, are permitted to approach the regent," he said. "The holiday is for citizens, and citizens alone. Do you think we want folks streaming in from thousands of pasangs about to rob us of our places?"

"I suppose not," I said.

"I do not think you are of Ar!" he said. "Give me your ribbon!"

"I would rather keep it," I said.

"Guardsman!" he cried. "Guardsman!" Then he quieted quickly, lifted up by the back of the neck.

"Do you know how Alars cut out a tongue?" he was asked.

"No," he squeaked.

"It is done with an ax," said Hurtha, "from the bottom, up through the neck."

"I did not know that," said the fellow, dangling.

"An ax much like this," said Hurtha, holding the great, broad blade before the fellow's face, from behind. "Do you understand?"

"Perfectly," said the fellow.

"Did you wish to speak to a guardsman?" asked Hurtha. "There is one just over there."

"Why would I want to do that?" asked the fellow.

"I have no idea," said Hurtha.

"I don't either," said the man.

Hurtha then dropped him to the stones and he scurried away.

"There may be a problem," I admitted to Hurtha. "I am not a citizen of Ar."

"How would they know?" he asked. "Are you supposed to be carrying the Home Stone in your pouch?"

"There could be trouble," I said.

"You could always ask for a clarification of the rules after you have seen the regent," he said.

"That is true," I granted him.

"What could they do to you?" asked Hurtha.

"Quite a number of things, I suppose," I said.

"Even if they boiled you in oil," said Hurtha, "as that is normally done, it could be done only once."

"True," I said, though remaining uneasy.

"The only thing you truly need to fear," said Hurtha, "is that your honor might be lost."

"I suppose you are right," I said. "Still I would not look forward to being boiled in oil."

"Of course not," said Hurtha. "It would be extremely painful."

"Stop pushing," I said to the fellow behind me.

"Move up," he said.

"You could always sing," said Hurtha.

"What?" I asked.

"That is what the chieftain, Hendix, did," he said, "in Alar legend, when captured by his enemies and put in oil. He shouted at them, and laughed at them, insulting them all the while. And then while boiling he sang merry Alar songs. In that way he showed his contempt for his enemies."

"Perhaps toward the end he lost the tempo or was a bit off key," I speculated.

Perhaps," said Hurtha. "I was not there."

"Greetings," said a fellow, coming up to me.

I remembered him. He was the fellow I had spoken to in the Teiban Market.

"Did you find lodging?" he asked.

"Yes, thanks," I said. "In the insula of Achiates."

"He is a splendid fellow," said the man, "though a bit of an avaricious scoundrel."

"Excuse me," I said.

"Yes?" he said.

"Come closer," I said.

"Yes?" he asked, coming over.

"Is it true," I asked, "that only citizens of Ar are permitted to approach the regent on this day?"

"You certainly need not fear," he said, "for though you came in from Torcadino, clearly you are of Ar."

"But what if I were not?" I asked.

"Are you not?" he asked, interested.

I considered judicious replies, rapidly.

"To be sure," he said, "your accent, now that I think of it, does not ring quite true. Perhaps you have been away from the city for a long time." Those of Ar commonly have a gentle, liquid accent. I think it is one of the loveliest of the Gorean accents.

"What if perchance I were not of Ar?" I asked. I looked about myself, noting the distance to the nearest guardsmen. I considered how long it might take to remove the ribbon and, hastily, hopefully without combat, disappear down a side street.

"Your question is purely academic, of course," he said.

I reached for the ribbon.

"No," he laughed, putting out his hand. "Stay in your place. I know you are not of Ar, or do not think you are of Ar, for that seems clear from your speech. I am just teasing you." He might have found his humor a bit less delightful had he seen Hurtha behind him with his ax. Hurtha lowered the ax. "Ones who are not citizens of Ar may approach the regent on this day as well as citizens, if they can get a place on the rope. It is all part of the meaning of the day, of the generosity and benevolence of those of Ar, and such."

"I was told by a fellow earlier that only citizens might be on the rope," I said.

"No," smiled the fellow. "He was just trying to get your place."

"Is that true?" I asked the fellow behind me.

"I hope so," he said. "I am from Venna."

"It is true," said a fellow behind him.

"Move ahead," said a Taurentian. We shuffled forward.

"You, there," said the Taurentian to Hurtha. "Move away from the rope."

The crowd must now stay to the sides, away from the rope.

A fellow moved in behind me, with a ribbon.

"Where did you come from?" asked the man from Venna. "The ribbons were gone."

"They are seldom really gone, at least until late," said the fellow.

"What are things like at the back of the line?" asked a man.

"Bloody," said the fellow. "But the guardsmen are dispersing people now."

"How did you get a ribbon?" I asked. I knew how I had gotten mine. Hurtha had given it to me. He had received it as a donation, of sorts, from a fellow who was not at the time in a condition to use it. I wondered if the regent was aware of the mayhem that attended the acquisition of the ribbons. To be sure, most folks who had come early had probably received them in a civilized and orderly fashion. I had had difficulty in getting Hurtha up this morning. It was our third day in Ar. Yesterday we had spent a great deal of time walking about the city. It is pleasant to see the slave girls. Feiqa, too, who was heeling us, I gathered, from the men turning about, the occasional intakes of breath, the various comments and observations, and sometimes the literal sex calls, some of the bold, obtrusive, hooting sort by which young men impolitely signify that something of extreme sexual interest has been spotted, and others of the sort, done as a compliment and joke, with which masters sometimes summon their girls running to them, attracted more than her share of appreciative appraisals. This was understandable. She was superb slave meat. I did not know where Boabissia was now. She was probably somewhere in the city. She had wanted to see more of it. Feiqa had probably been left in the insula.

"The guardsmen hold out some," he said. "I paid a silver tarsk for this one."

"I see," I said.

"Move along," said a Taurentian.

"Hail, Gnieus Lelius!" called a man. One could now see the chair on the dais. He was not wearing the purple of the Ubar, but his shoulders were covered with a brown cloak, rather of the sort worn by Administrators in certain cities, civilian statesmen, servants of the people, so to speak. I wondered if the regent knew about the business of selling the ribbons. Some, too, I supposed, would be sold by citizens who had received them earlier in the legal distributions.

"Move forward," said a Taurentian.

I clutched the letters from Dietrich of Tarnburg within my tunic. My hand was sweaty.

A fellow two places ahead of me, for some petition or other, received ten pieces of gold. That is a considerable sum. There were cries of pleasure and wonder from the crowd. "Hail, Gnieus Lelius!" I heard. "Hail, Gnieus Lelius!" Most of the folks, as far as I could tell, however, received only a kind word from the regent, or an earnest assurance that their petitions would be examined with care. Several individuals, however, to be fair, did receive handfuls of coins, mostly copper, from the regent, who, smiling, would dip his hand into heaping coin bowls near him, and then spill coins into the outstretched hands of the grateful recipients. "Hail, Gnieus Lelius!" I heard. Taurentians were about the regent, and, too, some scribes. Notes, it seemed, and names, were being taken. Doubtless a record of the claims, grievances, petitions, and such, was being kept. It seemed there was not an excessive amount of guards. So loved, it seemed, was the regent.

"Yes, Citizen?" said the regent. I looked up. He was a regal looking fellow, tall and gaunt. He seemed fair, and kindly. I thought he would probably be a conscientious and dedicated public servant, perhaps even a gifted statesman. Certainly he had been high councilor in Ar. Indeed, he was now regent.

"Citizen?" he asked. His voice was not sharp. It was kindly. He was not impatient. I supposed it was not unusual for a common citizen suddenly finding himself in the presence of one so great, to find words failing him.

I reached inside my tunic and drew forth the letters.

"He has a petition, or petitions," said one of the scribes. "Give them to me, fellow."

I drew back the letters, not handing them to the scribe.

"These papers," I said, "excellency, are for you. I will deliver them only to you. I am not a citizen. I have come a long way."

I turned the letters in my hand. On them, then, could be seen the seal of the silver tarn. I then turned them again in such a way that the seals could not be seen. Two or three of the scribes reacted. I saw that they recognized the seal. Another scribe moved toward me. He seemed dangerous, not like a scribe. I suspected, then, that some of the scribes about were perhaps not truly scribes, but guards.

"Thank you," said the regent, kindly. He took the letters, keeping the seals down.

"Who are you?" he asked. "And where do you lodge?" His voice was no different than when he had spoken to others. Yet I was sure he had seen the seals.

"I am Tarl," I said, "of the city of Port Kar, and I am now lodging in the insula of Achiates, in the Alley of the Slave Brothels of Ludmilla." This information was taken down.

"Write down," said the regent to the scribe nearest him, "that we have received petitions from Tarl of Port Kar, who is lodging in the house of Achiates, which we will take under careful consideration." This was done.

"I am grateful," I said, "that you will be pleased to ponder carefully the contents of these petitions. I assure you that I am quite earnest in this matter, and I attest with conviction to the veracity of what I take to be their contents."

"I understand," he said.

I bowed to him. "Excellency," I said. He inclined his head, graciously responding to my salute. I removed the ribbon from my body. My commission had been accomplished. I had delivered the letters. Dietrich of Tarnburg, and Ar, had been served. More I could not do.

The regent motioned that I should approach more closely. "Thank you," he said. "I have waited for such word for a long time."

"It is nothing," I said.

"Wait," said he.

I turned about. He poured coins into my hands, copper tarsks.

"My thanks, Excellency," I said, gratefully, as though I might have been another petitioner.

"Hail, Gnieus Lelius! Hail, Gnieus Lelius!" I heard, the crowd acclaiming yet again the regent's generosity.

I then turned about, and took my leave.

24: The Origins of Boabissia

"And this was found about your throat as a baby, in the wreckage of a caravan, by Alars?" he asked. He stood close to her. He looked at it in the light, holding it between his fingers. It was still on its thong about her neck.

"Yes," said Boabissia.

"It was on your neck?" he asked.

"Yes," said Boabissia. "And I have continued to wear it."

"I see," he said.

"Are you acquainted with the young woman inside?" an attendant had asked at the gate.

"Yes," I said. "I think so."

"It was here she entered," said Feiqa.

"Yes," I said.

"Please come in," had said the attendant. We had entered and followed him through the gardened courtyard, with its fountains, and, on the other side of the court, across the shaded portico and into the recesses of the house.

Hurtha and I had returned around noon to the insula, after leaving the area before the Central Cylinder. As soon as we had entered through the shuttered gate into the insula's small, dim vestibule, there, in the light, the dust in it, we had seen Feiqa. "Masters," she said, eagerly, rising to her feet, moving toward us. Then she stopped short. The shackle on her left ankle, fastening her to a floor ring, saw to this. She knelt at the end of the chain. The shackle looked well on her ankle. "Masters," she said.

"Where is Boabissia?" I asked. "I thought you would have been left upstairs."

"I was," she said. "But Mistress returned and fetched me. She had found something which greatly excited her. I must accompany her that I would know the place, and then, presently when you returned, lead you there."

"That is why you are chained here?" I asked.

"Perhaps, Master," she said. "But Mistress also, of course, may have thought of a slave's comfort."

I smiled. Boabissia was not the sort of person who would think of a slave's comfort. Indeed, she believed that slaves should be treated with great strictness and subjected to ruthless and uncompromising discipline.

"Why did she not wait for us?" I asked.

"She could not wait," said Feiqa. "She was in too great a hurry to get back."

"What is this all about?" I asked.

"She thinks she may have found the house of her people," said Feiqa, "that she might enter, that incredible fortune might be hers, that she might be able to claim her patrimony."

"I gather it was a fine house," I said.

"I think it is probably very beautiful," said Feiqa. "I caught a glimpse of the garden within, in the courtyard, and the house beyond, a large, lovely house, with a shaded portico, when she was admitted. Whoever owns it must be very rich."

"What makes her think that it might be the house of her people?" I asked.

"The tiny sign near the call rope," said Feiqa. "It is a Tau, much as on her neck ornament."

"The same form of Tau?" I asked.

"It is very similar," she said.

"Exactly similar?" I asked.

"No," she said.

"But very similar?" I asked.

"Yes," she said.

"Some clue, then, as to her origins, may be there," I said. Goreans are usually rather careful about such things as crests, signs, family emblems, and such. Sometimes such things are actually registered, and legally restricted in their use to given lines.

"I really think it is possible, Master," said Feiqa.

"If all is well then," I said, "let us rejoice for Boabissia, and her good fortune."

"It looks like a fine house?" asked Hurtha.

"Yes, Master," said Feiqa.

"Boabissia will like that," he said. "She has always been a spoiled, greedy little thing. It will not displease her to be rich."

"The family, too, if there is a fine house, and grounds, and such," I said, "may be powerful and of high station."

"She will not object to that either," said Hurtha.

"Where is this house?" I asked.

"It is not far, Master," said Feiqa.

"That is interesting," I said.

"There are some fine houses in this district," said Hurtha, "particularly over several blocks. We saw some yesterday."

"True," I said. Ar, as many cities, sometimes had rather contrasting neighborhoods in surprising proximity to one another. For example, the Avenue of Turia, nearby, was one of the finest streets in Ar. Yet, behind it, reached by a crevice between some buildings, only a walk of some two or three Ehn away, was the Alley of the Slave Brothels of Ludmilla.

"Where is the key to your shackle?" I asked.

"Over there, Master," said Feiqa, pointing. It hung on a hook, where it might be convenient to tenants or visitors, near the door that led to the apartment of Achiates.

I fetched the key. I returned to where she knelt, shackled. I looked down upon her. I wondered if there would be point in having her, there, suddenly, on the floor of the insula's vestibule, before I unshackled her. She was very beautiful.

"Master?" she asked.

I thrust her back to the floor, in a rattle of chain. "Oh!" she cried. It did not matter. She was only a slave. "Oh!" she gasped, and then was clutching me. "Disgusting," said a free woman, entering the insula, and then proceeding upstairs. I stood up. Feiqa was at my feet, gasping, shaken. Such things may be done to such as she. They are only slaves.

Feiqa reached to my foot and kissed it, tears in her eyes.

"Kneel," I said. I then removed the shackle from her fair

ankle. But I then held her ankle in my hand, substituting now for the clasp of the shackle the grip of the master. She gasped. She put her head down. She knew herself held, and as a slave. She lifted her head. She looked at me wildly. She was helpless. Once more I found her beautiful. I thrust her back, again, down to the stones of the dimly lit vestibule, and pulled her by the ankle to me. Then I saw to it, as it pleased me, at my caprice, for she was a mere slave, that she must again helplessly suffer the exigencies of her bondage.

"Oh, Master, Master, Master," she said, kissing me.

"Lead us to the place Boabissia found," I said.

"Yes, Master," she said.

On the way, following Feiqa, hurrying ahead of us, we saw a female slave, stripped, carrying a heavy yoke, tied on her, supporting buckets of water. Her master was behind her. Sometimes he poked her with a sharp stick, to hurry her along. Boabissia would have approved of that. She was in favor, I recalled, of stern treatment for slaves, particularly, it seemed, luscious female slaves, like the lovely nude struggling bound in the yoke, with its buckets, or Feiqa. We also saw a chain of female slaves, permitted tunics, but hooded, in neck coffle, and two slave wagons, with blue and yellow silk. This was the district of the Street of Brands.

"It is this house," said Feiqa.

"The wall is impressive and the gate is strong," observed Hurtha.

I saw the Tau near the call rope. It was indeed quite similar to that which was on Boabissia's small disk. I now recalled what Boabissia's disk had reminded me of. The resemblance, however, was not exact. There were at least two differences. That was good. The form of Tau near the call rope I had seen before, long ago, in Ar, on another street, and. more than once, at the Sardar Fairs.

"Is anything wrong?" asked Feiqa.

"Boabissia has already entered?" I asked.

"I think so," said Feiqa.

I drew on the call rope. We heard the bell jangle within. In a moment an attendant, a young man, had come to the gate.

*   *   *

"And this was found about your throat as a baby, in the wreckage of a caravan, by Alars?" he asked. He stood close to her. He looked at it in the light, holding it between his fingers. It was still on its thong about her neck.

"Yes," said Boabissia.

"It was on your neck?" he asked.

"Yes," said Boabissia. "And I have continued to wear it."

"I see," he said. "May I remove it?"

"Of course," she said. He delicately undid the thong. Boabissia smiled at Hurtha and myself. She had been there when we had been ushered into his presence. Feiqa had been put on a neck chain, just inside the gate. It was fastened to a ring, one of several there, fastened in the wall. It was sunny there. She must kneel. She must keep her head down. I gathered they did not pamper slaves in this house. We would pick her up on the way out. The fellow had greeted us pleasantly. It was almost as though he had expected us, or someone, to come. He had not, as I recalled, seemed surprised to see us. Similarly we had encountered no difficulty in being admitted into his presence, in spite of the fact that he was presumably an important man. It was a large, officelike room. There was a broad desk. There were many papers about. He was a distinguished looking fellow. I had never seen him before.

He was examining the disk in his hand.

"I think," said Boabissia, "that it may afford a clue to my identity."

"Perhaps," said the fellow.

"But surely it does," she protested.

"How could I know that you did not merely find this, or buy it, or steal it?" he asked.

"I assure you, I did not," said Boabissia. "It is mine. It was on me as an infant. I have always worn it."

He regarded it.

"Is it not the same as the sign on your house?" asked Boabissia.

"It is quite similar," he admitted.

"But not identical," I said.

Boabissia cast me an angry look.

The fellow looked at me, and smiled. "It is, however," he said, "what the sign was, some years ago, before its style was slightly changed."

"But that is right!" exclaimed Boabissia. "It was on me from years ago!"

"Precisely," he smiled.

"I would not have known that," she said. "Had I made a counterfeit, I would have done it, not knowing any better, in your modern fashion, and then you would have been able to detect, from the time involved, that the disk was a forgery, that it was fraudulent.

"True," he said.

"You see!" said Boabissia to me, triumphantly.

"Yes," I said.

"He is jealous," said Boabissia to the fellow. "He is almost beside himself with envy. He only wants to see me denied my fortune, deprived of my rightful deserts."

"Your fortune?" asked the fellow. "Your rightful deserts?"

"Yes, my rightful deserts, my rightful dues," said Boabissia. "I am determined to receive them."

"I understand," he said. "I shall examine the records. If all tallies, as I suspect it will, have no fear, you will receive, as you have put it, your rightful deserts, your rightful dues."

"All I want," said Boabissia, "is exactly what I deserve."

"I shall check the records," he said. "If it is within my power, I will try to see that you do indeed receive exactly what you deserve, precisely what you deserve."

"Thank you," she said, and cast an angry look at me.

"What is it, incidentally," he asked, "that you think you deserve?"

"Do you not recognize me?" she asked.

"I do not understand," he said.

"I may be your long-lost daughter," she said.

"To the best of my knowledge," he said, "I do not have any daughters, long-lost or otherwise. I do have some sons."

"Look at me," she said.

"Yes?" he said.

"Is there no general family resemblance?" she asked. I,

for one, surely did not note any. To be sure, members of the same family sometimes differ considerably from one another in their appearance.

"I do not understand," he said.

"You are perhaps my uncle," she said, "if you are not my father."

"Oh, I see," he said.

"Might I not be your niece, or a cousin?"

"An interesting idea," he said.

"Look at me," she said. "Look closely. What do you think?"

"You are curvy," he said.

"Curvy?" she said.

"I think I see now," he said, "what you have come here for."

"I am seeking my identity," she said.

"And perhaps a little more?" he speculated.

"Only what are my dues," she said, defensively.

"You consider yourself perhaps the heiress to riches?" he inquired.

"Perhaps," she said. "The caravan was a large one. Doubtless my presence there, as a mere infant, suggests great affluence on the part of my people. They might even have been the masters of the caravan. Surely you yourself are wealthy. This is a fine house, with luxurious appointments, with space and splendid grounds. Surely the sign on the disk is meaningful to you. You seem to have admitted as much."

"I see," he said.

"Surely in the fullness of your honor, as I conceive of you as a gentleman," she said, "you would not wish to deny to me what I have coming." I thought that was a rather nasty thrust on the part of Boabissia. It is seldom wise, incidentally, to impugn, or attempt to manipulate, the honor of a Gorean.

"No," he said, pleasantly enough, apparently taking no offense, "I would be one of the last to deny you exactly what you have coming."

"Good," she said, rather haughtily, putting her head in the air. Boabissia could occasionally get on one's nerves in this fashion.

"I believe that I am a wealthy man," said the fellow. "Too, I think it is fair to say that I have some standing in this city, and some power."

"That would be my impression," said Boabissia.

"You think there is some relationship between us?" he said.

"Yes," said Boabissia. "The disk, as you have as much as admitted, makes that clear. I invite you to consult your records."

"I gather you think you may be of my line, or of some pertinent collateral line," he said.

"Yes," she said. "I think that is altogether possible."

"If you are truly of my line, or even of some closely related collateral line," he said, "you would doubtless become overnight one of the most famous, one of the wealthiest and most powerful women in Ar."

"Perhaps," said Boabissia. She drew herself up proudly.

"I think that perhaps, as you seem to believe," he said, "there may be some relationship between us."

"The disk proves it," she said.

"I think you are right," he said.

"Consult your records," she said.

"Do you truly wish me to do so?" he asked.

"Yes," said Boabissia. "Indeed, I demand it."

"Very well," he said. "It will only take a moment." He reached for a small bell on the desk.

"Let us go, Boabissia," I suggested. "We could return tomorrow."

"Be silent," she said to me.

The man rang the small bell, to which, in a moment or two, an attendant responded. In a bit, then, the attendant, seemingly informed as to what was required, left the room. The man himself then sat behind the desk and put the small disk before him, to his right, on the surface of the desk.

Boabissia glanced at Hurtha and myself. She was terribly excited.

"Let us go, Boabissia," I suggested.

"Be quiet," she said.

"It will be only a little bit," said the man. "If you wait now, it will save you a trip back tomorrow."

"Leave, if you wish," said Boabissia.

"Why would they wish to leave?" asked the man, puzzled.

"I have no idea," said Boabissia.

"Nor do I," he said.

In a bit the attendant had returned with a large, somewhat dusty, oblong ledgerlike book. It was tied shut with a cord. It contained several pages. It was bound in leather. On the cover, though it was hard to see from where I stood, there seemed to be some designations, such as perhaps dates and numbers. "The older records, such as these," he said, "are kept here, together with duplicates of the more current records. The more current records, together with duplicates of the older records, are kept at the house."

I nodded. In that way two identical sets would be maintained, in different locations. This was not uncommon with Gorean bookkeeping, particularly in certain kinds of businesses.

"Is this not the house?" asked Boabissia.

"This is my personal residence," he said.

"You have another house?" she asked.

"Of course," he said.

Boabissia threw me a pleased glance.

"My place of business," he said.

"Oh," she said.

He untied the cord and blew some dust from the cover of the book. Its pages were yellowed.

"Do not dally, please," said Boabissia.

He opened the book. He put to one side, taking it from a shallow pocket within the book's cover, a punched copper disk, on a string, rather the size of that which Boabissia had worn, and put it next to Boabissia's.

"Look!" said Boabissia, joyfully.

"Yes," I said.

The disk also had some device on it, as did Boabissia's, but I could not see it well from the distance.

"The disk," she said. "It has something on it."

"Yes," I said.

"Doubtless it is the same mark as is on mine," she said.

"Perhaps not," I said.

The fellow began to turn the pages.

"Hurry!" said Boabissia.

He had then apparently found what he was looking for. He picked up the disk which had been Boabissia's from the desk, looked at it, and then checked it against something in the book. He then perused the entry there. Then he rechecked the disk against the book. He then rose to his feet and approached Boabissia.

"Yes?" said Boabissia. "Yes?"

"You were right, my dear," he said. "There does exist a relationship between us, and, indeed, I think as you suspected, a most important relationship."

"You see!" cried Boabissia, almost leaping in place, elatedly, triumphantly to Hurtha and myself.

"But, my dear," he said, "it is not exactly the sort of relationship which you anticipated."

"What are you doing?" she asked.

Then, suddenly, as she cried out in surprise, in dismay, he tore her dress down to her waist.

"Yes," he said. "You are curvy."

She looked at him, startled, not daring, under his fierce gaze, to raise her hands, to lift her garment.

"The relationship," he told her, "is that of slave to master."

"No!" she cried.

"Strip," he said.

"Do so, immediately," I said to Boabissia, sternly.

Trembling she thrust down her dress over her hips, and stood then within it, it down about her ankles.

"Your sandals, too," I said, "quickly!"

Frightened she slipped from them, too. When a Gorean orders a woman to strip he means now, and completely, leaving not so much as a thread upon her body. She stood there, confused, trembling and terrified. Her clothing was about her feet. It was as though she stood in a tiny pond of cloth.

"What is going on?" asked Hurtha.

"Do not interfere," I said. "It is as I feared."

"Here," said the fellow. He indicated the book and the

disk which had been within it, and Boabissia's disk. I went to the table. I looked at the disk which had been taken from the book. There was no number on it, but the "Tau" on it was identical to that on Boabissia's disk. Keeping the place where lay the apparently pertinent entry I looked at the cover of the book. On it was a year number, one dating back twenty-two years, and two sets of numbers, separated by a span sign. I examined Boabissia's disk. The number on it fell between the two numbers on the book's cover. I then turned to the page to which the fellow had had the book opened earlier.

"See?" he asked.

"Yes," I said. There, at the head of one of the entries, identifying it, and correlated with it, was the number which had been on Boabissia's disk.

"The caravan in whose wreckage you were found," said the fellow to Boabissia, "was a slave caravan."

Boabissia looked at him, regarding him with horror. She then looked at Hurtha.

"When you were found I was only a small boy," said Hurtha. "I did not know what sort of caravan it was. I do not think any of the Alars did. Apparently when found it was in much ruin."

"It was not traveling publicly as a slave caravan," said the man. "It was not, for example, flying its blue and yellow silk. In this manner it had been thought that we might keep secret its cargo, hundreds of beautiful females, a certain lure to the lust and greed of raiders. Our stratagem, however, it seems, was ineffectual."

Hurtha nodded.

"Was much left when the Alars came upon it?" he asked.

"No," said Hurtha. "I do not think so."

"I am not surprised," said the fellow. "The women, of course, would have been stolen. Doubtless they entertained their captors well, before being sold in a hundred markets."

"I was only an infant," whispered Boabissia.

"That may be why you were left behind," said the man.

"I could have starved, or perished of exposure, or have been eaten by animals," she said.

"Perhaps they did not find you," he said. "Perhaps, on the other hand, it was not of concern to them."

"Not of concern to them?" she asked, in horror.

"Of course not," he said. "Do not forget you were only then, as you are now, a slave."

She shuddered, her eyes wide with horror.

"Do not cover your breasts," he said. "Keep your arms at your sides."

She sobbed.

"It was my caravan," said the fellow. "I lost much on it. It took me five years to recover my losses."

"Your caravan?" whispered Boabissia. "What is your business?"

"I am a merchant of sorts," he said. "I deal in slaves, wholesale and retail, mostly female slaves."

"A lovely form of merchandise," I said.

"Yes," he said.

"But I was only an infant," whispered Boabissia.

"You were sold to my house in your infancy," he said.

"It is in the entry," I informed Boabissia. "Too, your slave number is in his house was the number on your disk."

"I was sold to you in my infancy?" said Boabissia.

"For three tarsk bits," he said.

"So little?" she said.

"You were an infant," he said.

"It is very little," she whispered.

"Would you rather have been exposed in the Voltai," he asked, "a wooden skewer through your heels?"

She shook her head, frightened.

"But why would I have been sold?" she asked.

"You were a female," he said. "Why not?"

The selling of infant daughters is not that unusual in large cities. Some women do it regularly. They make a practice of it, much as they might sell their hair to hair merchants or to the weavers of catapult ropes. Some women, it is rumored, hope for daughters, that they may sell to the slave trade. These women, in effect, breed for slaves. Too, there is a common Gorean belief that females are natural slaves, a belief for which there is much evidence, incidentally, and in the light of this belief some families would rather sell a daughter than raise her. Too, of course, daughters, unlike sons, are seldom economic assets to the family. Indeed they cannot even pass on the *gens* name. They can retain it in companionship, if they wish, if suitable contractual arrangements are secured, but they cannot pass it on. The survival of the name and the continuance of the patrilineal line are important to many Goreans.

"Stand straight," he said to Boabissia.

Boabissia, frightened, straightened her body.

Hurtha made a noise of approval, pleased at seeing Boabissia under male command. I, too, I must admit, was pleased to see this, to see Boabissia obeying. How marvelous and rewarding it is to control a female, having total power over her.

"Straighter," he said. "Suck in your gut, put your shoulders back."

She complied.

"If it is of interest to you," he said, "I did not simply buy you. Although your mother was a free woman I had her strip, and then put her through slave paces. I would attempt to assess the possibilities of the daughter by seeing the mother, by seeing her naked and performing, attempting desperately to please. When she was reluctant, as a free woman, I used the whip on her. Thus I obtained a better idea of what I might be buying."

"Tell me about my mother, please," she said.

"She was a comely wench, as I determined, when I saw her naked," he said. "She was curvaceous, and, when she realized I would not compromise with her, moved quite well. She herself, I am sure, under a suitable master, would have made excellent collar meat. She would also make, it seemed to me, an excellent breeder of slaves."

"Was she of Ar?" asked Boabissia.

"Yes," he said. "But she was of low-caste origins, of course."

"Oh," said Boabissia.

"But she had beauty beyond her caste," he said. "Indeed, I would be surprised if she had not, sooner or later, been caught and put in a collar. She may even now, somewhere, be serving a master."

He then looked upon Boabissia.

"I was only going to offer two tarsk bits for you originally," he said, "a standard price for a female infant, but after I had seen your mother, seen her fully, and performing, and under the lash, you understand, and considered how you might have something of her beauty, I raised my offer to three."

Boabissia nodded, tears in her eyes.

"Lift your head," he said.

"Excellent," he said. "Had I realized how well you would turn out, I would have offered not three, but five, or even seven, tarsk bits for you."

"Am I more beautiful than my mother?" she asked.

"Yes," he said, "and, clearly, even more of a slave."

She sobbed.

He turned to face Hurtha and myself. "Gentlemen," he said, "I must thank you for returning this girl to me."

"It was not really our intention to do so," I said. "She is surely herself primarily responsible. She saw this place, and, eager to inquire as to her antecedents and connections, entered of her own accord."

He turned to Boabissia. "And you have now satisfied your curiosity, haven't you, my dear?" he asked. "You have now learned what you wished to learn. You have now discovered your antecedents and connections, so to speak, and your exact place, or, perhaps better put, your exact lack of a place, in civil and social relationships."

"Yes," she whispered.

"But she has been with you, as I understand it," he said, turning to us, "and surely it is in your company that she came to Ar."

"Yes," I said.

"I thought perhaps it had been a joke on your part, something to amuse you, that you had let her enter here alone, first, before your arrival."

"No," I said.

"Nonetheless," he said, "surely some gratuity is in order, for abetting her return."

"None is necessary," I said.

We looked at her.

She was still maintaining a position of slave beauty.

"What do you think she will bring?" I asked.

"The market is depressed," he said. "Much of it has to do with the rumored affairs at Torcadino, the purported advances of Cosians, the crowding in Ar, the influx of refugees. But I would think, even so, she might bring two silver tarsks."

"A fine price for a girl," I said.

"I think she will bring that, even in the current markets," he said.

"I had not realized Boabissia was so valuable," said Hurtha.

Boabissia glanced at Hurtha, startled.

It is not unusual, of course, for a fellow to take a woman lightly, or for granted, until he learns of her interest to others, for example, what they are willing to pay for her.

Boabissia looked away from Hurtha then, swiftly, not daring to meet his eyes. She reddened in a wave of heat and helplessness from the roots of her hair to the tips of her toes.

Similarly, it is not unusual for a fellow not to think of a given woman in a sexual manner, or as an object of extreme desire, but when he sees her stripped, and as a slave, that changes instantly and dramatically.

"Please," she begged.

"Be silent," I said.

She was beautiful, and her life had changed. She must learn to endure slave scrutiny. Later she would perhaps learn to revel in it, brazenly.

"I had thought," said the fellow, viewing her, "that the caravan had been a total loss. I see now that I was mistaken.

She stood before us, viewed.

"I lost a mere infant," he said. "I am returned a beautiful slave."

She choked back a sob.

"Some gratuity, or reward, is surely in order," he said.

"None is necessary," I said.

"But consider the savings I have effected on feed alone," he said.

"Come now," I said. "Table scraps and slave gruel are not that expensive."

"I insist," he said.

"As you will," I said.

Boabissia regarded me with horror.

"You are more than generous," I said.

"Indeed," said Hurtha, approvingly. In my palm lay a silver tarsk. I put it in my pouch. Boabissia moaned.

He then reached to the small bell on his desk, and shook it, twice.

"I assume," I said, "in the light of the special circumstance of her case, she is not to be treated as a runaway slave."

"No," he said. "Or, certainly not at present, at least." Then he looked at the girl. "You do understand, however, do you not, my dear, the typical penalties for a runaway slave?"

She nodded, numbly.

"Excellent," he said.

"If I may be so bold," I said, "I would advocate a certain modest latitude, at least for a day or two, in her initial training. You must understand that she has, for many years, regarded herself as a free woman."

"Interesting," he said.

"Too," I said, "not only has she regarded herself as a free woman, but she has behaved as one, and has affected the airs of one."

"That is very serious, my dear," said the man.

At that moment a lithe, sinewy fellow entered, doubtless in response to the sound of the bell a few moments earlier. He whose office it was gestured toward Boabissia. Her hands were drawn behind her, and braceleted behind her back.

"But she did not understand she was not free, really," I said.

Boabissia pulled against the bracelets, weakly.

"She came here unveiled," said the man.

"True," I said. "But the Alar women do not veil themselves."

"She thought she was an Alar?" asked the man.

"She was accustomed to thinking of herself in that way," In said.

"But she should have known from her body she was not of the Alars," he said. "She is not a tall, strapping woman. Look at her. She is short, and luscious, and cuddly, and exquisitely feminine. That is the body of a woman of the cities or towns, and, if I may note the fact, it is a typical slave's body."

"True," I said.

"And what was her attitude toward female slaves?" he asked.

"She held herself immeasurably superior to them," I said. "She despised them. She hated them, and held them in great contempt."

"Quite appropriately," he said. "And how did she behave toward them?"

"With arrogance," I said, "and she enjoyed treating them with great cruelty."

"I see," he said. "You may kneel, my dear."

Boabissia knelt.

"Did you never suspect, my dear," he asked, "that you were a slave?"

"I did not dream I was imbonded," she whispered.

"But you were," he said.

"Yes," she said.

"It is an interesting case," he said, "a female who has been a legal slave unwittingly since infancy, and has only now, in the past Ehn, discovered her true condition."

"Yes," I said.

"But I fear, my dear," he said, "that you have somewhat misinterpreted my question."

She raised her head, regarding him, puzzled.

"I asked if you had never suspected that you were a *slave*."

She put down her head, reddening.

"Answer," he said.

"Are you speaking of legalities?" she asked, angrily.

"I am speaking of something far deeper and more profound than legalities," he said.

"I do not wish to answer that question," she said.

"Speak," he said.

"Yes," she said, "I have suspected it."

"You have been a slave from the moment of conception," he said.

She put down her head.

"Split your knees," he said. "More widely."

She complied. But then she looked up, half in defiance, half in tears.

"Yes," he said, "from the moment of conception."

She put down her head again, and sobbed.

"Leash her," he said.

The fellow who had come in, responding to the summons of the small bell, snapped one end of a long slave leash on Boabissia's throat. The leash is long to permit it being used in a variety of ways, for example, for binding the female or, looped, or loose, for giving her the encouragement of the whistling leather, or, if desired, the administration of more serious lash discipline. She looked up, frightened, knowing herself leashed, and on such a leash. Her eyes met those of the owner of the office.

"You came here," he said, "seeking to find out who you were. I trust you now know. Similarly, you came here to find riches, to seek your fortune. I trust you are now satisfied with the riches you have found, slave bracelets and a leash, though, to be sure, they are not yours, and with your fortune, that which you so avidly sought, which proves to be total bondage."

"Please," she wept, suddenly. "I did not know!"

"How demanding, how peremptory, and arrogant, and suspicious, you were," he mused.

"I am sorry," she said. "Forgive me, I beg you!"

"How insistent you were," he said.

"Forgive me," she said.

"How fearful you were," he said, "that you might not receive your dues, your just deserts."

"Forgive me!" she begged.

"Lift your head," he said. "Higher. Higher!" She looked up at him, her head far back, the leash on her throat.

"I think I promised you that you would receive exactly what you deserved, exactly what you had coming."

"Please," she said, trembling naked before a master.

"You will receive exactly what you deserve," he said, "and then even more. And you will get, my dear, not only exactly what you have coming, but that, I assure you, and then a thousand times more."

"Mercy, please," she begged, in her helplessness.

"And then," he said, "you will be sold."

"Please, no," she wept.

"It is amusing," he said, "that you held slaves in such great contempt, and treated them with such cruelty, for such is what you were all the time, and as such, revealed, in your full truth, you will now live."

She sobbed, helplessly.

"It is interesting," said the fellow, looking down at the distraught beauty, kneeling before us, almost beside herself with confusion and fear. "I have not seen this female since she was an infant. I remember tying the slave disk, with her number on it, about her tiny neck, opening her blankets that she might be exposed to me while doing so. Now, look at her, a beautifully developed, superbly desirable female slave."

"She is indeed beautiful, and desirable," I said. I had never seen Boabissia look so lovely. To be sure, I had not before seen her truly as what she was, a slave. Slavery, putting a woman in her place in nature, returning her to where she belongs, considerably increases her beauty.

"Who would have thought," he asked, "that that infant I bought for only three tarsk bits would have grown into something this marvelous. I am sure that I will be able to get at least two silver tarsks for her."

"Doubtless," I said.

"An excellent investment," he said.

"I agree," I said.

"You need not now keep your head in high-harness position," he said to the girl.

She moved her head. He stepped back a bit. She looked at him, frightened, his.

"It has been a long time, my dear," he said, "but you are now home."

She put down her head, sobbing. She had been returned to her master.

"Stand," he said to her.

She stood.

"You know what to do with her," he said to the fellow who held her leash.

"Yes," said the fellow.

"Do it," he said.

25: The Tunnels

"Enter," said the woman.

It was now in the evening of the day in which Boabissia had hurried into the house marked with the "Tau" near the call rope. That Tau was the design, or trademark, of course, of Tenalion of Ar, one of the well-known slavers of the city. 'Tau' is the first letter of the name 'Tenalion'. I had recognized it immediately when I had seen it near the call rope. Indeed, it was identical with that on his place of business, which I had passed at various times when in Ar, a large, formidable structure located in the heart of of Ar's slaving district, which housed various facilities pertinent to his trade, ranging from beautifully appointed sales rooms to discipline pits. I had also seen it at different times at the Sardar Fairs, at his display spaces.

I had not met him personally, however, until today. He had entertained Hurtha and myself, sharing some fine paga with us, of the House of Temus, my favorite, after Boabissia had been removed from the room, presumably to be transported to his house of business. By now she was doubtless marked and collared, and chained somewhere there, presumably in the lower pens, as she was for most practical purposes a new girl. He seemed a very pleasant fellow. The Tau on Boabissia's disk had reminded me, I suppose, of his Tau. On the other hand, it had been different, and Tau's, as other letters of the Gorean alphabet, are used in various designs and for various purposes. I had not realized, of course, that the current design of Tenalion's Tau had been changed from an older one, that which had appeared on Boabissia's disk.

"Enter," said the woman. "Enter the Tunnels." She was sitting on a stool outside.

I lowered my head and entered through the small iron door, and began to descend a dimly lighted ramp to the interior. At the foot of the ramp there was another woman.

"It is a tarsk bit," she said.

I put a tarsk bit into the copper bowl on the small table near her. To the woman's right was a barred gate. It was now open. Such gates are common in such establishments. They are generally open when the business is open, and closed when the business is closed. On the other side of the threshold hung a heavy curtain of red velvet.

The Tunnels was one of the slave brothels of Ludmilla, for whose establishments the street, the Alley of the Slave Brothels of Ludmilla, is named. She does not own all the brothels on the street, incidentally, nor the best of them, in my opinion, nor even the majority of them. It is only that several of them, five, to be exact, are owned by her, whereas no other entrepreneur owns more than two, this accounting apparently for the derivation of the name. Her brothels, if it is of interest are the Chains of Gold, supposedly her best, costing at any rate a copper tarsk for admission, a common price for a paga tavern, and, all cheap tarsk-bit brothels, the Silken Cords, the Scarlet Whip, the Slave Racks and the Tunnels. On this street, too, of course, among many other sorts of establishments, such as shops and stalls, and smaller residences, are several insulae, among them the insula of Achiates.

I moved to the curtain and brushed it aside.

"Welcome," said a woman. "Welcome to the Tunnels."

I stepped within, permitting the curtain to fall back behind me.

"Come this way," she said.

She was a large, strong woman, rather straight in body and coarse in feature. She was clad in brief leather. It was suggestive of that of a warrior. She wore armlets and bracelets. She carried a whip. Such is useful in keeping the slaves in line.

"This way," she said.

I followed her, threading my way among the small tables, and the mats, and the slave rings and clutching, moving, intertwined bodies, to a small table. I heard gasping, and a small cry of pain, and then a small cry of submission, and the movement of a chain on tiles. The room was crowded, but not too crowded. I heard conversation. Some musicians were playing in the half darkness. Some of these brothels are really not that much different from certain paga taverns. There, too, of course, girls go with the drinks, though dancers are commonly extra. The table was in the second row, or so, from the front of the room, where there was something of an open space. The musicians were on the right side of this, as I faced them. It was not easy to see at first. The room was illuminated, insofar as it was, with a soft, flickering, reddish light, the result of the flames of tiny tharlarion-oil lamps set in narrow red-glass enclosures on certain of the tables. In such a light, of course, interesting colorations, subtle, soft, constantly changing reddish hues, ranging, depending on the color of the glass and the mix of the lights, from dark, rose-colored pinks to creamy crimsons, are imparted to the flesh of white-skinned slaves. Too, there were many dark places and shadows. Some men are fond of privacy in such a place.

"Is this satisfactory?" she asked.

"Yes," I said, sitting down, cross-legged, behind the small table.

"Oh!" said a woman, near me, half rearing up on a mat, and I saw her eyes, startled, for an instant, and that she was blond, and that her flesh appeared interesting in the light, and then she, the chain on her neck fastening her to the slave ring near the mat, was thrust back on the mat. "Oh, yes!" she cried. "Yes, Master!"

"Are you he called Tarl, of Port Kar?" asked the woman who had conducted me to my place.

"Why?" I asked.

"I was told to watch for such a person," she said.

"Who told you?" I asked. I had come to the Tunnels in response to a message, delivered to me by Achiates, the owner of the insula in which Hurtha and I were rooming. He had, it seemed, if he were telling the truth, and I had no particular reason to doubt it, found the message thrust under his door.

She looked about. "I do not see him here now," she said. "Are you this Tarl of Port Kar?"

"I am called Bosk," I said.

"Oh," she said. This information did not seem to make much difference to her, one way or the other. I watched her. She did not, as far as I could tell, glance at any particular person, nor in any particular direction. I detected nothing unusual. I did not think, in any case, she would be more than the conveyor of a message.

I looked about. Various folks had entered after us. They, too, in their turns, were being seated. There were two or three hostesses, clad and accoutered similarly to mine.

One fellow was carrying a large sack over his shoulder. Even in the dim light certain curvatures seemed suggested within the sack. Too, there was a squirming within it which suggested that its occupant was bound. He was speaking to one of the hostesses.

"What is that?" I asked my hostess.

"It is a joke," she said. "He has captured a free female. We will put her stripped back in one of the tunnel alcoves. Her wrists will be braceleted behind her, chained to a slave ring. She will be unable to speak, being perfectly gagged. She will be left there in the darkness, helpless."

"But she might be used," I said.

"It is not impossible," she said. "It is a matter of chance. Access to her will be as unrestricted as that to a slave."

"Do you approve of such things?" I asked.

"If she is a feminine female," she said, "of course. Such belong to men."

"It is a splendid joke," I said.

"Yes," she said.

"What is done with them later?" I asked.

"Nothing," she said. "We just put them out naked in the back, in the morning. If they have been used, however, we tie their hands behind their back and, on a cord about their waist, suspend a punched tarsk bit on their belly."

"Why would someone do this sort of thing to a free woman?" I asked.

"Perhaps they found her displeasing in some way," she

said, "and thought it might do her a bit of good, to discover something about what it is to be a female."

"I see," I said.

"There she goes," said the woman. "She is being taken into one of the tunnel alcoves now." There are small exits from the larger room, on the other side of the open space, that lead to various tunnels, off of which may be found cells and alcoves. From such tunnels the establishment, of course, derives its name.

"Yes," I said. We watched the fellow crouch down and enter one of the small openings, the sack now, with its helpless, squirming occupant, dragging behind him. One cannot, on the whole, stand upright in the tunnels. Sometimes one must actually crawl.

The musicians had now stopped playing.

"Are you interested in free females?" she asked.

"Not particularly," I said.

"Let us show you one," she said. "Esne," she called. "Bring Lady Labiena."

In a few moments one of the hostesses had emerged from a side door leading a lovely woman, barefoot, in a wrap-around tunic, on a neck chain. She was brought to my table where, unbidden, she knelt.

"She is attractive, is she not?" asked my hostess.

"Yes," I said.

"She is a captive free woman," said my hostess. "We are keeping her for a friend."

"I see," I said.

"Open your tunic," said my hostess.

The woman parted her tunic, and held it to the sides.

"She is pretty, isn't she?" asked my hostess.

"Yes," I said. "Widen your knees," I told the woman.

She did so, continuing to hold her tunic open.

"Are you sure she is free?" I asked.

"Yes," said my hostess.

I regarded the woman. "It seems she might as well be a slave," I said.

The woman threw me a look of gratitude.

"No, she is free," said my hostess, "though now, to be

sure, she doubtless has some notion of what a slave's life might be like."

"One can have no adequate notion of that," I said, "until one has been truly enslaved."

"True," said my hostess.

"What is your life like here?" I asked the woman.

"I wear a neck chain," she said.

"I see," I said.

"You may lower your hands, but do not close your tunic," said my hostess.

"In what manner does she serve here, in this house?" I asked. To be sure she was barefoot, and was naked but for a tunic, and had a chain on her neck. These things suggested some answers to my question.

"Much as a slave, but with little of their skill," said my hostess.

"They will not tell me their secrets," said the woman.

"They have been ordered not to do so," said my hostess, "our orders countermanding any which she might give them."

"But they are *pleased* not to tell me!" she wept.

"Of course," said my hostess. "They are slaves, and you are merely free. Too, the secrets of slaves are perhaps best kept between themselves and their masters."

"We will not even give her training," said the hostess who had brought her in.

"That has cost me many beatings," said the free woman.

"Why not train her?" I asked.

"Training would be inappropriate for her, as she is a free woman," said my hostess. "Too, it might scandalize and horrify her. We would certainly not want that. Too, it is not likely that it would even be fully meaningful to her, as she is free, and would thus not be able to understand it as it is meant to be understood, in the helpless depths of an owned belly."

"Is she being held for ransom?" I asked.

"No," said my hostess. "But that was your hope, in the beginning, wasn't it, Lady Labiena?"

"No," said the woman, putting her head down.

"But when it was learned that she had been captured,"

said my hostess, "she was cast off by her family, and sworn from the Home Stone."

"My life as a free person was unsatisfactory to me," said the woman.

"Watch your tongue, prisoner," said the female holding her neck chain.

"It seems now," I said, "that you are neither fully a free person nor a slave."

"It amuses them," she said, "to keep me as a free person in their power, for their customers."

"Occasionally such women are available in these places," I said.

"You do not know what I have done here," she said, looking up, "what I have been made to do!"

"I can speculate," I assured her.

"But much of what she has done here," said the woman holding her neck chain, "has been simply servile. For example, we enjoy having her naked, on all fours, on a chain, scrubbing floors."

"But surely she has been put upon occasion to the uses of your customers," I said.

"Of course," said the woman holding the neck chain, "haven't you, Lady Labiena."

"Yes," said the kneeling woman, her knees wide, her tunic parted.

I regarded her.

"But I have learned things here," she said, "that I never dreamed of as a free woman. I have been able to sense here the ecstasies of bondage, the ecstasies of a life obligatorily sensual, a life under strict discipline, a life where I must obey, a life where I will, and must, surrender myself totally and, subject to penalties, and even death, if I am displeasing, live thenceforth solely for service and love."

"You sing the joys of a love slave, surely," I said, "not the woes of a woman who must crawl beneath the whip of a hated master."

"Do you not think a love slave crawls fearfully beneath the whip of her master?" she asked.

"The love slave is still a slave, you see," I said, "and perhaps more a slave than any other."

"Yes," whispered the woman.

"She is held in her bondage by the strongest of all bonds," I said, "that of love."

"Yes," she said.

"It is stronger than the chain on your neck," I said.

"I know," she said.

"It must then be very strong," laughed the woman who held her chain. She gave it a tug, jerking it against the side of the woman's neck.

"It is," I said.

"They give me to anyone here," said the woman. "Some are hideous, some smell, in the fetid breath of some I almost choke and die, and yet I must serve them, unquestioningly, although a free woman, according to whatever their dictates and whims."

I regarded the woman.

"I want a private master," she said. "I want my own master."

"It is a natural desire on the part of a female," I said.

Then she looked up, suddenly, piteously, at the woman who was holding her neck chain. "I want a collar," she said to her. "You know that. I have begged for it. Why will you not give me a collar? You have made me, in effect, a slave. Now I am good for nothing else. I have learned too much. Why deny me the mark, the collar? Why do you so shame me? Put me in a collar, that what I now know I am may be proclaimed to the world! I want to be sold! I want to find a master! I am ready to serve, and fully!"

"Be silent," said the woman who held her chain. "That is no way for a free woman to speak. Put your head to the floor, pull your tunic up over your head!"

Frightened, the woman did as she was told. The woman who had her in her keeping then called to another of the hostesses. "Three strokes," she told her. That woman then, with her whip, struck Lady Labiena three times.

"Replace your tunic and kneel straightly," said her keeper.

Lady Labiena, tears running down her cheeks, complied.

"We have told you, Lady Labiena," said my hostess. "We are merely keeping you for a friend."

"For whom are you keeping me?" she begged.

"That is for us to know, and for you to wonder," she said.

"Tell him, if you would," she said, "that his capture is now ready to be imbonded, that she is now ready to lick his feet and beg a collar, that she is ready to be used, or sold, whatever be his will."

"That is Lady Labiena," said my hostess. "See how feminine she is? See how right she is for a man?"

"Yes," I said.

"Chain her at his mat's slave ring," said my hostess.

"No," I said.

"What?" asked my hostess.

"No," I said.

"Clearly she is fit for the collar," said my hostess.

"True," I said. "But she is not yet in a collar. She is a mere free woman. She does not yet know the collar. She does not yet feel it in every part of her. Its meaning has not yet soaked into her brain, her skin, her belly, even to the tips of her toes."

"You are not interested in free females?" she said.

"Not particularly," I reminded her. This is not that unusual in one who has tasted of slaves. As women, there is no comparison between a free woman and her imbonded sister. Perhaps that is why free women so hate slaves. To be sure, there is something to be said for free women. It is enjoyable to capture, enslave and train them. That is interesting. But then, of course, in a matter of time, one is not then dealing any longer with a free woman, but only another slave.

"Close your tunic, you brazen slut," said my hostess to the Lady Labiena, who hurriedly drew it together, obeying. Then she said to the woman who held her chain. "Take her away."

The Lady Labiena was led from the floor, through the door from which she had earlier emerged. Presumably she would be fastened by her neck chain to a wall or floor ring within, until she was brought forth again on the floor.

My hostess then lifted her head and looked to the left of the open space, where several females huddled. It was hard to tell in the light, but I thought they were naked. She cracked her whip, and they scurried swiftly to the table, where they knelt. They were naked.

"Now these are slaves," I said. I examined them. How incredibly beautiful and sensuous they were, how soft and vulnerable, how owned. It was not merely that they were nude and that their necks were locked in steel collars. It was something else, almost indefinable, but very real, about them, which marked them as slaves, something which seemed to say, "We are slaves, Masters. We are yours. Do with us as you will."

The woman cracked her whip again and the girls inadvertently cringed and shrank back. They were slaves, and knew well that sound. Two of them had even cried out in fear. The woman then went to the line. "Straighten your bodies," she said. "You are in the presence of a man." She touched more than one with the whip coils, adjusting her posture, and, with the coils, lifted up the chin of another. Then she turned to me. "These are available," she said. "Perhaps you find one or more of them pleasing?"

I surveyed the women.

"Such," she said, "are fit for men."

"Yes," I said.

"They are pleasant, meaningless creatures," she said.

I did not respond to the woman. There was a sense, of course, in which the slave girl is meaningless, the sense in which she is nothing, the sense in which she is a mere property, a rightless object, fittingly to be scorned, to be treated as one pleases, to be made to serve, to be disciplined or whipped, to be kept or cast away, as one might choose and yet, in another sense, what meaning could a free woman even begin to have, compared to that of a slave at one's feet.

"Are they not pretty?" she asked.

"Yes," I said.

I regarded the slaves.

They knelt before me, in the half darkness, in a line. They had been well positioned. Their collars glinted, the steel reflecting the dim, reddish light of the tiny lamps. Their flesh, too, that of offerings of the house, so cheaply available, revealed the effects of this same dim illumination. The free woman, Ludmilla, proprietress of this establishment, and of several others on the street, had some concept, it seemed, as to at least one way in which female slaves might be presented before men. One does not, of course, buy a woman in such light. Preferably one considers them in strong light with great care. Indeed, preferably one does not put out any money until one has carefully examined every inch of her fair body. Even girls who are to be auctioned are commonly available, in exposition cages or display spaces, and sometimes for handling, for inspection before a sale, that one may determine whether or not he wishes to make a bid, and, also, of course, how high he might be willing to go to acquire her.

The woman turned about, and, lifting her whip, signaled to the musicians at the right side of the room. They began to play. She then cracked the whip again and the slaves sprang to their feet and began to dance before me, as only slaves can dance before men.

"How meaningless they are," laughed the free woman.

How incredibly meaningful, how explosively and thunderingly meaningful, how devastatingly meaningful, how momentously significant they were, these females of my species, presenting themselves before me in the modalities incumbent upon them, modalities constituting civilized and delicious refinements of relationships instituted and determined eons ago by nature, modalities which will always, in one way or another, in one nomenclature or another, be required of beautiful women by strong men, modalities most simply and directly thought of, and most honestly thought of, as those of the slave and master. One of the glories of the Gorean culture is that is has a body of law, sanctioned by tradition and mercilessly enforced, pertaining, without evasion or subterfuge, to this relationship.

"Yartel," said the woman, motioning to one of the girls who then, obediently, moved forward, writhing before me. She was a short-legged, creamy-skinned, voluptuous blonde. One difference between Gorean sexual tastes and those of Earth, I might mention, is that Gorean sexual tastes, at least in my opinion, are much broader and more tolerant than those of Earth, or at least of Western Civilization, and tend to run toward the statistical norms of the human female. For example, many women on Earth who are implicitly taught by their culture, for example, through pictures and accounts, that they do not fulfill culturally approved stereotypes of feminine desirability and beauty, might discover, presumably to their horror, that they would bring a high price in a Gorean slave market. If they should have any lingering doubts about the matter, and think perhaps to escape a discipline more appropriately applied to "true beauties," because they do not regard themselves as such, their delusions are likely to be quickly dispelled under their master's whip. Also, although I suppose the matter is neither here nor there, Goreans also tend to prize women for such things as their intelligence, emotional depth, charm and personality. It is a pleasure to own such a female.

The most fundamental property prized by Goreans in women, I suppose, though little is said about it, is her need for love, and her capacity for love. How much does she need love? And how deep and loving is she? That is the kind of woman a man wants, ultimately, one who is helplessly and totally love's captive, in his collar.

To be sure, it is also pleasurable, particularly in the beginning, to bend a woman, and to teach her her place. Few pleasures can compare, for example, with that of taking an unwilling female, preferably one who hates you, and, against her will, forcing her to yield to you the total and exquisite perfections of slave service. One may then, after she has learned herself a slave, after she has been brought to this self-understanding, do what one wishes with her, say, keeping her or selling her, doubtless now making a profit on her and putting her into the markets, where, eventually, if she is fortunate, she might eventually come into the hands of an excellent master for her, one whose devoted love slave she will beg to be.

"Louise," said the woman with the whip.

A short, slender, exquisite, very white-skinned, red-haired

girl moved forth immediately from the line, dancing before me.

'Louise' is an Earth-girl name. I wondered if she were from Earth. Often, of course, Earth-girl names are given to Gorean female slaves. They are almost uniformly regarded as suitable slave names. Similarly, girls who wear them are taken to be slaves. It is sometimes amusing to Goreans when an Earth girl shows up in a Gorean slave market, insisting that her name is such and such, a name taken on Gor to be a slave name. It is as though she were confessing her bondage. She may be given the name afresh, but now to be worn as a slave name chosen by her master, or, sometimes, presumably that she may better understand her dependence on men's will, and her subjection to male domination, she may be given another Earth-girl name. When more than one Earth girl is in the same lot, their names may be switched, the name 'Audrey', for example, being given to the former Karen, and the name 'Karen' now being given to the former Audrey.

Most often, however, the Earth girls are given Gorean names, and usually Gorean slave names. Many masters discover that this procedure often smoothes and hastens the transition between the background of Earth freedoms, such as they are, and the new reality of absolute bondage. When the former Stacy Smith or Betty Lou Madison discover that they are now, say, Sabita, Dilek, Tuka, Cicek, or Lita, it helps to convince them that their old life is now behind them, and is gone forever. They then hurry, and are well advised to do so, to become the finest, the most superb, the most desirable Sabita, Dilek, Tuka, Cicek or Lita they can.

I regarded the slender girl dancing before me. Her breasts were small, and well formed. The reddish light was particularly lovely, in its shifting hues, reflecting from so fair-skinned a body. The steel collar looked well on her neck.

"Are you from Earth?" I asked her, in English.

"Yes!" she said, startled.

"Do not stop dancing," I told her, in English.

"Are you from Earth?" she asked, wildly.

"Once," I said.

"I am an Earth woman!" she said. "Behold me in bondage!"

"I do," I said. "And you are very pretty in bondage."

Her fists clenched over her head, as she writhed before me. 'Right this wrong!" she begged.

"What wrong?" I asked.

"That I am in bondage!" she cried.

"Dance more superbly," I told her.

She writhed yet more lasciviously, more deliciously, before me.

"You look well in a collar," I informed her.

"Please," she protested.

"Quite well," I said.

"Rescue me from bondage!" she cried.

"No," I said.

"What!" she cried.

"Dance," I told her.

She wept, and danced, and danced well.

I examined her movements. Clearly they were those of a slave.

"The only wrong, my dear," I said, "would have been if you had not been reduced to bondage."

"Please!" she wept.

"How do you address me?" I asked.

"Master!" she wept.

I motioned that she might return to the line, and, sobbing, dancing, she did so. The collar looked well on her neck. Clearly it belonged there. In time she would come to understand that and would then, fearfully, live in love, rejoicing.

"Birsen," said the woman with the whip.

A tall thin girl, then, with brown hair about her shoulders, came forward. On Earth such a type, of such a structure, and with her beauty, I surmised, might have become a high-fashion model. I indicated that she might return to the line.

"Demet," said the woman.

A short, dark-skinned girl, plump and meaty, one about whose femaleness there could be no doubt, with long, swirling black hair, spun forward and writhed before me. She had soft, full, pouting lips, of the sort that seem made for the

raping of the master's kiss. If she had ever been a free
woman, doubtless she had been warned to keep those lips
veiled, lest they attract the attention of slavers. I forced
myself to remember that I had come here in response to a
message, that I was expected to be partner to some sort of
rendezvous. I had left Hurtha at the insula, with Feiqa,
though by now, a lusty fellow, he was doubtless somewhere
else on the street, Feiqa left behind, chained to her ring in the
room. I did not know if there would be danger, or not. At any
rate, if there were to be any danger, it did not seem to me
appropriate that I should enter my hearty companion of the
road into it. Such perils, if they existed, were properly mine.

"I see that Demet interests you," said my hostess. "She
was once a high lady in the Tahari, but, as you can see, her
lips made it inevitable that she would be sold into slavery."

I considered the movements of her sweetly broad love
cradle.

"Have you learned submission, Demet?" I asked.

"Can you not read it in my eyes, Master?" she asked.

"Speak," I said.

"Yes, Master," she said. "I have learned submission."

"You are one of our best girls, aren't you, Demet?" asked
the woman with the whip, moving it on her belly as she
danced.

"I hope so, Mistress," said Demet, frightened.

"Are you happy as a slave?" I asked.

"I beg to be sold," she wept suddenly, "that I may have a
private master." Then she cried out in pain, lashed by the
woman's whip.

"Forgive me, Mistress," she begged. She did not stop
dancing. The other girls, too, frightened, still dancing, shrank
back a bit. I saw that the hostesses kept these feminine
women under good discipline.

"Let us have her chained to your mat ring," said the
woman with the whip.

"Return her to the line," I said.

"Lale," said the woman with the whip, summoning forward,
with a gesture of the whip, the last of the slaves before me.

"I am Lale," said the girl, dancing meaningfully before

me. "Examine me. I can give great pleasure." I regarded
her. She was a medium-sized, full-bodied, stunning brunet. I
had no doubt that she could indeed give great pleasure. I
observed her with care. How beautiful women are in slave
dance. And what a splendid prelude it is to their subjugation
and ravishment.

"Master likes Lale," she said.

"Perhaps," I said.

She then, suddenly, danced very close to me. "Have Lale
chained to your ring," she said.

"Is the belly of Lale needful?" I asked.

"Yes!" she whispered.

I regarded her.

"Please," she said. "Lale has not been chosen in two
nights."

"You would have yourself chosen not for my pleasure, but
for your desperate need?" I asked.

"For both, please, Master," she said. "For both!"

"Perhaps," I said. She was quite beautiful. Until one has
seen needful slaves, one has not seen women.

"Too," she whispered, "if Lale is not chosen tonight, she
will be whipped. Do not let Lale be whipped. Master does
not want Lale whipped."

"I see now why you have not been used in two nights," I
said. "Apparently you are not satisfactory."

"No," she said. "No, Master!"

"Return to the line," I said.

"Master, please!" she protested.

"What is going on?" asked the woman with the whip.

"She is trying to influence my choice by extraneous
considerations," I said. "I choose not to accept this attempt
at manipulation."

The woman suddenly cracked her whip. The girls stopped
dancing. "Kneel," she said to them. "You, Lale, remain
where you are."

"What did she say?" asked the woman with the whip.

Lale trembled, and moaned.

"Nothing, really," I said. "It was merely that she attempted to elicit my pity, to win my choice, telling me that if she was not chosen tonight she would be whipped."

"Head to the floor!" cried the hostess.

Lale put her head down to the floor. The lash fell once, fiercely, across her back. Lale cried out in misery.

"It is not worth whipping her about," I said. "It is not her fault if she is not popular."

"Not popular?" laughed the hostess. "Oh, she is a sly one, the little she-sleen! She is one of the most popular girls in the house."

"Oh?" I said.

Lale cried out as the whip fell on her again.

"Look up, little fool," said the hostess, "and see the man you tried to manipulate!"

Lale looked up in misery, the tears streaming down her face.

"Does he look like the kind of man you could play your silly little games with, does he look like the kind of man you could manipulate with pity? Can you not see he knows what slaves are, and knows how to handle them. Head down!"

Again the lash fell upon Lale.

"I have told you about that trick!" said the free woman, angrily. "You have used it before! Perhaps that is the secret of your popularity! Perhaps that is why you are so often chosen, and are thrown sweets in the chaining bin as rewards! Is that how you compete with the other girls?"

"Please, Mistress!" begged Lale. But the lash fell twice more upon her.

I noted that the other girls, kneeling in the background, did not seem at all dismayed with the punishment of the errant Lale. If she were popular in the house, I gathered it was with the customers, and not with her chain sisters.

"And now you have lied again, and to a free man!" snarled the hostess. Three more times then the lash fell upon the hapless Lale, and then she lay on her belly, sobbing on the tiles.

"Kneel!" commanded the free woman. Lale struggled to her knees.

"Get on all fours," said the woman.

Lale was then on all fours.

"You are now in the modality of the she-quadruped," said my hostess.

Lale moaned.

"Esne," called my hostess. That woman, she who had earlier taken the Lady Labiena from the floor, came over. She, too, carried a whip, and was dressed in brief leather, rather like that of a warrior. At her belt was a chain leash.

My hostess made a sign and Lale was leashed.

"Can you understand me, my little she-quadruped?" asked my hostess. "Whimper once for 'Yes,' whimper twice for 'No.' "

Lale whimpered once.

"Good," said my hostess. "You are a bright little she-quadruped."

The chain shook, as Lale trembled.

"Have you ever served as a she-quadruped before?" asked my hostess.

Lale whimpered twice.

"But you understand something of what is involved, do you not?" asked my hostess.

One whimper.

"For two weeks," said my hostess, "or more, if I choose, you will be chained in the darkness, in one of the back alcoves, serving there as a speechless animal any who may come upon you or desire you."

Lale groaned in pain.

"Do you understand?" asked my hostess.

Lale whimpered once.

"Take her away," said my hostess. "Delta Tunnel, Alcove Twenty-One."

That would be on the left side of the tunnel, as one entered. The even numbers are on the right.

I watched Lale being conducted from the floor. Her head was down. Once or twice her head was jerked up, as the leash was tautened, Esne hurrying her along. Esne, like my hostess, was a sturdy woman. It interested me that the hostesses here were dressed in rather mannish garb. That was, I supposed, primarily to impress upon the slaves that it was a masculine type discipline to which they were being subjected. Too, of course, it is easier to move swiftly, and to kick, and use a whip, in such garb. On the other hand, it did seem a bit of an empty mockery. The hostesses, when all was said and done, were not really men; they were, ultimately, like their charges, only females. To be sure, they were free females, and this well qualified them for their posts. There are few things a female slave fears more than a free female. Female slaves, so helpless in their collars, so much at the mercy of any free person whatsoever, live in terror of such females, for they know that they despise and hate them.

"Return to your places," said my hostess to the other girls.

"Yes, Mistress," they said, and, leaping up, hurried back into the shadows, at the left, from whence they had been summoned, there to crouch and kneel once more, awaiting their next call forward.

"I am sorry," said my hostess.

"Perhaps you have others?" I asked. I looked about. As yet, as nearly as I could tell, no one had attempted to contact me. I assumed that they would attempt to make the first contact, either having seen me, presumably near the Central Cylinder, or having some sort of description. I would prefer, of course, to get a look at them first, and, if necessary, to count them.

"If you care to wait," she said, "some of these other wenches, on their backs and bellies on the mats, will be relinquished."

"Have you any others, available now?" I asked.

"Not really," she said. "We do have some new girls, in cages, recently brought in. They are not yet fully trained for the floor, however. Indeed, some are only recently marked and collared. We do have the girls in the alcoves, of course."

"Who is that woman?" I asked. I indicated a nicely bodied woman, barefoot, in a calf-length, sleeveless white gown, with a low décolletage, moving among the tables. The neckline left no doubt as to certain of her excitements. They were such as men might pay for in a slave market. I found it interesting that she, in this place, though apparently not a hostess, was clothed. The slaves I had seen here were stripped. Golden bangles encircled her ankles, and golden bracelets encircled her wrists. Too, she had golden armlets.

"She is a free woman," said my hostess.

"Here?" I asked.

"She has paid her tarsk bit," said my hostess. "Beware of her."

I saw the woman approaching a fellow at a table. She knelt near the table, in the position of the free woman. She smiled at him.

"Where are the cages?" I asked.

"I will show you," she said.

I rose to my feet.

My hostess paused for a moment beside one of the girls serving on a nearby fellow's mat. The chain on her neck ran to the mat ring. Becoming suddenly aware of the presence of the hostess, the girl, who was kneeling, swiftly put her head to the floor.

"Leitel," said the hostess, kindly.

"Yes, Mistress," said the girl, her voice quavering.

"You can lick and kiss more salaciously than that," she chided.

"Yes, Mistress," said the girl.

"Our customers do not come here," said the hostess, "for attentions which they could receive at home from their free companions. They come here for the kisses of slaves, and the the pleasures of slaves."

"Yes, Mistress," whispered the girl.

"Are you a slave?" asked the hostess.

"Yes, Mistress!" said the girl.

"Wholly?"

"Yes, Mistress!" said the girl.

"And is this a customer?" she asked, indicating the house's client in question.

"Yes, Mistress!" she wept.

"See, then," she said, "that you give him the pleasures of a slave."

"Yes, Mistress!" she wept.

"The total pleasures of a slave," said my hostess.

"Yes, Mistress!" she cried.

My hostess then continued on her way, and I followed her. We went past the girls at the left, Yartel, and the rest. They shrank back in fear as the hostess passed them.

"You keep these females under excellent discipline," I observed.

"Yes," she said.

"You seem to enjoy making them serve men," I said.

"Yes," she said, "it is enjoyable to make such women serve men. That is what they are for."

"Such women?" I asked.

"Feminine women, slaves," she said. "It is what they should be doing. It is their nature and destiny. Every truly feminine woman desires to belong to some man. No such woman will ever be truly happy until she is helplessly in the collar of her master, and subject to his lash."

I continued to follow her.

"Through here," she said.

"I see," I said.

Within this room there were some fifteen or twenty slave cages, some four to four and a half feet square, such confines dictated by the consideration that their contents are not to be permitted to stand upright within them, or stretch out, completely, within them. They may be comfortably knelt within, and curled up within, of course, postures suitable for slaves. Seven of these cages were occupied, the occupants stripped and collared.

One of the girls, seeing the hostess, scrambled, frightened, to the back of her small cage. She cowered there, not daring to look at the hostess. Her back was marked.

"Little Ila first learned discipline today," explained my hostess. The name 'Ila' was on a small card inserted into a frame on the front of the cage, at the upper-right-hand corner. "Do not disturb these two," said my hostess. "They have had a hard day." We saw two slaves curled up in their cages, asleep. They had tiny bits of blankets clutched about them. These did not, however, much cover them, or leave much doubt as to their beauty. Bits of blanket, too, floored some of the other cages. On these some of the other girls knelt or lay.

From the cards in the frames I noted that the two slaves, so tempting to awaken suddenly with a master's rape, were Sucha and Takita.

"Food," whispered a woman, extending her hand piteously through the bars, toward the hostess. "Please, I am hungry!"

"Learn your lessons better in the training periods," said my hostess to her, "and you may be fed."

The name of that one, I read, was 'Chelto'.

"Perhaps," I said, "she might do better if she had a more suitable name."

"What is wrong with 'Chelto'?" asked the woman.

"It is a rather masculine name," I said. "It is the sort of name which might be used as the nickname for a male sleen, or something."

"Perhaps you are right," said the woman, looking at the cage's occupant, a shapely, wide-hipped brunet. "What would you suggest?"

I shrugged. "I do not know," I said. "Perhaps 'Tula' or 'Tuka'."

"Please, no!" begged the woman in the cage, shrinking back. "They are such slave names! Mock me, if you will, with a name such as 'Chelto'. Better that a thousand times than names such as 'Tula' and 'Tuka', the names of slaves, of soft, perfumed girls who must helplessly serve in all things!"

The hostess removed a marking stick from her pouch and removed the card from the cage frame. She leaned on the top of the cage. She crossed out the name 'Chelto' and replaced it with another name. She then replaced the card in the frame.

"Mistress?" asked the kneeling slave within.

"You are now 'Tula,' " said the hostess. I saw that that was the new name written on the card.

"No, please!" begged the woman.

"What is your name?" asked the hostess.

" 'Tula'," said the woman in the cage, shuddering.

"Who are you?" asked my hostess.

"I am Tula," said the kneeling, stripped woman. She was pretty in her collar.

"And tomorrow you will learn your lessons well, will you not?" asked my hostess.

"Yes, Mistress," said the woman, trembling.

"And who is going to learn her lessons well from now on?" asked my hostess.

"Tula is going to learn her lessons well from now on," said the woman.

"And who is going to be a superb slave?"

"Tula is going to be a superb slave," said the woman.

We then left her cage. I glanced back, briefly. The woman was kneeling there, shaken, wide-eyed. It was almost as though some sort of explosion had taken place within her. She knelt there, as though trying to come to grips with what had been done to her, with what had occurred within her. She was now, by the will of masters, a new person. She shuddered. Then she widened her knees, trembling. She was now Tula.

We went to the next cage. In this one there was a blond girl sitting with her left side to the back of the cage, her knees drawn up, her head down, her arms about her knees, her left hand clasped about her right wrist. She looked up, dully, and then lowered her head again. Beneath her hair I could see the steel of the collar on her neck.

My hostess tapped on the bars with the whip. The girl then came forward and knelt before us, in the center of the cage.

The hostess tapped on the bars with the whip. The girl widened her knees.

"This one," said my hostess, "was to have been trained with gentleness, but she made the mistake of expressing a concern for her privacy. We then stripped her and put her in a slave cage."

"I see," I said. There was not much privacy for a naked woman in a slave cage.

"It was a mistake to have begun gently with her," said the hostess.

"It probably depends on the girl," I said. Some women, whose hunger for bondage is just under the surface, if not manifest, are probably prepared to be superb slaves almost instantly, with no pain, or perhaps no more than a modicum of pain, perhaps only enough to assure them of the reality of their condition, that they are truly slaves, and subject to the strict discipline of an uncompromising master. Such women, eager to serve, rejoicing in the achievement at long last of this profound fulfillment, hitherto only dreamed of, ask little more than what to do, and how to do it.

"True," she said.

"Did this one cause difficulty?" I asked.

"Not really," she said.

The girl in the cage looked up, angrily.

"Are you still determined to resist slavery, pretty Lupita?" asked the woman. That was the name on the cage card.

"Yes, Mistress!" said the girl.

"But you will not be successful, will you?" asked my hostess.

"No," said the girl, putting her head down, sobbing suddenly, "I will not be successful."

I looked at my hostess.

"She has had time to think in the slave cage," explained the woman.

The girl in the cage kept her head down. Tears fell from her cheeks to the bit of a blanket on which she knelt. The shadows of the cage bars made an interesting pattern on her flesh.

"For several days, I suppose as a matter of pride, she was pretending to resist slavery," said the woman, "though, clearly, to a trained eye, she wanted it, more than anything."

The girl looked up, in agony.

"That is true, is it not, pretty Lupita?" asked the hostess.

"Yes, Mistress," she sobbed.

"Give me your hands," I said to the girl. She extended them through the bars. I then drew her toward me, and moved my hands up her arms, until I held her near, high on her arms, until her right cheek was pulled against the bars. I held her there. "Your resistance, or pretended resistance, is now is nearly at an end, is it not?" I asked her.

"Yes, Master," she said. I then let her loose, and she fell back, twisting, on her shoulder, to the floor of the cage. She pounded on the floor of the cage with her small fists. She tore at the blanket on the floor with her fingernails, sobbing. Then she lay quietly. "Put me out on the floor," she said. "Chain me to a ring."

"Why?" asked the hostess.

"Because I am a slave," she said.

"You are not yet sufficiently skilled, slave," said my hostess.

The slave wept.

We then went to the next occupied cage.

Here a brunet, well-curved, with sweet, full thighs, knelt close to the bars, grasping them with her small hands, her face pressed between two of them. The bars in these cages are set about four inches apart, and are about an inch in thickness. They are heavy, sturdy cages. Here the card read 'Mina'.

"This is the former Lady Mina, a huntress, from the luxurious Noviminae villas in the vicinity of Lydius. But she is a huntress no more."

I regarded her.

"Speak," said my hostess to the woman.

"I went hunting," she said, "but it was I who was caught and put in a cage."

"How were you taken?" I asked.

"Please," she said.

"Speak," I said, "or will it be necessary to draw you forth from the cage and whip you?"

"I was the Lady Mina," she said, "of the villas of Noviminae, near Lydius. I set out in my hunting leather with crossbow, upon a pacing tharlarion, after tabuk."

"You were alone?" I asked.

"Yes," she said.

"A fool, fit for the collar," commented my hostess.

"I was after tabuk," she said, "but others, too, were abroad that day, who sought a slower, softer game."

My hostess laughed, and the slave clasped the bars yet more tightly.

"I did not suspect they were in the vicinity," said the slave.

"That is not unusual," I said. Such men, of course, commonly know their business.

"I spotted a tabuk, and set off in hot pursuit, across the fields," she said. "It was an agile, wily beast, and led me a splendid chase. Intent upon it I did not note the other riders, closing in upon me. The tabuk harried to exhaustion, helpless, lying gasping on the grass, I rode to it, my crossbow ready. It would not be a difficult shot. I would enter my bolt into its heart. I took aim. But the bow was lifted from me. 'Greetings,' said a man. 'How dare you interfere!' I cried. 'The tabuk is mine!' 'No,' he said, 'it is you who are ours.' 'What?' I cried. 'Greetings,' said he then, 'slave.' 'What!' I cried. But I felt then two ropes, from opposite sides, encircle my neck. I was dragged back off the tharlarion into the grass. I sprang to my feet. I reached for my dagger, but it had been removed from my sheath! I stood there, wild, on the grass, between them, the two ropes on my neck. Then in short order I was stripped and bound, my ankles together and my hands before me. I saw the exhausted tabuk recover and rise unsteadily to its feet, and trot away. I, on the other hand, was thrown on my back before the saddle of the leader of these men. Both my bound ankles and wrists were thonged to rings. I was in the place in which I would have brought home the tabuk, save I would have had him on his belly, so bound. My captor had put me on my back, I suppose, so that I might see him. We then began to move slowly toward a distant wood, that of Nina. It was in that place that they had their camp. 'Oh!' I cried. I had never before felt the hands of a man on my body. 'You cannot do this to me!' I cried. 'I am a free woman!' 'Be silent,' said he, 'slave.' I struggled wildly. Then he leaned down and seized me by the hair with his left hand, and pulled my head up, and then, then with the flat of his right hand, cuffed me, and then flung me back where I had been, as though I might have been a mere object. I could not believe it. He had cuffed me! Me! A woman from the villas of Noviminae! I lay there before him. We rode slowly. I could not believe what he was doing to me. I was a free woman! I dared not protest. I had learned my captor was not a weakling, and that he was quite capable of punishing me. Soon I began to squirm before the saddle. I could not even begin to understand such feelings. Some of the men laughed. At last, as we entered among the trees of the woods of Nina, he gave me respite. 'Thank you,' I said pridefully, in haughty irony. But in a moment I jerked helplessly, writhing, looking up at him, in frustration against the rings. The men laughed. 'Yes?' he asked. 'Nothing!' I said. I dared not confess to him how distressed I was at the stoppage of his touch, at the cessation of those intriguing, unfamiliar, troubling sensations which seemed to radiate through my entire body, seeming to change everything within me and my whole concept of myself. I dared not beg for more. We were then at his camp, and I was put bound on the leaves of the woods' floor. They had brought my tharlarion along. I supposed they would sell it. I wondered what my own fate would be.''

My hostess laughed.

"Go on," I said.

"There were other girls, too, in this camp," she said, "but they appeared to be mere peasant lasses. They were on a common neck chain, stripped, fastened between two trees. They seemed, unlike myself, suitable candidates for slavery.''

My hostess smiled.

"Continue," I told the slave.

" 'You will now beg to wear shackles and cook,' said the leader.' 'Never,' I said. They then untied me, but only to string me up by the ankles to a tree branch. In moments I begged to wear shackles and cook. They took me down, and, in horror, I saw the metal put on my ankles. They were close shackles, and gave me a play of no more than three horts. They need not fear I would run away. I then, though I was of the villas of Noviminae, cooked. It was the first time I had ever served men.''

"How did you feel about this?" I asked.

She looked down.

"Speak," said my hostess, sternly.

"I was unutterably thrilled, so to serve men," she whispered.

"Of course," said my hostess, "for you were not truly a huntress. You were only a slave pretending to be a huntress."

"Yes, Mistress," said the woman in the collar.

"The pretense is now over," said my hostess.

"Yes, Mistress," she said.

"What occurred then?" I asked the slave.

"There is little more to tell," she said. "After the meal I lay at the feet of my captors. I was docile. I hoped that they would touch me. After they had drunk they removed the shackles from me and I was passed about, among them. I could not believe the things I did, nor the feelings I experienced. There were cries of rage, and denunciation, from the other girls, who could see everything. But I did not care. I could not help myself. They had a wagon there, with a cage on it. They would leave the camp after darkness. When they left, I, and the others, were bound hand and foot, and put in gag hoods, so that we could neither see nor speak. We were then put in the wagon cage. It was locked. We then were taken from the woods of Nina. Eventually, when our solicitations for aid would be meaningless, for who cares about the lamentations of unknown females, our gag hoods and bonds were removed. Then, still sturdily encaged, but mercifully now only stripped, we were brought south. It was a long trip. In the beginning I was much at the mercy of the other girls, and was much beaten by them. They resented my behavior in the woods. Then, at a night camp, another girl was taken from the wagon, for the pleasure of the captors. She learned, too, she was a woman. There were then two to abuse, and beat. Then there were three. And, soon, there were more in the cage who now knew themselves than did not. The beatings then must stop, save for those administered, and often harshly, by the captors. Then, in time, there were none in the cage who had still to learn the meaning of their sex, none who had not now learned that they were slaves, and fully."

"Excellent," I said.

"We even began to beg for the attentions of our captors."

"Of course," I said.

"What had begun in the vicinity of Lydius, as, with the possible exception of myself, a cage of free women had become, by the time we had reached Venna, on the Viktel Aria, a cage of competitive, amorous slaves."

"Was it at Venna that you were legally imbonded?" I asked.

"Yes," she said, "it was there that the legal details were attended to. Our captors, quite rightly, adjudged us now ready for our brands and collars. The technicalities were attended to. We were legal slaves."

"I see," I said.

"It was only a short trip then," she said, "to the sales rooms of Ar."

"I understand," I said.

She, kneeling there in the cage, her hands on the bars, looked up at me. "I had been a rich woman of the villas of Noviminae," she said. "I think my captor enjoyed selling me to a brothel."

"Doubtless," I said.

She moved back a bit from the bars. She put down her head.

"What did you pay for her?" I asked.

"Three silver tarsks," said my hostess.

"That is a high price," I said.

"You had better be worth it on the floor, Mina," said my hostess.

"I will try, Mistress," said Mina.

"Perhaps you will come into the keeping of a private master someday," I said.

She looked up at me, tears in her eyes. "Such men," she said, "seldom buy girls out of brothels."

"Some might," I said. I looked at my hostess. "If someone were interested in her," I asked, "would she be for sale?"

"She is the only wench we have from the villas of Noviminae," said my hostess. "That is a rather special background. It is almost like once having been of high caste. That background is likely to be of interest to many of our customers. We expect her to be in frequent demand." She looked down at the slave. "Perhaps you can tell them of the beauty of the villas, and of how spoiled and rich you were," she said, "while you squirm in their arms."

"Yes, Mistress," whispered the girl.

"But if an offer were made?" I asked.

"It would depend, of course," she said, "on the offer."

"She is then for sale?" I asked.

"All our slaves are for sale," said my hostess.

"You could sell any of them to anyone then?" I asked.

"Of course," said my hostess. "To anyone who has the price."

We then proceeded to the next cage. It was the last one which was currently occupied.

This girl, like Mina, was a sweetly bodied slut, with luscious swelling breasts, a stocky, but considerably narrower waist, and wide hips, nursing a marvelous love cradle in which a man might lose himself with pleasure. She, too, like Mina, was nicely thighed. She, too, like Mina, was a brunet. She, too, like Mina, wore a close-fitting steel collar. She, kneeling in her cage, had not been unaware, of course, of our progress. When we appeared before her cage, she put her head down to the blanket, the palms of her hands on the floor of the cage, beside her head. It is a lovely gesture of obeisance, and required by many masters of their women.

"Her name is 'Candice'," I said, reading the cage card. "That is an Earth-girl name. Is she an Earth girl?"

"No," said my hostess. "She is from Tabor. We thought it a lovely name. We put it on her."

I nodded. It was a lovely name. If any girl were to appear on Gor with such a name, of course, she would be immediately taken to be a slave, and would be treated as such. She would soon be in a collar. Her fate would be bondage.

"A very attractive slut," I said.

"Yes," said my hostess.

"How much did she cost?" I asked.

"Two silver tarsks," said my hostess.

"Interesting," I said. "Her beauty seems quite comparable to that of her chain sister, Mina, and yet Mina brought a full tarsk more."

"It is the Noviminae background," said the hostess.

"Interesting," I said. "It seems then that sometimes what is being paid for is not the mere female herself."

"Of course not," said my hostess. "Suppose she was a Ubar's daughter."

"I see," I said.

"The daughter of a Ubar may bring ten thousand pieces of gold in a private sale," said the hostess, "but, as a woman, as a mere female on a chain, she may be worth far less than thousands of wenches one might lead home for a few copper tarsks."

"That is true," I said. And it is not unoften the case that such a common wench, of which little is expected, bought originally perhaps with the mere object of keeping her for a week or so and then reselling her, will be discovered to be an astounding value. Fortunate is the master who gets so much for so little. Fortunate is he who discovers that for his pittance he has purchased a treasure. He does not take her back in a week. She tugs at her chain; it is fastened securely to his ring. What counts ultimately, in my opinion, is not the cost of the merchandise, but its value, its quality; it is not what one pays that is ultimately important, but what gets for one's money. One day he considers himself, looking down at the slave at his feet; it is he whom she struggles so hard to please, as a slave must; it is he in whose complete power she finds herself; it is he whom she must serve so humbly, and who is so strict with her; it is he who is her master; he looks down into her eyes; he sees that she, looking up at him, unable to help herself, has become his love slave. He smiles. He fingers his whip. He wonders if perhaps he is her love master. She bends down, kissing his feet. He knows he must guard against weakness. He must never forget the whip. She understands the whip. All slaves do. He watches her, her hair about his feet, and feels her lips and tongue. The sensations are not unpleasant. If he does not find the relationship satisfactory, of course, he may always sell her.

"I think I will return to the table," I said. "Thank you for showing me these wenches. They seem superb merchandise. I think, in time, with training, they will all prove excellent upon the floor."

"That is our hope," said my hostess. "We want the Tunnels to be one of the best brothels on the entire Alley of the Slave Brothels of Ludmilla."

"Who is Ludmilla?" I asked.

"I have never met her," said my hostess.

We then returned to the floor. In our return we paused briefly by the girls at the side of the open space. "Yartel and Demet are now serving," said my hostess. "These two others are now open, ready for new rings." She indicated a blond and a brunet. "Ita and Tia," she said.

"Lovely," I said.

Louise, the Earth girl there, looked at me, aghast. Then she looked away. I gather she had not known that men from Earth, or once from Earth, could look in such a way upon women.

"But you will return to the table?" asked my hostess.

"Yes," I said.

"I shall have one of the slaves fetch you a drink," she said.

"That one," I said, indicating Louise.

"Certainly," she said. She snapped her fingers and Louise sprang up, and came to where we stood. Then she knelt.

I looked to one of the tables near my own. There was the free woman, in the sleeveless dress, with the low décolletage. She looked about. The fellow she had earlier approached was now slumped on the table. On the table was a bottle of ka-la-na. There were two glasses there. I saw her cut the strings of his purse and slip it inside her dress. On her left hand, as she did this, I saw a ring. I did not think she had had it on her hand before. I had seen such rings before.

"What would you like?" asked my hostess.

I had been considering a glass of paga, perhaps, if it were available in a place such as this, of the brewery of Temus. Now, considering the rather revealingly clad free female, I changed my mind.

"I think, upon reflection," I said, "that I shall order later."

"Very well," she said. Then she turned to Louise, kneeling in attendance. "When you are dismissed, if you are dismissed, return to your post," she said. "Do not neglect, however, to observe this table. When he wishes to order, and lifts his finger, hurry to him. Then obtain what he wishes from the bar."

"Yes, Mistress," said Louise.

"I may be ordering a bottle," I said to the hostess.

"The admission price was only a tarsk bit," she reminded me.

"Forgive me," I said. I then counted her out five copper tarsks. I did this a bit obtrusively. The free woman, she with the low décolletage, as I had expected, did not fail to note this. She glanced back at the fellow slumped over the table. He would not awaken, doubtless, for some time, perhaps an Ahn or more.

"Ah!" said my hostess. "You are generous! For so much whatever you might like in the house, and as much of it as you like, is yours."

"Thank you," I said.

My hostess then took her leave.

I regarded Louise.

She looked up at me.

"Master?" she asked.

"You are dismissed," I said.

"Yes, Master," she said. She rose to her feet, her head down, backed away a step or two, and then turned and hurried back to her place with the other girls. The female, I saw, was kept under good discipline. This pleased me. It is good for them.

"I see that you have dismissed a slave," said the free woman, she with the low décolletage.

"Yes," I said.

"Are you from out of town?" she asked.

"Yes," I said. The ring was not on her finger now.

"Are you enjoying Ar?" she asked.

I shrugged.

"It can be lonely for a stranger," she said.

"Would you care to join me?" I asked.

"I'm sorry," she said. "It would not be proper. I do not even know you."

"Forgive me," I said. "I did not mean to be forward."

She moved her left foot a little, causing the bangles on her left ankle to move slightly. Most free women, of course, would never wear such things. They are regarded as suitable and appropriate only for slaves. She moved the bracelets on her left wrist up her left forearm an inch or two. The tiny noise this made was exciting, slave exciting. With one hand she threw her hair back. It was loose. Slaves commonly wear their hair loose. She moved subtly, charmingly, seemingly inadvertently, within the dress. Then she seemed, suddenly, concerned with it. Could there be something wrong with it? She then, almost apologetically, adjusted one of shoulder straps of the dress, pulling it up tighter and more to the side. She did this as though not giving it much thought, and as though modestly, but in such a way, with such a movement of her body, and with such an effect, that she called dramatic and inevitable attention to the marvelousness of her breasts. Such breasts, I thought, would probably increase her value as a slave.

"That is all right," she said. "No offense is taken."

"I am really very sorry," I said.

"It is my fault," she smiled. "I should not have been so forward. I should not have spoken first."

"Please join me," I said.

She knelt at the table, in the position of the free woman.

"I spoke," she said, "for I was pleased to see that you had dismissed the slave."

"She is only an Earth girl," I said.

"So low?" she inquired.

"Yes," I said.

"I do wish they would put them in clothing," she said.

"They do have their collars," I said.

"True," she laughed.

"Are you sure you could not accept a drink?" I asked.

She seemed to consider the matter, and then, after giving it some thought, smiled. "All right," she said.

"What would you like?" I asked.

"Perhaps a tiny glass of ka-la-na," she said, "among friends."

I looked to the left. Louise, as she had been bidden, was watching. I lifted my finger. The Earth girl then leapt up and hurried to the table. At the table she knelt.

"A small bottle," I said, "of the Slave Gardens of Anesidemus."

"I have heard that is a marvelous ka-la-na," said the free woman, her eyes alight.

"So, too, have I," I said.

"It is very expensive," said the woman.

"Are you familiar with it?" I asked.

"Oh," she said, lightly, "I have had it a few times."

"Do you like it?" I asked.

"Yes," she said. "Yes!"

"Fetch it," I said to Louise.

"Yes, Master," she said, rising to her feet, and hurrying to the bar.

"That is the slave whom you earlier dismissed, is it not?" she asked.

"I think so," I said.

"You hardly noticed," she said, pleased.

I shrugged.

"I am so pleased to meet a man such as you," she said.

"Oh?" I asked.

"One who understands the value of a free woman," she said.

I supposed free women did have value. Slavers, for example, will pay for them.

"So many men," she said, "are interested only in slaves."

"Really?" I asked.

"Yes!" she said. "There is no understanding it. I find it unaccountable."

"I can see you are astounded," I said.

"What can a man see in any of those sluts?" she asked.

"A slave," I said.

"Precisely!" she said. "Disgusting!"

"Some men like them," I said.

"Is that what men really want?" she asked. "A woman who is totally theirs, one who is fully in their power, one who must strive desperately to serve them perfectly in all things, one who is absolutely and helplessly at their mercy, one who must lick and kiss at their least word?"

"I am afraid there are some men who do not object to that," I admitted.

"I am sure you find free women of some interest," she said.

"Certainly I find them of interest," I said. The most interesting thing about them, of course, was that they could be seized and enslaved. After that they might become of real interest to a man. The female slave, of course, yours in her servitude, is ten thousand times more interesting than a free woman could ever dream of being. In any contest of desirability the free woman must always lose out to the slave, and if she does not seem to do so, then let her be enslaved, and see how she then, suddenly, in a moment, competing then with her former self, becomes ten thousand times more desirable than she ever was as a mere free female.

"Master," said Louise, the nude, slender, red-haired Earth-girl slave, returning. She knelt near the table. She placed the small bottle of ka-la-na on the table, and two tiny cups.

"She is a pretty little thing," said the free woman.

I flicked my finger, dismissing the slave, not bothering to look at her. This pleased the free woman. I wondered how one of the usual, close-fitting Gorean slave collars would look on her own throat. Well, I thought. Such collars set off the beauty of a woman, the encircling steel, significatory of bondage, contrasting nicely with the softness of her throat, shoulders and breasts.

"Yes, please," said the woman.

I poured.

"To you," she said, lifting her glass.

"No," I said, "to you."

"Thank you," she said. I saw that she was flattered by this. She glowed. Her breasts were very nice.

We touched glasses. We drank.

"Oh, it is marvelous ka-la-na," she purred. I gathered that she had never before had such ka-la-na. True, it might run the buyer as much as three copper tarsks, a price for which some women can be purchased.

"I am pleased that you like it," I said.

"I am Tutina, Lady of Ar," she said, warmly, intimately, leaning forward.

"That is a lovely name," I said. To be sure, if I owned

her, I thought I would shorten it to Tina. That is an excellent slave name. Indeed, I had owned slaves with that name.

She basked in my praise.

"I am called Tarl," I said.

"Oh," she said, reprovingly, "that is such a fierce name."

I shrugged.

"It is a northern name, is it not?"

"It is common in the north," I said, "particularly in Torvaldsland."

"Men from Torvaldsland frighten me," she said. "They are so strong with women. You are not from Torvaldsland, are you?"

"No," I said. To be sure, I had been in Torvaldsland, and I felt that I knew as much as any fellow there about what to do with a woman at his feet. But then any true master anywhere knows as much. Indeed, although the men of Torvaldsland are fine and strong masters, they are generally rather direct and straightforward about what they are doing. In the south, in the cities, in my opinion, because of the richness in history and tradition, and the much greater cultural sophistication and complexity, a female is likely to find herself placed under a much stricter and more exacting bondage than in the north. To be sure, much depends on the girl and the master. Some girls thrive best with uncompromising barbarian masters who will put them on the oar or under the whip at the least sign of their being displeasing and others find that they did not truly understand helplessness and submission until they found their chain fastened to the couch ring of a gentleman.

"That is reassuring," she smiled. "Where are you from?"

"From the northwest, near Thassa," I said. I saw no reason to tell her I was from Port Kar. She might then have become not feignedly, but actually, alarmed. Most of the fellows of Port Kar have something of the ruthless lust of pirates in their view of females, coupled with some knowledge, because of a popular form of commerce in the city, of sophisticated techniques of slave handling and management.

"Where did you just come from?" she asked.

"Torcadino," I said.

"Oh," she said, disappointed.

"What is wrong?" I asked.

"You are not a refugee, are you?" she asked.

"Why?" I asked.

"Then you might have had a difficult trip," she said.

"I see," I said.

"I do not believe things are as bad in Torcadino as they say," she said.

"Oh?" I asked.

"No," she said. "They are just trying to frighten us." I saw her eye was on my purse.

"I came in by fee cart," I said.

"I see," she said. I saw she liked that information. I had thought she would. It suggested I had money.

"Are you of the Merchants?" she asked.

"I have sometimes bought and sold things," I told her. I saw that this pleased her. I did not tell her that many of the things I had bought and sold were much like herself.

"May I call you Tarl?" she asked.

"Of course," I said. She was, after all, a free woman. If she were to become a slave, of course, there would be no such liberty in such matters.

I poured her more ka-la-na.

She drank. She leaned forward, her elbows on the small table. Her breasts seemed to invite my touch. Her lips were warm and soft. "There was another reason," she said, "other than the splendid dismissal of a slut slave from your presence, why I came to your table."

"Oh?" I said.

"I feel drawn to you," she said.

"I understand," I said. I glanced at the fellow still slumped on the other table.

"And, too," she whispered, "I am lonely." Her hand then touched mine. I was becoming excited. I restrained myself. She belonged, really, to the fellow at the other table.

"Tarl," she whispered.

"Yes," I said. She knew her business, this woman. The sooner she was in a collar the better.

"Yes?" I said, softly, encouragingly.

"Oh, no," she said, drawing back, suddenly, seeming to wipe a tear from her eye, "I must not say such things to you."

"What?" I asked, kindly.

"I must leave," she said. "I must hurry away now." She put her hands out, that I might gently take them in mine, holding her at the table, restraining her sweetly, in earnest, gentle persuasion, from departing. But I, curious to see what would happen, apparently did not notice this opportunity.

She did not leave.

"I just do not know what to do," she said, turning her head from side to side.

"What is wrong?" I asked, seemingly concerned.

"How terrible you must think me," she said, wiping away another tear, it seemed, from the corner of her eye.

"Not at all," I said. I certainly did not think her terrible at all. Indeed, I thought she was luscious.

"I have been too bold," she said. "I approached your table. I have spoken to you first. I have permitted you, a man I scarcely know, to buy me ka-la-na. I am so ashamed."

"There is no need to be ashamed," I said.

"But far worse," she said, "I revealed to you my feelings. I told you of my unspeakable loneliness. Are you lonely?"

"Not particularly," I said. It is normally only free folks among free folks who are lonely, each so separate from the other. It is not easy for men to be lonely who have access to slaves. Similarly the slaves, so occupied, and of necessity so concerned to please the master, are seldom given the time for the indulgence of loneliness. Too, of course, the incredible intimacy of the relationship, intellectual and emotional, as well as sexual, for the master may inquire into, and command forth, and is normally inclined to do so, her deepest thoughts and feelings, which must be bared to him, as much as her body, as well as command, even casually, her most intimate and delicious sexual performances, militates against loneliness.

In slavery total intimacy is not only customary, but it can be made obligatory, under discipline. Masters like to know their girls. They want to know them with a depth, detail and intimacy that it would be quite inappropriate to expect of, or desire from, a prideful free companion, whose autonomy and privacy is protected by her lofty status. In a sense, the free woman is always, to one extent or another, veiled. The slave, on the other hand, is not permitted veils. She is, so to speak, naked to the master, and fully.

There is no doubt that slaves without private masters, or slaves in multiple-slave chains, arrangements, households, institutions, and such, may experience terrible loneliness. There is doubtless great loneliness, for example, in a rich man's pleasure gardens. Indeed, the presence of a lovely slave there might not even be known to the master, but only to her immediate keepers, and the master's agents, who may have purchased her, or accountants, who keep records of the master's properties and assets. Perhaps she must beg piteously to be called to the attention of the master. Some women in such a place, even those whose existence is known, or remembered, at least vaguely, might wait for months for a summons to the couch of the master, he perhaps selecting a ribbon with her name on it, from a rack of slave ribbons, and tossing it to an attendant, that she be brought in chains to his quarters that night, the ribbon on her collar. Too, it can doubtless be lonely in the house of a slaver, especially when the guards do not choose to amuse themselves with you, or have you perform for them, or, say, when you find yourself alone at night, perhaps a work slave, in the basement of a cylinder, chained in a cement kennel.

"Oh," she said.

"With you here," I said, "how could I be lonely?"

"What a lovely thing to say," she said.

I thought it had been pretty good myself. To be sure, it had required quick thinking.

"But mostly," she said, as though tearfully, "I am distressed at the boldness with which I spoke before."

"Boldness?" I asked.

"When I admitted, as I should never have done," she said, "that I was drawn to you."

" 'Drawn to me'?" I inquired.

"Yes," she said, lowering her eyes.

"I understand," I said. "You were drawn to me because

something within you seemed to sense, and delicately, that I might prove to be a sympathetic interlocutor, an understanding fellow with whom you might, assuaging therein to some extent your loneliness and pain, hold gentle and kindly converse.''

"It was more than that," she whispered, not looking up, as though she dared not raise her eyes.

"Oh?" I asked.

She looked up, as though distressed. "I felt drawn to you," she said, and then she lowered her head, as though in shame, ''—*as a female to a male*.''

I said nothing.

"Free women have needs, too," she whispered.

"I do not doubt it," I said. At the moment, of course, she had no real idea of what female needs could be. As with most free females they were doubtless far below the surface and seldom directly sensed. Their effect upon conscious life, because of her conditioning, would normally be felt in such transformed and eccentric modalities as anxiety, uneasiness, misery, discomfort, ill temper, imaginary complaints, frustration and loneliness. These things would be connected with her lack of feminine fulfillment, she not finding herself in her place, in her natural biological relationship, that of submissive to dominant, to the male of her species. These things, the result of her loss of sexual identity and fulfillment, too, often produced a sense of emptiness and meaninglessness. Too, they sometimes produced an envy and resentment of men, whom she, perhaps with some justice, would blame for this lack of fulfillment. When one sex needs the other to fulfill it, and the other refuses, what is to be done? One way of striving for vengeance, of course, is to attempt, socially and politically, to bring about the debilitation and ruination of anatomical males, whether they be men or not. This, of course, might prove dangerous, for it might provoke an upsurge of nature, like a natural phenomenon, in which her order, artificialities then scorned and abolished, would be harshly restored.

Another danger, and perhaps one more serious, is that a misdirected response would be provoked in which, say, angry males, perhaps unable to take direct action because of the numerous, carefully wrought political traps and snares trammeling them, would think themselves, consciously or subconsciously, to have no recourse but to engage in the undeniably masculine games of war, games which might destroy worlds, but, with them, perhaps, the walls within which they have permitted themselves to be imprisoned. It would be unfortunate, indeed, if the female, returned at last to her rightful chains, were to find herself kneeling in ashes.

"You are kind not to scorn me for my needs," she said. She looked up at me. "Sometimes they are very strong."

"I am sure of it," I said. She had as yet, of course, as a free woman, as I have mentioned, no real idea of what female needs could be. They were in her, as in all free women, muchly suppressed. She had no idea as to what they could be. Never had she confronted them wholly and directly. She was as yet alienated from the depth and richness of the extensive sexual tissues in her body; she did not yet understand how her entire skin, from her scalp to her toes, could awaken into life, startled and rejoicing, stimulated by the hot, surgent, wavelike irradiations emanating not only from her helpless, lovely, exploited centralities, but as well from all the other sensitive curvatures and beauties of her, curvatures and beauties so much at a master's mercy; too, she could not even now begin to suspect the momentous emotional dimensions of bondage for the female, its entire, totalistic matrix, of what it was to be a slave, the nature of the slave's feelings, how she is affected by what she is, and what can be done to her, of what it is to be owned, absolutely, to be under uncompromising discipline, of what it is to know that you must, and will, under strict and uncompromising enforcements, give yourself up wholly to service and love, no alternatives permitted.

"You are very kind to take pity on a woman," she said.

"It is nothing," I said. I speculated that her needs might be rather strong, as a matter of fact, for a free woman. Certainly her body suggested the influence of a rich abundance of female hormones. One does not get curves like that by being hormonally deficient. It might be interesting, I thought, to see what those needs might be like if permitted to develop fully under bondage.

"When I spoke your name before," she said, "I hesitated."

"I remember," I said.

"It was so hard to speak," she said.

"Yes?" I said.

"May I speak?" she asked.

"Yes," I said.

"I was thinking that I might perhaps let you see my body," she said, "that I might even permit you to touch it."

"Yes," I said.

"That I might tonight," she said, "as you have been so kind to me, and I am drawn to you, give you my body."

"I am overwhelmingly impressed," I said. This seemed to me a suitable response, as she was a free woman. It is really difficult to know what to say when one hears something so stupid. If she were a slave, I would have enjoyed hearing her try to speak in that fashion, speaking of "giving her body" and for such-and-such a period. That would earn her a swift whipping. If one could speak in that fashion, of "mere bodies," so to speak, and it was not typically Gorean to do so, she would not in bondage be considering whether or not to bestow her body, and for how long, but rather she would discover that it was his for the master to take, whenever he wished, however he wished, and for as long as he wished, for it would then belong not to her but to him, or he could order her to bring it to him, his property, in whatever attitude or posture he might please. But it is not typically Gorean to think in this fashion. The slave, for example, does not ask if the Master now wants the body of Gloria but, rather, does he want Gloria. In Gorean thought, and, indeed, Gorean law is explicit on this, what is owned is the whole slave. It is she who is owned, the whole woman, and uncompromisingly and totally.

"How kind you are," she said, "to a woman met in such a place, one so poor she cannot even afford sandals, a suitable gown, and proper veiling. Do you object that I am so revealingly clad, and am not properly veiled? Does it scandalize you?"

"No," I said. "Doubtless it is an inevitable concession to the cruelties of poverty."

"Yes," she lamented. "Perhaps you could try to think of me veiled," she suggested.

"That is a thought," I said. That much, surely, at least, could be said for it. I conjectured what she might look like, stark naked, save for chains, perhaps, holding her as a tight love bundle, for a master's pleasure, at a ring, and the locked, steel slave collar that belonged on her neck.

She looked at me, gratefully. In my imagination I tightened her chains a notch or two.

"Is it true that you are drawn to me?" I asked.

"Yes!" she whispered, daring to touch my hand.

"Then shall we leave this place," I asked, "and venture to your domicile?"

She drew back. As I had anticipated, she would not find a suggestion of this sort acceptable. She would not want her address known. That might put her at the mercy of furious, outraged victims. Too, it could make it simple for guardsmen, acting on complaints, to bring her in for identification and questioning, these details doubtless, in her case, to be followed by a hearing and sentencing, an almost inevitable reduction to bondage and then perhaps, initially, while her disposition is being more carefully considered, a placement in the public slave gardens.

"Perhaps then my room?" I suggested. "It is nearby."

"Sir!" she said, reproachfully. As I had thought, this would not be satisfactory either. She would prefer to complete her work here, where apparently it was tolerated, with the stealth of a drug, rather than go to the expense of employing confederates outside or take the risk of being recognized by others who might be in the vicinity of the victim's environs. "What sort of girl do you think I am?"

"Forgive me," I said, earnestly. "I did not mean to offend you." She was skillful at this type of game, it seemed, to provoke a male response, and then to claim she had been misunderstood, and was offended, thus confusing the male, keeping him off balance, and, in general, thusly guaranteeing, with a glance or tear, that she would have things her own way. She was, at least, manipulative in a feminine fashion. That I granted her. It said something for her femaleness. It is pleasant later, of course, to manipulate such women in a masculine fashion, by command and the whip.

"I knew I should not have come here," she sobbed, wiping away a tear, one at least in theory, from the corner of her eye. She made as though to rise but, as I did not restrain her, she remained where she was.

"I have been clumsy," I said.

"I do not really blame you," she sobbed. "What else could you think, meeting me here? Surely you must think me the same as these other, lower women."

"No, certainly not," I said. "You are quite different, obviously, from them."

"Thank you," she whispered.

I nodded. Of course she was quite different from them. That was obvious. She was not yet nude. She did not yet have a slave collar on her neck. She had probably never yet, in her life, felt a slave whip.

"Perhaps you are wondering," she said, wiping away yet another supposed tear, "what I, a gentlewoman, of breeding and refinement, am doing in this place?"

"Perhaps," I said, encouragingly. I tried to look puzzled. Actually I had a rather clear idea what she was doing in this place.

She looked down. "I think the real reason," she said, "under everything, as you may have suspected, is that I was driven here, almost helplessly, a woman in desperate need of love, daring to enter this terrible place, but one where I knew men were, by my desire to meet a kindly man, by my loneliness."

"Yes?" I said.

"But I should never have come."

"But then we would never have met," I said.

"Yes," she whispered, again touching my hand. "That is true."

"You spoke of a real reason," I said, "that having to do with your need of love, and such. That suggests, then, I take it, that there was some other reason, or pretended reason, for coming.''

She smiled, ruefully. "Yes," she said. "I am a proud free woman. I could not permit myself to recognize such things as my loneliness, or need for love. I must tell myself there was another reason for coming.''

"And what was that?" I asked.

"I am in need of money," she said. "I have a ring. I told myself that I would try to sell it, that I would try to find a buyer in this place.''

"I see," I said.

"But I have never been able to bring myself to part with it," she said. "It is one of the few things left to me from the time when I was proud and wealthy. It is so laden with memories. I could never really bring myself to part with it.''

"I understand," I said.

"Would you like to see it?" she asked.

"It is not necessary," I said.

"Please, let me show it to you," she said.

"Very well," I said.

From the tiny pouch, hung on strings at her belt, she produced the ring. She slipped it on her finger.

"Lovely," I said. Its oval stone was of white porcelain, mounted in a a red-metal bezel. On the porcelain, very delicately done, in red, was the representation of a Tur tree. The band was of gold.

"It was wrought in Turia," she said. I found that easy to believe. It had the Tur tree, emblem of Turia, in the southern hemisphere, on the porcelain stone. Too, I knew such rings were manufactured in Turia. Indeed, I had even seen them there. Rings of this design, however, though perhaps not of this purpose, were rare in Ar, in the northern hemisphere. Most fellows of Ar would not recognize the ring, or suspect its purpose. She had probably purchased it in an import shop on the Avenue of Turia, which was nearby. To be sure, perhaps the setting was solid, and not hollow. Many rings of this appearance are totally innocent.

"Would you let me buy it?" I asked. "Surely you could use the money.''

"Do not tempt me," she smiled. "I could never bring myself to part with it."

"I am sorry," I said.

"How fortunate I am to meet a man such as you," she said. "How understanding you are."

I shrugged.

"I am becoming excited," she whispered.

"Oh?" I said.

"I want to go to your room," she whispered.

"Let us go," I said.

"Oh, the wine is gone," she pouted.

That was true.

"May we have more wine?" she wheedled. "It would help me to get even more into the mood. With a little more wine I do not know if I could control myself. I might find myself hurrying after you, going to your room, heeling you through the streets like an amorous slave!"

"I will get some more wine," I said. I glanced over to the left. In a moment or two, I had managed to catch the eye of Louise. She had not, of course, after her initial command, been concentrating on our table. I was pleased that she was not in use. I enjoyed having her serve me. Had she been, of course, I would have made do with another girl, say, Ita or Tia. They were both very nice slaves. Louise was now looking at me, aware that I was looking at her. I lifted my hand. She leaped up, hurrying toward me. I noticed the fellow nearby, slumped over the table. He had not yet stirred. He might be out for another Ahn or so. I leaned over to where Louise now knelt and gave her the wine order. The collar, such fine, strong steel, looked nice under her right ear.

Lady Tutina smiled at me.

I, too, smiled at her.

"Do you like me?" she asked.

"Yes," I said. I thought, properly trained and disciplined, she would make an excellent slave.

"I wish that slave would hurry," she said.

"I'm sure she will be back in a moment," I said.

"Perhaps you should beat her," she said.

"An excellent suggestion," I said, "but let us give her a few more Ihn."

"I think I shall soon be in the mood," she whispered, confidingly, intimately.

"Excellent," I said. It amused me to hear her speak of moods, and such. I wondered if she might think, perhaps for the first few Ihn of bondage, until the hand, the whip or boot taught her differently, that she might make a master wait upon her pleasure, until, say, she might be in the "mood," or something like that.

"I suspect," she said, looking into my eyes, intimately, "that this meeting may change my life."

"It is not impossible," I said.

"Master," said Louise, arriving at the table, kneeling, another small bottle of wine on her tray. I removed it from the tray and set it near me. I then dismissed her.

I poured two small glasses of wine. I did not know how skilled the Lady Tutina was. I had known at least one fellow, Boots Tarsk-Bit, who was marvelously skilled at such things as misdirection and sleight of hand.

"She is rather pretty, isn't she?" asked the Lady Tutina, looking after Louise. She, the Earth-girl slave, nude and collared, hard to see in the flickering reddish light, carrying the tray over her head, was making her way back among the tables and mats to the bar. "In a trivial, servile way, suitable for a slave, of course," added the Lady Tutina.

"Perhaps," I said. I looked after Louise.

"That fellow seems to think so," said the Lady Tutina. A fellow had reached out to touch Louise's branded flank as she moved past his table. She withdrew, frightened, hurrying on, from the touch. Then the fellow sprawled to the side, drunk.

"Yes," I said.

Louise was lovely, indeed. She had not yet, however, I suspected, fully learned her collar. I did not think she, as yet, realized fully, in the depths of her, that she was a slave girl, and only that, and what that meant. She could, of course, be taught.

"She is a bit skinny," said the woman.

I shrugged. She was not skinny. She was slight, and

slender. But such often make superb slaves. Certainly for her size and weight, she was well curved.

"Let us drink," said the Lady Tutina. I decided that she was not particularly skilled after all. It is no great trick to put something in someone's drink when they are not looking. Boots, I was sure, could have managed it while engaged in face-to-face conversation. He, of course, was unusually good at that sort of thing.

"To you," breathed the Lady Tutina, smiling.

"No," I smiled, "to you."

She then sipped the wine. I, on the other hand, after lifting it toward my lips, merely returned it to the table.

"This is not the same wine," she said, lowering the glass. "It is different."

"Yes," I said. "Do you like it?"

"Yes," she said, smiling. "Of course. It is wonderful."

"Perhaps you will come to like it," I said. In the beginning perhaps it would be poured down her throat, her head held back by the hair, by masters. Later, she might find herself wheedling and groveling for it, grateful to have anything that good.

"You haven't touched your wine," she said, reproachfully.

"Come here," I said.

She came about the table, kneeling near me. It was the first time she had obeyed me. It pleased me to have her obeying me.

"Close," I said.

She came then quite close to me.

"Cuddle," I said.

She snuggled up against me. Her nearness made me master hot. Her breasts were exciting. I put my arm about her, that I might hold her to me. She looked up into my eyes. "You haven't touched your wine," she pouted.

"Oh?" I said.

"Drink, drink," she wheedled, picking up the glass, lifting it toward my lips. "Drink," she said, "and then we may hurry to your room, where I may serve you, even as a slave."

"You are luscious, and tempting," I said.

"Drink," she said.

I forced myself to remember that she was for the other fellow, the one slumped across the nearby table.

"Drink," she whispered.

I took the glass from her. I set it down on the table.

"What is wrong?" she asked.

"Encourage me," I said.

She then began to kiss me, and lick me, about the face and neck. She did it quite well. With training she would do it much better.

"Do you know the wine?" I asked.

"No," she said.

I turned the bottle so that she might read the label. It was a small bottle of Boleto's Nectar of the Public Slave Gardens. Boleto is a well-known winegrower from the vicinity of Ar. He is famous for the production of a large number of reasonably good, medium-grade ka-la-nas. This was one of the major wines, and perhaps the best, served in Ar's public slave gardens; indeed, it had originally been commissioned for that market; hence the name.

"Oh," she said.

"I hope you like it," I said.

"It's very nice," she said.

"I'm glad you like it," I said.

"Here," she said, picking up the glass, "hurry, drink. I wish to hurry to your room."

"Let us go to the room now," I said. I considered giving her this option, this chance to save herself. Did she accept it I would release her from the ring in the morning, with perhaps no more than an admonitory bruise or two.

"Hurry," she whispered. She lifted the glass to my lips. "Drink," she whispered, invitingly, seductively.

I smiled to myself. She had had her chance. To be sure, I had offered it to her only as an irony and amusement. That would doubtless sometime become quite clear to her. I had known she would not accept it.

"Drink," she whispered. I took the glass from her hand. "Drink," she whispered.

"But it is for you," I said.

"What?" she said.

"I bought the wine for you," I said.

"But I have had some," she said.

"Have some more," I said.

"You may pour me some," she said, uneasily.

"Take mine," I said.

"I could not do that," she said.

"Of course you could," I said.

"I do not want any more," she said.

"You were willing, a moment ago, to have me pour you more," I reminded her.

"I have really had enough," she said. She squirmed a bit. She was locked, kneeling, in my arm.

"No," I said, "you have not."

She looked at me, frightened. "I do not want it," she said.

"Of course you do," I said.

"No," she said.

"Is there anything wrong with it?" I asked.

"No," she said. "Of course not."

"Then drink," I told her. I lifted the glass toward her lips. She tried to pull back. "What is wrong?" I asked.

"Nothing," she said.

"Drink," I said.

"No," she said.

"You are going to drink this," I told her.

"No!" she said.

"Shall I call for a slave tube?" I asked.

"No," she begged. My grip on her was merciless. The slave tube is a device for force-feeding a slave. It is not a pleasant device. A round, cylindrical, truncated cushion, usually of cork or leather, with a circular hole in its center, is forced into the slave's mouth. This prevents her from closing her teeth on the tube. The tube is then introduced through the circular opening in the bite cushion into her mouth and run down to her stomach. There is a funnel at the mouth-end of the tube. It may be used for such purposes as feeding a recalcitrant slave liquids, such as juices and broths. Some tubes come, too, however, with plungers, so that semisolid food, such as slave gruel or hash, or even damp bread and tiny pieces of meat, indeed, about anything the master may please, may be forced into her stomach. The girl is usually on her knees when this is done, with her head held back and her hands tied or braceleted behind her. Afterwards her hands are usually left confined for an Ahn or so in this fashion, so that she cannot rid herself of the nourishment.

"Drink," I said.

"Please, no," she wept.

"Then you desire the slave tube?" I inquired.

"No!" she said. "Mercy!"

I pulled her head back, by the hair, with my left hand. "Open your mouth," I said. "Do not spill a drop."

She squirmed, helplessly. Her teeth were gritted.

"I see that it is your intention to be difficult," I said.

She struggled but then, by the hair, I held her precisely; where I wanted her. Her mouth remained tightly closed. I gathered she did not wish for so much as a drop of that liquid to cross her lips. It must be rather strong, I surmised. To be sure, the dosage had been intended for a male.

I looked up, and noted Louise, who had been returning to her place to the left of the open space, coming back from the bar. She was standing there, observing me with horror.

"We are going to give her a little drink," I said to Louise.

"Master?" asked Louise, frightened.

"The slave tube is not going to be necessary after all," I told the Lady Tutina. She looked at me wildly, her mouth tightly shut.

"A simpler, more primitive method, quite suitable for small amounts, is at our disposal," I told her.

"No!" she said.

I put the tiny glass of wine to the side, on the floor.

"Slave," I said to Louise.

"Master?" she said.

"Take the Lady Tutina's belt," I said, "and tie her hands behind her back."

"Master!" protested Louise.

"No!" cried the Lady Tutina.

"She is free," said Louise.

"Must a command be repeated?" I asked Louise.

"No, Master!" she said.

She took the Lady Tutina's belt off and pulled her hands behind her back, and tied them there.

"Good," I said. The Lady Tutina squirmed, on her knees, her hands tied behind her.

"Master," moaned Louise, frightened.

"Here," I said, handing her the tiny glass of wine. "Obey me, unquestioningly, when I speak."

"Yes, Master," whispered Louise.

"No!" said the Lady Tutina. "Oh!" I had then, reaching about her head with my left hand, pinched her nostrils tightly together between my fingers. She could now not breathe through her nose. With this same grip, and its afforded leverage, I pulled her head back. Perhaps I was not as gentle as I might have been, considering she was free. Still it might do her some good, like the binding of her hands behind her, to accustom her to being handled in this fashion. She gasped for air. I then wedged my right hand in her mouth and, with my thumb and fingers, my thumb on her upper teeth, my fingers on her lower teeth, forced it open, very widely. Held so, she could not bite.

"Now," I said to Louise. "Now."

The Lady Tutina whimpered. She squirmed. She tried to shake her head, but I held it in position, exactly as I wanted it. Louise carefully poured the wine into that lovely, widely opened orifice, that lovely, widely opened vessel that was the mouth of the Lady Tutina.

"Good," I said to Louise.

Louise looked at me, gratefully. She would not be immediately beaten, at least. She was pretty, naked.

I continued to hold the head of the Lady Tutina in place. As I had timed the matter she had not had a breath left at that point to exhale or blow the fluid from her mouth. She looked at me, wildly.

"I would suppose, sooner or later," I said, "that you would like to breathe. No breath, however, can enter your lungs until you have first cleared your mouth of the fluid in it. There is only one way for you to do that, in your present predicament. That is to swallow it. Perhaps your body will make the decision for you.''

She whimpered piteously in protest.

"There is not really much point in holding your breath," I said. "The matter is one of inevitability."

Another whimper.

"You are very pretty," I informed her.

Then wildly, tears plunging down her cheeks, she swallowed the liquid and, choking, gasped wildly for breath.

"You may now unbelt the hands of the Lady Tutina," I said to Louise.

"Yes, Master!" she said, hastening to do so.

"Oh, no, Lady Tutina," I said, holding her hands now. "You would not want to do that."

She jerked her hands, but could not remove them from my grasp. "I hate you!" she said. "I hate you!"

"There is nothing to fear," I said, "unless there might have been something in the wine."

"I hate you," she sobbed. She threw a wild look at the fellow slumped over the nearby table. He was still unconscious. She was clearly frightened. The dosage she had imbibed, assuming there might have been one in the drink, would doubtless have been one fit for a male. Accordingly, her own period of unconsciousness, given this possibility, might possibly last several Ahn, more than enough time to be carried to a cell in a praetor's holding area. She jerked her hands again, wildly, but I held them tightly.

"I hate you!" she hissed.

"Do not forget your loneliness, and your need for love," I said.

"Sleen! Sleen!" she hissed. She again tried to free her hands, and again, of course, could not. How could she expect to do so, with her strength, only that of a female? But this time, even so, it seemed to me she had pulled less strongly than before. Even her small woman's strength seemed now less than it had been. Apparently there had indeed been something in the wine. It was beginning, it seemed, to take effect. She seemed suddenly unsteady.

"What are you going to do with me?" she asked.

"When you awaken," I said, "you will discover what has been done with you."

"I love you," she said, suddenly. "Take me to your room. It was not necessary to drug me. I would have gone happily."

"It is nice to hear that," I said.

"I love you," she said. "You are going to take me to your room, aren't you?"

I regarded her, not speaking.

"I will serve you there—even as a slave!" she whispered. "Then you will let me go in the morning."

I did not answer her.

"What are you going to do with me?" she asked.

I did not answer her.

"You are going to take me to your room, aren't you?" she pleaded.

"No," I said.

"Then what are you going to do with me?" she asked.

"I do not think I am going to do much of anything with you," I said.

She looked at me, puzzled. She wavered.

I glanced at the fellow slumped over the nearby table.

"No!" she said. "No!"

"It is a pretty ring," I said. I then removed it from her hand. I put the ring on the floor. She leaned back. I did not think she could get up. She watched as I crushed it beneath my heel.

I glanced at Louise, who was kneeling to the side, frightened.

I looked again to the Lady Tutina. She was now slipped to the floor, beside the table, on the tiles, unconscious.

I took the unconscious Lady Tutina by the wrist and pulled her over a bit, onto a nearby mat, to the left of a nearby table. It was the table, of course, across which the unconscious fellow lay slumped. There was a heavy slave ring there, too, fixed in the floor. It was near the head of the mat. The mat and ring, both, of course, were those appropriate to the fellow's table. There, she lying on the mat, I pulled down her now-beltless dress until it was about her knees. In doing this I retrieved his purse. I tied it about her neck. I then, with some

binding fiber, cored with wire, from my wallet, bound her
wrists tightly together and then tied them tightly to the ring.

In tying the hands tightly to the ring it makes it harder for
the female to get her teeth on the binding fiber. But of
course, even if she should manage this, trying desperately,
determinedly and elatedly, with wild hopes, to free herself,
she would discover shortly, at least in this case, this discovery dashing these wild, absurd hopes, mocking all her efforts,
and plunging her into despair, the fiber's stern wire coring.
She was not tied there, in such a fashion, by a man, she
would then learn, that she might escape. It seemed to me
extremely unlikely that she would recover consciousness before the fellow. If that should, however, somehow occur, she
would still be found at his ring, awaiting his pleasure.

I looked down upon her. She lay there then, on her belly,
mostly stripped, her arms extended over her head, her head
turned to the side, her wrists crossed and bound tightly
together, lashed to the slave ring, his purse about her neck. I
considered matters. I then pulled the mat from beneath her,
and with my foot, thrust it to the side. She would lie naked
on the tiles, I had decided. Such a woman was not worthy of
a mat. I also kicked her belt over beside her. It was a small
detail, but it, like her dress, like herself, like all she was and
all she would be, now lay at the disposal of the fellow slumped
across the table.

I then returned to my own table. Louise was still there
kneeling. I had not yet dismissed her.

"Am I dismissed, Master?" she asked.

"No," I said.

She gasped.

"Are you any good on a mat?" I asked.

"But you are of Earth," she said. "And I am of Earth! I
am from Earth! You are from Earth! We are both from Earth!
You could not for a moment be thinking—!"

"Fetch a slave whip," I said.

She uttered a cry of misery and regarded me in disbelief.
Then she leapt to her feet and hurried away. In a moment she
had returned and knelt before me. She put down her head, as
she had doubtless been taught, in submission. She then

lifting and extending her arms, her head still humbly down between them, lifted her hands to me. The backs of the wrists faced me. This was rather as in several common submission ceremonies. With the backs of the hands in this position it is easier to pull them together and tie them. Indeed, in most of these submission ceremonies the wrists are presented already crossed to the male, so that he may the more conveniently lash them together. Every Gorean woman, incidentally, slave or free, is taught by the age of puberty how to render submission. Her life might depend on it. Now, however, held in these small, lovely hands, her hands about ten inches apart on it, lifted to me, there was an object.

"Yes?" I said.

"I bring you a slave whip, Master," she said.

"Yes?" I said.

"Use it on me," she said, "if I do not please you."

"Who are you?" I asked.

"Louise," she said.

"Again," I said.

"Louise brings you a slave whip, Master," she said. "Use it on Louise, if she does not please you."

"I will," I said.

She shuddered.

"And I might use it on you anyway," I said.

"Of course, Master," she said. One owns slaves and commands them. One does what one likes with them. One does not bargain with them.

"Go to the mat," I said.

"I am of Earth!" she said.

I shook out the blades of the whip.

She hurried to the mat, to kneel upon it.

I regarded her.

She looked lovely, nude, deliciously curved, frightened, in the glinting collar, in the flickering reddish darkness.

I folded back the blades of the whip and inserted them in their clip, near the butt end of the staff. By means of the hook at the end of the butt, I attached the whip to my belt. This action seemed to be greeted with relief on her part. Perhaps she thought, being of Earth, she would get off easily. Did she not know that she was now on Gor, and that a whip so easily placed on a belt may be as easily, and, indeed, even more easily, removed from it?

A girl cried out, nearby, moaning, sobbing, being well mastered.

I looked about, for a loose chain. In a moment or two I had found one, near another slave ring. I looped it in my hand, and carried it to the ring near my mat. The key, the same key fitting both the padlock-type terminations of the chain, was in one of the locks. I crouched down beside Louise and looped one end of the chain about her neck, where I locked it snugly in place with one of the padlock-type terminations. The chain depended from her neck, between her breasts. I then looped the other end of the chain about the slave ring and, with the termination at that end, locked it there. She had about five feet of play between her neck and the slave ring. That is more than sufficient to allow a female to perform. Many men give her even less chain, some only six inches or so, such adjustments being made with different length chains, and also, often with the same chain, by loopings, doublings and such, secured by fastening the padlocklike terminations through various links. She put her fingers on the chain. She surreptitiously pulled it a little. It was on her.

"Master?" she asked. I walked over to the wall and hung the key on a nail there, with other keys. That is where the key should have been in the first place. There it is out of the reach of all the slave rings. Too, in this way, it is easier to keep track of them, and a customer is less likely to inadvertently walk off with one. No chains hung there, incidentally. They were apparently, at least those usually there, in use or, like the one I had found, loose on the floor. I glanced around. The place seemed crowded. Ita and Tia were dancing, summoned forth by a hostess, before a customer. I recalled Louise dancing. She had done at least that well, surely. I wondered if she, an Earth girl, going about her business on Earth, had ever suspected that she would one day be so dancing on Gor as a nude, collared slave. I supposed not. I wondered what she would have thought if someone had suggested this to her. Doubtless she would have thought it absurd, or amusing

But then, a moment later, she might have felt the thick layers of the chemically treated cloth held firmly over her nose and mouth. Business seemed good this evening. Indeed, it seemed to be thriving. This Ludmilla, whoever she was, I conjectured, had something of a gold mine in this little establishment. Tonight's receipts, at any rate, would probably prove quite gratifying.

I returned to the slave mat.

"Master?" asked Louise.

She looked up at me, the chain on her neck.

I removed the whip from my belt, freeing the blades. I shook them loose.

"I am from Earth!" she said.

"Spread your knees," I said.

Swiftly did the Earth girl comply.

I looked down at her. She was incredibly lovely.

"Surely you will treat me gently, and with respect," she said.

"How do you lie on a mat, Earth girl?" I asked.

"However a master pleases," she whispered.

I gestured to the mat with the whip. Immediately she lay upon it.

"Perhaps you can interest me," I said.

"Please!" she said.

"Move," I told her.

She moved then, and turned, upon the mat, sometimes on her belly, sometimes on her back, sometimes on her side, sometimes kneeling, sometimes sitting, sometimes curled up, sometimes bending backwards, pausing every moment or so, for a moment or so, stock-still, posing, that I might feast my eyes upon her loveliness, revealing thusly for me her imbonded beauty in numerous and various attitudes. There were tears in her eyes. I saw that she had had some training.

She was then breathing heavily.

I let the loose whip blades brush her back. "Master?" she asked.

"Is that all you show Gorean men?" I asked. "If so, I am surprised you have not yet been fed to sleen."

"You are from Earth," she wept.

"And so you, a slave, think to cheat me, and give me less?" I asked.

"No!" she said.

"Do you dare, slave," I asked, "to think that you can behave toward me as a typical Earth female behaves toward a man of Earth?"

"No," she said. "No!"

"Do you think you can treat me as the typical females of Earth treat the men of Earth?" I asked.

"No!" she wept. "No!"

"Have you ever felt the slave whip?" I asked.

"Yes, Master," she said, terrified.

"Do you want to feel it again, now?" I asked.

"No, Master!" she said.

"Perform," I said.

"Yes, Master!" she said.

"Better," I said, "better. Remember you are no longer a woman of Earth now. More leg extension. That is behind you. You are now only a Gorean slave. Good. You are not even a person any longer. You are now only a lascivious animal that exists for the pleasure of men. Only an animal. Do not forget it. But an incredibly desirable animal. Lift your hand more piteously. Good. The most desirable form of animal in existence, the female slave. That expression, improve it. Let it show that you beg a man for his touch. Do you beg a man for his touch?"

"Yes," she cried, suddenly, "I do!"

"Use the chain," I said. "It is on your neck. Use it! Use it in this mat dance."

"Dance?" she wept.

"Yes," I said, "you can consider it a dance. You can treat it as a dance. You are writhing for a master, pausing now and then to startle him with your beauty, on your chain. There is even music here. Feel it in your belly. Deep in your belly! Deeper! Yes! Yes!"

"Take me!" she cried, in English. "I beg you to take me!"

I took her in my arms, and kissed her. She was helplessly hot and open.

"Oh, yes," she cried. "Now! Now! I beg it! I beg it!"

"As a woman of Earth?" I asked.

"No," she sobbed, "as what I am now, as a Gorean slave of her master!"

Later I used her once more, this time on her belly, that she might not forget she was a slave, nor grow too proud. I then turned her to her back. She looked up at me with tears in her eyes. "I am yours," she wept. "I want to live for you, and to serve you in all ways!"

I kissed her.

"Buy me!" she begged. "Buy me!"

"I think you will one day, now that you have learned how to serve, find a fine, strong Gorean master," I said.

"Then I, an Earth woman, will belong to a Gorean," she said.

"Yes," I said, "as do many others. And I think you will make him a splendid slave."

"Yes," she whispered, softly, "a slave!"

"You are a female of Earth," I said. "Such as you are fit only to wear the collars of such men."

"I know," she said.

"Aspire to nothing higher here," I said.

"I do not," she said.

"He would have you in no other way, of course," I said.

"I know," she said.

"Are you discontent?" I asked.

"No," she said. "It is a thousand times better to be the slave of such a man than to be an Empress on Earth."

I kissed her.

"Nor would I wish to be had in any other way," she said.

"Oh?" I asked.

"Because," she said, "it is what I have now learned I am, a slave."

I considered her softness and beauty, and her helpless, loving responsiveness in my arms. "Yes," I said. "You are a man's slave."

"I do not dispute it," she said. "I learned it indubitably while finding myself helpless in your power. You have taught it to me, and the lesson can never be unlearned."

I did not speak.

"Master," she said.

"Yes," I said.

"I think there are many slaves on Earth, only they have not yet found their masters. They do not yet wear their collars."

"Perhaps," I said.

"I think there are few men on Earth who can, or will, answer the cry of the slave in a woman."

"Perhaps," I said. "I do not know."

"Why will they not do so?" she asked.

"Perhaps it is too late for them to reclaim their manhood," I said. "Perhaps it is easier for them now, at this late date, their opportunities slipped away, surrendered to the enemies of manhood, to pretend to find it disgusting, or amusing."

She sighed.

"But here on Gor," I said, "have no such fears. Here, even for all their harshness, the cultures have not taken so unnatural, demeaning and debilitating a turn."

"True," she said.

"Here you will find men such as you have only dreamed of on Earth," I said.

"Yes!" she said, softly.

"Here you do not have to fear even initially that men will not answer the cry of the slave in you," I said. "You will probably not even have time for that. You will be too busy kneeling, and obeying."

"True," she laughed, and kissed me. "Master," she said.

"Yes?" I said.

"May I say something?" she asked.

"Of course," I said. "But if I am not pleased with it, I may beat you."

"Of course," she laughed.

"What?" I asked.

"Do you recall that I expressed a wish that I be treated gently and with respect?" she asked.

"Vaguely," I said.

"I do not think you treated me too gently," she said.

"Perhaps not," I said. She had been manhandled a bit, pu

where I wanted her, and so on, allowed to understand that she was an instrument of my pleasure.

"And surely you did not treat me with respect," she said.

"No," I said. "But then you are not the sort of woman who is to be treated with respect. You are a collared slave."

"I wait for my master," she whispered.

"I do not think, now, given the recent confirmation of these insights in you, you will have to wait long for your rightful chains, but, in the meantime, you will well serve the customers in the Tunnels."

"The customers!" she wept.

"Yes," I said, and then I turned her over, putting her again on her belly on the mat.

"Oh!" she said.

"Yes, the customers," I said, "of whom I am one."

"Yes, Master!" she said. "Oh! Oh! Ohhhhh!"

"Excellent," I said.

I saw that her fingernails had scratched at the mat. I put my hand on the mat, near her face. The mat was damp there, from tears.

"Master well knows how to use a slave," she said.

"You yielded well," I said.

"I cannot help myself," she said. "I am a slave."

"And only that?" I asked.

"Yes, Master," she said.

I gently parted her hair, putting it delicately on either side of her neck. In this way I could see the collar on her neck, and the small, sturdy lock at the back of the neck.

"I wonder who truly loves himself, and women," she whispered, "he who is true to himself and his nature, refusing to deny it or pretend it doesn't exist, and who fulfills women, as what they really are, or he who betrays himself, who lies to himself and who denies the true needs of woman?"

"It is true," I said. "There are two sexes, and they are quite different."

"Is that not heresy, for a man of Earth, to say that?" she asked.

"This is Gor," I said. I pulled at her collar a little. "Are you not aware of that, slave?"

"Yes, Master," she said. "I am aware of it."

"In a world where nature is free, a world not subjected to ideological poisonings, a world where she is not crippled, and hobbled," I said, "what is the place of women?"

"At the feet of men, Master," she said.

"And where are you, Louise?" I asked.

"At the feet of men," she said.

"Such does not prove, of course," I said, "that Gor is the ideal world, but it does indicate that Gor possesses at least one feature of the ideal world."

"Yes, Master," she said.

"To be sure," I said, "it is not unknown for females, free women, of course, to seek power."

"Such pursuits, to me," she said, "seem disgusting and unnatural in a woman."

"They are," I said. "But perhaps they are to be forgiven when men abdicate their responsibilities. Perhaps it is fit then that they be destroyed as males."

"No, Master!" she said.

"Why not?" I asked.

"For then we cannot be truly women, Master. The equations of nature would be disrupted. It would be madness and sickness. It could mean the end of a world."

"What do you think would happen if you were to seek power, Louise?" I asked.

"Doubtless I would be whipped and used," she said, "and then thrown naked, chained, into a tiny cage or slave box, and kept there until I learned my lesson, and begged to be suitably subservient. I might even be killed."

"Yes," I said, "but then you, of course, are a slave."

"Yes, Master," she said.

"You are not a free woman."

"No, Master," she said.

"That makes a great difference," I said.

"Yes, Master," she said.

"They may do much what they please," I said, "even if its ultimate objective is clearly the subversion of nature, involving the reduction and debilitation of an entire sex, a sex crime than which, it seems, none could be more heinous."

"How filled with hate they must be," she said.

"Perhaps," I said.

"Unable to be men," she said, "they try to destroy them. In this they fail also to be women."

"Perhaps," I said. "I do not know."

"They will attempt to use law," she said, "using men against men, using them as their dupes and tools, until the last man can be destroyed."

"That seems the intent," I said. "It is not even well concealed."

"No, Master," she said.

"It is an interesting concept," I said, "that legislation could be passed against manhood, that nature can be dismissed with a statute, that her reality and aristocracy can be declared illegal. Surely there is some sort of category confusion here. Laws cannot validly be passed against facts. Any such law is automatically null and void. It is like the English king who in the legend sat upon the beach and forbade the incoming waves to touch his robes."

"What happened?" she asked.

"He got wet," I said. "To be sure, he may have ordered the waves beaten, but, as far as we know, the ocean failed to take note of this."

"At least he moved before he was drowned," she said.

"Let us hope that all kings, however stupid they may be, would have that much sense at least."

"Surely they would," she said.

"Not necessarily," I said. "If they are sufficiently stupid, and sufficiently strongly conditioned, closing their minds to options, and such, they might remain right where they were, proceeding righteously to a watery grave. Such things are not unknown. Many people have given their lives for absurdities. Some are called heroes."

"Surely at least some of them were idiots," she said.

"That might seem a juster appraisal, scientifically," I admitted. "Still one might regret the tragedy involved, even in the case of the idiot."

"Yes, Master," she said.

I stood up.

"Master is leaving?" she asked.

I brushed her waist and flank with my foot. She shrank back a bit, on her belly, to the side. Women are so inutterably beautiful. I then put my foot on her, and let her feel a little of my weight, but not much. I then thrust down a bit, and stepped away from her. It had been an admiring, spurning caress. She lay there, the chain on her neck, on the mat. "I am through with you now," I said. "The hostess will soon come to unchain you, and send you back to your waiting station. The key is on its nail."

"And thus you leave me?" she asked.

"Yes," I said. I glanced over to the nearby table. The fellow who had been unconscious there, the free woman, the Lady Tutina, now chained half naked at his slave ring, she still unconscious, was showing some signs of reviving.

"Master!" said the girl.

"Remain on your stomach until unchained," I said.

"Yes, Master," she said.

I then stepped away from her, looking about myself. I had received a note to come to this place. I had waited, but no one, it seemed, had attempted to make contact. There could, of course, be various reasons for this. I did not think, however, that among these reasons would have been the inability to recognize me. Presumably the individual, or individuals, would be familiar with my appearance, either from the plaza near the Central Cylinder or from a description. This made it seem plausible, then, as they had not yet contacted me, that their business with me might be of a clandestine nature. One might think then in terms of the possible transmission of secret information, or, perhaps more likely, of the enterprise of the assassin, the covert business of unsheathed daggers.

I looked about. I did not think there would be more than two of them. I considered the openings to the Tunnels. The main egress, which served also as the entryway, would surely be under observation. The hostess, in earlier speaking to me of the free women brought in for a joke, had spoken of putting her out back in the morning, naked, and, if she had been used, with her hands tied behind her, with a punched tarsk bit tied on her belly. That suggested a rear exit. If they thought I were making for that they might move swiftly, hastily, too hastily. It would be dark in the tunnel. I glanced back at the Earth redhead on the mat. She was still on her belly, as she had been commanded. She looked back and up at me, pleadingly. I then left her. She was only a slave.

I walked past the waiting station. The only girl there now, the only one not now on a chain, this testifying to the traffic of the house, was Birsen, the brown-haired girl who seemed as though she could have been a fashion model on Earth. "Head down," I said. Immediately, kneeling, she put her head to the floor, the palms of her hands, too, resting on it. It is pleasant to own and master women. Too, it is correct to do so. Bondage is merely an institutional recognition and formalization of the proper and natural relationship between the sexes. In a moment I had come to the low opening of the Al-Ka Tunnel, the first tunnel. I glanced back. In the light I could not detect whether or not anyone was noting my entrance into the tunnel. Somehow I felt, however, that my entry therein would not go unnoticed.

26: I Take my Leave of the Tunnels

In a moment I was into the tunnel. Behind me there was a bit of light coming from under the door.

In a bit, however, I was beyond it. Soon I had to crawl. The ceiling of the tunnel, in this part, I now on all fours, was about a foot over my head. In parts the tunnel was carpeted, in other parts not, and one must move on the tile or stones. There were leather-curtained alcoves here and there along the tunnel, the openings of which were circular, and about two feet in width. Occasionally there was a small lamp within, its light detectable through the cracks in the leather curtain, and about it and under it, feebly illuminating the tunnel outside. For the most part, however, the tunnel was quite dark. In two or three of the alcoves, where there was a lamp, and the curtain was not fully drawn, I saw a master and a slave. One girl was kneeling naked with her back to the wall and her hands chained up and behind her, at the sides of her head, over her shoulders. She looked at me, wildly. Then she jerked back, the master caressing her with the whip. In another alcove a girl was chained on her back, her arms and legs widely apart, spread-eagled. She was lifting her body piteously to a man who now, apparently having aroused her to a point where she was in an agony of need, was merely toying with her. I supposed he might later concede to her pleas, if only because she was quite beautiful. In another alcove there was a girl on her stomach, her wrists tied to a slave ring. I did not know if she had put in that position for love, or for punishment, or for both.

Most of the alcoves, however, like the major lengths of the tunnel, were quite dark. Some were doubtless empty. I hoped

so, for I might have need of them. On the other hand many of
the alcoves which were in total darkness were not empty.
From within many I could hear, as I moved past, the small
sounds of chains, sometimes pathetic sounds, responding doubtless to the restricted, helpless movements of small, fair limbs
on which they were locked, and the soft love moans of used
slaves. Many of these women were doubtless forbidden to
speak. They found themselves responding in the darkness to
unseen masters merely as helpless, anonymous love objects.
In some of the other alcoves, of course, those not empty,
there were presumably slaves, girls waiting alone in the
darkness, in their chains, knowing that they would be at the
mercy of whoever might enter the alcove. In the Delta Tunnel,
in Alcove Twenty-One, the girl, Lale, I supposed, she now
reduced to the modality of the she-quadruped, might be so
waiting. Too, in at least one of these alcoves, I recalled,
though I did not know which one, in this very tunnel, there
was a chained, gagged free woman. I was suddenly very
quiet. I could hear something approaching me down the
tunnel. I expected, of course, that anyone interested in me
would be behind me. I unsheathed my quiva. I smelled paga.
Then a fellow crawled past me in the tunnel.

I continued on my way.

"More! More! I beg more! I beg more!" I heard a girl's
voice coming from one of the alcoves to my right. "Please,
Master, do not stop! No! Do not stop! Please! I beg more! I
beg more!" I heard the movement of chains, jerking helplessly against rings. "Please, Master!" she wept. "Please!
Please! I am helpless! I am at your mercy! Please, Master, I
beg it of you! Oh, yes, Master! Yes, Master! Yes! Yes! Yes!
Aiiiii! Oh, thank you, Master, kind master! Ohhhh. Ohhhh. Oh.
I am yours! You have made me yours! Buy me, I beg you. I
want to love and serve you! Buy me, take me home with you!
Own me! You have made me yours!" I then heard her
breathing, and gasping, and a small movement of chains.
"Master?" she asked, with a small movement of the chain.
"Master? Oh, Master! You are going to do it to me again?
No, sweet Master, I cannot prevent you. I must endure
whatever you choose to impose upon me. You choose to

make me again such a helpless, squirming, screaming thing, so much outside of myself, so helplessly at your pleasure? Do so, then, for I am a slave! I sense it! I sense it! Do so, then. I cannot stop you. Nor do I wish to do so. I am a slave. I am yours. Do with me as you will. Begin, I beg you. Oh, yes, yes, Master!''

I then continued again on my way.

The tunnel became more winding. It did not, however, become roomier. One can tell the alcove numbers by feel, if one does not have a lamp. I now felt the number to my right. It was Twenty-Six. The next alcove would be Twenty-Seven. It would be ahead and to the left. The alcoves are staggered. I suppose this is primarily for the sake of privacy. This arrangement also, of course, tends to reduce the number of unexpected face-to-face encounters in the hall. Goreans are sometimes nervous about such things. I conjectured I must be quite deep in the tunnel. The rear entrance, or the entrance into a rear corridor, I did not think, should be too far beyond this point. Perhaps I could simply leave by the rear exit, without difficulty. That might be very nice. I stopped. I listened. I was patient. Then I heard it. It was not a loud sound at all, but it was unmistakable, the sound of the movement of a piece of metal on the stones. For such a sound I supposed there might be many explanations. One of them, of course, which I found especially fascinating, would be that of a knife carried in the hand of a fellow crawling in the tunnel.

I continued crawling down the tunnel. ''Cicek,'' I said. ''Where are you? Where are you, little Cicek?''

''Hold,'' said a voice.

''Tal,'' said I. ''Did Cicek come this way? Did you see a slave come this way?''

''One sees nothing down here,'' growled the fellow.

''Perhaps you felt her then,'' I said. ''That might have been pleasant.''

''You are drunk,'' he said.

''Not at all,'' I said.

''What are you doing here?'' he asked.

"What does anyone do in the tunnels?" I asked. "What are you doing here?"

"Speak," he said, menacingly.

"To be honest, not much," I said. "Are you sure that Cicek did not pass you."

"No one has passed me," he said, a bit grimly, I thought.

"Perhaps she went the other way?" I said.

"Hold, who are you?" he asked.

"I am called Bosk," I said.

"Is there anyone else in the tunnel?" he asked.

"I think so," I said.

"Not in an alcove?"

"No," I said.

"Where is he?" he asked.

"He is ahead of you," I said. That was certainly true. I was ahead of him.

"Thank you, Citizen," said he.

"You are welcome," I said. I then turned about and began to crawl back down the tunnel. "Cicek," I called. "Where are you?" Fortunately none of the girls in the alcoves were named Cicek. Otherwise it might have been rather embarrassing.

If there was no one at the other end of the tunnel, I supposed I might just as well go out through the front door.

"Cicek," I called.

"Hold," said another voice. This fellow sounded fully as grim as the last fellow. The voices were not those of fellows that one, or most folks, at any rate, would be likely to look forward to meeting in a dark alley, or, as the case might be, tunnel. I couldn't see him any better than the other one, nor, I assume, could he see me.

"Did a slave pass you in the tunnel?" I asked. "Cicek? She is not very big, but she is very nicely curved."

"No," he said. "Who are you?"

"Bosk," I said.

"Have you seen anyone else in the tunnel?" he asked.

"It is pretty hard to see anything in the tunnel," I said.

"Is there someone in the tunnel who is not in an alcove?" he asked.

"Yes," I said.

"Where is he?" he asked.

"He is ahead of you," I said. That is exactly where I was.

"What is he doing?" asked the man.

"He is just staying in one place," I said. That is what I was doing at the time, of course, just staying in one place.

"I thought so," said the fellow, decisively. "Thank you, Citizen."

"That is all right," I said. "You are sure you have not seen Cicek?"

"No," he said.

"Maybe she is in the other direction," I said. I turned about and started down the tunnel.

"Enter an alcove," said the man. "Keep the tunnel clear."

"Do you know a good one?" I asked.

"Move," he said.

"Very well," I said. I saw no point in being disagreeable. They were all probably nice enough.

I moved back down the tunnel. I was reasonably well pleased. As far as I could tell there were only two of them, one at each end of the tunnel. They were two in number doubtless to spring a trap in a tunnel. The invitation had been to the Tunnels. They might have assumed, thus, that I, sooner or later, from curiosity, or, perhaps growing wary, and attempting to escape, would enter one of them. Too, surely they would not wish to wait until morning to locate their quarry. I no longer found it judicious to speculate that their intent was merely to make polite contact and transmit information. I suspected somewhat more serious things were on their minds. As I had not emerged from the tunnel, or tried to emerge from it, they would assume that I was waiting within it. They would also assume, presumably, and I had encouraged them in this belief, that their quarry might be in the tunnel and not in an alcove. In a tunnel he might swiftly move in whatever direction seemed opposite danger. In an alcove, it might seem he could be too easily trapped. Actually, of course, given the structure of the alcoves, as I had determined it, it could be extremely dangerous to attempt to enter it if it were defended. Indeed, one would only have to stay there until morning, at which time, presumably, they would feel obliged to make away. The fellow I had left behind me was probably the leader. Presumably he would wish to signal his fellow down the corridor in some way.

I heard, in a few Ehn, a soft whistle behind me. It carried well in the tunnel. It was answered, momentarily, by another soft whistle, ahead of me. I moved ahead. I felt the alcove numbers. There was another whistle behind me, closer now. The answering whistle, however, was still rather toward the end of the tunnel. The fellow there, not the leader, it seemed, was less eager to move forward into the darkness. I, for one, did not blame him.

I had then come again to the area of Alcove Twenty-Six. It was well down the tunnel. I had felt it before. I thrust back the curtain. "Master?" I heard, within, and a sound of chain. I then again closed the curtain. I moved to the next alcove. That was Twenty-Seven, on the left. I moved back the curtain. I heard nothing within. This one, I thought, would do nicely. I then entered the alcove. I then listened to the whistles approaching more closely.

It is normal practice, in a situation of this sort, to separate the enemies, meeting first one, and then the other, substituting two one-to-one conflicts, so to speak, for one two-to-one conflict. This works best, of course, when one can see what one is doing. Too often, darkness neutralizes skill; too often chance thrives in darkness. There are, of course, tactics for fighting in the darkness, such as misdirection, the casting of pebbles to encourage an opponent to make a move, the use of back kicks, giving extension to one's striking capacity while providing a minimum exposure of vital areas, the attempt to lure a blow from a distance, with full-arm knife probes, to encourage an opponent to lunge and overextend himself, and so on, but, in the true darkness, very different from what commonly passes as "night fighting," there is probably no really satisfactory way to reduce risk levels to tolerable limits. I prefer to avoid it. Accordingly, in entering the tunnel I had determined, from the beginning, in the event it was unlighted, that I would prefer to arrange matters in such a way that the

considerable risks involved be taken by the other fellows. I
myself did not care for the odds.

I stuck my head out of the alcove. "Who is there?" I
called, as though alarmed. "Is there anyone there? Who is
it!"

I then heard another whistle, from my right, toward the
entrance to the tunnel. This was answered by one from my
left, toward the end of the tunnel. There was then another
insistent whistle from my right. It was no closer. The whistle
from my left, then, was a bit closer. This was what I had
hoped for. They would hope to coordinate their efforts, to
take me between them, at the same time.

"Who is there?" I called again, once more as though
alarmed.

"Do not fear," called a voice, from the right. "We mean
you no harm. Are you Tarl, of Port Kar?"

"Yes," I said. "I am he!"

"We have a message for you," said the voice.

"Yes?" I said.

"Remain where you are," said the voice. "We will bring
you the message."

"You are certain that you mean well?" I inquired.

"Yes, yes," said the fellow to the right, soothingly. I
could now hear the small sound of the metal, presumably a
knife, on the stones, coming from my left. Did they really
think I would believe that two fellows were needed to deliver
a message?

"I am not certain of that," I said.

"Do not be alarmed," said the fellow to the right.

"You have a message for me?" I asked.

"Yes," said the fellow to the right.

"I am drawing my sword," I said. I then withdrew the
blade from the sheath a good deal more noisily than was
necessary. I did not want them to mistake the sound. I
thought that that would give them something to think about. I
wanted them to be somewhat alarmed. Then, when I sheathed
it, they might be inclined to act more swiftly, more
precipitately.

"We are friends," said the fellow to the right, in the darkness.

In their intentness, in their hunt, in the darkness, I did not think they would be keeping track of the alcoves. They would, in any case, have had to feel carefully for them. They would be thinking, I expected, only in terms of the tunnel and its walls. I had, further, led them to believe that I was in the tunnel itself. Too, surely this would seem reasonable to them. I had further confirmed this suspicion by the drawing of the blade. Presumably such a draw would not take place in the close quarters of an alcove, wher. there was little room for its wielding. To be sure, there was not much room in the tunnel either, though thrusting could surely be dangerous. With the sword drawn I did not think either would care to be the first to make contact with me. With it sheathed both, for all I knew, and particularly the fellow on the right, might be eager to make the first strike.

"Sheath your sword," said the fellow on the right.

"No," I said.

"We will then not deliver the message," he said.

"Very well," I said.

"But we must deliver it," he said. "It is a matter of life and death."

"That sounds serious," I granted him.

"It is," he assured me.

"From whom does this message come?" I asked.

"From the regent himself," said the fellow.

"I see," I said.

I doubted, personally, that the regent would be sending me messages, and, if so, that he would be doing it in this fashion. I was prepared to believe, however, that the business to which these fellows were about might have its origins in individuals close to the regent. Their mention of the regent, of course, convinced me that they were not common assailants, after a purse. Run-of-the-mill brigands would surely refrain from allusions so dubious and exalted, allusions so incredible that they would be sure to put a normal fellow on his guard.

"How may we convince you of our good intentions?" he asked. I heard him come a foot or so closer.

"I would consider that to be your problem," I said. "Not mine."

I heard the fellow on the left come a little closer.

"Are you armed?" I asked.

"We will slide our knives, sheathed, along the tunnel floor," said the fellow at the right. "That way you will know we come in peace."

"Excellent," I said.

In a moment two objects, presumably sheaths, though I doubted from the sound they contained knives, with some buckles and straps, came sliding along the tunnel floor, one from the right, the other from the left. I judged the two fellows to be about equidistant, each about ten feet away. They had a good idea of my approximate location, it seemed, from my voice.

"I am convinced," I announced. Actually I was not quite candid in this announcement.

"Sheath your sword," said the fellow on the right. I heard them both coming a little closer.

"There," I said, thrusting the blade back in the sheath. I then drew my head back. "Where is the message?" I asked.

"Here!" I heard, from the right, this cry coupled with the rush forward of a body in the darkness.

"Die!" I heard, from the left, with the sound of another rapidly moving body.

I then heard some very ugly noises in the tunnel outside the entrance to the alcove. I was within the alcove, my quiva in hand. If anyone tried to enter these limited quarters, it would be quite easy in the darkness, he in such an exposed position, to cut fiercely at the head and neck.

I listened.

There was not much noise outside. I could hear some gasping, and also some coughing, and spitting. Someone's lungs seemed to be clutching at breath. Not very successfully, it seemed. From the sound of the coughing, that of the other fellow I think, I conjectured that the mouth might be filling with welled-up blood. I think both of them were there. I think they were both just outside the alcove, perhaps locked in one another's arms, or now, leaning against one another, supporting one another. I wondered if they realized what had happened, or if each, puzzled, thought he had closed with this fellow Tarl, of Port Kar. Then I heard one of the bodies take another thrust. Then they seemed, both, to fall to the side, and then, it seemed, one was trying to move away, crawling. That might have been the fellow who had been on the left. I could hear the movement of the knife on the stones. Then whoever it was, coughing, and with a grunt, sank to the stones. The knife was then quiet. It had been a short trip. Doubtless the stones would be sticky. They would have to be cleaned in the morning. Slaves could do that, or, perhaps, the free woman I had been offered earlier in the evening, she who had been in the wrap-around tunic, the Lady Labiena, who was being "kept for a friend." I supposed the hostesses might enjoy having her do such things, perhaps monitoring her work with a whip or pointed stick.

I continued to listen. I now heard nothing.

I think both of these fellows had probably been reasonably skillful. They probably knew their business. I did not think this task would have been assigned novices. They had just mistaken their victim.

I continued to listen patiently for a few Ehn. It was now quiet outside the alcove. I heard nothing. Then I heard a tiny sound behind me. I had not realized I was not alone in the alcove. I spun about, quiva ready. It was now again quiet. I put the quiva in my left hand, extending my left arm. I then silently drew my sword. The quiva presumably could act as a probe and defense. The sword, the quick, short, double-edged Gorean *gladius*, was drawn back for a thrust.

"Who is there?" I asked. It was absolutely quiet. "Speak," I said, "or I strike." I then heard a tiny, almost inaudible, desperate, protesting, whimpering sound. I heard, too, the desperate movement of bare feet, moving back and forth, and pounding, on the stones. I heard, too, the jerk of chain against a ring.

With the sword and quiva, protecting myself first with one and then the other, and probing about, using them alternately, and generally keeping away from the source of the sound, I determined to my satisfaction that the alcove was empty save for myself and the source of the sound. Then, using the side of the sword, moving it twice laterally in the darkness, touching the object in the darkness on either side, as it hastily and fearfully, scrambling, pulled its legs back, and up, and whimpered, I specifically located the source of the sound. I sheathed the sword.

I then silently approached the object on its right side. Reaching forth I took it by its hair that I might locate it and hold it in place and moved the point of the quiva, the blade held sideways, that it might slip between the ribs, a tiny bit into its side, about half the width of a drop of blood. There was a protesting whimper. The object did not move, held in place. I let it feel the point a little more. It was then absolutely quiet, and immobile. I drew the point back a bit, but kept it mostly where it was. The object could feel it in contact with its skin. I then moved my left hand downward from its hair to check the wrists. They were shackled behind its back, chained to a ring. I tested the shackles. They were light shackles. But they would be quite effective, if locked, for such an object. They were locked. It was sitting then in the alcove, its hands back-shackled, its back to the alcove wall, close against it, its knees drawn up. I sheathed the quiva.

I then felt round to the object's mouth. It was well gagged, with Gorean efficiency, with packing and binding. It made tiny whimpers. These whimpers, of course, had been female noises. They are unmistakable, even with the gagging, that stern impediment to expression which her captor, or captors, had chosen to impose upon her, that device, inflicted upon her, by means of which it had been decided that she would not be able to speak. I lowered my hands. She whimpered, perhaps trying to call attention to her desire to speak.

"Be silent," I said. I crouched beside her in the darkness. I wondered if she were a slave. I moved my hands up her body, to determine whether or not she was collared. She whimpered, in desperate protest. "Be silent," I said, "or you will be cuffed." She was silent. I felt her throat. It was innocent of any metallic circlet of bondage. She had been nicely breasted.

"Are you a free woman?" I asked, interested.

She made some noises, which I took to be affirmative whimpers.

I recalled the device that my hostess had used in communicating with the slave, Lale, a not uncommon one, or, at least, one of a not uncommon type, for females put in the modality of the she-quadruped. "You will whimper once for 'Yes,' " I said, "and twice for 'No.' Do you understand?"

She whimpered once.

"Would you like to have your gag removed?" I asked.

She whimpered once, eagerly.

"Are you a free woman?" I asked.

She whimpered once.

Then she scrambled back against the wall, pushing back against it, uttering urgent, protesting whimpers.

"I do not detect any brands on your body," I said, "at least in the normal brand sites. Perhaps you are telling the truth." The most common marking sites for a Gorean slave are on the left or right thigh, high, near the hip. Others may wear their brands variously, for example, low on the left abdomen, on the inside of the left forearm, on the left breast, or, very tiny, behind the left ear. I myself do not approve of brands on the breast. A woman's breasts, in my opinion, are too beautiful for a brand. On the other hand I do not object to temporarily marking them in such a place, say, with a grease pencil, lipstick or paint, as many slavers do. The ideal, of course, given the necessity of marking women, the importance of which anyone recognizes, is to do it in such a fashion that it does not detract from a woman's beauty, but rather enhances it, and considerably. The thigh brand, for one, has this effect. It also, put in her flank, below her waist, helps her to understand what her slavery is all about.

Her breasts, of course, in which so much of her luscious femaleness is naturally manifested, do not escape notice in her bondage. They are as open and available to the master as any other part of her. After all, he owns the whole slave. Accordingly she knows that they, so sweet and soft, so delicious and marvelous, so wonderful and exciting, will, like the rest of her, without a second thought, be submitted to attentions appropriate to her status. For example, they may be lovingly handled, and kissed and caressed by the master however and as long as he pleases. Too, they might be emphasized and accentuated by various forms of garments and bindings. The tying of slave girdles, for example, and the arrangement of binding fiber, often has this subtle, delicious feature in mind. Too, of course, they may be confined, if one wishes, in open brassieres of cord, or netting.

She whimpered once, angrily.

"Surely you cannot criticize my curiosity," I said. "One does not usually expect to find a free woman chained naked in a slave alcove in a brothel." My investigations concerning brand sites had, as a side effect, of course, informed me that she was unclothed, except for her shackles.

She made a number of angry noises.

"Are you displeased?" I asked.

She whimpered, once, angrily.

"Are you angry?" I asked.

She whimpered again, once, even more angrily. Then she made a number of other angry noises.

"Do you wish to speak?" I asked.

She whimpered once, angrily.

"You would like me to remove your gag?" I asked.

She made a single, short noise, very insistently. I waited. She repeated it.

"Oh," I said. "You do not want me to remove your gag."

She then whimpered twice, insistently.

"You do want me to remove your gag?" I asked.

She whimpered once, very definitely, very clearly, just once.

"But I have not done so, have I?" I asked. "Perhaps you think I have forgotten to do so, that it has somehow slipped my mind. That is not it at all, however. I was merely inquiring, before and now, if you would like to have it removed. That is what I was interested in. That is all. I have never had any intention of removing it. I am not interested, for example, in hearing from you."

There was a startled noise, and some puzzled ones.

"No," I said.

I then put my right hand on her neck under her chin and forced her head up and back.

She made a frightened noise.

"You are in no position," I said, "to be displeased, or angry, or impatient, or peremptory, in any way."

She was silent.

I then put my hand on her, and she whimpered, and drew back, pushing back, frightened against the wall of the alcove. I then took her ankles in my hands. I let her try for a moment to resist me. Then I spread her ankles, widely. "Do you understand?" I asked.

She whimpered once, frightened.

"Good," I said. I then released her ankles and she drew them hastily back and together, pulling her knees up, and close together, and, as she could, turned her right side to me.

"Were you the female who was brought in in a sack, earlier this evening?" I asked.

She whimpered once.

"Are you beautiful?" I asked.

She whimpered twice.

"Then there would be no point in my having my way with you, would there?" I asked.

She whimpered twice.

"I think that I shall strike a light," I said.

She whimpered twice, piteously.

"And if I find that you have lied, and that you are beautiful, I shall use you—and as a slave."

Two whimpers.

"Very well," I said. "I shall give you another chance. Are you beautiful?"

She whimpered once, in defeat.

"Or at least you think you are beautiful," I said.

She whimpered once.

"Then perhaps I should use you," I said.

She whimpered twice, piteously.

"If you are a free woman," I said, "then, from what I have heard, there may be something around here." I felt about the alcove. "Yes," I said, "here it is." I had located some binding fiber at the side, and a leather thong, with a coin, presumably a tarsk bit, threaded on it. That was to be used, I recalled having heard from my hostess, if she was used in her stay in the brothel. "There is some binding fiber here," I said. "Do you know what it is for?"

She whimpered twice, frightened.

"For binding you," I said. "If you are used tonight you are to be put out naked in the morning, in the alley, your hands tied behind your back with this binding fiber."

She whimpered twice, in protest.

"There is also a coin here, a tarsk bit, I think, threaded on a leather thong. Do you know what that is for?"

She whimpered twice.

I took the thong and coin and, putting my arms about her, tied the thong about her waist, fastening it behind her back. The coin was then at her belly. With my thumb I pushed it back into her belly, that she might clearly feel its shape and know its location. Then I let it dangle there, resting on her belly. "This coin," I said, "when you were put out in the morning, if you were used tonight, was to be tied there. It signifies to all who see it that you have served a man. You are given the coin because you are a free woman. That is your payment. To be sure, it is the smallest-denomination coin in common circulation. It is, thus, a comment on your value."

She moaned in protest. I removed the thong and coin from her waist. I laid it, with the binding fiber, to the side.

She whimpered gratefully.

"I know you are a free woman," I said, "but are you prepared now, in the light of your recent experiences, to reform your behavior, to be at least minimally polite, to observe certain basic amenities, and to conduct your life and business at least generally in accordance with simple canons of common civility and courtesy?"

She was silent.

I put my hand on her.

She whimpered once, quickly.

"Good," I said. "Since someone put you here, presumably as a punishment, I gather you have been something of a she-sleen."

She whimpered once.

"But that is going to change now, isn't it?" I asked.

One whimper.

"You see," I said, putting my hand on her thigh, she trying to pull back, "this is not really much of a punishment. Many other things could have been done to you. For example, from a place such as this, it would be no great trick for you to be delivered to a slaver. Indeed, perhaps a slaver has an appointment with you in this alcove before morning. I do not know."

She whimpered in fear.

"You could be branded and collared before morning," I said, "and shipped out of the city, then a slave, hooded, gagged and helpless, for your first sale."

Two whimpers.

"Indeed," I said, "perhaps I am that slaver."

She whimpered twice, wildly.

"But I am not," I said. "Oh yes, I have done slaving, and doubtless will again. There are few occupations so pleasant and rewarding."

She was silent, trembling.

"Would you look well at a man's feet?" I asked. I put my hand on her throat. ":Answer truthfully," I warned her.

She whimpered once, in agony.

"Or you think you would?" I asked.

One whimper, a fearful whimper, in misery.

But do not be afraid," I said. "I have no intention, at least at present, of carrying you into bondage. Are you grateful?"

She whimpered once.

"Besides," I said, "I have not even seen you."

She whimpered in fear.

"Accordingly I reserve the right of carrying you into bondage later, if I wish," I said. "Perhaps you are too beautiful to be free. I do not know."

She whimpered twice, fearfully, protestingly.

"Be quiet," I whispered. "Someone is coming." Down the tunnel I could see a flicker of light, doubtless from a tharlarion-oil lamp. Although it was a very small light, it seemed very bright in the darkness.

I heard a woman gasp, seeing, I suppose, at least the first body in the tunnel. "Ai!" she cried in a moment, the wash of the light moving, lifting, in the darkness outside. I saw it reflecting on the other side of the tunnel, and a bit into the alcove. She had then seen, a bit further down the tunnel, I suppose, the second body. I moved back, to the side of the alcove entrance. I saw the light approaching more closely.

"What has gone on here?" she asked, under her breath, not really speaking to anyone. I gathered she was alone. Her surprise seemed genuine. She made no attempt to call back to anyone. She was now close to the alcove entrance.

"Are you all right in there, little slut?" she cooed. "Are your chains too tight? Would you like to be let loose from the nasty old slave ring? Have you learned now what it is to serve men? Have you squirmed well? Is your pretty little body tired of being chained? Is it sore? Does it ache? It is getting late, my beauty. Would you like some clothing? Of course you would! I have some pretty binding fiber in there for you to wear and, if you have given pleasure to a man, as seems likely by now, a pretty coin to tie on your belly. It is cold out in the alley this morning, and gray. The binding fiber will help keep your wrists nice and warm." She lifted the lamp outside the alcove. "There you are," she said.

The girl, whom I now saw was blond, slender and lovely, with sweet breasts and beautiful thighs and calves, shrank back against the alcove wall. I told myself I could have had her in the darkness, but had not done so! Had I realized how attractive she was I might have done so. She did have the look of a wench that belonged in a collar. She had nice slave curves. I thought that she, objectively considered, would make a very nice slab of slave meat. I would not have minded, for example, seeing her naked on a block, in chains, being put through her paces, under whip discipline, dancing, writhing, squirming lasciviously for the interest of men, being auctioned to the highest bidder. I myself might have made a bid. I forced myself to remember that she was free.

The woman outside held the lamp inside the alcove entrance. I then seized her wrist and drew her forcibly, swiftly, she crying out, on her belly, through the narrow opening. The lamp, spilling oil, briefly flaming in a rivulet on the alcove floor, went to the side of the alcove, and went out. I knelt across her body. She was carrying only her whip and some keys. I removed these from her. She struggled fiercely, silently. She was strong for a woman. She would have been much stronger than the chained girl. Still, when all was said and done, her strength was only that of a female. It amused me. I let her struggle for a time, until she realized the futility of her efforts. With a sob she ceased struggling. I then removed her leather from her. I thought perhaps the free woman might be able to use it. "Be silent," I warned my captive. She was silent. I then felt on the floor for the binding fiber. I had it in a moment and tied my captive's hands behind her, and then took her ankles and, crossing them and pulling them up tightly behind her, bound them to her wrists. She would not be going anywhere.

"Who are you?" she hissed, on her side in the darkness, pulling at her bonds.

"Tarl," I said, "of Port Kar."

"They were looking for you," she said.

"They found one another," I said. I then thrust my captive to the side. I then felt about for the lamp. I located it almost immediately, and swirled it a bit. There was a tiny bit of oil left in it. I relit the lamp with the lighter, or as the Goreans say "fire-maker," from my pouch. It is a standard flint-and-wheel device, with its tiny wick and reservoir. Goreans do not smoke, of course, but, as they commonly use natural flame for cooking and light, they find such a device, and others like it, utilizing springs and pyrites, with cartridges of oil-saturated tinder moss, and such, of great utility. The common sulfur match, on the other hand, so common on Earth, I have never met with on Gor. The chemistry involved in such a device, interestingly enough, is forbidden on Gor. It is regarded as constituting a violation of the Weapons Laws imposed on Goreans by Priest-Kings. This is not as farfetched as it might sound at first. Sulfur, for example, is one of the primary ingredients in the composition of gunpowder.

"You!" exclaimed the captive. "You told me you were called Bosk!"

"I am called Bosk," I said. "You appear to be well bound."

She struggled briefly.

"Yes," I said, "quite well bound."

"Release me," she said.

"One of these keys," I said, "has a 27 on it. That, I take it, is the key to the chains in this alcove."

"Yes," said the captive, sullenly.

I took this key and assured myself that it opened the manacles of the blond prisoner.

She threw me a grateful look.

Then I reclosed the manacles, leaving her chained precisely as she had been before. She regarded me wildly, puzzled, in consternation. She jerked at her hands. They were still manacled to the ring behind her. The captive on the floor laughed.

I crouched in the alcove, looking at the blond girl. "She is a pretty thing, isn't she?" I said. She drew her knees up, and shrank back against the alcove wall.

"Yes," said my captive. "Take her, use her. We can then put her out in back, with a tarsk bit tied on her belly."

"She looks like she would make an excellent slave," I commented.

"Yes," said my captive. "Look at her. She is that kind of woman."

"She looks like the kind of woman whom you manage, then slaves, of course, in the brothel."

"Yes," said my captive. "She is exactly that sort of woman. She belongs in a collar. Doubtless one day she will find her neck in one. Who knows? Perhaps one day she will even be here, subject to me, as one of our girls."

"Would you like that?" I asked.

"Of course," said my captive.

"You would make her serve men well?" I asked.

"Yes," she said.

"You enjoy making women such as she serve men?" I asked.

"Yes," she said, with relish, "I do. And I would see to it that she served men superbly."

"Why?" I asked.

"I despise such women," she said.

"Why?" I asked.

"They belong to men," she said.

I picked up her whip. "Doubtless she would look well kissing the whip," I said.

"Yes," laughed my captive.

"Kiss it," I said to my captive, holding it before her.

"What?" she cried.

"All women belong to men," I said.

She tried to pull back from the whip, frenziedly. She struggled.

"Be careful," I said. "You may cause your bonds to cut into your limbs."

She looked at me in helpless fury.

I loosened the blades of the whip. "You will kiss it now," I said, "or after you have felt it. To me it is a matter of indifference. The choice is yours."

"Do not whip me," she said.

"You are a free woman," I said. "You have doubtless never even felt a slave whip."

"I will kiss it," she said.

I held it before her. Many free women, before they have felt it, are skeptical of the efficacy of the slave lash. Their skepticism vanishes, of course, as soon as they feel it. On the other hand, I did not think this one would be. She was quite familiar with it. She doubtless used it regularly in her work. It was one of her tools, a useful device for the instruction, correction, discipline and punishment of slaves. She would be quite aware of its power, from its effect on her helpless charges.

"You can do better than that," I said. "Better. Very good. Now, with your tongue. Come now. That's better, much better. Excellent. Now, again, kiss it. More lingeringly, more lovingly. Splendid." I then drew the whip back.

She looked up at me. "I have kissed your whip," she said.

I then turned her to her belly and freed her ankles.

"No!" she cried.

In a few Ehn I turned to the blond captive and ungagged her, carefully removing the gag binding and drawing the wet packing from her mouth. "I am not looking forward to hearing a great deal of noise from you in the immediate future," I said. "Is that clear?"

She nodded, not speaking.

"Aargh," said the captive on the floor as I pushed the wadding into her mouth and bound it in place. "Nor from you," I informed her.

I then took my quiva and addressed myself to the rather mannish leather I had removed from the captive. I shortened it, considerably. I cut away the sleeves, deeply. I find the arms and shoulders of a woman attractive. I cut down the neckline, opening it considerably, and then slashed it almost to the belly. This would be pretty, I thought. I then slashed the tunic on both sides, up to the waist. A flash of thigh is nice on a woman, even if the thigh is not branded.

The blond prisoner, her hands chained behind her, watched. I then freed her hands from the manacles and pulled her hands up and over her head. I then slipped the improvised tunic, cut now in a more feminine fashion from the mannish leather, on her body. Swiftly she pulled it down about her thighs, as far as it would go. Swiftly, too, then, did she kneel, her knees now tightly together, in the fashion of the free woman. She looked at me, frightened.

I glanced back to the captive, her wrists still tightly bound behind her. She was on one elbow, and her hip now, on the alcove floor. Her hair was down about her face. Her eyes seemed filled with disbelief, as though she might be trying to understand what had been done to her.

"Look," I said to the captive, indicating the blonde.

The blonde tried to pull the tunic further down her thighs. She clenched her knees more closely together.

"She does look as though she belonged in a collar, doesn't she?" I asked the captive.

The captive looked up at me.

"Doesn't she?" I asked.

The captive uttered muffled noises.

I seized the captive's head, pulling it up. "Doesn't she?" I asked. "You may whimper once for "Yes," and twice for "No." I am sure you are familiar with the procedure."

She looked at me with fury. I shook her head. She whim

pered once. "What?" I asked. She then whimpered again, once, clearly. "Do you wish to be beaten?" I asked. She whimpered twice, clearly. "I see that you are familiar with the procedure," I said, I then thrust her back to the floor of the alcove.

I again regarded the blonde. "What are you going to do with me?" she whispered. I put my hands on her upper arms. "What?" she asked.

I forced myself to remove my hands from her arms.

"What?" she asked.

"We are going to get out of here," I said. I then looked back at the bound captive, and then located the leather thong with the tarsk bit threaded on it. She looked at me wildly over the gag. She shook her head. She whimpered twice, again and again, desperately. Then the thong was tied about her waist, knotted in the back and the tiny coin, threaded on the thong, dangled at her belly. I pushed it into her belly so that she could feel its impression, and then released it. I then took her by the hair with my right hand.

"Come along," I said to her. I picked up the tiny lamp with my other hand. "Follow us," I said to the blonde. I then left the alcove, holding the lamp, drawing the bound captive by the hair after me. The blonde followed. The one body in the tunnel was to the right. In a moment or so we had crawled around the other one, that which had been to the left. Their message, according to the fellow who had been on the right, had been a matter of life and death. I supposed that had been intended to be a witticism on his part. Doubtless he would have enjoyed reporting on the manner and the words with which he had delivered the "message." He had spoken truly, it seems. But it had turned out to be a matter of my life and their death.

In a moment or two, as we were near the end of the tunnel, we came to the back corridor. We could stand up there. We came to the rear entrance. There was a small lamp there, in a niche, and I extinguished the lamp I carried and put it down. In a moment I had left the building, pulling the captive behind me, her head held down at my waist, in leading position. We were followed by the blonde in the brief leather garment I had fashioned for her. The door latched behind us.

We emerged into a yard, where the slaves presumably could get fresh air and be exercised. There were some treadmills there, and some wooden platforms, with chain holes in the planks, where, in good weather, girls might be secured for tanning. Beyond this yard was the narrow alley behind the buildings. The gate to this yard also latched behind us. We could not re-enter from the outside. It was still very early, and half dark. It was also quite chilly. I recalled that my captive had told the blonde that her wrists might be kept warm by the binding fiber. She herself now, of course, though I do not think she had counted on it, had the benefit of that narrow, encircling garmenture.

I pulled my captive around and between buildings, and emerged onto the street called the Alley of the Slave Brothels of Ludmilla, and then I went between more buildings and emerged on the Avenue of Turia. This is a splendid avenue, and there are many shops on it. There I put my captive on her knees, her back to a slave ring, fixed in a wall a foot or so above the level of the pavement. I then slipped the extra binding fiber dangling from her wrists, that with which I had earlier tied her ankles up behind her, to her wrists, through the ring and then crossed her ankles and knotted it securely about them. Once again then were her wrists fastened to her ankles, though she was this time secured as well to a slave ring.

"This is a very busy street," I said, "though it does not seem so at this hour. Doubtless you will soon attract your share of attention. Doubtless some of the customers of the Tunnels will recognize you. You may consider what you will say to guardsmen, to explain your presence here. You might consider in particular how to explain to them the meaning of the tarsk bit on your belly. But then they may be familiar with such things, and their meanings."

She looked up at me.

"Farewell, Free Woman," I said.

She extended her head toward me, whimpering, tears in her eyes.

"Do you beg for mercy, for release?" I asked.

She shook her head, negatively.

"Surely you know I would not give it to you," I said.

She nodded, tears in her eyes.

"I am not that sort of man," I said.

She nodded.

"What then?" I asked.

She reached toward me with her head. I crouched down beside her. I touched her gently on the left side of her face. She pressed her cheek, the gag binding drawn back tight between her teeth, against mine. I felt her tears.

"You are not unattractive," I said. "And in you somewhere there is a female. Do not despise any longer other women, for you, too, are a woman. Let your female emerge and become one with you, until there is only you, who is the female."

She whimpered softly, piteously, gratefully.

"I do not think you will long be much good for working at the Tunnels, at least in your former capacity," I said.

She put her head down.

"For you have now discovered how inordinately precious and glorious it is to be a woman," I said. "It is its own thing, and it is different from being a man. Too, it is not even to be a pseudo-man or facsimile male. It is quite different. Such things are unnatural and despicable. It is its own place, in its own country, and a whole marvelous life and being."

She kept her head down.

I stood up, and looked down at her. "Have no fear," I said. "You look well kneeling at the feet of a man."

She raised her head, tears running from her eyes.

"A rag, or a bit of silk, would become you more than the masculine leather, so amusingly outlandish, so silly and absurd on your female body, which you seemed so fond of affecting," I said, "if, indeed, a master would permit you clothing at all." I regarded her. "Perhaps you should feel the whip," I said. She shrank back. "And your neck is rather bare," I said. "It could use an ornament—perhaps a steel collar." I stepped back. "Yes," I said, considering her, "you are not unattractive. You would make an acceptable possession. You yourself, like the girls you so terrorized and dominated, like all women, as you have perhaps guessed by now, are ultimately and appropriately the property of men.''

She nodded, and lowered her head. Tears fell from her eyes to the pavement.

"Come along," I said to the blonde.

"You will leave her here, like this?" she asked.

"Of course," I said. "And it is much what would have happened to you except that you would have been free, naked and bound, the tarsk bit at your belly, to try and make your way home."

I then, leaving my former hostess behind me on her knees, naked, her hands and ankles tied behind her to the slave ring, the tarsk bit on her belly, conducted the blonde back between the buildings to the Alley of the Slave Brothels of Ludmilla. It was on that street that there was to be found the insula of Achiates.

"There is the Tunnels," I said, crossing the street. "It is there that you were taken last night."

"Free women scarcely speak of it except in whispers," she said, shuddering. "It is one of the lowest of the slave brothels in Ar."

"It is there that you were taken," I said.

"What a grim and terrible place it seems," she said.

"It does look a bit grim now," I admitted. "But then you are not seeing it at its best. It is closed now, and it is early morning. It is hard to look one's best this early in the morning, I'm sure you will agree. In the evening now, when it opens, it looks much better, warmer, cheerful, lit up, even perhaps a bit gaudy. You would have known that last night if you could have gotten your head out of the sack."

"I'm sure of it," she said.

"Perhaps you could drop by some evening, and get a better idea of it," I said.

"Perhaps," she said.

"But I would not come unescorted," I said.

"No," she said. "I do not think so."

"It is not really a terrible place at all," I said. "I think it is rather nice."

"You were not chained naked in a slave alcove," she said.

"Look at it this way," I said. "Consider it an interesting experience. After all, how many free women have ever been chained in a slave alcove?"

"I am one of the lucky ones," she said.

"Certainly," I said.

"I must thank you," she said.

"What for?" I asked.

"In the alcove," she said, "I was much at your mercy."

"You were totally at my mercy," I said, correcting her.

"Yes," she said, thoughtfully. "I was. And so I want to thank you for not using me."

"That is all right," I said.

"But you were thinking about it, weren't you?" she said.

"Yes," I admitted.

"But you did not do so," she said.

"No," I said.

"Why not?" she asked.

"What?" I asked.

"Why not?" she asked.

"I do not know," I said. "I suppose because you were free, and so helpless."

"My helplessness would not have made a difference if I were a slave, would it?" she asked.

"No," I said. "One often makes a slave absolutely helpless, and then does what one wants with her. One commands and uses a slave totally. That is what they are for. They must serve completely. They must deliver, at so little as a word or gesture, immediately and unquestioningly, whatever the master desires. One gets from a slave all that a man could possibly want from a woman, and more, simply taking it from her, or ordering her to provide it."

"She is so helpless," she said.

"Of course," I said. "She is a slave."

"But you did not use me," she said.

"No," I said.

"Because I was free?" she said.

"I suppose so," I said. "I did not know how attractive you were, of course."

"Had you known," she asked, "would you have used me?"

"I do not know," I said. "Perhaps. I am only human."

"Is that why you have dressed me as you have?" she asked. She looked down, demurely, pulling down at the short hem of the leather she wore.

"Yes," I said.

"This is very revealing," she said. She pulled together the sides of the neckline, closing the garment there to some extent.

"Yes," I admitted.

"It bares my arms and shoulders," she said. "That would generally be done only with a slave."

"True," I admitted. She did not mention it, but it was not merely her arms and shoulders which were bared. One could see a good bit of her legs, a sweet suggestion of her shapely breasts and, at the sides, going to the waist, a high slash of thigh.

She looked at me.

"It is a bit large," I said. The hostess had been a larger woman than she.

She pulled it more closely about herself. This more accentuated her figure.

"You put me in this garment," she said. "And it is the sort of garment a slave might be put in."

"Probably not in leather, however," I said.

She nodded. Leather is generally not permitted to slaves. Softer and more feminine fabrics, silk, rep-cloth, and such, often brief and clinging, not only stunningly attractive and aesthetically pleasing, but also indictive of, and reflective of, their subjection to masculine domination, are generally required of them.

"But I see what you mean," I said.

"Do you think I am a slave?" she asked.

"Of course not," I said.

"Oh, I do not mean *legally*," she said. "I mean *really*."

"Oh," I said, "then of course."

"Of course!" she said.

"Yes," I said.

"Beware!" she said. "I am a free woman!"

"Not *really*," I said.

"Not really?" she asked.

"No," I said. "You are really a slave. All you lack are some minor legal technicalities, such as the collar."

"This garment," she said, looking down, quickly. "It is so brief, so revealing. It makes me feel so strange."

I shrugged.

"How dare you have put me in such a garment?" she asked.

"It pleased me," I said.

"It calls attention to my sexuality," she said.

"It calls attention, at least," I said, "to the potentiality of your sexuality."

"Am I beautiful?" she asked.

"Yes," I said.

"Am I sexually desirable?" she asked.

"Yes," I said.

"Am I beautiful enough and sexually desirable enough," she asked, "to be a slave?"

"That is a strange question for a free woman to ask," I said.

"Am I?" she asked.

"Yes," I said.

"Thank you for rescuing me," she said.

"You are welcome," I said.

"Could you really have carried me into slavery," she asked, "as you intimated in the alcove?"

"I could still do so," I said. "We are not far from the Street of Brands. Within the Ahn I could deliver you into the clutches and metal of a slaver. He would take one look at you, as you are now, and there would be no questions asked."

"You would then get money for me?" she said.

"Yes," I said.

"But it is not your intention to do so?" she asked.

"No," I said.

"Why not?" she asked.

"I do not need the money," I said.

"Please," she said.

"You are free," I shrugged.

"It is cold," she said, shivering.

"It will grow warmer later in the day," I said.

"What time do you think it is?" she asked.

"Somewhere between the fourth and the fifth Ahn," I said.

"It is so cold," she said, "and so dark and gray."

I turned away.

"Wait!" she called.

I turned back. "What?" I asked.

"I do not live in that direction," she said.

"So?" I said.

"Where then are you going?" she asked.

"To my room," I said. "It is late."

"No!" she said.

"No?" I asked.

"No," she said. "Aren't you going to take me home?"

"Can you find your way home from here?" I asked.

"Yes," she said.

"Then do so," I said.

"Wait!" she called.

"Yes?" I said.

"See how I am clad!" she said.

"I do see," I said.

"I cannot go through the streets like this," she said.

"Many women," I said, "in collars, go through the streets with much less, and in full daylight, among crowds."

"They are slaves!" she said.

"And so, too, *really*," I said, "are you."

She looked at me, angrily.

"Would you rather do it naked?" I asked. "That can be arranged." I took a step towards her.

"No!" she said, putting out her hand, stepping back.

"Very well," I said. It did amuse me to think of her trying to make her way back to wherever she lived, probably a good way from here, as she seemed an educated, refined, perhaps affluent woman.

"What if I am surprised?" she said. "What if I am caught? What if slavers pick me up?"

"I really do not think there is much chance of that," I said, "not at the present hour, with it getting light. This is not an ideal hour, too, as you are probably aware, for the practice of activities such as slaving, raping, capturing and such. It is just too miserably early. Don't you really think so? What self-respecting rapist or slaver would be abroad at this hour? What would he expect to find? A miniature domestic sleen among the garbage cans? A brawny teamster bringing in produce from the country? Similarly I assume you live in a frequently patrolled, well-to-do district. I really do not believe you will be in any danger whatsoever. Run along."

"Run along?" she said.

"Yes," I said.

"Just because I am dressed like this, do you think you can dismiss me like a slave?"

"I would go while I can," I said.

She looked at me, suddenly. "This is the Alley of the Slave Brothels of Ludmilla," she said. "Escort me at least back to the Avenue of Turia."

"Very well," I said.

She then led the way back across the street, to the opening between the buildings, one of several which joined the Avenue of Turia, in this section, with the Alley of the Slave Brothels of Ludmilla. She walked well before me. A few yards into the passageway, which was winding, and about a hundred yards long, with some side passages, she stopped, and turned, and faced me.

"I am cold," she said.

"Oh?" I said.

"Put your arms about me," she said.

I did so. She fitted well within them.

"Is that better?" I asked.

"Yes," she said. She looked up at me. "You have saved me from an unspeakable fate," she said, "one worse than death, that of a man having his way with me, against my will."

"Do not be absurd," I said. How seriously some free women took themselves! Such ridiculous vanity! A week in a collar would straighten her out on such matters. She would then know what women were for, and all about.

"However that may be," she smiled, "it is to you that I owe my rescue from the shackles of a slave alcove."

I began to think I had probably made a mistake. I should have left her there.

"I owe you much," she said. "I am grateful. I would show my gratitude."

"No thanks are necessary," I said. I wondered if she knew what she was doing.

She lifted her lips. I felt her in my arms rising up on her toes. "There," she said, kissing me.

"Beware of what you do," I said, "dressed as you are." Her body was luscious, rounded and slave soft. I forced myself not to seize it to me, and crush it in my arms.

"There," she said, kissing me again, "can a slave kiss like that?" This second kiss, with its remark, was a mistake on her part, an irrevocable one.

"You know nothing of kissing," I said. "If a slave could not do better than that, she would be whipped."

"Sleen!" she cried, and tried to strike me. I caught her wrist with my right hand and twisted her suddenly and forcibly about, startling her. I took her left upper arm in my left hand, holding her, making her helpless, and with my right hand forced her right arm up suddenly and angrily behind her back. She cried out in sharp pain. I held her in this position for a moment, letting her know how helpless she was, keeping her in pain. She was high on her toes to relieve the pressure on her arm. She did not so much as move. Then I released her. She spun about, looking at me, wildly. She rubbed her arm. She had been in a man's power. She looked small then. "You hurt me!" she said.

"Was it not your intention to hurt me?" I inquired.

She looked down. She seemed small, and beautiful. She continued to rub her arm.

"What you attempted to do would earn a slave a beating at least," I said, "if her hands were not cut off, or if she were not fed to sleen."

"I wouldn't have done it, if I were a slave," she pouted.

"No," I said, "I do not think you would have, Free Woman."

"Must I throw myself at you?" she asked.

"After that second kiss," I said, "that would not be necessary."

"What do you mean?" she asked.

"I am going to give you what you want," I said.

"No!" she said. "Not that! I mean— I mean—!" But I had swept her into my arms and carried her a few yards down the passageway and then into one of the side passages, where, sticking out from a rear area, I had seen the corner, in the mist of other garbage, refuse and trash, of a discarded, ragged, thick, roughly woven reed slave mat. "No!" she said. "Not now! Not this way!"

"Be silent," I said. What was she complaining about? I had even carried her to this place in honor, in my arms, as a free woman. I had not thrown her over my shoulder, her ass to the front, her head scornfully to the rear, as properties are commonly carried, such as sacks of grain and female slaves.

With my foot, not yet putting her down, I dragged the mat free of the garbage and trash, and kicked it back to where I wanted it, back further in the rear area, between the high walls. I then threw her down upon it. "Get your clothes off," I told her. "Be quick!"

Sobbing, she stripped herself.

"Please!" she begged. "No! Please!"

"Perform obeisance," I said.

"I am a free woman!" she said.

"Out of your own mouth you have said it," I said. "You are a woman."

"I do not know how to do so!" she said.

"There are many ways to perform obeisance," I said.

"I am a free woman," she said. "I know none of them."

"I shall instruct you briefly in three," I said. "First, kneel before me, back on your heels, yes, with your knees wide, wider, your hands on your thighs, your back straight, your breasts out, good, your belly in, good, and now lower your head in deference, in submission."

"Like a slave!" she said.

"Do it," I said. She looked well. "Now that," I said, "may not be exactly a performance of obeisance, for authorities do not all agree, but for our purposes we shall count it as one. It is, at any rate, a beautiful position, and it is, certainly, a common position of slave submission."

"Slave submission!" she cried.

"Yes," I said, "and you do it well. It looks natural on you."

"Now," I said, "and this is clearly a form of obeisance, bend forward and put your head to the mat, the palms of your hands on the mat. Good. Now lift your head a little and come forward, substantially keeping the position. Forward a little more."

"But then my face will be at your feet," she said. "My lips will be over them!"

"Yes," I said. "Good. Now put your head down and lick and kiss my feet."

"I am a free woman!" she said.

"You are a woman," I said. "Now, softly, lingeringly and lovingly. Good."

"I am not a slave," she said.

"All women are slaves," I said. "Imagine what this would be like if you were truly a collared slave."

She gasped.

"Good," I said. "Continue."

Frightened, she did so.

"Now," I said, "for a third form of obeisance. You may 'belly' to me."

"I do not understand," she whispered.

"There are various forms of bellying," I said, "and bellying may be suitably and pleasingly combined with other forms of floor movements, approaching the master on all fours, turning to your sides and back, writhing before him, and so on. We shall take a very simple variation, suitable for an ignorant free female who has not yet even begun to discover the depths of her sexuality."

She looked up at me.

"On your belly," I said. She backed off a bit, and went to

her belly. Her hair was before her face, as she, now on her belly before me, looked up at me.

"Now inch forward," I said, "remaining low on your belly, and when you reach my feet, once again, as before, lifting your head a little, tenderly and humbly, and beautifully, as though you were a slave, lick and kiss them. Good. Good. Now take my foot and place it on gently on your head. Very good. Now place it again on the mat, and kiss it again. Good. You may now belly back a little, humbly. I have not yet given you permission to rise, of course."

She looked up at me, through her blond hair. There was a sort of disbelief and awe in her eyes. I think she could not understand the emotions that had gone through her, as she had performed these overt actions, understanding and internalizing their meanings.

"You may now kneel," I said.

She did so, obediently.

I then crouched down before her, and took her by the upper arms.

Our eyes met. "I did not know it could be like that," she whispered.

I said nothing.

"I performed obeisance," she said, shaken, wonderingly.

"Yes," I said.

"I have never felt so female," she said.

"You have not yet even begun to get in touch with your femaleness," I said. "You will discover that it is a wonderful thing, that it is deep and marvelous, and, I think, fathomless. A voyage of discovery lies before you, through lands of love and untold sensuous wonders. A great adventure lies before you, filled with life and meaning. In this adventure you will find your fulfillment, as what you truly are, a female, not as something else, not as something different."

"I understand," she whispered.

I touched her.

"Ohh," she said, softly.

"Interesting," I said. "Though you are a free woman, you are rather vital, even at this stage."

"Please do not embarrass me," she said.

"In time," I said, "it is my hope that you would grow proud of your body and its responses. I do not think you will find them embarrassing then, unless perhaps, say, strapped in a slave rack, you are forced to exhibit them publicly before scornful men or contemptuous free women. I think rather then that you would come to welcome them, and to exult in them, and rejoice in them."

"Please," she protested.

"Slaves," I said, "are generally quite open, and loving about their bodies. They tend to understand themselves, and their nature, and love it."

"I am not a slave," she reminded me.

"That is true," I said.

"What are you going to do with me?" she asked.

"What do you think?" I asked her.

"Will you be kind to me?" she asked.

"Not particularly," I said.

She looked at me, startled. Then I pressed her back, down, on her back, onto the mat.

"I am a virgin," she whispered.

I kissed her.

"You will be kind to me, won't you?" she said.

"Not particularly," I said.

"This mat is hard," she said. "It is rough." She squirmed a little, moving her back upon it, on its rough fibers.

"It was designed for the instruction of a slave," I said, "not for her comfort."

"I am not a slave," she smiled.

"The mat does not know that," I said.

"It is my hope that you know it," she smiled. "Oh!"

"I have forgotten it," I told her.

"Be kind!" she said. "I am not a slave!"

"You will be treated as I please," I said, "and exactly so. Now be silent."

"I have strange feelings," she whispered. "I feel that I should call you Master."

"Do not do so," I said. "That is only for slaves."

"Yes," she whispered, "—Master."

"Very well," I said.

"Oh, yes!" she cried, softly.

"Never let me go," she wept, clinging to me.

I thrust her back, gently, to the mat, disentangling her from me.

"Let me hold you," she begged.

"Not now," I said. "Keep your arms at your sides."

"In your arms—" she said, "in your arms—!"

"It is not I," I said. "It could have been any man. It is rather that you were ready."

"I am prepared to be a love slave!" she said.

"Keep your hands at your sides," I said.

Her small hands and arms writhed at her sides. "I want to touch you. I want to hold you!" she said.

"Keep them at your sides," I said.

"Be my love master!" she begged.

"You are a free woman," I reminded her.

"Please, please be my love master," she begged.

"Doubtless he somewhere exists," I said. "But I am not he."

She moaned.

"Do not be so overwhelmed," I said. "This is only a simple initiation into the world of the senses."

"Simple?" she asked. "Initiation?"

"Yes," I said.

"I did not know there was anything in all of life like this," she said.

"And you are not yet even a slave," I said.

"I want my love master," she moaned.

"Search for him," I whispered. "Perhaps you will find him—after a thousand collars."

"Let me hold you," she begged.

"You may do so," I said.

She put her arms about me, pulling me toward her, that I be pressed against her softness.

"Ohh," she said. "You are strong again."

"You are very beautiful," I explained.

*   *   *

"You are calm now?" I said.

"Yes," she said, "you have calmed me."

"A woman sometimes finds her first experience, of the sort you had before," I said, "before the last one, that is, one of unusual emotional impact, at least compared to what she has hitherto experienced."

"I understand," she said.

"So, then," I said, "now that you are in a calm frame of mind, and are fully rational, and the experience is at some distance, what are your feelings?" I asked.

"They are quite simple," she said.

"Yes?" I said.

"I want to be collared. I want to be branded. I want to be a slave."

"I see," I said.

"Do you think a woman can forget such an experience?" she asked. "That she is stupid, that she cannot remember it in the belly of her, that she is incapable of learning from it?"

"No," I said.

"It is what I now know I am," she said.

"I see," I said.

"And you knew it before, didn't you?" she asked.

"Yes," I said.

"I suppose some men are better than others at seeing the slave in a female," she said.

"Perhaps," I said. To be sure, some men are quite remarkable at this. Certain slavers, for example, at a glance, find it easy to assess slave potential. Otherwise, I suppose, it would be very difficult to explain their unusual success in deciding which women, even of women in crowds, and veiled and clad in the robes of concealment, are likely to be the most beautiful and make the best slaves, and those women, of course, are the ones most profitably stalked. It is their business, of course.

"Oh," she said, "you are not calming me now!"

"Oh?" I said.

"No," she said. "You are exciting me! You are doing it to me again! How dare you! I am a free woman! Is this how you want me, as an irresponsible, helpless, whimpering, yelping, squirming, animal, unable to help herself, leaping and crying out, half mad, beside herself with passion, responding almost as a slave in your arms?''

"Yes," I said.

"Beast!" she said.

"Oh, yes!" she cried. "Yes!" This time it seemed it had taken her hardly any time at all. Her reflexes were clearly honable.

"Shhh," I said. "Someone is passing by, in the passage between the buildings." To be sure, they couldn't see us where we were, unless they had entered this particular side passage and followed it to its termination.

"The shops may be open on the Avenue of Turia by now," I said.

"Yes," she said sweetly, her head on my chest.

We could see the sunlight on the walls high above us. It was now warm between the buildings.

"What time do you think it is?" I asked.

"The eighth or ninth Ahn," she said.

"Probably," I said.

"How will I get home?" she asked. "There will be many people about now? Will you buy me robes and a veil and bring them back here?"

"Do not count on it," I said.

"Do you think the free woman you tied at the slave ring has been freed by now?" she asked.

"Probably," I said. "I do not know."

"Do you remember the second time I kissed you," she asked, "the time when you told me that if a slave had not kissed better than that she would have been whipped?"

"Yes," I said. That was the time she had tried to strike me, and I had not permitted it, but instead had punished her. I had shortly thereafter carried her to the slave mat.

"Is that true?" she asked.

"It depends on many things," I said, "such as the master, the familiarity of the girl with her collar, for example, has she yet learned how to kiss, and the mood, the situation, and so on."

"But some slaves," she said, "might have been whipped for not kissing better than that?" she said.

"Certainly," I said.

"How do I kiss now?" she asked, kissing me.

"Much better," I said.

"As good as a slave?" she asked.

"No," I said.

"Oh?" she asked.

"No," I said. "You will not kiss as well as a slave, until you have become a slave, and then, probably, only after you have learned your collar for a few months, and perhaps even have had some training. Also, there is a whole indefinable modality to the kisses of slaves, that has to do with bondage and that they are literally the properties of the master. It is an entirely different sort of kissing from that of a free woman."

"I understand," she said. "Perhaps one day I will be a slave. And then I will kiss like a slave."

"Perhaps," I said.

"I know that I am a slave," she said. "I have learned it here, on this mat, in this place."

I said nothing.

"So what should I do?" she asked.

"What do you mean?" I asked.

"What does a free woman do," she asked, "when she learns she is a slave?"

"You are free," I said. "The decision is yours. But beware of certain decisions, for if you make them, you would then no longer be free. Your decisions then might rather be concerned with such things as how to best please your master, within certain latitudes which he might permit you."

She was quiet, her head on my chest.

"The self-enslavement decision is an interesting one," I said, "for it is a decision which is freely made, being made by a free individual, but, once made, it is irrevocable, for the individual is then no longer free, but only a property."

She lifted her head. She was then on her elbows beside me. Her breasts were lovely. "You could take me to a slaver's, and sell me," she said.

"True," I said.

"Do so!" she said.

"No," I said.

"Why not?" she asked.

"Because it amuses me to treat you like a slave," I said.

"Beast," she said, and put her head down again on my chest.

"You could turn yourself in, to a slaver," I said.

"True," she said.

"You call upon him, dressed in your finest veils and robes of concealment," I said, "probably first having made an appointment. That would be a common courtesy. He may, after all, be a busy man. Then, in the privacy of his office, as he observes, you strip yourself. You do this as gracefully and as well as you can, without training. You reveal yourself to him completely. You are absolutely naked. He will presumably put you through some simple slave paces, forming some conception of your capacity to move well before men. In the process of this, you are, of course, being assessed. You then, when permitted, kneel. You then humbly beg his permission to bind yourself into slavery before him, thereby making yourself a slave, and, in the context, submitting yourself to him as your first master. You keep your head down, and await his decision. In your case, I am sure the decision would be affirmative.

"Various things might then happen. He might have you sign a slave document, in the presence of witnesses. As soon as your signature is on the document, of course, you are a slave. On the other hand, he might proceed even more simply. He might merely have you utter a formula of enslavement, though, again, doubtless in the presence of witnesses, who might sign a paper certifying their witnessing of your declaration. Let us suppose you utter such a formula. The simplest is perhaps, 'I am a slave.' You are then a slave. He will perhaps then say, 'You are my slave.' This claims you. You are then his slave. This is sufficient in the context for in that context you have been momentarily an unclaimed slave, who may be claimed by the first free person who chooses to do so. Too, in this case, there are, of course, no counterclaims to be adjudicated. He is there first, so to speak. His claim is fully warranted, unchallengeable and legally indisputable. This is again done presumably in the presence of witnesses, who may be asked to certify their witnessing of the action. You might then say, though it is not necessary in the context, for you are, anyway, by this time, clearly his slave, 'Yes, Master, I am your slave.' By this utterance you officially acknowledge him as your master. It is sometimes thought that this sort of thing is good from the slave's point of view, that she hears herself say this. It is legally unnecessary, but it is sometimes thought to be a psychologically useful act on the part of the slave. She, in this pronouncement, at any rate, clearly acknowledges that she knows who owns her. This, too, of course, may be attested to in writing by the witnesses.

"There is then little left to be done with you, except perhaps to take you below, to the pens. There you will presumably be branded and fitted with your first collar. You might also then be given your first whipping in order that you learn almost immediately to fear, and terribly fear, the slave whip. You might then, afterwards, when you can eat, be given a handful, or two, of moist slave gruel. You might also be permitted to lap some water on all fours from a pan, or from a puddle, where it has been poured onto the floor. You might then be chained in a training kennel. In the morning I suppose your training might begin. On the other hand, perhaps you would be simply shipped out of the city to a distant market, there to be put on the block for your first sale."

"My sale," she whispered, excitedly.

"Yes," I said.

"Do you think I would bring a good price?" she asked.

"Yes," I said. "I think so."

She shuddered with pleasure.

"I think I will take you home now," I said.

"I thought you would not take me home," she said.

"No," I said. "I will do so."

"Why this sudden change of heart?" she smiled.

"I am not sure," I said. "Perhaps it is because I now know you better. Perhaps it is because it is now later in the day."

"Or perhaps there is another reason?" she said.

"Perhaps," I said. "I am not sure."

"Bind me, and take me instead to a slaver's," she said.

"No," I said.

"I would not have the courage to turn myself over to a slaver," she said. "I would be afraid."

"I understand," I said.

"I could be killed," she said.

"If you are obedient and pleasing," I said, "there is usually little to fear, other than the normal rigors and exactions of bondage."

"Surely they are fierce enough," she said.

"Sometimes," I admitted. Not all masters were pleasant with their properties.

"But I could be killed," she said.

"You are in far greater danger of being killed as a free woman," I said. "Just as it would not occur to most men to kill a pet sleen or a kaiila, it would not occur to them to kill a slave. She is, like other such domestic animals, not a person, but a property. She, like them, has certain sorts of work to which she may be put, and very pleasurable work often, and, like them, has her many values and uses. If a city is taken, while free folks may be fleeing about, and be subject to indiscriminate slaughter, she is likely, instead, to be secured and protected. She is, you see, like the sleen and kaiila, part of the clearly understood spoils of victory. Surely you can understand that you yourself, for example, might make delicious booty."

"I?" she said, softly. "Booty?"

"Yes," I said, "if you were slave."

"I understand," she said, trembling. I saw from the way she said this, so softly trembling, so thrilled, that she belonged, truly, in a collar.

"To be sure," I said, "the slaves in such a situation would be well advised to be as obedient and pleasing as possible."

"Of course," she said.

"Particularly as the killing lust might still be upon the men."

"I understand," she said.

"But slaves are generally well trained in placatory behaviors," I said.

"Of course," she said.

"And they serve well, naked, in the victory orgies." I said.

"Yes," she said.

"But then even free women may be used in such orgies," I said.

"I do not think they would long remain free," she said.

"No," I said. "That would presumably be their last night of freedom."

"Do they serve naked at the orgy, as do the slaves?" she asked.

"Of course," I said.

"Are such women sometimes enslaved before the orgy?" she asked.

"Yes," I said, "presumably that they will then understand the totality of what will be expected of them at the feast. Too, some commanders think this is an excellent introduction to her new condition for a former free woman."

"They are probably right," she said.

"We must get you home soon," I said.

"Why?" she asked.

"You are tempting," I said.

"But if I were a slave," she said, "I would be subject to penalties."

"Yes," I said. "The master would own you."

"I could even be killed," she said.

"Yes," I said.

She was silent.

"It is one thing, of course," I said, "to be subject to penalties, and it is quite another for them to be inflicted."

"That is true," she said.

"For example, it is one thing to be subject to the whip, and to know that that subjection is quite real, that the master can, and will, whip you, and well, if you are not pleasing, and something else to be actually whipped."

"I understand," she said.

"But in general it is similar with all the penalties," I said.

"even those which are seldom, if ever, inflicted. She must know that they exist, and that, for her, they are real possibilities. She must know, whether they are inflicted upon her or not, that she is truly subject to them."

"I understand," she said.

"This is the sense in which she knows that anything can be done with her, that she might even be killed."

"I understand," she said.

"Without this," I said, "her slavery would be incomplete. She would not be a total slave."

"That is true," she whispered.

"Most simply put," I said, "she belongs to the master, fully, totally."

"I understand," she said.

"So let us now return to your residence," I said.

"I could accept that risk," she said. "It would be part of my fulfillment. Indeed, without it, I could not truly, fully, belong to him."

"You are so confident of your ability to please?" I asked.

"I am confident of my ability to try desperately to please," she said.

"We must be on our way," I said, sitting up.

"Take me to a slaver's," she said.

"No," I said.

"Are you a true man?" she said, petulantly, rising up on her knees.

I regarded her.

"Are you?" she challenged.

"You belong in a collar," I said.

"Take me to a slaver's!" she said. "See that I am put in one!"

I did not speak.

"Let it be such that I cannot remove it!" she said.

"It would be such, I assure you," I said.

"Take me to a slaver's!" she said.

"No," I said.

"Are you afraid?" she asked.

"No," I said.

"Look upon me," she said. "Am I not the sort of woman who might suitably be taken to a slaver's?"

"Yes," I admitted.

"Do so," she said.

"No," I said.

"Look," she said, but inches from me, as I sat there, observing her. She suddenly rose up a bit on her knees and thrust her belly forward, toward me. "There!" she said. "Would any but a slave do that?" she asked.

"No," I said. Perhaps it would have been better for her, I thought, if she had not done that. She was attractive.

"Take me then to a slaver's," she said.

"No," I said.

"You are no true man!" she said.

I then stood up before her. She looked up at me, puzzled, I then, after regarding her for a time, suddenly, with the back of my hand, struck her fiercely back from the mat, she twisting and falling back, flung to the side from her knees, almost half on her feet for an instant, then losing her balance, then falling back into the trash at the side of the wall. She, from the midst of the garbage, half on her side, looked at me wildly, her hand at her mouth, blood between her fingers.

I pointed to the mat. "Here," I said. "Kneel."

She hastened back to the mat and knelt before me. She looked up at me in wonder, blood at her mouth. She had been cuffed. "Did you strike me because I challenged your manhood?" she asked. "I did not really mean it. It is only that I was terribly angry. I did not think."

"You were not struck for such an absurd reason," I said. "You are, after all, a free woman, and free women are entitled to insult, and to attempt to demean and destroy men. It is one of their freedoms, unless men, of course, should decide to take it from them. You were struck, rather, because you were attempting to manipulate me."

She nodded, putting her head down.

"Do you recognize your guilt, and the suitability of your punishment?" I asked.

"Yes," she said.

"Also," I said, "I would not, if I were a free woman, go about moving like that before men."

"But I am not really a free woman," she whispered.

"You are at this time in your life," I said, "legally free. Do not forget it."

"Yes," she said, "—Master."

"Do not call me 'Master,' " I said. "That is for slaves."

"Yes, Master," she said.

"You seem to have a curiosity as to the slave experience," I said.

"I am a slave," she said. "It is only natural that I would have some curiosity about what it is to be a slave." She put down her head. She wiped some of the blood from her mouth.

"You have no idea," I said, "about what it is like, truly, to be a slave."

She did not respond.

"Perhaps I can change your mind about its desirability," I said.

"Master?" she asked.

I then took her by the hair and, twisting her about, as she cried out, flung her forcibly, on her back, on the mat. I then, ruthlessly, angrily, swiftly, caring nothing for her feelings or sensibilities, exploiting her, employing her in the role of a mere, lovely object, used her unilaterally for my pleasure. I then, in a moment or two, stood up beside her, and rolled her to her side, spurning her, with my foot. She lay there on the mat, gasping, her legs drawn up.

"So," I asked, "Free Woman, what do you think?"

She turned about and looked up at me, through her hair.

"It is thus that a slave may be used," I said.

She looked up at me. In her eyes there were tears.

"How did you like it?" I laughed.

She went to her belly and reached for my foot. She put her lips over it and kissed it, tenderly. Then she looked up at me, again, her hair about her face. "I loved it," she said.

I cried out with rage, and pulled my foot away from her.

"Put on your garment," I told her, angrily.

"Yes, Master," she said.

In a bit she had donned the brief leather garment. It amazed me that it could take her so long to get into so little. To be sure, she had had to smooth it out, and had not been hurrying. She looked down at the garment, now on her. She pulled down a bit at the sides. "It is not very large, is it?" she said.

"No," I said.

"But I suppose," she said, "if I were a slave, I might be given things much less than this to wear, and things far more revealing."

"Quite possibly," I said. I saw no point in telling her that that was almost a certainty.

"But I am a free woman," she smiled. She looked down at the garment, ruefully. "Are you really going to take me through the streets in this?"

"Yes," I said. "I certainly have no intention of buying you a new outfit."

She laughed. "No," she said. "I suppose not." She looked at me. "Clad like this," she said, "I suppose I should heel you."

"No," I said.

"You will permit me to walk beside you, as a free woman, though I am clad so shamelessly?" she asked.

"No," I said.

"You are not going to accompany me then?" she asked, disappointed.

"I will come with you," I said.

"I do not understand," she said.

"You will precede me," I said.

"Of course," she laughed. "You do not know the way."

"Of course," I said.

She laughed. "That is not the true reason, is it?" she asked.

"No," I said.

"I have seen masters walking their girls before them in the streets," she laughed. "Doubtless they enjoy seeing them walk before them."

"Doubtless," I said.

"That is your reason, isn't it?" she laughed.

"Yes," I said.

"You do find me attractive, don't you?" she asked.

"Yes," I said.

"I will try to walk well before you, Master," she smiled.

"Do not call me Master," I said.

"Yes, Master," she smiled.

"Let us go," I said.

"I will never forget this place," she said. "It was here I became a woman, and learned my slavery."

"Let us go," I said.

"Take me to a slaver's," she said.

"No," I said.

"Shall I now precede my Master?" she asked.

"You may precede me," I said.

She then preceded me from the back passage, into the larger passage, running between the buildings, leading to the Avenue of Turia. She did walk well. I wondered why I had decided to accompany her to her dwelling. I was not certain about the matter. Surely she could have found her way there safely, and particularly now, in the full daylight. I did have extra binding fiber in my pouch.

On the Avenue of Turia, to the left, we saw a small crowd. "Wait," I said. "Let us investigate that." We went a bit closer. Then, between people, we saw the hostess from the Tunnels. She was still on her knees, tied to the slave ring. Though it must have been the tenth Ahn, she had not yet been released. Her head was down. Much, I gathered, had she been suitably mocked. "Look, Mother," said a child. "She is naked !"

"Come away," said the mother.

"I know her," said a man. "She is from the Tunnels."

"Look," said another fellow, "she has a tarsk bit tied on her belly!"

"Yes!" laughed another. I did not think that that free woman would be likely to return to her work at the Tunnels. That sort of thing, I thought, was behind her. I did not think that she would be any longer wearing leather. Other garmentures would now be more appropriate for her, I speculated, such as tiny rags of rep-cloth or brief tunics of silk, bound with girdlings of binding fiber, and perhaps, about her neck, closed closely about it and locked shut, a graceful ornament of steel, a slave collar.

"Let us continue on our way," I said.

"Yes, Master," said the blonde.

She then took her way in the opposite direction, which would have been to the right, as we had emerged between the buildings. Behind her I was in an excellent position to see the looks she received, which were many, the admiring glances, the intakes of breath, the sudden delights at seeing such a female. To be sure, she walked well. She did belong in a collar, I thought. I put the binding fiber in my pouch from my mind. I must not think of it. She was a free woman. Yet, to be sure, she was desirable and exciting, and should be a slave.

"It is here," she said, after a long walk.

"In that tower?" I asked. We were on one of the lower bridges.

"Yes," she said.

It seemed to soar to the clouds.

"You must be wealthy," I said. We were in one of Ar's finest residential districts, that of the seventeen Tabidian Towers.

She shrugged.

"Quite wealthy," I said.

"Yesterday, I thought so," she smiled.

"That seems a strange thing to say," I said.

"Oh, in one way I suppose I am one of the wealthiest women in Ar," she laughed. "But in another I think I am perhaps one of the most miserable and poorest."

"I do not understand," I said.

"My life was unsatisfactory," she said. "It seemed empty and meaningless. I only this morning learned what happiness, and fulfillment could be."

"Helpless on the mat of a slave?" I said.

"Yes," she smiled.

"Perhaps it was the masculine domination, and you finding yourself in your place in nature, as what you are, a female," I said.

"Perhaps," she said.

"I wish you well, female," I said.

"I must climb the high bridge alone?" she asked.

"Yes," I said. "I think it is better that I leave you now, quickly."

"Why?" she asked.

"I think I do not trust myself," I said.

"Oh?" she asked.

"You are an exciting female," I said.

"Do you really think so, truly?" she asked.

"Yes," I said.

She came close to me. She looked up at me. "Bind me then," she whispered. "Take me to a slaver's."

"No," I said.

"You know I am a slave," she whispered, "that I am truly a slave, that I belong in a collar!"

I did not speak.

"Please!" she begged.

"Turn yourself over to a slaver," I said. She looked down in frustration. She kicked with her right foot at the flooring of the bridge. Her feet were bare. "I can't," she said. "I can't!"

"Farewell," I said.

"Do not go!" she pleaded.

I turned to face her.

"Some women can do that!" she said. "I can't!"

"Very well," I said.

"I am afraid!" she cried.

"I understand," I said.

"Please!" she said.

"Is freedom not precious?" I asked.

"Perhaps for others," she said. "To me it would be a thousand times less precious than my slavery."

I looked at her.

"I want my master to be free," she said, "but as for me, I want to belong to him, totally, to be his, fully, like a sandal or a sleen!"

I did not respond to her.

"Let him treat me as he pleases," she said. "I do not care.

It is his prerogative. He is the master. Let him neglect me or be cruel to me. Let him whip me or chain me. Let him do with me as he wills. I do not care. I want to belong to him. I will kiss his whip with joy! I want to love him, with all that I have to give as a woman. I want to serve and love him, selflessly, only his mastered slave!''

"Turn yourself over to a slaver," I said.

"No!" she wept.

"Very well," I said.

"Help me!" she begged.

"No," I said.

She wept, and raised her fists as though to strike me, but then she put her hands down, quickly, frightened, thinking, perhaps fearing that I might not be pleased, and might punish her. She had learned earlier that not all men will accept humiliation at the hands of a woman, even a free woman.

"So," I said, "turn yourself over to a slaver."

"I do not want it done that way," she said, tears in her eyes.

"Farewell," I said.

"Farewell," said she, looking up at me with tears in her eyes, "Master."

"I have told you about calling me Master," I said.

"Yes, Master," she said.

She turned about and began, slowly, to walk up the long bridge. The soaring, lovely tower, one of the seventeen Tabidian Towers, lay ahead of her. In it was located her residence. It would presumably be on the upper levels. Those are usually regarded as more exclusive, and safest from attack. They are usually approached only by the higher, narrower bridges. Her apartments, doubtless, would be luxurious and well appointed, perhaps involving portions of more than one level. Perhaps she might serve well as a slave in such a place, I thought. The particular bridge, colorfully paved, graceful, narrow and ascendant, on which she walked, barefoot, blonde, her hair moving in the wind, in her exquisitely brief leather, gave entrance to the tower at something over half its height, other bridges about, as well, some giving access at different levels, and others leading to other towers, and to other bridges, and down to the streets. Gorean cities, given the bridges, can be traversed, often, at different levels. She looked very small, and forlorn.

Part way up the bridge she turned about. She looked back. She lifted her hand. I did not deign to respond to this gesture. She was, after all, only a female. She then lowered her head and turned about, and, slowly, continued on her way up the bridge.

I caught up with her at the height of the bridge.

"Stop," I said.

She stopped, startled.

"Do not turn around," I said.

"You," she said. "I know your voice."

"Do not turn around," I said.

She did not turn, but continued to face the other way.

"The leather you are wearing is rather brief," I said.

"Yes," she said.

"It seems more fitting for a slave than a free woman," I said.

"Yes!" she said.

"You may call me Master," I said.

"Master?" she asked.

"Yes," I said. "Begin to form the habit of calling free men Master."

"I do not understand!" she said.

"Place your wrists, crossed, behind your back," I said.

She did so. "Oh!" she said. I had whipped binding fiber about them, securing them in place. "It is so tight," she said.

"Now that you are bound," I said, "you may turn and face me."

She spun about, wildly, trying to free her hands.

"You cannot free yourself," I said.

"No!" she cried, elatedly. "I cannot! Oh, What are you doing?"

"Leashing you," I said.

"That is not necessary," she said.

I snapped the slave leash, taken from my pouch, about her neck.

"Be silent," I said.

She looked up at me, startled.

"The proper response," I said, "is 'Yes, Master.' "

"Yes, Master," she said, wonderingly. "Master!"

"Did you ask permission to speak?" I asked.

"May I speak?" she asked.

"Yes," I said, jerking the leash twice, rather hard, against the back of her neck, testing it. The leash collar was a high, sturdy one, and fitted rather closely about her neck. Girls do not slip such leashes. It had two buckle fastenings. These I had fastened in the front and then turned to the back. This had brought the sturdy leading ring, on its plate, riveted into the leather, to the front, under her chin. This is the common position for front leading, the girl behind you, whether she is on her feet, as it was my intention to lead this girl, if only to save time, or, say, on her belly or all fours. The back position is commonly used when the girl is in front of you, and you are controlling her from behind, she either on her feet ahead of you, or, say, beside you or ahead of you on her belly or all fours. The front position is generally preferred as leash pressure is then received at the back and sides of the neck, not the front. To be sure, a girl is likely to be much more wary, and fearful, and docile, when the ring is at the back.

I had then snapped the leash strap on the leading ring. In one's pouch or pack the leash strap is normally coiled inside the collar, whether it is snapped on the leash ring or not. I usually do not keep it on the collar because in that way I am free to use it independently as a binding device or, doubled as an admonitory lash. Also, I think it does a girl good, and it had seemed to do this girl good, to hear it snap on the collar ring, either at the back of her neck, when she is to be back-controlled, or just under her chin, when she is to be front-led. Leashing, of course, of either variety, is excellent psychologically for the female, as it confirms her bondage upon her and helps to make clear to her her animal status. Similarly, the jerking of the leash, to test its strength, is good for her. It helps her to understand that it is truly on her.

This leash pressure, in testing, of course, either is done with the ring in the front position, to avoid damage to the throat, even if the collar is then to be turned and she is to be back-controlled, or, if the ring is left in the back position, in such a way, say, with a thumb or fingers inserted at the front of the leash collar, as to take the pressure of the testing, and protect the throat. The general consideration here, of course, is to avoid pressure to the front of the throat. It is general Gorean practice to avoid even the slightest of pressures here. This does not represent a relaxation of Gorean disciplinary practices, incidentally, for discipline may be, and will be, if there is the least cause for it, inflicted outside the strictures of the leash. Too, if the ring is in the back position, if the girl is not compliant she puts this pressure on herself. An excellent example is the choke leash, which cannot be slipped, but can tighten. The least bit of resistance on the part of the girl closes the loop. In such a device, girls, after the first moment or two, follow without resistance.

"What are you going to do with me?" she said.

"I am going to take you to a slaver's," I said. "I think I know one who will not ask too many questions."

"To a slaver's!" she cried.

"Yes," I said.

"Why?" she cried.

"Why do you think?" I asked. "To make some money on you, of course. It will probably be the first time any man ever made any money on you, but I assure you, it will not be the last."

I then turned about and began to stride rapidly down the bridge. She was running behind me, on the leash, laughing and crying.

27: I Sell a Blonde

I threw the blonde to her knees before Tenalion, slaver of Ar. It was he to whom Boabissia had earlier, inadvertently, returned herself, his slave. We were now, however, in his house of business, in his office there. She knelt inside an outlined yellow circle. It was a few feet before his desk. This circle had a diameter of about seven or eight feet. The border of this circle, delineating it, was about seven or eight inches in width, and was formed of yellow stones set mosaiclike into the smooth scarlet flooring.

"I bring you a woman," I said.

He rose from his desk and came about it, to stand a few feet from the blonde.

I removed the leash from her neck. I separated the collar and strap. I coiled the strap, placing it within the collar. I then returned the two parts of the leash to my pouch. I glanced to the blonde. "Kneel with your knees more widely spread," I said.

She obeyed. I could see she was frightened, now that she was here. Perhaps she was having second thoughts. It was a bit late, however, for such thoughts. She squirmed a little, on her knees. She was attractive, doing so. This squirming, I think, was genuinely due to her fear and agitation, but, even so, I thought it might add to her price. She moved well. Her hands were still tied tightly behind her.

"What is her brand?" asked Tenalion.

"She is a free woman," I said.

"I thought so," he said.

"You are in the house of a slaver," he said to the blonde. "You kneel within a circle of assessment."

She looked down at it. "I did not know," she whispered.

"It is about the size of a slave block," he said.

She nodded.

The circle, of course, was flush with the floor. The slave block, on the other hand, is normally about a yard to five feet high, and is designed to raise the girls above the crowd, so that they may be more easily seen by the bidders.

"Have you ever seen a sale of female slaves?" he asked.

"No," she said.

"Perhaps you have some idea," he said, "of what they are like."

"Yes," she said.

"Usually the merchandise is exhibited stark naked and sold to the highest bidder," he said, "whose slave they then are, in all ways."

"I understand," she said.

"You are to be assessed," he said.

"I understand," she whispered.

"And eventually, doubtless," he said, "in one way or another, you will be sold as a slave."

"I understand," she said.

"Is she a virgin?" asked Tenalion.

"No," I said.

The blonde blushed hotly.

"I did not think so," said Tenalion.

The blonde put down her head.

"You are beautiful, my dear," he said.

"Thank you, Master," she said.

"Are you sexually responsive?" he asked.

She looked at me, wildly. "I do not know," she said.

"Yes," I said, "quite so, at least for one who is still substantially a free woman."

"In your opinion," asked Tenalion, "she shows slave promise?"

"Yes," I said.

"May I see?" asked Tenalion.

"Of course," I said.

"Oh!" cried the girl. "Please no! Not here! Not like this! I beg you! No! Oh, oh, Master! Master!" I could scarcely hold her then, squirming, bucking, on her knees. It was almost like trying to hold a small sleen. Her body was very strong in its passion. Then she looked at Tenalion, tears in her eyes, revealed before him as a superbly responsive female, in a man's hands no more than a slave.

"Excellent," said Tenalion.

"I would suppose," I said, "of course, that she might improve considerably, and indefinitely, in such matters, when she is truly a slave, when she is legally and fully imbonded."

She looked at me with wonder.

"Of course," said Tenalion.

The blonde put down her head, shuddering.

"Girl," said Tenalion.

She lifted her head.

"Are you prepared to enter slavery?" he asked.

"Yes, Master," she said.

"Will you strive to be a good slave?" he asked.

"Yes, Master," she said.

"Many masters are not patient with slaves," he said. "Do you understand what that means?"

"Master?" she asked.

"You are well advised to be fully pleasing to your masters," he said.

"Yes, Master," she said.

"It is not pleasant to be whipped," he said.

"No, Master," she said.

"Similarly, it would not be pleasant to be subjected to many other conceivable punishments, or, say, to be thrown alive to hungry sleen," he said.

"No, Master!" she said.

"Be a good slave," he said.

"Yes, Master!" she said.

"Do you think being a slave is merely a matter of crawling about your master's legs, and licking and kissing, and serving his intimate pleasures?"

"I do not know, Master," she said. "I have never been a slave."

"Do you think you would look well dancing before your master?" he asked.

"I do not know," she said.

"Absolutely naked, of course," he said, "as you are now."

"I do not know, Master," she said.

I, frankly, thought she would look quite well doing this. No one, however, had asked my opinion.

"Still," he said, "such things are only among the more obvious sexual modalities."

"Yes, Master," she said.

"Your entire life," he said, "will now be pervaded with sexuality, with your femaleness. Your life will now be a sexual one, a life in which your femaleness, for the first time, will be of undeniable and paramount importance, a life in which it will be overwhelmingly central. Everything else will take its coloration and meaning from that."

"Yes, Master," she said.

"It will be a life of total femaleness, and dedication, and service and love."

"Yes, Master," she said.

"The smallest tasks in your life, how you clean your master's leather, how you set out his clothes, how you cook, and sew, how you shop, how you clean and launder, even the tiniest and most servile tasks, all such things, will become sexual, all will become expressions of your femaleness, fitting and joyful manifestations of your worthless but helplessly proffered, gladly tendered love and service, that of only an insignificant slave."

"I understand," she said.

"The life of a female slave," he said, "is a life wholly given over to love. It is not a compromised life. It is not one of those lives which is part this, and part that. It is a total way of life, a total life. The female slave seeks to give all, selflessly, knowing that she, as she is a mere slave, a rightless animal owned by her master, one who can be bought and sold at his least whim, can make no claims, that she deserves nothing, and is entitled to not the least attention or consideration. There are no bargains made with her, no arrangements."

"Yes, Master," whispered the girl.

"And it is for such women," he said, "that men are willing to die."

She put down her head, humbly.

"What do you want for her?" asked Tenalion.

I shrugged.

"Two silver tarsks?" he asked.

"Fine," I said.

"Not a thousand gold pieces?" asked the blonde.

Tenalion smiled. "You have very unrealistic concept of the market," he said. "Too, you are no longer a free woman, and priceless. You are now only one slave among others, and now, within certain limits, have a specific monetary value."

"But so little?" she asked.

"Prices are useful in helping women to understand themselves and rank themselves, at least in certain dimensions," he said.

"So little?" she asked.

"That is a high price," I told her. Indeed, when Boabissia had returned herself to Tenalion, only one silver tarsk had changed hands.

"Oh," she said.

He reached to a bell on his desk and rang it. It was not unlike the bell which had been on his desk in his residence. Tenalion, I gathered, like most efficient people, was a creature of habit. This frees the mind so that it may better concentrate on important considerations. In a moment, as before, a fellow had entered the room.

"This is a slave," said Tenalion, indicating the blonde. "Take her below. See that she is fittingly marked as such. We do not want there to be any confusion in the future about the matter."

"Yes, Tenalion," said the fellow.

The blonde saw Tenalion place two silver tarsks in my hand. She looked at them, wonderingly. The slave, she, herself, so easily, now had a new master.

Tenalion's man, taking her by the upper arms, from behind, jerked her up to her feet.

"You do not even know my name!" she cried to me.

My right hand, reflexively, flew up, striking her across the mouth, lashing her head back.

Tenalion's man, angrily, threw her again to her knees, before me.

She looked up at me, startled, frightened, blood about her mouth.

"You do not have a name," I told her.

"Yes, Master," she gasped.

I regarded her, idly. She was attractive, naked and bound, and on her knees.

"Do you not wish to know who I was?" she asked.

"Who were you?" I asked.

"I was the Lady Lydia, she of the High Merchants, she whose wealth was in gems and land, she of the Tabidian Towers!" she said.

"An excellent catch," smiled Tenalion. "I shall enjoy having her in my pens for a time, the lovely Lady Lydia, before her sale."

"Lydia," she said, "of the Tabidian Towers!"

"Does it matter?" I asked.

"No," she said, crushed. "It does not matter."

"You are now only a nameless slave," I said.

"Yes, Master," she said, head down.

"Take her away," said Tenalion.

The slave was pulled to her feet. She was roughly turned about. The hand of Tenalion's man was then in her hair, fastening itself deeply therein. It was like the closed talon of a bird of prey. She, bound, held, was helpless. She cried out softly, so held, startled, in pain. Then, bent over, her wrists confined in the cruel, encircling binding fiber, that which I had earlier put well on her, holding them so mercilessly, so helplessly, behind her back, her head at his hip, stumbling, weeping, she was conducted swiftly from our presence.

"She will be branded shortly," said Tenalion. "If you wish, a little later, in the afternoon, you might visit her in her pen."

"You are a kind fellow," I said.

He shrugged. "It is a weakness of mine," he said.

28: Tenalion Accords Me a Favor

"Girl," I said.

She moved in pain, in the straw. She lifted herself to a half sitting, half kneeling position. There was a sound of chain. "It is you!" she said, softly. The heavy chain was on her neck. "They branded me," she said. "I am branded."

"Thigh," I said.

She, wincing, turned toward me, in the straw. "An excellent brand," I said. It was the common kajira mark, as I had expected, small, delicate, and beautiful, the cursive Kef, the staff and fronds, lyrically feminine, but unmistakable, a brand marking property, worn by most Gorean female slaves.

She looked at me. How helpless and soft she was, so perfect, now that she was enslaved.

"It is beautiful," I said, reassuring her.

"Thank you," she whispered.

"What is your name?" I asked.

"I have not been given a name," she smiled.

I too, smiled.

"Do you think I would so soon forget my cuffing?" she asked.

"No," I said. "I did not think so."

"The other girl had a name, or thought she did," she said.

"I see," I said.

"So I shall answer promptly to the name given me," she smiled.

"That would be my recommendation," I said.

"I hope I am given a good name," she said.

"You are pretty," I said. "You will probably be given a pretty name."

"I hope so," she said.

"But if you are not pleasing," I said, "it may be removed from you."

"I know," she said.

"Some masters force a girl to serve superbly for months, before being given any name, let alone a lovely one."

"That is cruel," she protested.

"You are at the mercy, totally, of anyone who buys you," I said.

"I know," she shuddered. The chain on her neck made a small noise. Chains look well on the necks of women.

"Have you received your first taking, after your branding?" I asked.

"No," she said.

I nodded.

"I am naked, and the straw is soft and warm, Master," she said.

"You are very beautiful," I said. So beautiful are slaves!

"My Master, Tenalion, of Ar, has permitted you here," she said.

"Yes," I said, looking down at her.

"He has doubtless planned this," she whispered.

"Are you resistant?" I asked.

"No," she laughed. "I am not resistant! I am a slave! I shall do my best to be responsive, and pleasing. I wish to be pleasing to my masters."

"Perhaps you do not wish to be beaten, either," I said.

"True," she laughed. "I do not wish to be beaten, either."

I smiled.

"I think Tenalion is kind," she whispered.

"Do you think he would be slow with the whip, if you were not pleasing?" I asked.

"No," she smiled. "I do not think he would be slow with the whip."

"Does your brand hurt?" I asked.

"A little," she said.

"Prepare to be taken," I said. I removed my tunic. I

looked down at her. She was lovely in the straw, at my feet.
"How do you wish to be taken?"

"I am new to my chains," she said. "Gently, lovingly, please."

"Very well," I said, "this first time."

29: Soldiers

"Hist!" whispered the fellow in the doorway.

"Ho?" I asked.

I saw then that it was small Achiates, he who was the landlord of the insula in which I lodged, which shabby structure now lay only a stone's throw away, down the Alley of the Slave Brothels of Ludmilla.

I approached him. It was now well past the fourteenth Ahn, late in the afternoon. I had intended to be back somewhat earlier, indeed, rather in the neighborhood of dawn, but I had dallied for a time in the house of Tenalion, or, more specifically, in one of the pens, off one of the labyrinthine corridors, beneath his house. I remembered the heat and softness of her lips and beauty, her readiness and eagerness, and the chain on her. I thought she would make an excellent slave.

"Surely the rent is not due so soon?" I inquired.

"Here, come out of the light," he said.

I stepped into the doorway with him. He looked about. He then drew back his head.

"What is wrong?" I asked.

"What have you done?" he asked.

"Nothing," I said. I think it is generally a good rule to protest one's innocence with vigor.

"Come now!" he said.

"I do not know," I said. "I have done quite a few things. Have you anything particular in mind? Has the room been damaged?" I feared Hurtha might have been practicing with his ax. Another alarming possibility was that he might have decapitated, either as an honest mistake, or intentionally, another tenant, perhaps one who had been so bold as to object to the declamation of poetry in the halls. Hurtha had the habit of composing orally. Still that would be something he had done, not that I had done.

"No," said Achiates, nervously.

"See," I said.

"They are waiting for you," he said.

I watched a free woman hobble by, carrying a sack of suls on her back.

"Hurtha and Feiqa, the slave?" I asked. I blinked. Perhaps I had not had enough sleep the night before. That was possible, I thought, as I had not had any sleep.

"No!" he said.

"You are thinking of raising the rent?" I asked.

"No!" he said. But I had noted his eyes had glinted for an instant. I should not have said that. It had been the lack of sleep, I gathered. One must be careful how one speaks to landlords. One must be careful not to put ideas into their heads. It is generally better to complain loudly and frequently, keeping the fellow on the defensive, so that the very thought of having the rent raised under such conditions would seem an unthinkable, outrageous affront.

"Who, then?" I asked. I noted a slave passing by in the street, the lower portion of her body in shadows, the upper portion bright in the late afternoon sun. She was shading her eyes. Her collar was close-fitting. Her dark hair fell about it. She was probably on an errand. A coin sack was tied about her neck. Some slaves are not allowed to touch money. Many, on the other hand, on errands, carry coins in their mouth. This, however, is not unusual on Gor, even for free folks. Gorean garments generally lack pockets. She was barefoot. She moved well. In time, I supposed, the former Lady Lydia, whom I had left behind me in one of Tenalion's pens, one of his newer acquisitions, would be put on the block and sold, and would then, eventually, in one city or other, probably not Ar, find herself only such a girl. Such slaves are not allowed outside the city gates, unless accompanied by a free person. I recalled how the former Lady Lydia had showed me her brand. It had been an excellent one, lovely one. How pleased she had been that that was the case. I smiled. Slave girls are so vain about their brands.

"Soldiers," he said.

"What?" I said. I felt suddenly alert. This seemed, suddenly, a serious business.

"Soldiers," he repeated, looking about himself.

"City guardsmen?" I asked.

"No," he said, "soldiers."

"Taurentians?" I asked.

"No," he said. "Soldiers."

"What do they want with me?" I asked.

"I do not know," he said.

"Did you ask?" I asked.

"Yes," he said.

"What did they say?" I asked.

"Nothing," he said. "They only wanted to know when you would return."

"What did you tell them?" I asked.

"I told them I did not know," he said.

"How long have they been there?" I asked.

"Only a little while," he said. I found that of interest. Planned arrests are normally made at dawn.

"Why are you informing me of this?" I asked.

"You are a tenant," he said. "Too, you have paid your rent. Too, I do not want any arrests made in my insula. That might be bad for its reputation."

"Thank you," I said. I pressed a coin into his hand.

"That is not necessary," he said, but took it. He was, after all, a businessman.

"You are Tarl of Port Kar?" asked a man.

"Aiii!" moaned Achiates.

"Yes," I said, "Captain."

"May I have your sword, please?" he inquired. There were now some fifteen or twenty fellows behind him. There was not much room in the doorway to draw, let alone to wield the weapon. Yet I was not covered by crossbows. Too, none of the men had lowered their spears or drawn their weapons.

"On what grounds?" I asked.

"You are under arrest," he said.

Achiates moaned.

"You may leave, Citizen," the fellow informed Achiates. Achiates then, like an urt, spotting an opening between sleen, darted away, hurrying toward the insula.

"Your sword, please," said the captain. Surely he realized men do not lightly surrender their weapons. Too, clearly he must realize I could force myself from the doorway, and, in an instant, be in the open, the blade free. I wondered if it were his intent to encourage such a movement on my part, in order that this might provide a plausible, legitimizing circumstance for the employment of their own weapons. But I really did not think so. They could always attack, surely now that Achiates was gone, and we were alone, as they wished, and fill out their reports, if necessary, in any way they saw fit. In that way they would have risked very little, if anything. Too, they had permitted Achiates to slip away, in spite of the fact that he must have been engaged in the business of warning me. I did not think he was in league with them. If he were he could simply have let me walk into their midst as I entered the vestibule of the insula. Interestingly enough, I did not think the officer was engaged in making a standard arrest. His generous treatment of Achiates suggested this. Interestingly enough, I did not think he anticipated any resistance.

"Please," he said.

I handed my blade, in its sheath, the straps wrapped about it, to him.

"Thank you," he said.

"I do not wish to be bound," I said.

"That will not be necessary," he said.

"What is going on here?" asked Hurtha, coming up to us.

"Do not interfere," I said to Hurtha.

"It appears," said Hurtha, unshouldering his ax, "that a battle to the death is in order."

"Who is this?" asked the captain.

"My friend," I said.

"Greetings," said the captain to him.

"Greetings," said Hurtha. Hurtha was a friendly Alar. He was not one of the suspicious, remote, aloof ones. He enjoyed being on good terms with fellows he was preparing to fight to the death.

"Where are we going?" I asked the captain.

"To an arranged place," he said, "one of secrecy."

"There?" said Hurtha.

"Yes," said the captain.

Hurtha, too, I suspected, had not had a great deal of sleep last night.

"And what is to occur there," I asked, "in this place of secrecy?"

"One awaits you there," he said.

"Who?" I asked.

"An august personage," he said.

"Who?" I asked.

"His excellency, Gnieus Lelius, regent of Ar," he said.

"I am comging with you," said Hurtha.

"He is to come alone," said the captain.

"Look after Feiqa," I said to Hurtha.

"Do not think you can rid yourself of a tenacious comrade so easily," said Hurtha. "I am an Alar."

"Please," I said, "do not make things harder for me."

"I refuse to be left behind," he said.

"Please," I said. "This is hard enough. You must try to understand."

"Consider all we have been through," he said.

"Hurtha," I pleaded. I did not wish to weep. I put the two silver tarsks I had received for the blonde in his hand.

"Where did you get these?" he asked.

"I sold something," I said.

"Was it pretty?" asked Hurtha.

"Yes," I said, "very pretty."

"Not Feiqa?" he asked.

"No," I said.

"But another candidate for the collar, one you came across, somewhere, one for whom the collar is as fitting, perhaps, as for Feiqa?" he asked.

"Yes," I said. "That is true."

"Well, farewell," said Hurtha.

"Farewell?" I said.

"Yes," said Hurtha.

"Shall we go?" asked the captain.

"Yes," I said, somewhat irritated.

I then fell into step within the column of men, marching in their midst. The captain was in the lead, my sword in its sheath, slung on its strap, over his shoulder. I looked back, once. Hurtha, now at threshold of the insula of Achiates, waved cheerily. I wondered if killing an Alar, Hurtha, in particular, would count, strictly, legally, as an act of murder, or if there were some more sensible, benign category under which it might fall. Then I turned my mind to more pleasant thoughts, such as recollecting the pleasures men may take in slaves. I recollected, in particular, most recently, the former Lady Lydia, that particular slave, how she had looked, the straw about her body, and in her hair, the chain on her neck, her eyes, her cries, her pleading kisses and touches, her utter helplessness, and the joy of doing ownership on her.

"Let us step lively," said the captain.

We moved more quickly.

To be continued in
RENEGADE OF GOR,
to be published soon.

DAW

Do you long for the great novels of high adventure such as Edgar Rice Burroughs and Otis Adelbert Kline used to write? You will find them again in these DAW novels, filled with wonder stories of strange worlds and perilous heroics in the grand old-fashioned way: